The Glass Horse

A novel by Lynn Miller

Davila Books

The Glass Horse

First Edition/First Impression

Copyright Lynn Miller, 2008

ISBN 978-188521020-3
Fiction

*On the front cover: The Percheron Stallion
pictured was photographed at the Butte Fair &
Fiesta, Chico, California in 1937 He belonged to
Fred Franklin and was registered as
"Canto 182337"*

Published by Davila Books
an imprint of SFJ Inc.
P.O. Box 1627, Sisters, Oregon 97759

Dedication

*To the starchy and melodious
departed spirits of Bruce and
Carl Leonhardy, brothers who
both loved the smell of the high
desert's hidden stories.*

part one
Dry

chapter one

Crooked River

"Who then, is the invincible man? He whom, nothing that is outside the sphere of his moral purpose can dismay."
- Epictetus 101 A.D.

The tie chain ratcheted through the manger ring and made a slapping sound as his head jerked back to give his clear grey eye a view of the black mare John led into the barn.

The man with the mare looked to the stallion and said one word as a calm warning, "Now?" The stallion snorted in pig-like disagreement and forced his long nose into the manger of hay as if to say "we'll see about that."

There were only the three of them in the bottom floor barn space, the grey Percheron stallion in his single tie stall, the black draft mare heading into the double stall, and the magician farmer, John, also known as Sloop. The one light bulb hollowed out the morning core of the cavernous dark wood building's interior defining the edges of posts, wisps of hay, perched guinea fowl, harness hangings and the packed earth floor. The mare sighed deeply as she entered the stall and waited for him to snap her lead rope to the manger. Then her nose examined the empty grain box before slipping into the waiting hay, showing to her big lips which cured grass and legume patch might be best. Sloop stroked her neck and listened to her chewing and breathing. Over the stall wall, "Glass" his stallion, played a light see-saw racket with his tie chain.

John would be harnessing these two and hitching to the great wooden feed sled. Cattle and horses, by welcome force of habit, played anxious with their digestive juices and leaned their waiting eyes against the gate they knew would deliver to them their feed. But first steps needed to be taken. John entered his stallion's stall with curry comb and brush. "Step over" he in- sisted and the big animal obeyed moving against the right side partition. John entered on the left and set his brush hand on the high waiting withers while his right hand drew the steel curry comb over the muscled back. The slightest movement gave knowledge to the man that his horse both tensed and relaxed in complete appreciation for his touch. John thought, yet again, of what a simple and complete ritual this was. Horse in comforting, safe, space receives excellent feed while his friend scratches his back, legs, and neck. Done twice a day, every working day, week after week, month after month, and in this way the partnership is cemented.

John went to the tool box for the scissors to clean up the Stallion's bridle path and heard the beep followed by the vibra- tion. Annoyed, he fished out the pager. The numbers were assur- ance rather than interruption. His confirmation that the transac- tion had concluded satisfactorily. No need for him to call anyone. John Ogdensburg could continue his morning ritual which he likened to the finest of Bach's piano variations. The forms and disciplines, the repetitions and patterning, were always there but the nuances, soft subtle and vital, were his to shape and relish every winter morning.

He kept the wind wings open otherwise the windshield of his old pickup frosted over. And he wore a heavy sheep-lined jacket with blankets wrapped around his legs.

It was cold and snowing.

The ash-like snowflakes raced at him only to separate and vanish into swirling apparition before touching the glass and exploding deep in his eyes, deep in his thoughts. As if by companion magic, the windshield edges thickened in a wide cord-like frame of ice. He drove on a highway that was a packed and dusty white sheet. It lied to him. He recognized the lie and kept the truck's speed at thirty or less. The flakes which floated and then threw themselves at his windshield suggested faster speeds, much faster. He slowed even further and at one point stole a quick glance at his speedometer. He was only going ten miles an hour. Even so, he gripped the wheel leaning forward and gritting his teeth as though he were speeding through a life-threatening gauntlet. He blinked hard and shook his head. Forcing a false calm, he had to keep his evening brain free of those familiar drifting thoughts - they fed into the dizzy snow view and made him sleepy. It was a high-speed, slow-motion dream state. He fought sleep. He slapped his own face. He muscled his eyes open. He fought sleepy. A "good-bye, I'm done now" sleepy. A deadly drowsiness. He rolled his window down and stuck his head out into the cutting cold and hollered with numb face,

"... dreaming of a white Christmas."

The slow snow tickled his hot eyes.

What!

Exploding from around a tree-shrouded corner came the high sharp lights of an oncoming semi-truck. This was the top side of fear and surprise, whiter than snow, colder than cold. The empty everything races to fill. Slamming against himself, against his dream state, within that fraction of a second before the swelling pain of fear takes hold. It was all happening at a crawl, too slow, a confusing warp for his alerted senses.

It should have been an easy matter. Duden was already driving slow and the oncoming truck approached cautiously, yet the light-crazed swirls of snow confused the view. It was a magnetic mirage, a tightening tunnel of a steep and bottomless white. He slowed the old blue pickup but couldn't seem to counter the sensation that he was being sucked directly into the oncoming cluster of lights. He wasn't going down but it felt like he was. In his crippling panic he almost stopped his vehicle completely. The big truck passed and for a moment he was blind. Pulling to the right, his front wheel bit a seat for itself in the roadside snow berm and, clutch engaged, the engine died.

Staring into temporary blindness the young man came gradually to feel, from pained stiffness, just how tight his hands gripped the large, hard-rubber steering wheel. He felt a brittle cold as if the inside of his body's shell had been rubbed with dry ice. Enno wasn't frightened. But he felt the pain. He was used up, spent; exhausted, separated, drifting.

Deep sighs, head back, opening the door he pulled the blankets off his lap in preparation to get out to view the damage.

That's when he saw it.

The late model caramel-colored Chrysler was half-buried in the snow drift twenty feet ahead of him. He might have hit it. His first thought; it had been abandoned after stuck. From the seat of his truck, he looked harder and felt his breath tighten. He thought he saw the driver's door open just a crack and then suck back to almost latch.

Better see if someone needs help. Later he would wonder at his recklessness. Much later he would smile nervously about the whole affair.

Stepping full into that high mountain blizzard his face instantly became thin crystal with a small concentrated pain inside at the bridge of his nose. His boots crunched down past the powder and through earlier packed snow. He reached out to brace himself against his truck. Sticky snow blew into his eyes. He had difficulty seeing. Cautiously his fingertips traced a guidance along the car's side panel.

When he saw her it set him back and he almost slipped, almost fell. She was an out-of-focus silhouette in the window. Hugging himself he went to her door and, faced with glass between them, asked the question loud, but more as an observation.

"Need'n help?"

Rapidly she shook her head no. Then her head went back, way back, then forward to her chest. She turned to look over her shoulder and through the window at him. Through the fogged glass all he could make out were the wet, white-framed eyes of terror. With her entire body she seemed to say "go away" and "help me" and "leave me alone" and "What am I going to do?"

And all the moves, half sounds, snow softened edges, unpleasantness, inconvenience, refused apologies, denied gratitudes, and threadbare panic flowed together. He looked around, listening, stepping back from the inset, stepping back from the logic of the circumstance. He looked down and through the window.

"Maybe I can pull you out. I've got a chain." He said this with hand signals and an exaggerated mouth. It was as if he expected she'd be reading his lips. He didn't wait to see her shake her head no. He knew instinctively that he had to get back into the rhythm of purpose or he'd float away with the snow and the cold.

Walking briskly back to his truck he climbed into the rear and brushed the snow pile off a big handmade plywood tool box. He lifted the lid and pulled out a long heavy chain with a hook on each end. The cold steel stuck to his damp leather gloves and pulled at the hide like a hungry animal. He looped its length over both outstretched arms and walked, slowed by weight, to her rear bumper. She had cracked the door open to speak through.

"No, no, someone is coming ... to help me. My husband will

be here any minute."

She spoke to the night, to the snow, to the shadows of snow-ladened fir trees, but not to him. "Him" she wanted to disappear.

He ignored her in the selfish blindness of his helpful intrusion.

"Okay then, I'll just get my shovel and clear out your back wheels for you," dry words from numb lips, "that way you'll be ready when he gets here."

"No, no, no ..." she trailed off as her window went up.

He didn't hear those last soft words. It was cold and he needed to move. Chain returned, shovel out, he dug at the snow. He thought, 'A lot of snow, it would take some time. Why was he doing this? Had to. The woman was stuck, stranded. Don't know if anyone else will stop tonight on this blizzard-covered mountain pass. But why would they anyway? This car is half-covered in snow and looks abandoned. Most people worry about stopping to help and then getting in trouble.'

Why? He could hear Sam Riven's voice coming up from inside him, from between shoulder blades, crawling up the center of his neck until it burst into his skull and spread fingers around his brain.

"Digger, you're a mess, a boob, a cub, a child, you're fragile, your easily broken, always will be. You'll never make it, no focus, no strength man."

He shook his head hard and continued to dig but the voice remained.

"You've got to toughen up, only way you'll get that farm."

He tried to think of something else. Billie and the day they spent on Sloop's farm. Vicky and that way she looked at him. But Sam's remembered voice cut through it all. Duden knew he wasn't that breakable boy, someday Sam would find that out.

"It's no different than being a small time fisherman. You've got to be tough as Croc's knuckles. You've got to sway in the back like a boneless eel. The land, people, the ocean; they're all the same. Throw everything at you cuz you're puny, insignificant, practise-bait, alone. If you don't bend they'll pitch you and you'll suck water 'til you are dead.

"For us orphans, and low cast, life's a constant storm, a dragon but with a soft underbelly - tickle there and she'll release you to fight again. The way you tickle, not with talent or tools, but with a blow-by-blow don't-care-if-you-die 'you'll never see funny again' nastiness.

"Liars and thieves only ones who get elected or go 1st class or sit out the storms. And you don't get it. You won't ever know what I'm talking about. You kid - are - puny ...."

A dry sharp tear in his upper nasal chamber. He had to stop letting people talk to him that way, slammed his shovel against a small exposed piece of Chrysler bumper. CLANG. Didn't see the tightly wound passenger inside jump.

Sam's words, the sound of them, their shape, their furred-over quality, their absolute insolvency, Sam's words ... hungry Enno felt the words in waves of internalized echoes. They had some of the power and all of the flavor of tragic loss, of failure. Why was he drawn to splintered Sam Riven? A bankrupt poetry? Riven the New Zealander of limitless prejudice. Riven the bounce-about, the *never-belong-no-where*. Enno Albert Duden, orphan son of a single dream. Were they a pair? Ridiculous, they weren't a pair. They weren't even friends, as if friendship makes a pairing.

'There, one wheel dug free.'

... dug free ....

Some time ago that other man had said 'you'll never get yourself dug free.'

Enno remembered sitting across from him in that chemical-scented, death-grey government office.

"n - o - dud - in." The man read slowly from the form.
"No sir. Excuse me, but it's 'Eeno Doodin'."
"What sort of name is that? What nationality?"
"Don't know, sir."

"Don't know your own family?"

"I'm an orphan, sir."

"That is, of course, unfortunate. This won't take long Mister Doodin. I'm rejecting your application. You've got no experience, no collateral, no security. It's pretty cut and dried. Bad loan. Besides you don't seem to have any business sense."

"But Mr. Hert, the sheep I buy and the lambs they have will be the collateral. What I don't know, I will learn. And as I told you, the man I'm renting the farm from said he'd co-sign. There's your security."

"I heard you. It doesn't make sense why anyone would stick his neck out to guarantee a loan for a kid. No, I have to, in good conscience, deny this application. I'm doing you and Mr. Adams a favor. Besides, if you did buy 200 killer ewes to try to lamb out you'd be so far gone in debt you'd never get yourself dug free."

"I don't mean to be disrespectful sir ..."

Enno may not have meant to but he felt disrespectful. He hoped it didn't show.

"... but I know you're wrong."

Jack Hert looked hard at the young man. He needed to understand what the boy's eyes worked so hard to hold off. No, he didn't need understanding, he didn't want understanding, he needed license. License to squash. He tapped his desk blotter with the pencil point. An electrified warning hung unspoken in the air.

"I know this will work. It won't be easy, but I'm not looking for easy ..." he choked back apologetic pleading ... "If you can't make the loan is there any place else you might ...."

Hert tapped too hard and the pencil broke. He forced a chicken-butchering smile and said in a loud whisper,

"Listen, kid ..." long, wheezed, small flame, pause ... "Mister Dooodin, we CAN make the puny little loan. Farming is no longer some romantic backwoods adventure like you seem to think it is. Farming is now big business where powerful science and strong industry produce commodities. Stronger people than you with a lifetime of experience and inherited farmland are being forced out of agriculture by the thousands everyday. They can't make the grade. Change is here now and for the

better. Cheaper food. Better food. If those other people can't cut it, you
with your little joke of a dream won't even get in the front door.

"Time for you to go. I'm busy."

Cold slowly returned to his face. Duden shook his head and
noticed that it had stopped snowing. He went up on one knee,
leaning on the shovel, and was startled to see a woman standing
near him.

She wore a long, expensive, cheap, champagne-colored
down coat that almost matched the color of her strawberry-grey
hair which was flecked with sparkling snowflakes. She looked
down on him. They were tired old hollow eyes. A trace of terror.
Gloved hands clutched purse to chest.

"Oh, hi," he said standing up and brushing snow off his
knees.

She mumbled something.

Leaning forward to hear he offered an "I'm sorry?"

"Cold." It was a barely audible whisper switching her whole
body into a slow standing stagger.

"Oh Geez," he said with spring-loaded yet hesitant outstretched hands. He turned to run to the truck, stopped, went
back to her, stopped, looked at her car.

"Here." He took her elbow in both hands. Gently he suggested, with giving pressures, that she walk with him.

She looked so out of place sitting in his five window '52
Chevrolet pickup. Her smell. It's smell. His smell. The odors
wrestled. She hugged herself into her smallest size. He started
the engine, poured her a cup of coffee from his thermos, and
stepped out of the cab to brush snow off the windshield. She
hovered over the coffee, soaking in the safe small heat and
wrinkling her nose at the old, oily, nut smell. She was guarding
her silence. She knew she was thin glass.

"The snow's stopped, thank heavens, and it's not too far into
Mascara. There'll be places there where you'll be safe and warm
and can get to a phone. My name's Enno." He spoke and drove

and looked at her.

"Enno Duden."

A hiccup of a pause.

"I'm a carpenter, or really just a carpenter's helper. It's temporary till I can get a farm job."

She showed no sign of knowing he was even there. He tried silence but it was just too tight. So he talked.

"Rough spot for you ... to be stuck up here in the snow, I mean."

Her eyes flicked right, away from him and his voice which crowded her.

"I shouldn't ha' been coming over myself but I'm looking at some property over here and I wanted to start out first thing in the morning. Only get the next day and a half off. Lucky I got this old truck - it's like almost a four-wheel drive. I call it *mystery drive*. Always seems to get me where I'm going."

Why'd his mind spin off to a picture of Sloop and his big black team? The remembrance of Billie's whistle of admiration for Sloop's horses smiled on Enno. And the smile heated as the mental picture slid into the confusing warmth of Vicky's *why won't you* eyes.

The sound of the woman's unexpected voice came like a stick in the ear.

"You're too young. Too young. Only old people dread the word waste. My husband said I wasted my life. That it is, was, spent ... and on nothing. Said he needed to be with someone whose life still had coin. His big joke - coin - that's his last name - Coin. Bo Coin."

Enno made quick motionless glances at the woman as she spoke. He recognized the name - big shot developer - Coin Bros. Realty. Signs and ads everywhere. Young Mr. Duden felt a warning chill but couldn't picture why.

Without looking at the rescuer she continued,

"I don't know where I'm going. I guess I should thank you. Yes, I'm sorry. I do thank you." And with this she turned towards him and put a tentative gloved hand on the seat between them as a gesture.

He caught sight of her small outlined eyes, a melting black line traced them. Her mouth was kind. She had to be somebody's lovely mother, somebody's lovely aunt, somebody's lovely grandmother.

Enno had jumped a cog and jammed his human interaction gears. By her conversation she was reaching for him. He hunkered down like a wrongly accused child, he couldn't talk. The silence tightened.

"My name's Nettie, Nettie Coin."

It was her turn.

"He's got an office in Mascara. Comes over quite a bit. Times I've been over I've always found it beautiful but frightening. Lived my whole life in the city. Doesn't seem natural for forests and animals to spill into where people live."

He thought about what she said. Strange thoughts, hers.

They were going down a steep, packed-snow grade so he played with the truck's brake pedal. He thought about farms.

"I don't know why I'm coming over here. When I left I knew this is where he'd go. I don't want to see him but I called his office just the same, left a message that I'd be coming. That's why I knew he'd be driving up to find me. I've been too long."

Oncoming lights. Slow. As the patrol car passed, Enno's eyes met the searching glance of a county sheriff. The boy's first and only thought was to be glad someone was on duty.

"Bo says I'm incapable of an original thought. This proves it, going to Mascara I mean. I'm not following him, I just needed to be someplace else. I couldn't stay in our house, there are pictures of him everywhere."

She was crying. No sound. No motion. Her head turned away. But he knew she was crying. It was his turn.

"I grew up in the city. In an orphanage."

That did it, that one word, orphanage, altered her posture. She chose to listen. She had to.

"Don't remember a time when I wasn't daydreaming about a little farm of my own. Fence rows, the cluttered backsides of chicken houses, the cobwebby beams of old barns, corrals full of muddy manure ... don't know how those pictures got into my head, but they did."

He offered an awkward soft chuckle and added,

"Guess I'm the exact opposite of you. I've always dreamed of a place where the forests and animals mix right in with where I'd live."

She was looking at him hard. Looking to remember him, know him.

He saw a pulsing bar of colored lights in his rear view mirror. It was a long ways off and around corners and bouncing pretty off the snow covered fir trees. Here it came and he knew it, emergency lights of some sort. He slowed down and pulled to the plowed snow berm to let it pass. It was the sheriff's patrol car and it pulled in behind Enno and stopped.

Flashlight on, the Sheriff's deputy cautiously approached the old pickup. Enno rolled down his window. The beam of light pierced the truck cab.

"Mrs. Coin?" Came a low tentative grumble.

Enno didn't see her nod yes.

"You, out of the truck, hands on your head. NOW!"

Enno saw the drawn pistol. It was like a mouthful of turpentine, how he felt.

"But, I don't under..."

"Do it, NOW!! Excuse me, Ma'am, you just stay there for a moment."

Enno stumbled out and felt himself being spun and pushed up against the truck cab. His wallet was taken.

"Officer, what are you doing? Stop this ..." came Nettie's small, weak, worried demand.

"You have the right to remain silent ..."

"The law of sacrifice leaves the last word to the cowards and the timorous since the others have lost it by giving the best of themselves. The ability to speak always implies that one has betrayed."

-Albert Camus

chapter two

Klamath

"If your daily life seems poor do not blame it: blame your-self, tell yourself that you are not poet enough to call forth its riches; for to the creator there is no poverty and no poor indifferent place."
                              - Rainier Maria Rilke

Mascara, unwilling to consider itself a real town, it's a made-up congestion on a secondary highway, an accidental destination, a thin picture post card, a burg in the drug store fairy-tale sense. It's a small-time Realtor's dream come true, and a spoiled teenager's empty cup. It's a matronly shopper's once-only paradise. The serious panhandler's worst nightmare. As if a movie set, behind the all-pretty-from-a-distance false front buildings and Plymouth Navigator tinted glass, it is every bit premature, all sterile, all cheap upscale, senior assisted-living decor, brittle, synthetic, temporary.

East side of the Cascades squatting over the once beautiful Sage Creek, the village humility forgot. Sign post said 800 but the population was in excess of 8,000. Particle board false false-fronts screwed to wafer board buildings painted fashionable dusty colors to give a sense that here, at last, was a palatable sanitized safe wild west. A tourist commune which had successfully slowed highway traffic by the allure of 122 similar gift shops. A community less of like-minded folks and more of event managers and Realtors. A curio setting always for rent and grossing hundreds of millions in revenue but unwilling to bankroll its own police department. The county maintained law and selling-order by a sheriff's housekeeping in the Mascara City Hall.

No jail. There wasn't any. Enno Duden sat handcuffed in the back of the Sheriff's cruiser. Inside the city hall Nettie Coin fought waves of emotional sauce. She was becoming, with her hardened mind flailing, a frameless picture with fragile vibrating edges, misplaced instincts, heavy chest, pulsing temples.

"No. You listen to me. You two half-wit gorillas! I want that boy released this minute. If you don't I'll see to it that he gets an attorney and sues you for false arrest - even before I file for divorce."

Nettie's glare was fully leaded, sharp, stained glass; a burning directed light.

"And Mr. Coin," (slow drawn out Mister) "get a tow truck up there this minute."

"Honey, calm down," said Bo, hands outstretched, soft palms forward as if facing a warming fire. "We've already got Jonesy up bringing down your car."

"Not my car, his pickup truck! Now!"

She looked at his familiar big *Baby Huey* bulk, small facial features swimming in the large soft roundness of his face. Even thicker neck blending into an absence of shoulders heading for swivel-chair hips. In a flash familiar melted away, she saw him as a stranger who had cheated her out of 33 years of life. She reached out with force and deliberation, like she was clearing a table in anger, and slapped him hard. Slapped him to peel off his presidential grin. It worked. And it hurt her own face worse.

Slumped forward, hands cuffed behind his back, Enno sat looking at the wire grill which, in most of the Americas, kept dogs, potheads, drunks, murderers, and angry wives from reaching the well-armed county chauffeurs. In Mascara, the barrier usually kept office supplies and coffee makers from spilling onto the front seat when the cruiser's frequent high speeds were ungraciously interrupted by deer crossings or lady joggers.

Something caught Enno's eye, a movement. Without straightening he swiveled his head to see a small twisted man rifling through the city hall dumpster. Baseball cap, torn down vest, heavy leather belt with two metal rings tied to which were the braided remnants of rope and twine reaching down to the patient collars of two seated dogs. Long-haired, tri-colored dogs of somebody's favorite mix.

The little man pulled a handful of crumpled papers up out of the dumpster and waved them in the air triumphantly. The back of his head felt a watcher and he turned to see. Duden there in the sheriff's car. Duden watching him.

Enno smiled in recognition. Jimmy Three Trees. Mascara's only town vagrant, token vagrant, necessary social apology, necessary 'evil', necessary dirt. Enno knew Jimmy, liked him, helped him, misunderstood him. Recognized him as possible. Never felt any natural pity. Felt need, all around.

Jimmy limped to the patrol car. The front passenger window was open. Turning his contorted face sideways, he jammed his nose and lips into the crack. Enno made the soft, throated, air sound of someone who might laugh hard under different circumstances.

"You. Kid. Good kid. Come ow out ow ow ow out. They - da fillin shorts blis'ered mo'ers - I got 'em. See here, ow, ow out."

He fanned his fist full of papers.

"Da badges says Jimmy prove it. Broke my jaw. Kicked Sally dead, she's dead."

Enno's face jerked. What?

"Your dog Sally's dead?"

Little, screwed-up, crying, horizontal, old man's face nodding yes, sideways.

"Oh God, not Sally. Jimmy, not Sally." Eyes closed, in an

altered grief position.

Duden had heard something, Riven talking to Ogdensburg weeks ago, something about Jimmy Three Trees found beat up in the alley. They said he was okay. But Sally, sweetest little Border collie Sally, Jimmy's third dog. (He tied each to a different tree at his forest camp hideout. That's where the nickname came from.) Enno found the camp and took two paper sacks full of empty soda cans and a box of dog biscuits last summer. The other dogs, no names, barked and snatched presented biscuits. Sally wagged her tail, tenderly took the offered treat, set it down and licked Enno's hand. He'd told himself someday he'd have a dog like this.

His upper torso seesawing, Enno's forehead made soft gentle sad taps against the separating grill.

"Get away from there. You! Get away!" Came the deputy's snarl as he came out the city hall's back door to see Jimmy up against the cruiser window.

Enno, handcuffed, locked up, embarrassed, felt himself swell instantly with indignant anger, stupid anger, brave anger, worthless anger, blind anger. "Leave him alone!" It was a roar. Enno's surprising, forceful roar.

"Shut up." Came the inadequate official response. Odd, though, that it was accompanied immediately by Enno's release from the car, the cuffs, the custody.

"Deputy ..." was a soft 'Nettie' warning from the Hall's open door. Deputy went soft and into his car. Enno went to Jimmy. Nettie went limp. Bo went for a drink. Jonesy went back for the old blue pickup.

"This is a brand new century and it's our turn. We have four maybe eight years to turn this country around. We have the key players in every secondary position, policy's been inserted and legislation is on deck. But things need to happen to set every-thing in motion. There are at least three up-coming battle fronts and the Middle East ain't one of them: They are in order of importance: number one - a united Europe (we don't want it), number two - a healthy Asia (we don't want that either), and number three our own economy. The Middle East, Africa, South America, even as messy as things are now, these regions are still ours, we control them, we own them. The true enemy, gentlemen, is class warfare, it's the haves versus the have-nots. But let's call it by its more accurate name, terrorism - in all its various forms - terrorism, because that is what it will become. We do not have the time to convince people that our free market is the solution and that it is something which, at all costs, must be protected. If terrorism wins out, the free market will fall and we will have anarchy. Everything we hold dear; our life-styles, our incomes, our good schools, our churches, our restaurants, our oil, our media infrastructure, our corporate dividends, our power base will be gone. And it can happen very quick. The U.S. would look like another Cuba or Nicaragua or North Korea or, heaven help us, another France. A new form of defacto Marshal law, one which is implied by urgency rather than ordered by the executive branch ... **that** is, in our opinion, the only appropriate next step.

"We have to take people's minds off the economy and the ridiculous, unimportant, mess in the middle east. What we need is an event, something which will focus John Doe on his own survival and the survival of this country. We've got to scare the living crap out of people again and make 'em even madder. It's got to be big. Big enough to grant us, overnight, new heightened powers of surveillance, seizure and interrogation. But we can't afford the screwup of last time. We need to make sure that any loss of property or life is targeted. Mistakes happen and this is war but we don't want to lose friends or votes. That's why your government, in these dangerous times, is approaching you gentlemen. We are asking that you set aside your differences with the Justice Department and join the outlined religious and business consortium, and, of course, **your** government, in this critical endeavor. For this we are willing to offer absolution, pardon and profit sharing but only, gentlemen, if we all recognize that the U.S. Attorney General's office will be command central."

The 35 suited men in the private back room of the Las Vegas Benadryl Arms Hotel all nodded silently as the Attorney General drank from his water glass and canvassed the room with rubbery, grey eyes.

Piero Gambizzi knew the ultimate opportunity when he saw it, he also recognized the idiot pigeon, attorney general Larry Berry, as a small-time ego-maniacal culture pimp. Someone who mistakenly believed that a nuanced law was evidence of, and an instrument of, absolute control. Gambizzi only respected enforceable authority. And, having in respectful fashion duly erased any authority beyond his own, trusted his magnificent ability to create new undeniably effective forms of enforcement.

Back to Mascara's outer edge:

Four of Enno's friends were all seated with him around the table in the kitchen of Sloop Ogdensburg's farm. Sloop's wife of ten years, Helga. Billie Blue-Chevie and his half-sister Nancy Simmons. Enno finished his story.

... "My God man, a nightmare, a stupid nightmare. Maybe you should'a never stopped?" Blond temporarily sincere Billie.

"He had to, Billie. He'll always have to. It's him." Smiling, lovely, dark-haired Nancy with words towards Billie and eyes towards Enno.

Sloop, bearded, graying, thick inside and quixotic, sat still and quiet, watching.

"Are you hungry, dear? I can fix you a sandwich, heat up some soup ...?"

"No thanks, Helga. My stomach's all tied up in knots," answered Enno.

"So'd you find out about Jimmy and his dog?" asked Billie.

"Some teenagers tried to get him to buy them cigarettes and

beer at the convenience store. He was going to do it, too. But you know how Jimmy talks funny and spaces off into things he remembers. Well, I guess they thought he was saying no, so they beat him up. Sally I figure tried to defend him and they kicked her repeatedly. She died. Jimmy tried to get the cops to do something. He being a vagrant, they just shined him on. Told him to knock off the cheap wine. Told him that he needed official documented proof. That's what he was looking for in the city dumpster, documents, any documents."

Silence.

"Yeah, it's time to pivot." Sloop said, each word measured.

They all straightened up, everybody at uneasy attention, all uncomfortable and apologetic as if caught not listening. All with left-over grief. All with paid memberships in some cosmic order of the disenfranchised.

"Don't let this suck you in. Justice belongs to the gangsters of commerce." He paused and rubbed his hands together. "Fairness we make for our loved ones, but only in small doses and in those out of the way corners we call home. Little Sally dog was a nurse-queen. No doubt she'll be reborn and in the fullest armor of beauty, capable of teaching the world that passion is a force to the good. Jimmy?" He chuckled looking down in thought. "He's, he's currently a punctuation mark in some indecipherable foreign language. He'll come back as a judge with an unexplainable urge to larger than average doses of fairness." Sloop looked up at nothing, his folded hands settings till on the table.

Nancy glanced at this silly farmer chieftain and shook her head softly, catching herself before she fell, right on the thin line of embarrassed. She felt contradictory electric jabs in her emotional center mixed with uncertain advances all questioning. Misjudged. She had misjudged. Something else, something changeable. Why did it feel like this was where select people came to get direction? To get orders? To get clarification? It was her first moment in the court of John Ogdensburg.

Helga felt each of Nancy's glances at Sloop. She felt them as

maddening pin pricks. She felt them as welcome acknowledgments. She hoped her husband noticed. She knew he needed this,
he could never admit it, but she knew. She could no longer give
it. She was in love, deep inside her; slow, familiar love where
emotions and movement have thickened like forty-degree honey.
John needed the flaring light which accompanies falling into the
abandonment of new attraction, new love. True to her though he
was, he still needed the heat she couldn't provide. For Helga the
fall had long since concluded. She had hit bottom and the flares
had flickered out. Her love for John was possessive, protective
and apologetic.

"Enno, don't you have an early morning appointment?"
Sloop said in his *Johnny Cash* voice..

"Yeah," with an exaggerated release of held-over air,
"maybe. It was with someone at Coin Brothers Realty. Don't
stand much of a chance with that now, do I?

Nancy asked, "What was it about?"

"Raw land." Enno

"The farm thing." Billie

"Never apologize." Sloop

"I'll make some coffee." Helga

Nancy leaned her sharp, pretty chin into her curled waiting
fist and gave Enno her full-force smiling eyes. He, she could
enjoy in comfort, he was an easy read.

Enno looked back into those eyes and rested there. It wasn't
fair. She was a fruited 33. He, an awkward enthusiastic bumbling
21. And he was in love with her. Nancy casually loved goodness,
never wasting much energy on sincerity. She liked to move her
emotions around because she was hopelessly attracted to fresh
doses of other people's imagination. She couldn't bring herself to
settle on one attraction, not yet anyway.

They talked late. Fairness. Raw land. Short growing seasons.
Courage. Grapes. Futility. Politics and manipulated public paranoia. Plowing. Permits. Poultry. The force of their shared values
made the time hover and lengthen. Their talking like this, to-

gether and separately, made the momentary gather, moisten and
itch.

Later, unable to sleep, Enno spent the short night on Sloop's
couch worrying. His old farmer friend, his *mentor*, had repeatedly
advised him to quit his valley job and move to this other side of
the mountains, insisting he needed to be right where he wanted
to be if he was going to make his dream work. That's what Sloop
said.

Next morning he went to his meeting with a "Brad" at the
real estate office. He went in his own good old blue truck.

"Hey. Have a seat."

Ever noticed how some people will get all the visual information they need in one short quick glance and then look away
while they make an assessment? Brad did this and quickly told
himself - disillusioned, kid, dirt-poor, kid, enthusiastic, kid, poor
family, why am I wasting my time?

"Mr. Duden, this is not really farm country. Oh, people do
farm here but its rough. Short seasons. And land values are high.
They're high because successful folks want to live here. Some
will try to tell you that land prices go up and down. Well, that
only happens when a community hasn't formed yet. Around here
we have successful people, many of them retired, who want to
live amongst others just like themselves."

Brad pursed his lips and touched the fingertips of one hand
to the other. He was rehearsing a Rotarian speech and only
vaguely aware of Duden.

"And here, in Mascara, land prices are up and only going
higher."

He stood to signal the meeting's closure.

"But what about that thousand acres at Snake Flats you've
advertised?"

"That's not land. That's a huge slab way off in the corner of
the county. Scab rock, Juniper and rattlesnakes. No power, no
water, no county road, no phone, no neighbors but forest service
and timber companies."

Enno knew more. The property included an abandoned failed homestead. He was keenest about the low per acre price.

"I'd like to see it. And I've got some questions ..."

"I'm sorry young man but something's come up and I couldn't possibly show it to you today. My best advice to you is that you forget this area and look around east of here. Cheap land and people you'll understand. Now, if you don't mind ..."

Enno had been refused, politely, rudely, softly, in the wash and wear fabric of "qualified buyers only" salesmanship. He had been judged unclean, unworthy, unwanted. Next time maybe he would take Sloop's suggestion and not be so damned honest.

Walking out of the office and past the glossy photo of Bo Coin, Enno had to wonder ...

On the sidewalk, leaning against his pickup's fender waited Vicky Wood.

"Hey, cowboy," she said with a magazine cover smile. "Buy me breakfast and we'll deal with the rumors later." Duden blinked a nose-hair blink.

Blond, tall, exotic. Broken flattened nose, God feared her attitude. Her full head-to-toes beauty would have destroyed entire congregations of the pious. Vicky Wood. She had sensors, though young raw sensors. Her unschooled intelligence trusted them. First she heard someone say "Duden's different, he'll be something." Then she watched.

Hers was a curvature of anticipation, new parts of herself cradled by a fresh forested wondering. She was ready to surrender to not-a-clue comforts, if she picked them. She felt needy. The animal attraction was complete. Sensors worked. "He's mine," she decided.

He was confused.

To Enno, Vicky was an off-balance mystery. Common thoughts; Why was she teasing him? Flirting? Couldn't be interested? Duden saw himself as fifty percent short of ordinary. Vicky was the earned love focus of every Mascara building contractor's daydreams. (And this little developer's dream village had more licensed contractors per capita than any incorporated city in the Milky Way.)

"What do you say?"

"Hi, Vicky, nice coat."

Combination fur, leather and porcupine quill coat with sophisticated imitated native design. Glistened on the tip ends from the morning frost. A man with money had said, "I'll buy you anything!" She took him a fancy catalog and pointed to the 4 figure coat. It came to her apartment address. So did he. She told him he was a dope. Sent him back to his wife.

"Yeah, I suppose so." With her fingers on the collar of his old denim jacket she asked, "What's with the Realtors?"

There came a honk. She didn't look up but waved over her shoulder, certain the call was for her. New pickup, gold contractor's name and license number on the door. She kept her eyes on Enno. She certainly had focus. Duden was insoluble but his knees weren't told this, they were directly connected to deep-seated glands with other ideas.

"Oh, tried to get them to show me some property but no soap. Guess I'm not good enough for 'round here."

"The farm thing?"

"Yep. I'm gonna make it happen, Vicky. One day I'll make it happen."

"Well, get it out of your system, honey, 'cuz soon as you and I get hitched I got plans for us and farming ain't in the cards." She laughed brittle. Sad for her, no way yet to understand why. Enno wanted to believe it was all a joke. Somewhere three contractors just had to be looking. Exchanging bets. Somebody's practical joke. They had put her up to this. It just didn't make any sense otherwise.

"Vicky, if I ever get married it'll be to a woman who can chop firewood and shovel manure." His face was hot and red, soon to increase.

"Yuck!" She tugged on his little ears with long cold fingers and jabbed a soft kiss on his lips.

"Just for that you can eat alone, see ya." And she walked off as two new pickups nearly hit one another. On the second floor of the Coin Bros. Realty office, Bo picked bacon from his teeth as he watched Vicky's departure.

Enno stood at his pickup, hand on the door handle, the moment lost. Morning sun ricocheted off the crusty snow piles. The green pickup pulled up slowly. Sam Riven's red face pushed forward towards Duden. He rolled down the passenger window. "Kid, let's talk."

Enno looked up slow. When his eyes met Riven's they said 'Leave me alone.' When his eyes moved back to see Riven's dog they softened. He had the oddest name. Riven called his dog "Resumé." Large tri-colored Border collie/McNab cross. Supposed to have been legendary with sheep. Now he just slept in the back of Sam's truck and came to life barking only when the truck started out, only leaving.

"Come on. Get in." There it was, that musical condescending New Zealand accent. Riven opened the door and pushed it towards Duden.

"What do you want?"

"I want to talk to you. Got a plan. Need your help. Get in. We'll be walking back but it's not far and a beautiful morning for it." Clean speech though somehow still cascading out like a slurry of cuss words.

Across the street Nettie Coin sat in the restaurant watching the two men. Why did she feel such an ache when she saw that boy?

Enno sat bolt upright expecting some speech about his ineptitude, about his being a loser. This time it didn't come.

"The time's now for a change. Me, I mean. I need a change, big change. Big Sur is gone, Maui is gone, Paul's dead. Drank too much rotgut, did a swan dive into an empty pool. Why'm I telling you this? You don't have a clue what I'm talking about. Edges, I'm talking about edges. We walk edges, jump canyons, kiss married women, let the air out of patrol car tires - we live -

got that? - live. We don't live in a roll-over position, we live in a broad jump position."

Piece of silence. Then Sam started to shake his head softly.

"I'm not talking about you kid. Not talking for you, either. I'm talking to myself - about myself - that's all any of us do, ever."

Enno looked at him almost understanding. Until he saw the moisture in Sam's eye. "I'm leaving kid. Think I'll head for Central America. Nicaragua I think. So I need a favor or two. Want you to move into my cabin till it sells. I'll give you a key to a lock box at the Greyhound station in Bend. Put all my mail in it every week or so. Also, when the cabin sells I'll have you put the money in that box. Don't want anyone knowing about this. Just you. Got that? Can I trust you? Don't want any rent. You can stay there as long as it takes. Okay?" The voice of a down-under Robert Preston.

"I don't know what to say, Sam."

"Say 'thanks buddy,' 'sure buddy'."

"No, I mean I don't know if I'm ready to move over from the valley."

"Oh, geez, well bust my bongos but you're a lame one. Rent free, man. My cabin, rent free. You'll be here only a few miles from Sloop's farm. Don't tell me you don't want that."

Enno was looking out the side window. Thinking.

"Where we going?"

"To the Fingerhut quarry." Pausing, Riven took a thoughtful glance at Duden. "I'll give you my dog. If you do this for me, I'll give you my dog."

Enno turned quickly to look at Sam.

"Resumé?"

"Yeah." Riven was smiling, a used-car dealer's smile.

Enno sat looking straight ahead exhaling in little preparation bursts. Without looking at Sam he asked a curious,

"Why?"

"Holy mother of sterile cattle! Because I'm getting wrinkled and I need to be tickled by women who speak another language. Because ..."

"No, I mean why did you name him Resumé, your dog, why did you name him Resumé?"

Sam started to laugh.

"So we've got a deal, kid?"

"Why did you?"

"Because I always enjoyed being able to say 'and here's my resumé' while pointing at the mutt."

"He's not a mutt."

"Okay, kid, anything you say. He's yours now."

They drove past the quarry entrance. Around up the side to the top where teenagers sometimes went to smoke weed and make out. Sam drove right up to the edge.

"Okay, Duden, get out and tell the dog to disembark."

Enno felt icy. Sam had a new different grin. He peered off at the open expanse ahead of them and above the massive hole. It was as if he expected the pickup to fly.

"What'a you gonna do, Sam?"

"Us, boy, you and me. We're gonna push this six thousand dollar bucket of bolts off this here cliff."

"What! No, Sam, why?"

"Insurance money, boy. I need to get me to those Central American beaches and soon. You push, I'll steer and jump but first get your dog out of the back.

"I won't do it, Sam. Can't."

"You better get that dog!" Sam put gloves on, wiped the steering wheel clear of finger prints and played with the clutch and the gas. Enno jumped out and called Resumé. Just in time. The truck went slowly off the cliff. Sam opened the door and bent over, leaning out to jump but stopped midway, his coat caught on the handle, he clawed at the swinging door. He broke free but missed the cliff edge. Enno, shocked, watched as both truck and Riven disappeared side by side. Resumé ran to the cliff. Whining and barking.

chapter three

Alsea

*(From notes best left in: wet it all, way back, so that
each moment spreads like a stain. Let each spreading
moment run into and join with adjacents if it was meant to
happen. Let the inside/outside stink of each character build
mounds of emotional debris which give modest elevation to
the presentation of personality. Sink down to human, coil
tight and push to the surface for air. Forget the readers.)*

Rhododendrons. Fiddleneck fern. Moss fingers and blankets. Nettles. One hundred forms of water. Pacific the neighbor.
Designated rain forest riddled with light in three dimensional
lacings, pieces floating off into meandering mists. Dirt covered
rocks. Moist crawlers. Big trees. Firs as big around as God's
thigh. A black-haired half-breed girl mumbling to herself as she
searches for the creamy frills and lace of Chanterelle mushrooms.
From a distance she's tall. Up close, short. Last name Intoit. First
name Shirley. Not pretty. Less than lovely. But a presence of pure
floating joy. Happiness incarnate. Met by the right eyes she was
not to be forgotten.

One hundred and sixty miles east of Shirley Intoit's fungal hunt, a young man in a sheep-lined coat and cheap jeans raced to the edge of a quarry cliff arriving second behind a dog named Resumé. The dog bobbed back and forth, whining and barking. Sam Riven's ticket to central American beaches, his green pickup truck, stood on its crushed nose at the bottom of the quarry. It looked like some sad circus elephant standing on its trunk. Inappropriate, unnecessary, curious.

"Oh, this is fat, just fat!" Sam's voice.

Enno looked left. Spread eagle on the crushed rock face of the cliff, there was Sam looking the part of a sky-diver whose chute never opened. But he was moving, like a huge slow spider, fingering and toeing the wall. He was moving down.

"What can I do?" offered Duden.

"You can join the dinking D.A.R. for all I care!" Sam had forty or fifty feet to navigate to the bottom. Resumé couldn't stand it anymore and flung himself off the cliff. The old stock dog immediately changed his mind in mid-air, turning like a torso-twisting cat to face up cliff and paw at the loose, facing gravel materials. A miniature avalanche rained down on the New Zealand spiderman. It was a worthless defense, but he spewed a torrent of unfamiliar language at the canine. Resumé's digging did nothing to slow the dog's slide right into, over and beyond prone Sam.

"Dog, when I catch you I'm gonna give you to some fat woman in a trailer park who'll practice those Parisian haircuts and dye jobs on your sorry carcass."

"Sam, there's a car coming."

"Oh man! I don't need this... Kid, you, get out of here! I'll be all right. Don't let anyone see you. Forget everything. I'll be in touch. Now get lost. I mean it! Beat it before you end up just another iron-on patch!"

Made perfect comfortable sense to Enno. He didn't want to be there anyway. He looked around and picked a likely back-door route to walk to town.

Second-hand rough-out Tony Lama boots on Duden's bony
feet pretty much promised an uncomfortable hike. He folded up
the big, woolly, coat collar and pulled his dirty brown cap down
over the lock-tite ridge ringing his dark brown head. With his
shoulders pinched together and hands deep in pockets he did a
fair imitation of the worthless posture of a sorry, cold man. Even
from a distance he looked sincere, determined, lost in thought.
He didn't look like he'd ever make a good motel manager or gas
pump jockey. This was a young man who would only look good
self-employed. He walked to avoid the scattered snow piles. The
freeze-dried sagebrush, juniper branches and pine needles joined
Enno's riding heels to play out a crackling percussion to the boy's
thoughts.

'Better just get back to my truck ... get on home. Whole trip's
been a flop, a mess. If I stay around here I'm just liable to get into
more trouble!'

Under those thoughts came Sloop's advice to move on over
to Central Oregon. The business about Sam's cabin - it was just a
bad joke.

He had this trick whenever he was confused and anxious.
He had learned it from a man out of his past, Sig, the one who
called himself a Buddhist monk. Enno walked and as he did he
put his mind nowhere. That was the trick. To do this he pulled
up from his memory an image of *Pascal's Triangle*, an obscure
mathematical design.

One on top, two ones on the next row. Third row, a one, a
two, and a one. Fourth row, a one, two threes, and another one.
Fifth row, one, four, six, four, one. Pascal's Triangle, an arrangement of numbers in which each number is the sum of the two
numbers to the right and left of it in the row above: made up of
the coefficients of the binomial expansion, each successive row
representing the next higher power. Duden didn't understand the
words of the definition but he could, at almost any time, call up
the visual image of the triangle and *see* its math. He understood
how and why the numbers sat where they did. And when he saw

them in their proper places a wash of gratitude and calm flowed over him. He became a zero.

Sig had quoted a South America librarian/essayist/philosopher, Borges, to explain: "The learned doctors of the Great Vehicle teach us that the essential characteristic of the universe is its emptiness." Sig had said that out of embraced emptiness comes the nothing of everything, the rock hard mirage, the quenching dream drink.

It didn't take long. From zero, it took an instant and he was down a familiar path. He was on his farm. His mythical farm. Walking down a neat imagined row of plain unpainted buildings. Fences connected the buildings, the functions. Animals. A low "milk me" moan from the Jersey/Ayrshire-cross beauty lay like a soft, heavy, flannel blanket over the egg squeezing staccato shrieks from the layer house and the "I'm over here" pig squeals.

Enno was well placed in the *other*. Smells, pains in the milking hands, soft moist forehead pressed against her flank, the burn of the poultry ammonia, all in his head, all imagined.

Elsewhere parallel and still cognizant of this limited real world, he could see the road, the actual road. Ducking beneath brittle, monkey-tail Pine limbs, he made for it while trying not to spill his dream. Head down in a duck, his eyes made a small arcing sweep behind his left side. A dog? Resumé?

The boy stopped, still bent over, still looking back. The dog stopped and sat down.

"Where's Sam? He okay?"

The dog got up, made a complete circle in place, lifted his leg without target and sat down.

Enno smiled. What was 'said' was not important. Enno sat down on the big nearby lava rock. He aimed his smile at the dog. Resumé scratched behind an ear and licked his own nose.

"You want to come with me? 'Til Sam shows up?"

Resumé stood up, grinned with double winks, wagged his tail stub and entire fanny and sat down.

Duden reached a hand out to pet him and with invisible

speed the dog had his jaw clamped around the offered palm. Teeth pushing into the flesh with precise gentle gripping pressure. He held it there the length of a statement, released, and licked.

"You're smarter than I am. Aren't you?

The dog laid down, front legs straight forward, head cradled and eyes looking up in perfect apology.

Enno Albert Duden felt his torso fill with the juice of longing and his knees collapse with unexpected arrival. He wanted this dog, this dog, another man's dog. He didn't like seeing his as a thin character. Built on two wants, a farm, a dog. Wants. Did he, could he ever warrant them? Wants, warrants. Could he? Would he ever...? It was the dog. Somehow he'd gone from confusion, to the dream state and into a loss of hope. He looked down and noticed the thaw heave-marks in the soft forest floor, the fragile top soil mimicking the action of an opening flower.

Resumé knew to do something. He bounced up, trotted on tip toes past Enno, turned and barked a rapid 5 times.

"Going someplace?"

Five more barks.

"Oh, we're going someplace? Okay Rez' lead on."

The dog was in heaven. Finally someone who understood. Finally a home for his talents. Maybe a partner. The dog was in heaven.

Enno smiled as he followed Resumé, marvelling at how it seemed the dog's feet never actually touched the ground. His smile broadened as he understood. He had wanted this dog. To possess it. Turned out the dog, for now, possessed him.

Twenty-one years before: Charmaine Lebow believed. It mattered less what she believed. It mattered most that she believed. The strength of her believing was a life force. The fashion of her believing was a cultural force. Attractive but. The intensity of purpose drained her of any easy beauty. Made her grey and stiff and demanding.

Reflected juxtapositions, layered over allowed memories, pushing up against maybes, cupping songs of passion; felt beauty; knowable beauty, Charmaine "Charley" Lebow's deliberation denied all this. She wasn't cold, she was linear. She was incapable of retaining the wax finish that comes of collision between impossible longing and junkyard circumstance. She was spiritless. Her work in a Berkeley food coop shoveled the woman towards a grainy purity of purpose. The poetry of an argument or a cause had no impact on her. She was charged by incomplete logic. The end of the string had to be known to her. Comic accidents of drunken repartee and crazed devotion turned "Charley" and pointed her at saving whales. Here was a thing to do.

Alaskan natives were harpooning whales, she would stop them. Bunch of social changers and Charley went to try. The cold, sparse piece of a native village welcomed the changers then spit them out. All but Charley, she needed the end of the string. Son of the tribal leader fully waxed, round faced; taught patient eyes, persistent eyes, seeing eyes; the spirit of many lives in one waiting hungry destined leader; Oochuck knew to read panic in a quarry, in that thing that was hunted. He knew to read comfort, knew to read self-defense, to read defiance, to read love. He knew how to read lust. Oochuck could not read Charley.

Ms. Lebow learned Oochuck would lead a whale hunt the next day. She spent nine hours communicating 30 seconds worth of simple bargain to Oochuck. Nine hours to ask "is there anything in this world I might do to prevent you from leading tomorrow's hunt?"

The end of her string almost in sight, his answer was simplicity. His answer was glacier. His answer was his answer.

"Empty woman stays with Oochuck 'til fall. All that time Oochuck not hunt whales."

Bargain. Bargain struck. Bargain misunderstood. Bargain made plain. Bargain made interesting.

Meanwhile Ahchuck, Oochuck's younger brother, took the whaling parties out. Day after day. It was made clear to Ahchuck that "Charley woman" was not to know the purpose of the excursions. On the seventh day Ahchuck struck whale. Charley went outside to understand sounds of mass female commotion and discovered bloody blubber. Oochuck shrugged, Charley left for Berkeley. The end of the string proved frayed beyond understanding. The empty woman remained empty, save for Oochuck's baby in her belly.

In California, within seconds of her tiny daughter's birth, Charley knew something was wrong. This baby had spirit, too much spirit, many spirits, watching eyes, understanding eyes.

One month old child bundled, Charley headed north for Oochuck.

"Here, she's more you than me. Her name's Shirley. Her burps stink. You're the father."

With that Charley disappeared from our story.

Shirley Intoit grew to be an insatiable comedienne and magician. She left Alaska at fourteen. In search of her mother and something, anything, resembling a farm. Her maturing burps had changeable odors.

Side image: Some many years before, Louis Armstrong headed for Chicago with his horn and a trout sandwich his mother had made. He was 21.

One happy, one circumspect, old man dog and young dog man hike the paved road edge toward town. Cars and pickup trucks passed going both ways. Comes a Chrysler from behind them. Slows as it passes. Stops just ahead. Inside Nettie anxiously clears the seat next to her for a passenger. Enno recognizes the car and he nerves up. He's startled further as a second car stops beside him and Billie's welcome voice pours out.

"What're you doing out here? Isn't that Sam's dog? Want a ride?"

Duden opens the passenger door of the '62 Buick Electra and gets in. With the speed of a frog's tongue Rez' lands in Enno's lap and offers four sharp small barks. Both young men laugh shoulder-shaking silent smiles.

"Okay? The dog I mean. Is it okay if he comes with us?"

"Isn't that Sam's dog?" Asks a nodding Billie as he drives off.

"I'm not sure. I think he's mine now. How much you know about Sam?"

Billie has a distant look, preoccupied.

Nettie watches in the mirror red faced as Enno and Billie and Resumé drive up alongside.

Billie nods to Enno. "Open your window and ask if she's okay."

"Drive on by Billie! Drive on by! That's her. That's Mrs. Coin."

The Electra hesitated and then accelerated. From the corner of his vision Enno thought it looked like Nettie was crying.

"Jeeze," he thought, "that's one mixed-up old lady."

"Whoa, I'm glad you saw who that was."

"Yeah," long breath, "what about Sam Riven?"

"You were asking if I knew something about him: not much. He's strange but no more than most. I did hear a funny story about him recently. Back last fall, during the harvest festival, Riven rented a room for 2 days at the big motel west of town. Even though he's got that cool cabin on the backside of Bailey Butte. Can't figure it. As the story goes he wanted to deprive at least one tourist of a place to stay that weekend. Middle of the night he couldn't sleep so he went out in his underwear and paced the motel halls, counting room numbers. Memorized them. Then he went back to his room. By now it was 4 a.m. so he dialed each room number and let the phone ring once, hanging up quickly.

One hour later, at five, he calls each room again. This time he lets it ring and when people answer he says *'this is your five a.m. wake up call.'* Weird, huh?"

"How'd you hear 'bout this?" Enno asked.

"Sam told me."

"And you believed him?"

Resumé, laying all over Enno's lap, made spasmodic vibrating jerks. He was laughing.

Nettie was frightened and feeling silly, still sitting roadside, when Sam Riven opened her car door, got in, and told her to drive on, quickly.

Dropped off by Billie in Mascara, Enno and Resumé went, via 5 window '52 Chevy pickup, to Sloop's farm. Rez' rode on top of Enno's plywood tool box leaning into the cold air. The dog hoped Sam never returned. This answerless boy was perfect modeling clay to an old dog whose lineage could be traced clear back to Cleopatra's appointment secretary.

chapter four

Williamson

"There may be a great fire in our soul, but no one ever comes to warm himself at it, and the passers-by see only a little bit of smoke coming through the chimney, and pass on their way. Now, look here, what must be done, must one tend that inward fire, have salt in one self, wait patiently yet with how much impatience for the hour when somebody will come and sit down near it, - to stay there maybe?"
    Letter to Theo by Vincent VanGogh

She gripped the wheel, looked straight ahead, and spit out, "No."

"Please, lady, just drive. We get away from here and I'll get out. Honest, Please!"

Nettie turned and looked at Sam Riven.

"Are you married?" She asked this with tight eyes demanding the truth. She was shopping for samples to understand.

"What? Married? Anything you want lady, just drive, please!" Sam was tired. Sam was an old, disillusioned, visionless priest. Sam was a frightened boy. Sam was a prolapsed sarcasm. He was a bad taste in his own nose. Sam, the womanizer, was a heart which had never known the free fall flight of love. He was a debt unto himself. Sam was used to having his way.

So, so slowly Nettie started her car to roll. So quickly she spoke, out of tune with the realities of the moment.

"I'm married to a loser, a slob, a a a bad person..."

The pause was too long.

"So what do you want me to say lady? Gee, I'm sorry? Welcome to '*this is your reality*'? So your husband's a slob, so what?"

Nettie slammed on her brakes reached into her purse pulled out a small pistol and shouted.

"Get out of my car, right now!"

Sam opened the door, opened his mouth and she shoved him with her pistol fist while stepping on the gas.

Sam Riven spilled to the pavement in a roll, cracking an old knee and a posture.

Nettie Coin driving away dropped the unloaded pistol into her purse and allowed her eyes to crinkle with power.

Resumé and Enno Albert Duden pulled into Sloop's farmstead. The gate was framed in carefully stacked rock. The sign beside the gate read "Please go away. This miracle is fragile."

Somewhat sheltered from roadside view by a tight row of Poplars, the Ogdensburg farm buildings seem to rise out of a fertile fantasy brocade of pretty goodness mixed with the blinding beauty of a deep grass deceit. Here was that place birds remembered if allowed to choose where to die. This was that lowest hollow in Mother Nature's back that men in search of place moan for. This was an electric home to biological allowance. This was an eclectic home to possibility in any pattern. This was a choral masterpiece of funky recycled sheds set against orchard set against fanciful wooden fences set against massive stone barn set against a home which was a cluster of gathered cabins connected by screened porches and shirted by open veranda encircled by a hand-holding ring of homemade rocking chairs which went on forever.

Each time Enno entered this magic domain he felt re-
charged. He felt his dream swell. He saw the light increase
around that goal deep in his head. This place of Sloop and
Helga's was the proof that one day, some day, he would begin to
build and gather his own dream farm.

Straight ahead of him he saw the eave of the Ogdensburg tin
shop lined with Helga's Guinea fowl, heads bobbing and bubble
shrieks spurting out, heralding an intruder.

To their right Sloop was pitchforking compost into a manure
spreader while two black, harnessed horses waited patiently. To
their left Helga, wrapped in sweaters, was yanking feathers off a
steaming chicken carcass. They both smiled and waved.

Enno parked by the shop and walked towards Sloop. Rez
plopped down in the old truck bed for a late winter's nap. Walking by the small stone tool shed, Duden snagged a favorite six
tine fork. Sloop nodded, said nothing. The silence was a gift.
They forked together.

Spreader nearly full, Sloop put a hand on Enno's shoulder
and pointed a nod at the driver's seat. Duden acknowledged with
raised eyebrows and a nervous grin.

Folding the seat back, Duden started to step up onto the
wheel. He felt a hand on his shoulder and saw the finger pointing to the coil of driving lines hanging round the spreader
handle. "Oh, yes" he nodded silently. He took the lines in hand
while climbing into the spreader seat. The team of horses rustled
slightly, waking in anticipation.

With a look at Sloop for approval Enno said a soft questioning "Pete, Jewel?" The horses leaned and, on receiving a clicking
sound, pulled the loaded spreader ahead. First hesitant, then
quick, then quicker. Sloop spoke,

"Steady guys" to his horses

and

"Be a teamster" to his young apprentice. Enno tightened up
the lines, slowed the team and asked,

"Will I be able to tell where this stuff goes when I get out there?"

"I'll walk along and show you" answered Sloop.

The horses roll in their harnessed walk, side by side, step by step. Close harmony. Pulling with ease. Pulling in comfort. Pulling satisfied. Pulling determined. Leaning into their collars for the correct placing of this working moment of their thankful lives. The boy is revisiting a massive right-now enchantment. His tight-set lips conceal a deep-dish smile. Spreader creaks. Chains clank. Horses breathe. Appreciation is everywhere and heard.

Shirley Intoit was back in the old airstream trailer she called home. Stirring Chanterelle mushrooms and butter in the frying pan and watching the evening light ping and flicker around the insides of the glass horse she kept on her window sill.

She was thinking about something her father had written to her. "A life may be small, thin, brittle. A life may be wafer thin and wide as time, elastic with humor and memories. Or a life may be piled high, thick, dense and dangerous. Most often it is all three."

Her life had become all three.

"So what did the kid want?" Bo Coin asked, standing at "Brad's" desk.

Took him a minute.

"Oh, now I know who you're talking about. Wants to buy a ranch around here. Can you believe that? Wanted me to show him your thousand acres out at Snake Flats. Told him to take a hike."

Bo Coin had a thoughtful look on his face which on another man might have been attractive.

"And the blond with the broken nose, which Deli you say

she works at?"

"Clios, behind the pawn shop."

Billie Blue Chevy and Nancy Simmons were sitting in the Gun Club Cafe eating sandwiches. She picked at her teeth and when he looked up she offered,

"That Sloop is fascinating."

After saying it she closed her eyes to make it go away.

"Down Sis, he's married."

"Oh stop Billie, you know what I mean."

"Yes, I do."

"Excuse me," interrupted Nettie Coin standing just behind Nancy, "are you friends of Mr. Duden? Enno Duden?"

Shirley soaked up the last of the sauté with her bread and ran by the plan once again in her musical brain.

'Up to Portland, pulling the Airstream behind her International pickup. Get the strong box from the train station locker but not until a two day canvas satisfies her that no one's watching. Stow the box in the hole she's created by removing the little trailer's water heater. Up the Columbia River and then south down 97. Visit Payout and Wasco friends on the reservation. Leave them some of the 'find', but without letting them know where it came from. Then further down 97 to Central Oregon to see if she could locate someone her father said was a school chum of "Charley's." At this stage, Shirley didn't want to know her mom. She just wanted to complete her search. Some sense of the end of a string. Maybe this Helga person would know something.

"Lady you got him into a lot of trouble. Why should we tell you anything?" Billie had glass-clear blue eyes walking out of a perfectly sculpted face pockmarked to demand tender reflection from any opposing eyes lonely enough to pause there.

"Billie don't be a toad." Nancy was looking into Nettie Coin's eyes as a nurse might.

Nettie's gaze rotated calmly to Nancy's and finding messy comfort. "The business about the police: that wasn't my fault. Oh, maybe it was indirectly. I just never had a chance to thank him. He saved me. Rescued me. Found me. Oh, you know what I mean, he bothered to stop and try to help. I'd like to know how to reach him. Does he have a mailing address where I could send a note?"

"It can't hurt, Billie. Give it to her."

"Don't have it. Not on me. I can get it. Helga and Sloop's got it."

"Here's my address. I'd sure appreciate if you would send it to me."

Pause. Looking down.

"It was my stupid, soon-to-be-ex husband that got that Sheriff's deputy worked up. It was Bo who caused the trouble. I couldn't help but notice the young man going into my husband's office this morning. You wouldn't happen to know what that was all about, would you? I just don't want that fathead to cause the young man any more trouble."

"He went there to meet with some Realtor. I'm sure it wasn't Coin. He would have said something about that last night. Enno was hoping to look at a chunk of raw land the Realtor had listed. Some big piece out at Snake Flats. Only the hotshot salesman sent Enno packing. He never got to the piece." answered Billie.

Nettie's eyes got smaller for just a split second, and she nodded with understanding. Nancy saw it all.

Shirley was getting gas at an Aurora truck stop when up walks what looks like a western-version of a Buddhist monk with an empty bowl in the white hand extending out from his robe. She smiled a chuckle and offered a longish "Yes?"

"Goodness is an illusion."

"You got that right, brother." She put the cap back on her gas tank and handed the sleep-walking station attendant a twenty.

"An illusion with a growth cycle. Plant goodness. Water her. Weed her. Aim the sun at her and she will grow..."

"You want money? You want food?"

"Actually," his tone changed from droning chant to California casual, "I need a lift."

"Out of luck, I travel alone, have to. Sometimes my burps stink. Real bad."

"Are you Alaskan? Intuit maybe? I got drunk once with an old buck near Ketchikan. He was Intuit. Never forget his name. It was Ahchuck. If I hadn't been sitting with my back to the wall his rotten egg burps would have sent me to the floor. That's when I discovered there was life the other side of meditation. Learned as much with Ahchuck as I did in Somalia or Uganda. Learned the best survival has a melody. The worst survival is a kind of live burial in a tub filled with coincidence and non-aligning relevance."

"Hop in," she said.

"Don't you want to know where I'm heading?" he asked.

"We've just decided you are heading my way," she offered.

"Which is?"

"North and maybe east. 'Til we're done," she answered.

"What made you change your mind?"

"Ahchuck Intoit is my uncle," Shirley said with slow relish.

Jimmy Three Trees walked up the main street of Mascara with a large, half-full burlap sack. Two dogs, tied to his belt by hemp ropes, followed because they had to. The sack contained road-kill soda / beer can and bottle empties destined as convenience market trading stock certain to secure temporary possession of cheap wine. Jimmy's face is a small theater of twitches and shakes. As if he were an old Prairie dog being attacked by an army of gnats. His lips move endlessly, yanking on facial muscles, creating winks, frowns, and homeless smiles. Not as indication of madness, instead as if he were a preacher consumed with the final remembering of a soon to be hurled sermon. But to listen. Up close. The words:

"Fa, fa, fa, far the bad whatsit you guys. Guys? Dogs in the grass up my _____. Trees can itchitchitch. Once, Once, I would wait. But there's blood. No, no, no! No more blood. Tastes wrong. Can we cans, cans, cans...."

Jimmy sees a cosmetically intensive, fat knuckled, sixtyish, female, bourgeois tourist coming his way. Middle income, winter high-fashion. She sees him and misses a blink as her face tightens and she feels a thickening neck. Tighter lips, same length of stride, no change in her deliberate faraway face but her walking speed is halved almost to reverse. These things signal him. He stops and yanks his dogs around backing into a doorway. Not to make room, to hide. The industrial bill cap comes off and he holds it behind to cover his butt. Her speed builds. She walks with dynaflow ease changing gears seamlessly until reaching walking overdrive as she passes Jimmy. Her acknowledgments of his existence contained solely in the blipped pattern of her trajectory.

As Jimmy watches the woman pass, from the opposite direction Billie and Nancy approach.

"Hey, Jim, you hiding?"

Jimmy jumps straight up. Startled. Free hand to his forehead. Hat hand still capping his fanny. Eyes wide as two tight little nervous holes can be. He points at Billie and mouths soundless words as the dogs growl. Billie grins. Nancy jabs Billie and scowls.

"I'm sorry he scared you Jimmy." All sincerity, all Nancy.

Now Jimmy's pointing towards the retreating tourist woman.

"Watchout! Disease! She wants wah, wah, wants Jimmy. My butt's for work. Hu, Hu, hu, huh, humm. Dogs sniff it. Can't help it. Diamonds. She's disease. You," he jabs a finger in Billie's chest, "pretty baby listen! Disease kill slow, burn all over. Oh, Oh, Oh, Oh, Oh." Jimmy's crying now. Wipes his face with a sleeve half-composted. "Here Jimmy show you, hu hu hu huh. When Diamonds comes, see you, back quick into dark hole and cover your butt. Yes, Yes, yes, Yes. Do it! Practise!... Any cans?"

"Sorry Pal. Not today. Busted. Couldn't afford a beer if I wanted one." With that Billie put a hand to Nancy's elbow and started them to walking.

"You are one creepy toad! Did you have to scare and tease him that way?" She pulled from him.

Billie enjoyed his big, blushing, satisfied quiet grin. "What did I do?!"

Jimmy watches them walk off and his sadness swells. The dam won't hold. He knows what has to be done. Like a fat old woman in felt slippers towing two confused dogs Jimmy Three Trees breaks into a sliding feet-never-leave-the-sidewalk, high speed shuffle. His bag of cans jangle. One hand searches a pocket. When he reaches Billie, tears are flowing out of Jimmy's twitching, multi-colored, horror-viewing, edge-of-death eyes. A little dirty fist throws a crumpled bit of paper at the "pretty baby" face and Jimmy runs off. The dogs now catching on, provide some happy towing action.

"What was that all about?" laughs Billie.

Nancy's kneeling down. Picks up the greenish ball of paper. Flattens it out. It's a hundred dollar bill.

"Right down through here. Along the edge of the last load."
Sloop was pointing. "Make 'em walk."

Resumé was sitting up in the back of Enno's pickup. On the
toolbox. At attention. Looking. Listening. There. There he was.
Enno sitting on that spreader. Out in the field. The dog whined
did a circle in place then remembered he has not been ordered to
"stay." He leaped and ran, low to the ground, young again. This
was purpose. This was fun.

Enno put the beaters in gear and selected a speed for the
conveyor chain. Rez was slowing as he neared the back of the
spreader and tried to gauge how, where and when to leap in.
This boy. His boy. Not leaving without 'ol Rez.

Enno spoke to the team. Knowing the work, they gave an
extra shove to get the loaded apparatus going. The beaters
whirred and clanked. The conveyor ratcheted. The compost was
carried into the beaters and made to fly out the back in a fan of
debris. It rained down on one confused old dog. Resumé was
determined. Squinted his eyes. Bit at a few offending compost
missiles. Though in a hail of manure the dog kept on following
the spreader and his boy.

Sloop watched. Mouth slightly open. Arms crossed. The dog
made him smile.

Vicky stood at the saloon bar. She was a post-modern Venus
in levis and transparent muslin blouse. The toe of one booted
foot flirted with the brass rail. Four fingers of her left hand
lightly rested on the bar's edge. With one long forefinger she
drew patterns on the melting frost of her beer glass. She wore a
polite smile and faraway eyes. The only part of her which acknowledged the man on her left was her nose. Her broken nose.
It pointed sideways, towards the man.

The large old male looked to be mounting the bar, his feet
pushing hard on the stool leg bracing. His left side torso

sprawled as it curled to pedestal his neck and head across, around, and at Vicky Wood. Fat snake, his eyes went almost everywhere, almost. They avoided her nose. Bo Coin was alive. He was pumped. He was disgusting. This young woman, he thought, was definitely worth a few beers. He murmured stupid offensive little words. The Realtor in him recognized a rising "no sale" sign and it made him work all the harder.

Vicky had completed an upside down V on her glass.

He backed up just a little and asked an important question.

"Do you know someone named Duden? Enno Duden?"

Her drawing finger stopped. He missed that clue and she gave him no others. Someone stepped to the bar and whispered in Bo's left ear. Vicky drew on the glass, making an outline of a barn and smiling to herself.

"Gotta go. Honey, you want another beer tell the barkeep to put it on the Coin tab. I'll see you later."

"I don't think so." She looked through him to the far side of her own passion.

Bo gave an insincere shrug and felt his insides ache.

"Will that dog mind you?" asked Sloop.

"I think so." Looking at the rapt attention on Resume's face. "Yes, I know he will." Enno had no idea where his sense of assurance came from.

"Well I'm walking up above to move my heifers. You're welcome to come. Both of you. But keep him in check. No cow chasing, hear?" Enno felt heat where Sloop's hand rested, at his shoulder.

The farmer/rancher carried his worn old planting stick. It had been a gift from an Anasazi elder. Push it into the soft ready earth. Make a hole. Drop a seed into the hole. Cover with a foot. Press it down with a foot. Move a step. Repeat. A planting stick. Plain. Waxed smooth. Ordinary. Magic. Rituals passed through its grained interior electrifying its core with alignment and purpose and the lint of possibilities. Sloop, too, was a planting stick.

Almost dusk. Cold. They walked a packed trail to the side of a hay field checked with snow patches. Bearded sweaty aromatic gypsy farmer Sloop walked in brisk delight. Looking first here then there. As if in the emotional guise of a woman discovering a meadow of wild flowers.

Enno hungered to know what the man saw. Hungered to see that way. Knew it was a clue.

Resumé shook his head. Repeatedly. A couple of pieces of compost down in his right ear. Driving him nuts.

A coyote yipped too many times. Rez crowded Enno's leg and growled. Sloop said,

"Look at this. See. Here, where it's sandy. Turkey. And right on top of the track. This soft round spot. A Bobcat's toe and claw."

"How do you know what that is?"

"Same way you know about that dog. Mix a few parts of experience with a trust of intuition and put a blanket of romance over the whole thing. You see what you're looking for but only if you're open to it."

Enno nodded from his belly.

"Romance?"

"Yeah, as in lovin' longing. It makes gratitude flow like saliva."

They walked. Quiet. To a scattered bunch of blue and strawberry roan heifers voluptuous in their purposeful symmetry. In their growthy promise.

Sloop slowly raised his planting stick and clicked. The thirteen lovely teenaged bovines gathered on cue and walked away with the nonchalance of Italian debutantes.

He pointed his stick at them and turned to Enno. Tears were flowing from Sloop's eyes.

"This. This is a patch in God's quilt. The quilt that spells out beauty." He turned his head away and up.

Sam was a wreck. Cold. Bruised. Confused. And vengeful. Add that he could only drag his leg. He tried to drink the styrofoamed coffee. Tasted like counter wipings from a hardware store.

The deputy sheriff knew this man wasn't telling the truth.

"A woman? An old woman? You want me to believe that an old woman hijacked your truck. Pistol whipped you and left you for dead and took your truck? You put up much of a fight?"

Sam was elsewheres. In his head he was messing with his own stupidity and the people who put him stupid. He wasn't thinking consequence. He wasn't trying to align his lies. Not beyond insurance claims. He saw a momentary glimpse of denied generosity, denied complicity. He blurted,

"She had a big kid helping her. He stole my worthless dog. Don't care about that. But the truck... Geez... Can I get a copy of your report for my insurance guy?"

chapter five

Cowlitz

When you see a fire from a distance,
never wish it not to be your own home.

The town of Mascara wasn't named, it was designated. The
natives had, for a thousand years, referred to the area by their
word, which in loose translation suggested the words *face paint.*
The nomadic peoples, in their comings and goings, had gathered
vegetable and mineral substances in the area which they used as
coloring. And they had interesting, mostly unpronounceable
names for the collective curvature of three and a half mountain
peaks which now crowded the town of Mascara. Generally
known as the Mascara mountains, or Mascara peaks, it wasn't
until the 1950's that the popular names evolved to Holloweye,
Drynose, Lumpylash and Sunkencheek. The latter of course
being the lower most telling southernmost volcanic crater remains of a mountain. Even today the natives couldn't think of the
peaks by name, they thought of them in their essential presence.
Both the natives and the mountains were convinced that the

Europeans would be replaced soon by Hispanics and Asians and that they in turn would disappear, leaving the ground to break out in boiling pots of steam and mud as a prelude to a truly sacred state of constant explosion.

Horses, dogs, birds, winos, art history majors, menopausal women, and lizards could feel the ground shudder ever so softly. The winos appreciated it as a cosmic foot massage, the art history majors and women fought the paranoia it created, all the others took it as early warning and counted on being advised of any updated urgency.

Resumé's head on his lap, Enno Albert Duden guides his old mystery-drive six cylinder pickup over the mountain pass. Periwinkle morning blue sky with a snatch of dollhouse fabric, snow so bright eyes are useless. In his rock-climber shielded sunglasses, brown-haired Enno looks half-mercenary, half-carnival. Sunglasses give sight-deny sight. The road he cautiously guides the truck over he knows. The road in his head, surprises him. Remembered voices and images blend to create unknowns. The unknowns are desired and they are repulsing.

Yesterday Sloop had talked him into quitting his job in the valley. Moving in with he and Helga. A place to stay and food for some work. Plenty of time available should he want to get a paying job off the farm.

He was on his way to his valley apartment to gather his meager belongings. Carefully pack his precious pile of old farming books. Rent a small trailer for everything. Quit his carpentry job and head back to Sloop's soon's the road condition on the pass allowed. Daytime. He would stick to daytime. Daylight for driving this road. He shook off a memory of the Nettie Coin mishap.

Down his internal road he feels the new confusions. His piece of a day, yesterday, with Sloop had refilled his farm dream to overfull. His time had also reminded him of how much there was to know, to learn, to feel first hand and up-front. Sloop hadn't said it in words but Enno felt the looks. Duden wanted his farm, now. But he also wanted to learn, now. He needed to. He had to. And Sloop needed an audience, an apprentice. Sloop needed something else, expected something left unspoken. In time Enno would be asked to do something, a payback perhaps, he wasn't worried. Should he have been?

Then there was Helga, sweet Helga, strong Helga. Helga of the secret stubbornness, Helga of the thousand skills, Helga of the juxtaposed heart, Helga of the wet grass memories, Helga of the barren womb, Helga of the anguished braids, Helga of the two eyes, one looking forward as for a lost child; one looking back as for a corrected path. Helga, who, in her Berkeley youth, had succumbed to the allure of political urgencies. The crest of the wave had been giddy to the misplaced daughter of a European milk maid. Giddy enough to shield. A young man had loved Helga then, many years ago. Loved her to ruinous completion. Loved her long enough to leave on Helga's soul a soft strong insistent pattern of focused passion and focused devotion and desperate need. Helga's response had been giggles.

When she learned of the accident which took his life she fell off the wave, never to return. The silliness, the girlishness left her forever. She would never know if she might have loved him. She would always know that she had been loved to the top, over the top. For nine months of her young life she had been at the core of an intense blaze of directed light. And she, in her stupidity, had giggled and opted for political meetings and thin friendships. How was she to know that those thin, casual friendships would cut the intense young man into desperate, bloody, jealous chunks.

The young man had left a note for her with his watch. People still wondered how he had managed to tie the bandana over his eyes as he road his Indian motorcycle. They also wondered at how the pearlescent orange fuel tank had survived the accident without a scratch, landing up in the hawk's nest, in the Pine tree directly out from the cliff he had sailed over. Having made it into the lyrics of a Tom Waits song, the particulars and curiosities would only swell over time to become like a pepper flake in the mayonnaise of bay area culture.

But for Helga it was an emotional tourniquet. She would never forget consenting and then watching as her friend, in an effort to help Helga forget, set fire to the suicide note. She would never forget grabbing the watch in fears that it too would melt to horrible ash. Almost immediately began the ever changing flood of memory engendered visitations from and with him. In death he was to never leave her side. She would wake in shudders even now. Regret was a torn shirt she would wear forever. Yes, she loved Sloop, her husband, this other man, completely. But what was wrong? How could her true feelings for this man of her todays not have the strength to protect her from the regret she felt about the other, her ever present man of her yesterdays?

Her husband's today love of her? Sloop's love of her. She was but a piece of something larger, almost as if she belonged to him. Together they worked their land. He conducted, orchestrated the farming. She was an extension of him. Most of what they did resulted in manifest poetry, perhaps because of their fragile co-mingling. They each had their personal barriers, walls of secret strength and weakness, through which the other was never allowed. They talked to one another with tenderness, limited understanding, thick unforgivable familiarity and sympathy but without abandon, without reckless poetry, without silliness, without naked trust. Sloop knew of the memory, the legend, the regret. He had recognized it in her from the beginning and it was an attractant. But he insisted to himself he wanted to know nothing more, ever.

None of this could be shared with Enno. What he felt was the view from outside, that Helga, sweet Helga, was the strongest, happiest, sad, weak woman he would ever know.

With that sappy wandering wonder he found himself look-

ing into a daydream of Nancy's face. He shook it off. He was not
to know her the way he longed to. He stroked Resumé's head.
Pascal's triangle was called upon and thoughts about learning to
plow with a team of horses came into him like a welcome stream
of water.

"If you're French... this name - Sigis Mondo - isn't that Latin
or Italian or something?"

"The name's a holdover. From another time, another life."

As they drove and spoke Shirley had a growing uneasiness.
This "Monk" felt wrong. Her father had insisted that coincidence
was God's clue that change was coming.

"The hunter makes the coming change his own. The hunted
misreads coincidence as good luck or as unimportant."

It was too easy. This monk knowing her uncle. Too damned
easy.

"And you, young lady, you're on some sort of quest. I read it
all over you." The monk interrupted her day-dream hookup.

"That was deep." She observed sarcastically. "You use new
age clichés like some men pick their noses."

She worked her throat hoping to hook onto a ripe and
offensive burp. Failure.

He smiled with superiority, with half-concealed purpose.
His smile was Zenless and premature. For most prey, the look of
him was an attractant. For Shirley, the look of him was a warning.
She could see how it was he saw. To her, the monk saw as though
through the unassailable eyes of a hunter drunk with the proximity of its prey. She saw his eyes as two cups full to overflowing
with digestive juices. Nothing sexual, it was all portal, doorway,
stepping stone, all throw away, all trespass.

Shirley remembered a feeling, a guidance. It was impossible
to see through her glass horse. The bouncing colored light became everything. She had to look away to see. She looked at this

man and couldn't see him. Then she looked away and knew she would ditch him at the next stop.

Helga opened her farmhouse door and invited Billie and Nancy in.

"Sloop's off cutting rails. Not sure which direction he went." She knew exactly where he was. She knew exactly why she lied.

Nancy's head was turned slightly and she tried to look hard at Helga without being obvious.

"You know, if you folks got a telephone you'd probably get less drop-ins like us," offered Billie chuckling.

Helga said nothing. She was actually enjoying the dangerous competitive measuring warmth of Nancy's gaze.

"We've come hoping you've got an address for Enno. The Coin woman might be wanting to dump a rescue reward on him, or something."

Without taking her eyes off Nancy, Helga said,

"It's here. This is his address. Sloop's invited him to live with us. He went to get his things."

"Whoa, wait 'til Vicky hears about this," said Billie.

As if in an aggressive trance Helga spoke in a firm monotony to Nancy, "you are wondering about my husband, about me..."

Nancy's mouth parted. Her eyes grew and radiated the crytaline color of embarrassed pain across her face. She offered a slight hesitant sideways shake of her head.

"...I need my husband, he does not need me..."

Nancy squirmed and inappropriately continued to shake her head no.

"...My husband is complete. I am incomplete, like you."

Nancy reached for Billie's sleeve without finding it.

"...I love my husband for who he is, what he does, what he can do. He feels the same way--about himself. I wish he were

someone else, someone simple, someone who needed me completely." She was looking deep into the apron she curled in her
red hands.

Nancy took the moment, the pause, and allowed herself
composure; thin, pained, contrived, drugstore composure.

"My husband's like his stallion..." she was looking up at the
kitchen ceiling and drying her hands in her apron - over and over
again, "...you think you can see right through him. But you can't.
Its his passion and those secrets. They hold you off. A glass
which hides, which conceals."

And with that Helga turned and walked from the kitchen
leaving Billie and Nancy alone.

"We better go," Nancy said.

"You got that right, Sis. Whoa, this woman really needs a
phone!"

"Yes Billie, you're right. She needs someone to talk to."
Hearing herself, Nancy felt small. Feeling small Nancy reached
for sad. It didn't take long for her to settle for cheap.

Outside they walked through an oozing mud with thin
wafers of ice as skin. Approaching was a black and grey team of
horses pulling a rubber-tired wagon piled high with Juniper rails
stickery with hairy bark and sharp limb remnants. Sloop drove.
He had seen their car and knew someone was visiting.

"Hey," Billie said as hello.

Sloop kept his eyes on Nancy and nodded. Nancy was
mesmerized by the grey horse. Beautiful broken-egg-shaped
white dapples each surrounded by shimmering black. Powerful,
muscular, erect with an oily smooth haircoat, glistening, almost
suggestive. He was harnessed and hooked to the wagon but with
an individual, towering strength which denied any appearance
of servitude. By comparison the beautiful black mare, in her long
winter coat matted by sweat, looked dull.

Nancy's eyes caressed the form of the stallion, marvelling in
the perfect firmness and correct curves, rejoicing in the skin's
color pattern. Her eyes were like fingers tracing along his skin,

up the erect neck to the proud defiant head with the blinderless bridle. His eye, the stallion's eye, stopped her in a crashing waterfall of ice.

She stepped back and shuddered. His eye was a clear grey, like milky glass with a light which shot out from deep inside. He was looking at her. He was inspecting her. His nostrils flared and pumped.

He was expecting her.

Nancy's trance was broken by Sloop's words.

"Glass. His name is *Glass*."

She looked at Sloop and had to look away quickly when she saw his nostrils flare to the same rhythm as the stallion's.

Brad looked up from his desk and swallowed his gum. Vicky Wood was standing there smiling, looking wreckless, available, alive. Looking certain of her boundless appeal to masculine wilderness. She was wanting something.

Brad's voice broke in a squeak when he offered a questioning "Yes?"

"Hi." She took a long time with that one word. "I'd like some information about some property you have advertised."

Brad shuffled papers, slid back and forth in his chair and blushed as they talked about the property at Snake Flats.

"Brad, can I see you for a minute?" came Bo's voice from the mezzanine above.

Shirley couldn't remember the last time she had laughed so hard. Her big rear view mirror afforded a perfect long look at one brown-robed, French, Buddhist monk, hemline pulled up for running and exposing hairy skinny white lower legs sprouting out of two Converse high-top tennies. His john time at the rest area had proved to be her perfect opportunity to ditch him. It would be one of the first times any one would laugh at the image of *the Monk*.

Bo was chewing hard on his good luck. Alone with Vicky in his posh new Landcruiser and headed out to the most remote corner of the county. She wasn't buying any property. She was inviting him. Looking at the fit of her clothes he almost hit a tree.

Eating a cucumber sandwich and watching the train station, Shirley remembered how the strong-box business started out.

There had been a letter from Uncle Ahchuck with a scribbled confusing map and a request. 'Send money.' A key was included with the letter. The note read:

"Ten year ago up on Elk Knee fell onto rough cabin. Man inside fevered wants to die. Tells story like already dead. Falls from sky. Hides. Buries box. Comes north to laugh and wait. Wants to keep laugh. Tells me draw map to where he buried ticket to a thousand thousand beers. Must be February shadow Uncle dig two February's for thousand thousand beers. Crazy man laugh in wind. Now you little one. Spread beers around if there. Send hundred dollars today. Key yours."

The crude map showed a Columbia River mile post, a back water slough, a raised railroad bed and a row of willows with one large cottonwood. At 10 in the morning in February, the sun shining on the cottonwood was supposed to cast a shadow across a gully on the slough bank. Mark the spot and return later to dig there two feet down, but only at night. You will find a double metal ammo box. The key was for the lock.

Shirley spent two weeks at the site last February.

"So what's your game? We both know you're no 'qualified buyer'. You didn't bring me way out here because you want this worthless old homestead." Bo was still angry at her rejection.

"You brought me out here. And I'm glad to know this property is, in your words, worthless." Her maybe smile was maddening, completely maddening. Vicky knew exactly what she was doing. "I want this property."

Bo tried not to scratch himself as he appraised the situation.

"Whether I think its worthless or not doesn't matter."

"Don't embarrass yourself, Bo. I know this property belongs to your wife."

"Still takes money. You got money?" He was not concealing his sarcasm.

"I got what you want." Vicky said it slow.

Bo said nothing.

"You get property all the time without spending a penny. You trade for it, you shuffle it, you foreclose on it."

"Are you proposing we trade?" He couldn't conceal his smile.

"No honey, I'm not. I'm telling you I want this property and you want me. You aren't going to get me. I'm going to get this property. You've already helped me. Anyway what I've got is worth a darn sight more than this property."

"This is the way it works. I know you're lying to me. All the way. I know it." The Sheriff's deputy was pointing a loaded finger at Sam. "You blew it, fingering Mrs. Coin. Either I charge you with filing a false report or you sit down with the lady and get your stories straight. Both of you need to come in here and correct this paperwork. Do you understand me?"

Sam was ten years and several brain cells older than the deputy but he still felt like a juvenile delinquent.

She insisted on meeting at the Deli. Sam didn't like it because there was no room for the bum leg and no privacy. His urge for Central America was looming large.

"I'm older than my husband, ten years older. It was my father's money. I know that now." Nettie was playing with her frozen yogurt.

Sam wanted a French cigarette, some Oozo, and a professional woman who understood abstract expressionism. Sam's leg hurt.

She hadn't followed the instructions about night time digging. Maybe that was part of the reason this whole business still made her nervous. Though there were lots of reasons to be nervous. It was broad daylight, middle of the afternoon, when Shirley's little folding shovel struck metal on the slough bank. Pulling the box out had taken better than a half hour. She hadn't wanted to wash it off in the river for fear she'd further damage the contents. Spreading newspapers on her trailer table, she'd brushed at the small lock with an old toothbrush. It was evening by the time she'd finally given up getting the key to work and had cold-chiseled the box open.

Inside, on top, were two newspaper clippings folded neatly into a zip lock sandwich bag. Under this and clearly visible, though discolored, were several plastic bags full of money. Shirley took a deep breath, looked up at her glass horse, and carefully opened the limp newspaper clippings. They were of two headline stories from The Oregonian about a sky-diving hijacker who called himself D. B. Cooper.

Titus made an entry in his journal;
" How far out dare we go? They will come to our efforts and find

vain excess, which they will enjoy excusing, and find expressed aban-
dons and loose-jointed advance, which will confuse and frighten them.
Then, torches in hand, they will come in force to remove us from our-
selves. Only later will they claim our efforts as their own. Only later,
after we have gone away, will we become ourselves to them and finally to
end as nothing of what we were.

"We are exceptional. Those in charge are not. They want exceptions
deleted. They will disregard us to our death, or, if we insist on ignoring
their disregard, they will make a mess of us and themselves. It is not a
natural law, it is the plastic law of mediocrity."

He paused, took a slow drink of his iced peach nectar and
read what he had written. The arrogance and rationale he saw
there bothered him so he crossed out the second paragraph and
wrote;

"The penance of Wagner's Klingsor, a comedy of layers and
manners. An unnecessary meal. A pretty vulgarity. A thick kiss. A
chorus of sympathy pains.

"Let us pretend we are going to live."

He closed his journal and opened the book of Rimbaud
poetry.

Chapter Six

Rogue

"Mosaic law instructs people what they should believe,
not, or not only, how they must act."
- Louis Menand

Chores done, Helga and Sloop drove their generic pickup
to Mascara. It was dawn. They made this trip every Wednesday.
Sloop's visit to the post office. Helga's walk past closed shops.
Both sharing breakfast at the truck stop. Then to the hardware
store, next to the feed store to deliver eggs and herb sachets.
Then Sloop disappears into a repair shop complex in the industrial park while Helga reads her mail in the truck. When the
bank opens, they trade places and Sloop sits in the truck as Helga
visits her safety-deposit box at the bank. Most every Wednesday,
same routine.

This morning Sloop went into the post office box area
thankful that no one else was there. A quick look around and he
produced from his pocket four different keys. At each box he
carefully removed the contents, head side to side, eyes watching.
Some items went into his coat pockets, some items went into a
brown bag, while he accumulated Helga's letters in one hand.

He frowned, still no response to the new ID request. One
more day, then he'd have to consider recycling "Kenneth

Church." Kenneth could go away. That's okay. But no one should be looking for Kenneth. John B. "Sloop" Ogdensburg, Kenneth Church, King Simmons, and Clyde Taylor were all aliases...

Helga's expression was empty as she glanced into the shop windows. Blank, empty, expressionless until she saw the travel poster of Sydney, Australia. It caused a changing, she felt small like a stuffed doll being encircled by large gentle hands. Her psyche was being massaged. She stood wistfully gazing at the poster until a faint smile of possibility crossed her lips. A flashing memory of her chickens and garden sadly woke her. She moved on, glancing once over her shoulder at Australia.

At the truck stop diner over the formica table Sloop handed Helga her small bundle of mail. He noticed what was perhaps a fresh face color, transparent, lain over her normal steady sadness.

"See something today?" he asked.

"Yes." Long pause. "Have you ever thought about traveling? I mean, seeing new places."

"I think about it often. It's why getting the kid to stay with us is important." He answered as he opened a letter and sipped the cafe's dishwater coffee.

"You know what makes dull? Dullness makes dull. Didja' ever notice how it is that an exciting person is never dull? And a dull person?" Sam was looking at Nettie hard.

"What are you trying to say?" She almost stopped herself from asking.

"You, lady, are dull with a capital D. Now don't go grabbing for your little gun. I'm trying to salvage 'our time together'." He made fingered quotation marks around the 'our...together'. And he sneered.

She sucked in a whimper and exhaled a used-tissue forgiveness.

Sam stroked his knee and looked out the deli's window. "Dull," he whispered, "this town is dull."

She inched closer. "What?"

"I said this town..." He turned his head to face her and was surprised to find her so close, "...is dull." He frowned as he looked at her. "You know, you're not a bad looking broad... just dull... you do it to yourself, you know?"

"We can't change how we look. Who we are." She fiddled, red-faced, with her little handbag.

"Wrongo, lady, wrongo. Hang out with dull people, become dull people. And vice the versa. Who decides who you hang out with? Huh? You do." He turned to look back outside. "Like this souvenir town, a hangout for dull people. Perfect name, Mascara, 'cause women with thick makeup, controlling attitudes, costume jewelry and neutered husbands run this fake town. Good place to hide. Not worth much for anything else."

Nettie looked over his shoulder and out the window. She saw Coin Bros. Realty. She saw the lavender Landcruiser pull up. Plump boyish Bo heaved himself out. Then she saw lovely Victoria Wood exit the other side. It surprised her. Her ambivalence surprised her.

"Mr. Riven, in spite of the fact that men like my husband run this town, I still think it's a fine place. Just fine."

"Fine equals dull. Don't you understand? Can't you see!?"

Jabbing her finger at the window she shouts, "My husband's not dull! She's not dull!"

Looking out the window, Sam answers, "Your husband's as boring and predictable as a load of wet laundry. Not an ounce of real passion in him. He's human waste, fat, madeup, bebobbled, pushy. He's a woman! Your husband's one of the women who run this town. As for the blonde, she depends on depravity and her fragile looks. Can't handle mystery or the emotional hydraulics of reality."

"What a lump!" Nettie was smiling a new smile. "You are what they mean when they say *'so and so is full of himself'*. Mr. Riven, I'm not going to defend my creep of a husband nor that that that lady, I'm through with all that. But you, you misogynistic creep! You are something else!" It surprised her to feel the volume and freedom in her voice. She was in the fight.

Riven noticed.

"Call me Sam, honey."

"Why on earth would I call you 'Sam honey'?"

She caught herself and started to laugh.

Marvin Seesaw was a big Payoute. Two hundred eighty pound tribal elder, casino consultant and many times grandfather. Marvin lived to drag stories out. He was less interested in surprise or mystery or illumination. His game was repetition. Shirley Intoit was his match, she was born to the game.

"Seeds belong to our Mother Earth. Our mother the earth is the keeper of the seeds. The belonging seed rests cupped in Mother Earth's fat hand. When..."

"Forgive me Marvin, but the seeds also belong to the birds who eat them and to the winds which carry them. And..."

"Shirley Intoit, your wisdom will grow with time but you complicate and you confuse. Seeds belong to our Mother Earth. Her care of the seeds is simple and as it should be. There is the story of how our mother the earth came to be the keeper of seeds. It was a time when..."

"Forgive me Marvin, your wisdom is legend and I would never question it. In fact I tremble" (smiling she says this) "to remind you that the lowly seed chose Mother Earth not the other way around..."

They continued to a point of laughter. Marvin's face changed. Instantly stern and distant. "Little one, we laugh and play pat ball, while the Yeewiz are killing our seeds."

Shirley backed away from the game they had been playing. She knew it was time to wait and listen.

"The Yeewiz are making our seeds sick so that the money comes always to them, only to them. It is for this reason I ask you to take your uncle's beer money and give it to the Glass Pirate 'horse Victor'. He waits in hiding with powerful weapons against the Yeewiz. But he needs help to stay invisible. You, little one, have been sent to help Victor."

With these last words, Marvin's head dropped. He was lost in emotion, exhaustion and meditative measure. She knew she was being asked to go.

As Shirley was leaving Marvin Seesaw's old Airstream trailer confused and intrigued, she noticed, nearby, a white woman hanging underwear on the polycord line which stretched between the TV antenna post and a knarled Juniper tree. Shirley introduced herself and dove, head first, into her curiosity.

"Who or what are the Yeewiz?"

"Honey, ain't you never heard of 'GeeWhiz', that huge corporation that makes everything from corn oil to underwear, from rat poison to baby formula. They even invented a way to make seeds! Marvin's" (with a thumb over her shoulder) "skeered of 'em. Says they are death to everything."

Shirley nodded non-committally.

"Who's this Glass Pirate, Victor?"

The woman chuckled. "Nobody knows 'cepting maybe Marvin. Sometimes I think it is Marvin. But he's too old and slow 'cus of his wisdom'. All I know is that once a week, Wednesdays, Marvin and his grandson, Carl, drive all the ways to Mascara. When they come back Marvin's smiling and laughing and thumping stuff and talking 'Glass Pirate'. If you ask me its some kind of senile gang stuff. You know, 'private club'."

Bo was fascinated and more than a little confused. The man who sat opposite him wore expensive big city clothes, perfect toasted skin tones, shellacked fingernails, shiny blue black hair and the demeanor of a sun-soaking snake. Bo had known all along that the real power, the real money, would someday come to Mascara, come to him. He slid his big bottom back and forth on the polished carved swivel chair seat. Bo had known this time would come and he had assumed he'd know what needed doing. But what Brice Liner wanted made no sense.

Helga sat in the truck counting the cash she'd received for her delivery to the feed store. Sloop headed 'round the building. He unlocked the metal door and went inside what appeared to be a small storage room with boxes and brooms. He locked the door behind him and removed a circuit breaker lid inserting a slim rod into a hole in the back of the panel. The side wall of the closet slid silently sideways. Revealed was a small room. Clothing along one wall and three live computers on the opposite wall. Sloop closed himself in and went to the conventional door with a tiny fisheye viewer. Looking through he saw that Jack and Titus were the only ones there. Fishing in his pockets he brought out two of the morning's post cards. At the computers he typed in stuff while reading the cards. Then he changed into his disguise while waiting for the printout. Another look through the fisheye. He could see they'd all arrived. Carl had brought Marvin again.

Enno and Resumé arrived in Mascara needing gas for the truck, food for their bellies, and an emptiness addressed. The long trip over the mountains had been time enough for wandering thoughts to stagnate, to set promise to melted jell. Enno wondered if he'd ever get a farm of his own. He could handle the waiting if at the end he was where he wanted to be. As if he had the cosmic authority, he insisted that he would not wait for the paint to dry on anything less than his heart's design for a farm.

As for the dog, Resume', he wore Enno's longing, anxiety and passing depressions like tight underwear. They'd only been together for days and already the dog was consumed by his new partner. It was a wide awake trance.

Enno stopped at the Mascara market and asked Resume' if he would like to chew on a nasty warm beef and cheese burrito. Resume' smiled and allowed a long tongue to hang wet from the left corner of his mouth. Enno correctly interpreted this to mean "do you have to ask?"

Walking to the market door he noticed two filthy tennis shoes sticking out from around the corner of the garbage dumpster. The dog seated at the end of the frayed cord immediately confirmed who it might be.

"Jimmy?" The shoes drew in.

Around and up against where dumpster met greasy wall sat Jimmy Three Trees. A bottle of Thunderbelly wine, a plastic tub of synthetic cheese spread and hard bread sticks adorned the mumbling old jester.

"Hey," said Enno.

"C.I.A. - rags to break in in in in a a where they hook fingers into your empty holes and and drag you till you..."

Enno sat down, politely refusing the offered appetizers.

Not expecting an answer, appreciating the value, he asked, "How you been Jimmy?"

The old man looked at 'Digger' Duden in a series of uncontrolled winks. "Heard something bad. Pretty boy is being looked for. And and and big shot mean Realtor wi' wi' with C.I.A." He put his finger to his lips, screwed already tight eyes to cautious slits, looked around, and stood up. He looked in the dumpster and yanked on the dog's cord. When the dog came to him, he clamped his hands over its ears and whispered.

"Pst, they're ugly rags, flug, always ugly to watch you. Going to find you where you go. Your holes. They and and and they will drag you. They they pay for what you know."

Enno frowned. What Jimmy lacked in coherency was always outweighed by his sincerity, essential accuracy and truthfulness. What Jimmy lacked in coherence made him a fool to most everyone. Not to Enno.

"Jimmy..." Enno started to speak and stopped when he glanced up and saw, ten feet away, the tall craggy, slender, grey-haired cowboy with the grocery sack. The man was watching them with a strangely animal-like sewage-free stare. Just as casually he turned and walked to a pickup truck.

Jimmy was up frantically gathering his stuff. "Not safe, not safe, not safe."

In the market Enno learned that the old cowboy was a sculptor/rancher named L.J. Shoulders. He tried to remember what Sloop had said about Shoulders.

Helga was in the bank vault alone with her large metal safety deposit box. The clerk had greeted her with a "here's Helga, it must be Wednesday" smile. That was thankfully past. Now she was alone with her box. Helga's two rough hands rested on the lid as she said her ritualistic, silent, eyes-open, prayer. Inside the box were several large envelopes and a soft black cloth draw-string bag. She removed a thick manila envelope closed by a rubber band. She opened it and added this week's egg and sachet money. It was a tight fit. She would have to remember to get another envelope. Soon she'd have to rent an additional box. That would make four. With the little pencil stub she recorded the week's two hundred plus dollars. Her almost ten year total had now reached just under ninety-five thousand dollars. She acknowledged the number with the softest sad blink and no enthusiasm. Envelope closed, she trembled as she took hold of the little black bag. Still trembled. After more years than she cared to count she still trembled. She took out his pocket watch. Opened the cover. Reset the time and wound it carefully. What she wanted were those searching blue-grey eyes looking sideways deep into her. She only remembered them now because of this weekly visit to wind his watch. It was the only thing which remained of him and the possibility of 'them'.

"I wish I knew bright, like in shiny" Nettie mused as she came down from a relieving laugh.

Sam Riven, face altered now to reveal a compote of nervousness and certainty sprinkled with humor, gently took her hand. Nettie's face wrinkled and she made a limp attempt to pull away. Very slowly he began to unbutton the sleeve of her cream-colored silk blouse. That was too much, she pulled her hand away quickly.

Sam smiled, almost gently, and wagged a finger at her. Without words he pulled her arm back towards him across the delicatessen table and unbuttoned her sleeve as she watched shocked, thrilled, suspicious, anxious, and nervous. Goosebumps raced each other across her body. She looked all around the restaurant as he folded the sleeve back two turns. The action was repeated on the other sleeve. Sam leaned back grinning with palms outstretched and up.

"Brightening, my dear, you are brightening."

"What? Because of two rolled-up sleeves?"

"No, because your skin is alive and your brain is peeking into places you don't know. Undo your collar button."

Nettie's neck grew longer.

"Let's just say I'm in research and development. My company's done some investigating. Important work's being done here. We're not sure by whom or exactly where, some clues. We need to know, and now. It's important to us and worth paying for. Mr. Coin, here, says you might be in a position to help."

The young man dishes up a disbelieving smirk, looking from bloated merchant to blighted mercenary.

"Let's cut to the chase, shall we? We know your small inheritance is about gone and that your pretty little life of, shall we say, modest leisure is threatened. We'll pay you well to keep tabs on a few people and report everything to me." Brice's fingertips were poised against opposing twins in a constant, rigid pyramid.

"Who's on your list?" asked Billie grinning.

"John Ogdensburg, Kenneth Church, Sam Riven, Lloyd Shoulders, Victor Armanhope and Enno Duden. That's for starters. The list may grow or shrink as we move along. And rapidly, I suspect."

Those fingertips had to be glued together, still no movement, no flex.

Billie glanced at Bo who was fidgeting.

"Well Mr. Big," looking at Brice and turning to Bo "that is what you called him, isn't it?" Coin wanted to strangle Billie. "Well, maybe you've made a mistake. Maybe I can't help you. You see, I only recognize three names on your list. And one of them is a friend of mine."

Brice was looking forward to snapping this arrogant brat, snapping him in two.

Just then Bo's second story office window shattered as a paper-wrapped rock dropped to the floor.

"What the...!?"

Billie picked it up. Brice raced, hand inside Armani coat, to the window. He couldn't know he was watching Vicky help Jimmy across the street and that he in turn was being watched from above.

"There's a note tied to the rock." He opened it. "It says,

> Bo Creep and Geewhiz stooge,
>   First we stamp out complicity.
> Next we destroy agency
>   Passports current?
>   - Milk Man "

"That's impossible, there is no way they would know I'm here." Brice looked at Billie as if he were already dead.

On the roof of Coin Bros. Realty a slender form crawled to the waiting ladder.

Chapter Seven

Owyhee

*"...in that instant he had lost his head. His head was
always most valuable when he had lost it. In such moments
he put two and two together and made four million... it was
real inspiration - important at rare crises - when whosoever
shall lose his head the same shall save it."*
- Chesterton

Helga was ever so slightly animated on the way back home.
It was because of the Fork family.

Towards Sloop's farm, the last seven or eight miles of infrequently maintained dirt road, wandering from pine grove to juniper thicket to bunch grass and sage country, was often in poor condition. But the deeply rutted, narrow spur trail splintering off the main road and accessing the Fork family holding, was always miserable. A miserable way in to a harmonious, sheltered haven.

It was Jackson, Franklin and Mahalia - the three Fork children - they always delighted Helga. Changed her outlook, her posture, even if only for the moment. Those children and their parents always made her smile.

To get on the Fork road you had to half circle a big old ponderosa pine. That tree always reminded Sloop of Jefferson

Fork. His tree trunk-like torso, ramrod straight, supported a huge
cross timber of shoulders off of which hung thick arms.
Jefferson's black skin shone with varied rich burnt sienna under-
tones coming together in a visual treat. He was a happy, happy
man married to a big, magnificent, Jamaican beauty, Brenda, who
everyone called 'Yummy'. And to round out the household there
was Titus Ibid, family friend, and co-conspirator.

The farm road wiggled in tight serpentine curves down a
ten percent grade into Preacher's Hollow. It felt like many other
secluded spots in Central Oregon where deep canyons sheltered
rivers and creeks. But this was different. Preacher's Hollow was a
dry box canyon.

Somewhat dry.

Maybe not really dry because there was the seep and swamp
at the center of the Fork holding.

The gradual north and fanning south slopes going into and
forming the hollow were designed by Jefferson's personal God to
pour sunlight into the hole. The steep east and west walls protected the spot from winds. The hollow's bottom undulated with
thickets and ribbons of poplar, willow and cottonwood trees
framing the geometric orchard quilt squares of late winter peach
and apricot branch fuss.

On the bottom, Sloop's driving came upon the first fenced
pasture, a long narrow fringed by a young pine thicket and
bordered on one side by the rough road. They saw a familiar tall
thin silver-haired white man driving two black mules which were
pulling a chain harrow. The man was Titus Ibid, Jazz bassist
extraordinaire and agrarian Sancho Panza to Jefferson Fork's
comic effort to reconcile his own Quixotic nature.

Astraddle the one mule's withers, hanging on to hame balls,
rode five year old pretty and black Mahalia. Titus stopped the
mules when he saw Sloop's pickup. He waved. Mahalia waved.
And she bounced on the mule's back as she hollered "Helgies
here, Helgies here!"

Trying to keep it to herself, Helga squirmed a little too. She

wanted to hug that child. Sloop knew. Sloop was anxious all
week for these moments when Helga's sad guard dropped and
she became someone else, sugared and fresh from life's oven.

They drove on, around the next bend and came to the edge
of the oldest orchard. Gnarled, worried, healthy, old Peach trees
threatening in their collective bare-branch, tip-fuzz to swell and
burst. Sloop always marvelled at how Jefferson and Brenda had
worked such miracles and complex patience with their fruit trees.
The universe has many centers. Sloop believed the Fork orchards,
indeed the entire Fork Holding, was one of the centers of the
universe.

It was Jefferson who insisted from the beginning to call their
place 'The Fork Holding.' Most Wednesdays there was an important lunch meeting of a small handful of agrarian magicians.
Jefferson loved the image of the 'Fork Holding' as home to such
glorious lunches - all in attendance were revitalized, all.

It was for this place, to this place, that Sloop had drawn
Enno a map.

("Drop your trailer off in town and join us for lunch at this
farm. I want you to meet some people and a place." Sloop had
said. Nothing more. Sloop had never previously mentioned the
Forks to Enno. He had been saving this.)

Just past the willowed edge of the peach orchard another
pasture unfolded. This one contained the unusual view of twenty
water buffalo, cows and new calves, eating on a row of loose hay
Jefferson had spread earlier. That field concluded up against a
tall wall of silvery Poplars. Hidden temporarily were irrigation
handlines, a meager string of old farm implements, and three old
Suburbans kept for parts. Next a board and batten polebarn with
the words "FORK HOLDING" and a brand painted in white high
up in the gable under the hay door. The brand was a three
pronged fork coming out of the bottom of a heart. Juniper and
Pine rails around the barn. Rock Cornish Game hens pecking the
farm lot, it was clean, orderly, nothing left laying. Snug up
against the barn lots was a rustic new-made, salvage-materials

home with covered porch. Smoke wafting from its chimney. A
row of bright, common laundry was freeze-drying on the porch
cord. The walls of the house held a symmetrical organization of
old windows and doors. Tied to the porch rail was a winter-
haired, 13 hand, black and white Pinto wearing a child's saddle.
Under the porch were three sleeping Redbone Hounds.

Sloop pulled up and parked. Helga looked in the direction
of a squeal. From out of the stone and old window greenhouse
came running a coat-bundled four year old Franklin, his arms
filled with a towel in which lay steaming fresh-picked lettuce,
peas and herbs. He shouted 'Helgie, Helgie!' And his *Los Lobos*
ball cap bounced precariously on his little head.

Each dog barked once and went back to sleep.

Helga swooped up Franklin, squeezing and kissing him as
he giggled and softly rubbed his forehead against her pink ears.
Sloop, on the porch, lifted his nose and closed his eyes. 'Ah, this
ritual!' he thought. The kitchen odors from Yummy's Wednesday
lunches always swelled his chest and made him itch behind the
knees. 'Ah, yes' he thought.

He was rudely roused.

"You're early," said a stern seven year old Jackson. "Mom
and Dad are wrestling. In the bedroom." He guarded the front
door. Hands on hips. Sloop grinned and held his porch spot. In a
short minute Jackson's little form seemed swallowed from behind
by the massive bulk of his father. Jefferson stood behind the boy
tucking his shirt tail into his jeans.

"Son, let John in. Let him pass." Rich baritone.

"John." Nod. "Jefferson." Nods, winks, suppressed grins,
ripe respect all around.

Enno and Resume', having split the deli-equivalent of a
gastro-intestinal depth charge, release runaway gases as they
continue trailerless to their meeting with Sloop and Helga.

"Sloop, I need to be in the trenches with you. You know that. This battle belongs to all of us." Jefferson and Sloop were standing by the wood heater talking in half-muffled tones. Sloop was looking at the autographed photo of his friend Jefferson with pianist/composer John Q. Lewis.

"Jeff, this is sneak work. Nobody can know who any of us are. How we gonna' disguise your big black carcass?"

Enno and Resumé double-checked their scribbled map just before circling the big Ponderosa and taking the Fork spur road. He noticed a "serious," four wheel drive, camouflage-painted, high-rise pickup truck coming up behind him. He made his turn to clear their way and was chagrined when they too made the same turn, right in behind him. With the road so narrow Duden continued on in search of a wide enough spot to let the other truck by.

Helga was in the Fork home holding little Franklin and listening to Jackson's narrative. She was smiling. From across the room Sloop watched his wife. His slow, self-comforting nod did not escape Jefferson's gaze.

Then the bedroom door came open like a ship's sail and "Yummy" Brenda Fork floated into and across the room on big bare feet, the other end of a smile warm enough to roast chestnuts. All six foot of her perfect black, Rubenesque torso welcomed everyone and anyone to her home.

"Helga, in the kitchen darlin'. I need you. And Choo Choo, baby, you better get your sweet watermelons out marching and fetch in the professor and baby girl. Mornin' John. 'Member love belongs to lovers. And that man, "(she pointed to her husband Jefferson) "is a lover. Go with him and get him to explain that little pinching thing he does. Choo Choo honey, if you played that Piana the way you play me there'd be lettuce growing in here what already had French dressing on it. Go now, go."

Both John and Jefferson were grinning and blushing as they headed out the door.

They were following him close, real close. Their pickup was half again taller than his old chevie. When they backed off a few feet, he could make out two men in camouflage outfits, painted faces, lots of rifles. Hunters, he thought, impatient hunters. Well, he couldn't and wouldn't go faster. He wondered what or which hunting season would be open late winter. Resumé sat next to him, chin resting on the seat back as he watched the following truck. Every so often he bared teeth and made a menacing, almost mechanical sucking sound. Looking over at the dog, Enno smiled. He marvelled at how such a new short-term friendship could feel as though it were the result of a lifetime together.

They continued for a handful of miles with no place to turn off. Twice the following truck had stopped and it seemed perhaps they'd lost them. But both times they roared back to within inches behind Duden's bumper.

Ahead, maybe a solution, the road widened adjacent to what looked like a long narrow field. Enno saw the farmer just before he pulled over. His tall shiny silver-topped form. Even though coated he was thin like an Ichabod Crane. Duden pulled his truck to a stop making sure there was ample room for the other pickup to pass. He was mesmerized by the sight of this farmer walking behind a harrow which was being pulled by two big black mules in harness. Atop one mule rode a young black girl, maybe five or six years old. Enno drank in the sight, the combing action of the implement, the softening of the pasture's look as the dark stains and piles of livestock droppings were broken up and spread. The Preying Mantis form of the farmer teamster appearing less in necessary control and more along for a pleasant walk.

Enno had for a second forgotten about the following pickup. He rolled down his window readying himself to wave. That's when he heard the strange voices from behind. Laughing, taunting, spitting out cuss words, horrible sounds, deadly stupid questions. That's when...

Enno turned in his seat, disbelief opening on him. Locked doors in his brain, worst memories, terrible baptisms, all came up in his throat to stain his nature.

Behind him the two camouflaged men stood beside their truck with beer and rifles in hand. Hollering into the brisk air, one of the brockle-faced men said,

"Hey, little girl, 'sat 'yo daddy?" Mean laughter.

"No, no, Joe. I got it! You see that is her daddy only he's like a double freak seein' as he's a black albino!" Peels of laughter.

Enno's skin stretched to bursting. He remembered the orphanage, the savagery, the time they tied him half under the bed naked from the waist down, his little friend's 'forced' accidental drowning, the pain of being always left out. Enno's eyes grew and grew yet his eyelids were hard and larger than his eyes. A ring of cold air circled each eye ball and his mouth shrank to a small tight pucker. Resume' looked at him and wondered. As the young man opened his truck door, consumed with corrective purpose, Sloop and Jefferson were watching the scene from through the bordering Pine thicket. They were coming to call in Titus and Mahalia for lunch when they first caught sight of what was unfolding. Sloop's hand was on Jefferson's shoulder. Titus had stopped the mules and taken the sobbing Mahalia in his arms. And the two 'hunters', cocky in their confidence, continued,

"Hey, little girl, come here a second. We just want to talk to you." Smirks. "Come here, right now, you hear?"

He was so outside of himself, so inside of himself, he was

invisible. They didn't see him coming. The first thing they heard was a low panther-like, "What is this?" Coming from the quick wide eyed intruder.

The crazed Duden stepped to within inches of each of them and clamped a rapid hand on each rifle, yanking them loose before a reflex response was possible. He tossed the rifles, crudely, into the back of the truck.

The one 'hunter' came jerking alive and in anger made a sweeping move on Enno - but a second too slow. Duden grabbed both of the man's ears in his gripping fingers and yanked the painted face to within an inch of his own. Pained, the man pulled unsuccessfully at Enno's wrists.

"Please listen to me." Came Duden's porcelain/nitro whis-per. Pulling out and hard on the ears with a strength belonging to the poisons of regretted loss he continued,

"You will get in your truck and you will drive away from here and you will never come back. You will do this now."

The hunter's partner stood motionless except for his eyes. Enno's lunatic strength and determination angered and fright-ened him. He thought about his pistol hidden in back. He thought to do something.

Then he saw the others. The two men just inside the trees. The big black man and, and... He knew those eyes. He knew what that crazy old white man could do. Had done. He rotated his eyes to look at Enno. 'Geez, they could be kin', he thought. He wanted out of there right then. He grabbed his partner's arm just as Enno let go. Cursing and mumbling they got in their truck and drove off.

Enno wiping the sweat back, off his forehead, started in awkward deliberation, to walk back to his own truck.

Resume' sat in the road. Head cocked sideways. Mouth open in disbelief. Stub tail reluctantly wagging.

Titus and Mahalia watched. Watched enough to reach through space and touch Duden with their directed attention. He looked their way and said,

"I'm sorry. Gosh, I'm sorry. I wish none of that had happened. I'm sorry."

He and Resume' got in the truck and drove off real slow. They didn't see Jeff and John cross the road to talk with Titus.

Enno didn't drive very far. Stopped. Lowered his head to the steering wheel. He was exhausted. Sat that way for long minutes.

Came a tap on his window. Looked up, startled to see the thin man, mules just past him, girl riding again. Rolled window down.

Man's long arm came slow into the cab. A bony hand arrived and rested on Enno's shoulder. A warm strong pressure from that hand. A smile without assumption. No words.

"I'm okay." Offered Enno without prompt. "Looking for a man named Sloop."

"Almost there. I'm Titus. She's Mahalia. You must be Duden. Please follow us."

The mule team ambled up the dirt lane as if pickup and man were in tow. Girl frequently turning to look back at Enno. The old blue pickup crawling along in low gear, giving boy and dog good time to take in the unfolding of the Fork holding.

Sloop and Jefferson went quickly back through the trees anxious that Duden not know they had witnessed his confrontation.

Chapter Eight

Illinois

"There are no isolated sacrifices. Behind each individual
who sacrifices himself stand others whom he sacrifices with
him without asking their opinion."
- Albert Camus

His slow entry into the sheltered canyon ranch of the Fork Family had erased the burning mood of the incident with the hunters. Enno felt the same emotions he felt every time he entered Sloop and Helga's farm except with greater concentration. The tapestry of the place was all brand new to him and there was so much to see and taste. He parked a little distance away from Sloop's rig trying to be perhaps a little out of sight. He left his vehicle and walked the few steps to try to understand an unusual nearby building.

Duden stood in the arched entryway to a stone and timber structure. A reminder of one of those depression-era, WPA project, campground buildings. It was massive, symmetrically balanced, open on all sides. There were wide eaves and it had a concrete floor. A craftsman-style Appalachian storm cover for picnics. Only this one had an unusual use. Enno smiled.

The building was full to 3 foot high with a steaming mound

of manure compost over the top of which brightly plumed chickens pecked and scratched.

A short person had come up on him. Little Jackson Fork stood alongside Enno, one of his dark hands slowly, cautiously, hooked into Duden's front jean pocket. Minutes before with a pointing nod of his silver head Titus Ibid had directed young Jackson towards Enno who was just stepping out of his pickup. To the seven year old welcoming committee of one, just standing alongside the stranger was good enough. He looked up and saw the wonder reflected in Duden's eyes which were still directed at the building and its function. Jackson tugged on Enno's pocket.

"It's poop. Lots a' poop from the animals. And mommy's garbage. Know what it's doin'?" asked the anxious boy.

"Compost." Came Enno's slow marvelling answer as his gaze took in the meaning and measured value someone had poured into the building.

Little Jackson was hurt not being able to offer the answer to his own question. But that small hurt fell away as he stared at the rapt "Digger" Duden.

"Wow. How'd you know it was compost?"

Enno smiled and let his eyes wander to other distinctive elements of the Fork Farmstead. The handmade stone and used-window greenhouse. The wooden silo next to the pine barn with the Fork brand painted in the gable. The tidy sawbuck rail fence along the back lane. The water buffalo cow and calf in the budding orchard. Wow, water buffalo! The curious low, hugging, used-materials house with the wrap-around porch. The sleeping Red Bone Hounds. The Juniper smoke smell. The parking area full of eight cars and pickups. The child's teepee in the fenced raised-bed-fringed side-yard. It was all a marvel. He had thought only Sloop's place could do this to him.

"Well Mr. Duden, lets go inside and meet folks," came Ibid's voice. "Jackson, you take care to unharness."

The little boy looked so worried. "Okay, but don't tell anyone he knew about the compost. Wait for me, okay? I want to be the one who tells. Okay?"

"My promise, son. Now go to the mules, they're waiting."

Little Jackson patted Enno's leg. Smiled the smile of anxious dance. Smiled up at his new discovery. His new smart friend. And then he ran to the barn.

"He's so small. How can he unharness those mules?" asked Enno.

" A stool. And the mules like him. They help."

Titus too was enjoying this young Duden. Enjoying watching him drink in every little fragment of the place. New and wide open. Moments like this were tonic to Titus. They yanked at his infrequent complacency. Titus understood Sloop's choice. And he approved.

"Oh, what about my dog? Can I let him out?"

"Chase stock?"

"Its funny. But he listens to me." Enno said this with such a sad smile that the old man heard a song in the response and felt himself nod the rhythm nod. That nod which makes the buttocks sway slightly.

Resumé's eyes were glued on Duden as the three approached the house. The dog allowed himself to wonder about this intense fixation he had for the boy. But his thoughts were secondary. First came a passionate need to be with him, to please him.

Titus smiled at the dog. And at the young man. This was what Titus Ibid had been created for. This and playing bass. For the 'next one', whoever he or she might be, he was a sympathetic guide to the universe. Rhythmic counterpoint, grandfather, backdrop, over-qualified sidekick. His grin itched.

Cruising south of Madras on Highway 97, Shirley felt the road through her music tape. (Cooder's *Buena Vista Social Club*). She was in that cushion space, in-between, tasting befores and

afters mixed together. Zero apprehension. Full float. She thought
about all that money. Didn't touch her. Felt like laundry. Somebody else's. She thought about the mission to learn about her
mother. Maybe this Helga woman would have answers. If not
she'd keep looking. But something else was cooking too. A new
small hunger. Maybe she'd take some time to find herself a
puppy. One out of working stock. She got happy thinking about
that. About the companionship. Thought for a flash of a second
about what it might mean to have a man for a pet. Shook that off
violently. Looked in the mirror. That sedan again. At the Crooked
River Bridge construction project she pulled off on the shoulder.
The car went by. When she got back on the road she noticed the
sedan had pulled off at the wayside ahead. The male form driving the offending car waited until she and 3 cars were past before
pulling back out. So that little rental car WAS following her.

Oochuck had frequently told his daughter that the best way
to disappear was to stop moving. And that the best place to hide
was out in the open wherever you belonged. The best place to
hide was in plain sight.

Mascara was just ahead. She'd ditch him there. Didn't know
the town. Confidence held her.

'Who was it?' she wondered. It bothered her just a little. Not
knowing when the tail had started.

Town of Mascara. She watched her rear view mirror. NOW!
She turned hard, fast, without signalling. Into the gas station.
Past the two pump islands. Left again between station building
and vehicles filling. She stopped her pickup and trailer. The grey-
blue sedan went past, then left at the sandwich shop and
stopped. Shirley pulled out. Now she was heading back the way
she came. Back to the little trailer park outside of town. A self-
pay low-rent setup. She pulled into the frontmost space and
quickly unhooked the old airstream. After dropping the pay
envelope into the slot she pushed her black hair up into a ball
cap, pulled on a hooded sweatshirt, and headed back into town
in her pickup truck. She was a little surprised to see him still at

the sandwich stand. Beside the sedan. Looking puzzled, up and down the main drag.

He looked different in regular clothes. But he couldn't hide from her. She remembered, with a smile, his skinny white legs under the raised monk's robe.

She was hungry and noticed the deli sign. Eat. Then she'd stalk him.

"These are, well, they are, beautiful. I think. Yes, yes. I do. They're beautiful."

Nettie barefoot. Nettie walking slowly around the big table. Nettie, both hands wrapped around the coffee cup. Looking down at many small full-colored prints of fanciful gravity-defying design. The colors showcased Alizarin Crimson against golden yellows against Ultramarine blue surrounding rich Cadmium reds all punctuated with small marks of translucent dark greens and black. The designs were Moorish geometries violated by floating figures of animals and women. Nettie hummed in conversation with the pictures. That over-obvious tired age she had carried before was gone.

Sam leaned against the studio post. Watching her. Playing with his cigar stub. They were at his place and a hundred years had been packed into a handful of hours. Impossible things had happened. He was off balance. He was absorbed. He was adjacent. Somewhere alongside what he thought he would always be. And he knew he'd never be the same again.

"Why would you, why would you hide this part of you? The artist part?"

"Don't think of myself as an artist. I'm more of a light-industrial graphic doodler." Then he added, without thinking, "keeps me tuned up for my real work doing fake identity papers." "Geez!" he thought, "why'd I say that?!"

But no need to worry, it was obvious she did not take him literally. She'd think it was just more of his extreme nonsense.

Coffee cup to her lips. She looked at him beneath lowered brow. Two ear-to-eye smiles. Curved mouth-like grins at each lower temple. Nettie had become someone she always thought she could be. Except for the subliminal terror. It was so frightening to think of a fluid living and doing. She was expected to always be 'in waiting,' as a living posture, her entire adult life.

And Sam was taken also.

But he wasn't ready. He felt the need to push in other directions.

"Come with me to Central America. We'll spend your money and my youth, what there is left of it. I can see you with crossed ammo belts and a loose fitting bikini."

Nettie stuck her finger tips into the coffee and sprayed him with droplets. "Maybe, except for you dressing me, but first I have things to do." Her breath quickened listening to her own words.

"I know, I know, the Duden thing. I still can't figure that out. If you feel like you owe him something for helping you... I can understand that. But this business of just handing him over a big chunk of land... Sweetie, it just don't fit."

She set the cup down and cut short a sigh.

"I don't expect you to understand. And frankly, I don't understand your Central America attraction. This is something I have to do." Her face was blank, turned inside out. Then it returned in a 'come here' smile "But I do expect you to help me."

Sam was grinning from ear to ear. "You what? You are shameless." He squinted, "what's that? You have a little flake of something at the corner of your eye. Come here a second. Let me look..." When they were near one another he whispered, "of course, I'll help you. But nobody knows about it. Got that? And I'll be difficult every step of the way."

"Just the way I like you, I think," chewed Nettie.

"Six years ago two hundred million dollars were siphoned

out of Chasm Hattan Bank. Embezzled. Stolen. Some clever cracker took it. At the time the suspect was a man named Armanhope."

Billie Blue Chevie picked his teeth with a broken toothpick. He struggled to maintain composure. Brice continued;

"Armanhope disappeared. I think he's here in the Mascara area."

"Be pretty hard to come here with all that money and go unnoticed," offered Billie.

Brice smiled a vengeful paint-stripping smile.

"Chasm Bank received several notes from what they believe to be Armanhope's group explaining how the money was successfully 'redistributed' to Latin American and African farmers.

"Group?"

"Had to be. Operations were too spread out."

"Then its true, about the redistribution?"

"Don't know if it all went out but the evidence is clear that those idiots actually gave away millions in seed, plows, tools, food, even medicine to those poor slobs. Gave it away! Gawd, I still can't believe it!"

Billie registered the depth of Brice's anger and disgust. The theft Brice admired. The total disregard of that money's higher value drove Brice Liner to want to break things.

"So what do you know about this group? What's it got to do with this corporate sabotage you're working on?"

Brice looked at Billie a very long time. Billie was up to it, or thought he was.

"Remember the note on the stone? *Milk Man* he called himself. Chasm got a similar note from Mexico, several years ago. I saw it. It was signed 'Milk Man'. THIS TIME they won't get away. THIS TIME I'll find out who he is. Next time he disappears it will be for real."

Billie bit down and broke the toothpick into two unusable short sticks. Brice noticed.

"Before we go in." Titus stopped Enno, "Humor me a second. We sometimes share the weather, we humans. This outside weather. Most of the time our inside weather, inside our heads, we have to go alone. Often though there is such a storm or gloominess deep inside, it comes out through our skin. Blinds us to what's outside trying to get in."

Enno was looking down, feeling as though he'd had many hundreds of such talks with the gentle old man he'd just met. Also a little miffed. Why him, why Enno? Why was it that old guys just naturally seemed to gravitate to him and try to psyche him out?

"We get ourselves in a bad funk. There's times when we miss out on the good outside weather. The clue is to find 'in-between'."

"I'm sorry. I don't mean to be disrespectful but I don't have a clue what you're talking about."

"It's not that complicated. You're here now. You decide what or where here is. You have some place where you want to be..."

"Yeah, I do."

"So between here and there is a place that is entirely of your choosing. And you can make it a perfect filling for today." Long pause. "Where is it you want to be?"

"Farm of my own."

Slow spreading smile across Ibid's unsurprised face.

"And you're here, all messed up with fear and courage, anxiety and calm, need and maturity, curiosity and patience, thirst and thirst. My suggestion to you is that you make of today a time to drink-in introductions. You're being formed, this place, this day. These days to follow, will loom very large throughout the remainder of your life. Some people read palms, I read futures. I trust my internal measurements and you, son, will live a very long life of enormous challenge and consequence. Today is your day to take measure, not to measure up. Don't waste it on anxieties about a farm. You will have your farm, over and over again."

Titus turned and opened the house door for a confused Enno.

"Nettie, young Duden's a loser. He's a vacuum. Don't get me wrong. I like him. But he's just a piece of glass sitting too close to the shelf edge, waiting to fall off and break. He'll never amount to anything. Certainly not, if you give him land. The only chance the boy's got is to earn it slow and hard."

Nettie pursed her lips and yanked three gathered Sam Riven chest hairs out by the roots.

"Geez woman! That hurt."

Shirley Intoit stood in the deli line behind two middle-aged hog-sausage day-trader types, Brice Liner and Bo Coin. The menu was interesting. More so than the *'come to me baby'* garbage the boys were shovelling at the pretty sandwich clerk.

Wasn't that interesting, Shirley thought? The way the broken, flattened nose, set the woman's face to a visual cantata. Hard not to look at her.

Brice Liner was leering at that deli clerk, Vicky Wood He reached across the order counter and grabbed her hand. His left arm hung off away from his torso like a wrestler's. His legs were spread, probably to aid the circulation of air to overheated well-larded areas. He acted as if no one else was present. Or, perhaps more accurately, as if no one else would dare to intercede. Shirley noticed the oak display barrel with the 30" long bread loaves in brown paper bags. Without thinking she pulled two loaves from their bags and quickly slapped the baguettes up, one into the waiting armpit, the other between Liner's spread legs. Brice instinctively jumped and clamped legs together and arm to his side. Vicky's hand came free and went to her gaping mouth. She struggled to keep from laughing. Liner looked as though he'd been run through with Baguette swords. A jealousy-splattered Bo, hesitant with fear 'til now, started to smile and quickly backed away and into the deputy sheriff who had just entered the deli. Shirley calmly stepped forward, winked at Vicky, and said,

"I'll have a Salmon-Cucumber on pumpernickel. Hold the white man, please! No pickle, no rhyme, no slime. Oh and I'll have a half caf/decaf/slider pecan Latte with caramel, hold the cilantro. The names Shirley. I'll take it outside in the yard."

She left a $10 bill on the counter and turned to leave. Bo was pointing at her and Liner was crushing a baguette under foot.

"You'll have to pay for that." Vicky offered.

"No, I changed my mind, don't make him do that, it's too embarrassing." With a puckered pout mouth she added, "Instead put it on his tab." Shirley pointed to Bo Coin and nodded to the curious deputy.

Vicky choked on hard laughter.

As he slowly entered the Fork home, Enno's senses were swimming in a whirlpool of stimulus. Low ceilinged, the first room spilled into other rooms around posts and exposed circular stairway and bookshelf islands. To his right the front room merged with what looked like a child's bedroom that had three rope swings hanging from a weight bearing beam. Straight ahead was an enormous dining table up against a room with a grand piano, an upright piano, a stand-up bass and instrument cases piled up. From the left came the smells. Rich aromas. 'Cooking stink' as little Jackson Ford would say, 'cooking stink.' The second sweep of Enno's eyes peopled the space and they were looking at him.

Titus chimed, "Everyone, this here's Sloop and Helga's

friend, Mr. Duden."

Enno felt her coming before he saw her. Brenda Fork. He turned to have his shoulders received into two big black hands. The look of "Yummy" unsettled him. Six foot tall, a striking full beauty with translucent brown eyes. Eyes forty-two feet deep. She held Enno and looked at him.

"Honey, you beloong here." With that she kissed his forehead and returned to her kitchen.

Sloop was approaching when the front door opened and a form vaguely familiar to Enno entered. An old cowboy. Fit, erect, handsome, almost proud. Enno felt a tinge of worry. This was the man who had so frightened Jimmy Three Trees. This was the man who had been listening to their conversation. This was the one they called Lloyd Gerald Shoulders. They said he was a cattleman and a sculptor. They said he was an old fashioned gentleman, and he was a hermit. He walked casually past them and into the kitchen to receive a hug and a kiss in exchange for the bottle of wine he brought. Only Enno paid him any mind and he held on to that for now.

Sloop led Enno to the big table. He was looking at the boy through a new eye, a new prism. At the table three men were talking. Sloop put Duden in a chair next to a big black man with a smile as deep as Brenda's eyes.

"Well, I don't care," a man from across the table said, "if we worry about those things, and hold back, in just a few years the entire world's food supply will be at risk. We're heading back to the middle ages except, instead of evil Kings, we'll have evil corporations."

"Where the leadership? Why's nobody screaming? Why's nobody working for change? We need some courage in government," said another face.

"It's not about leadership or government. It's about dogma. It's about how our culture, if we truly have one, pushes us all." Titus was reaching for an open magazine as he spoke. "Listen to this, these are the words of Jacques Barzun; *'around 1890 art joined science in spreading the twentieth century dogma that latest is best.*

Modernist man looks forward, a born future-ist, thus reversing the old presumption about ancestral wisdom and the value of prudent conservation. It follows that whatever is old is obsolete, wrong, dull or all three.'"

"So, is he saying that artists have sold us out?" asked 'Jeff,' Jefferson, Fork.

"I think so, in a sense, yes, but that sense is collective and has been spurred by the so-called tastemakers, the critics and historians who in their desperate need to explain everything in a connected stream have forced the issue of a depleting, pervasive, artificial modernism." Titus.

"Since you insist on reading to us, where's that quote you showed me the other day from that California-based British painter?" Sloop.

"You talking about Hockney?" Titus

"Yes, I think that's the one. Here, let me see that. Listen to this; *'If we are to change our world view, images have to change. The artist now has a very important job to do. He's not a little peripheral figure entertaining rich people, he's really needed.'"* As if asking for a response Sloop turned to face Lloyd Shoulders, who was standing up against a post. Shoulders said nothing and seemed separate from the conversation.

Enno listened and looked around, attracted to the fabric of the words but completely lost to their meaning. This stuff was way over his head.

Another redfaced man spoke up, "This is getting a little far fetched, the real issue is how corporate greed is destroying humanity and the planet and you guys are trying to tell me it's the fault of Shoulders and other artists like him? Come on, let's get real here. Old farts with too much education and time on their hands, people like Ibid," he nodded towards Titus, "they're the problem, thinking too much, analyzing too much. Nothing's gonna change until we can understand what turns the crank for young people. What about you kid, what is it you want out of life?"

"That's enough Joe," warned Jeff.

"No, I mean it. I'm prepared to go to jail or die because of what I believe in. Is it too much to ask that I know what the kids, who I'm sacrificing for, expect out of life?" He was speaking too loud.

Jeff and Sloop slid in on either side of the man, Sloop took the wine glass from his hand and Jeff lifted him by the armpit. They moved towards a back room and the man hollered over his shoulder, "What's trump kid, if you don't know we're all screwed?"

Enno felt himself shake, he wanted to slip out, this wasn't his place. What stopped him cold was a low string riff, turning he saw Titus plucking at a stand up bass and winking at him. Then came piano, tumbling, cascading, tap dance piano. It was a surprise to see big Jefferson Fork bent over the upright keyboard tickling out a Walleresque rendition of 'Kind of Blue.' It made Duden smile and look around to see if Sloop was there to share the moment. The back room door was shut and there was no sign of Ogdensburg. But he couldn't help but notice Helga and Brenda together. Both of Helga's hands were together inside of both of Brenda's.

The moment was shattered with a boy's scream. The front door flew open and young Jackson came falling in, breathing hard, and stuttering. Jefferson's huge bulk was to his boy's side immediately.

"What is it son?" Was interrupted by

"It's Marvin! He's outside, bleeding. Carl says somebody shot him!"

His friend had beat it. Mumbled something about a crazy old white guy in the brush, with a big black. But nobody was pushing Charlie Hopkins around. Maybe he wasn't smart. But at least he was tough. That shot he had just fired, into the old yellow pickup, would bring the kid out. And Charlie would shoot the man's ear off. That's all he wanted, just to give him a taste of how it felt. He simultaneously stroked his rifle barrel and his own bruised ear.

There were seven picnic tables outside of the deli. Scattered along the bank of a grassy ditch somebody wanted to believe was a creek. This brisk late winter morning the sun warmed only two exposed table surfaces. The others were shaded and wore a frost fuzz. At one table sat the bent odd shape of an old man who seemed to have a dog tied to his ankle. Shirley sat at one table. Jimmy Three Trees looked to be shivering. He was mumbling and beeping strange noises.

"Are you okay?" asked Shirley.

Jimmy's eyes looked at her but his body refused to acknowledge. In a minute he offered.

"Ba, a, ba, it, it, ba. The Enno boy, bo, bo, boy."

Shirley stood up and moved cautiously to his table. She didn't talk but her body language asked slowly, gracefully, if she might join him. She sat carefully trying to read his face.

Jimmy started to cry. It was like the marriage of a biblical flood to a feeble epileptic seizure.

Shirley sat still in attendance.

Vicky Wood came out carrying Shirley's sandwich and coffee order. She came gleefully anxious to meet this funny warrior woman. At least until she saw her sitting with Jimmy. At least until she saw Jimmy crying.

Shirley looked up quickly, "Think we should do something for him?"

"That's Jimmy. He's Mascara's token homeless person. Found him yesterday nearly hysterical. Can't understand him..."

With that the crying stopped and Jimmy wheeled around, clasped a chicken claw of a hand on Shirley's arm and fired a torrent of babble at her.

Vicky noticed it immediately, she was astounded. This strange young woman understood him, she actually understood him!

"What's he saying?"

Shirley held one hand up, and watched Jimmy intently. He slowed to a whimper.

"There's somebody name 'Doodin,' 'Eeeno Doodin?' I take it it's a young friend of his?"

"Yes, yes, I know him, Enno Duden."

"This man says that Duden is being set up. Somebody named 'Chevie,' somebody whose supposed to be a friend, is double crossing him. He says Duden's to be found and hurt. Hurt bad. Jimmy here thinks they might want to kill him?"

Just then the little bell on the deli's back door jingled. The women looked up and saw the menacing form of Brice Liner. Shirley felt something and turned to watch Jimmy Three Trees scrambling to run away, dragging a whining just awakened dog. Turning back to Brice's direction she saw the bad man had disappeared.

They had all run outside partly because of Jackson's announcement of Marvin's being shot. But most certainly because the three children, Mahalia, Franklin and Jackson had all run out. Brenda was calling loud and anxious to her children.

"Franklin get back in here, NOW!"

Helga and Brenda flew like furious hens out the door. All the men scrambled. Enno had a horrible premonition. Everyone's eyes were to the children and Carl's yellow Ford pickup with the shattered passenger window, everyone except for Enno. His eyes were everywhere else. Instinctively he grabbed the first person he could reach, it was Sloops' shoulder. Enno hollered, "Wait, everybody, come back quick!" The shot rang out and Enno felt the air trail of the bullet push on his cheek. Children screamed. Sloop saw Enno's face, a thousand year old face, a visage torn to despair by regret. A face turning to locate source, a face paralyzed. A face unable to scream NO.

Brenda had Mahalia and Jackson heading back to the house. Helga ran to scoop up baby Franklin. As she stood between Sloop and Enno with the child in arm, the second shot rang out.

She felt the surprise of the bullet entering her head. She felt Sloop's arms. She thought of the children. She thought of her chickens. She was in Australia. Her last thought was of his watch.

Chapter Nine

Little Luckiamute

"I see, gentlemen, that Hell hath let out for recess."
- Howard Mosher

Sloop was on the ground. Helga's bleeding head in his lap. Brenda phoning for help. There was confusion mixed with stun. Except for Enno. He was looking very hard at one particular spot of sage, rabbitbrush and scrub juniper.

There, he saw it.

The pattern moved again. He looked around quickly, did anybody else see it? Mouth open. Ready to holler. Saw Sloop's intense stare directed at him. He also saw Sloop's slow side pass of the head. Sloop was telling him not to say anything. Sloop was willing Enno to keep quiet.

Duden dropped to one knee and whispered to his friend, "But I know who it was! I know where he is!"

"So do I. So do I" came Sloop's response as his eyes made an arc towards the road hunter's hiding place. "And, I know how to find him later. Right now, this time belongs to Helga."

"Air Life chopper's on the way," came Titus' report.

Ibid saw John "Sloop" Ogdensburg's war zone clench. He

saw Duden's assigned guilt. He saw John's eyes move to the brush spot. And they anxiously, guardedly, nodded to one another.

"She's alive. She's still alive," came someone's insistent report.

Away from any news of the trauma, Nancy Simmons, half-sister to Billie Blue Chevie, registered nurse on self-imposed sabbatical, worried from too much emergency room trauma, thirty-three year old 'professional' woman. Too long dedicated to her career and now anxious about life missed. Not ordinary life, not the usual stuff. It never had much attraction for her. She was interested, keenly interested, in those things which tax imagination while making life emotionally expensive. But today, now, she had to deal with the tawdry small realities.

"Billie, I need a loan. I'm almost broke. I may have to go back to work soon. Hope not, I'm not ready yet." Pause. "I've got to pay some bills."

"Sis, I'm sorry but I can't help you. I'm 'bout broke myself. Got a scam going that might pay off. But today I can't help you."

"Thanks anyway. Guess I'll put an ad in the local paper. Maybe I can get a quiet live-in nurse job and avoid the emergency room a while longer."

Yet another spot, a ramshackle cabin on the back of Bailey Butte. The smaller wildlife, looking out from warm holes, thought they detected a hesitant warmth coming from the cabin windows. Before the light had always had a cold sarcastic brightness, now it had a pink tinge and a barely audible hum.

"I see myself as scum. I do virtual virtuality. I justify it by not accepting payment."

"There you go again. What are you talking about?" she asked.

"Scum. As in bad stuff."

"I got that part. Yes, dear, you are scum. Lovely scum. It's the other part I didn't understand."

Sam Riven thought for a second. But only a second. This was new for him. It was a free fall. He looked at Nettie and felt the melt. He had to go with it or lose it. He reached into his wallet and pulled out his driver's license.

"See this? I make these for people. Only the ones I make are fakes. You want a new birth certificate or driver's license? I can make you one that will fool anyone."

"But that's illegal, isn't it?" She sounded like the surprise wounded her.

"You betcha. Seriously illegal but in my view highly moral. And I aim to keep it that way."

"Moral?"

"Baby, you ever think about this system that has to number, name, tag and catalog every fool one of us? Why do they have to do this? Against our will. Why do they? It's worse than police state tactics. Its kennel or feedlot management. It denies individuality, liberty and a bloke's right to be anonymous. So anything I can do to gum up the works I figure is my duty. Besides, I try not to help degenerates and I never accept money. Got it whittled down to just 3 'brokers.' Might whittle more. Titus is the only one I really trust." Pause. "Won't meet or know any of the actual 'customers.' 'Ids' I call 'em. The brokers handle the Ids. Nobody knows me, I know nobody."

Lights cigar, feels old, lonely creeping in and tries to swat it away. 'Don't go back there!' He says to himself.

Nettie's mouth was open. She had backed out of the new warm *Sam* circle. She had been in that circle. She was slipping out. Out and away from him.

"I'm losing you." Sam twinged, porcelain fear he'd never known before.

"This is so, I don't know, so scary. So different from anything I've known." Inside Nettie's head she had a question in the form of pictures. The pictures asked 'what am I doing? I see futures, I see pleasures, I see confusion, I see possession, I see belonging. Too fast. Isn't this too fast?'

"I shouldn't have told you."

"Why did you tell me?"

"Maybe because for once in my life I was letting myself see an escape from my cranky, lonely self. Secrets, especially ones with any passion, can hold you down. I guess I thought I could unload a little of the weight."

She took the driver's license from his hand. While looking at it she said,

"Maybe we're both going too fast." Pause and then, "Did you do this one? Are you really Sam Riven?"

He chuckled, "No, I didn't do that, its real - mine are better - and Yes, I'm Sam."

When he smiled like that she wanted to cup her hand, softly, against his rubbery old face. In a very short time he had lifted her out of those predictable, artificial, internalized, deadening expectations and hurled her at the speed of emotion into a posture of strength and magnificent inevitability. She wasn't an old woman now. She was elegance, grace, naughtiness, empathy, and adventure. A reprieve. He had done that to her, for her. Without trying, without ulterior motive, he had done that. A quick glimpse over her shoulder at what she used to be, days ago, hours ago, and she knew there was no going back. She chose to hold on to this new muscle tone, these new trembles, this new positive. She slid her hand up inside the sleeve of his snap-button denim shirt and stroked his arm. His eyes brightened from the electricity.

Same time, a distance away and inside a trailer, a young half breed woman took measure of recent events. Shirley and Vicky struck a chord. Vicky's concern for Enno and Jimmy. Shirley's curiosity about all that and the fact that Vicky knew of this Helga Ogdensburg. They agreed to meet when Vicky got off work.

There was a chance this Enno Duden and Helga might be at the same spot.

Meanwhile, Shirley had a 'date' with the man who had been tailing her. It was her turn to stalk him.

Brice Liner, the thug, had apparently disappeared. He should have been a larger concern.

The Air Life chopper had landed in the pasture next to the peach orchard. Radio calls to specialists to aid in diagnosis had determined that the wounded woman needed to get to the Bend Hospital for immediate surgery. They invited Sloop to ride with them.

"Just a second."

"We haven't got seconds," came the paramedic's response.

Sloop turned to Titus as he moved to the copter. He handed him a slip of paper with the road hunter's license plate number. "Come to me at the hospital with the address, tell no one else."

Titus turned without a word and left in a fast walk.

Sloop looked at Enno a few yards away and thought fast. "She'd want you along too." They both climbed into the helicopter. It took off. The water buffalo cow and calf scurried to the distant pasture corner followed by a crystalline spray of chopper chased snow.

Resumé watched his buddy go up in the air. He whimpered and loaded himself in the back of Enno's old pickup and laid down. 'He'd better come back real soon.'

Sig stood in neighboring porch shadows. He watched Shirley get into her pickup and drive away. The dark Lincoln Towncar pulled out slowly behind Shirley's old International pickup. Just as Sig was set to go to his little rental sedan he saw the little old crippled man, with a dog, jump up from behind a dumpster and hurl a rock at the Lincoln. It struck the trunk with a sharp thud. The car stopped. Brice's well-dressed ugly bulk jumped out of the car but Jimmy Three Trees was already out of view around the store corner. It gave Sig a chance to see Brice and click a quick photo with the digital camera.

"This guy," he thought, "will definitely be of interest to the boys."

Brice failed to notice Sig. He loaded back in his car and sped off to try to find that girl.

Next to Sig was the high-powered high-tech brief case they had supplied him with. Sig used the 'company' cell phone modem and laptop to send the digital image to the 'boys.' He did this while following Brice's Lincoln. Something told him that Aachuck's niece no longer needed to be followed. She could be found at the end of this 'thug's' fishing line. He hadn't expected to see an obvious 'urban professional' in this little 'designer' western town. Follow the Lincoln, he thought, and there might be a double payday in this.

`Sig Maltesta aka Sigis Mondo- French/Italian monk, martial arts signatori, mercenary soldier, bounty hunter, collector of fine porcelain figurines and now on contract to the big boys as a private operative .

They stepped outside of the hospital waiting room. Helga was in surgery. Doctor's weren't saying anything yet. Enno was coming apart emotionally. He was responsible for what happened. The bullet had been meant for him. And sweet sad Helga laid on the operating table. He knew who did it. Not by name but certainly by looks.

And Sloop, he was being so weird, so strange, so solidly calm; sad but calm. Enno leaned forward and reached out with his young face to tell Sloop... But he was stopped.

"No need, son. Let me spare you. I too know who did it. More than that I also know why. I know he was aiming for you. Because you embarrassed him when you stopped the two of them from bothering Titus and Mahalia. I was there. Behind the trees. Watching."

Enno was stopped. He felt an odd anger swelling. He couldn't think of anything to say.

"This is not a question of blame. We're all to blame for everything that happens everywhere all the time. The only chance for dilution of blame, the only chance for earned peace of mind, does not come from disengaged reflection and guilt. It comes from action. Back there this morning you took action. That was right. You were right. It was beyond question. Don't lose sight of that. What happens next is mine. I have no intention of letting you get there first."

Glass, Sloop's Grey Percheron stallion, was nervous. Something was wrong. He rattled and banged against his pen gate. Half an hour of bumping and pushing and the gate came open. He was free. Off at a run. No interest in the other horses. He had somewhere he had to go.

Little Franklin Fork stood by the back of Enno's pickup chewing his gum. Every ten to thirty seconds he'd crook his little finger and say "here boy, here boy, it's okay." Resumé ignored him. But with the passage of time the old stock dog became fascinated with the little black boy's rhythmic jaws.

"What does it mean, this forever back and forth up and down?" thought Resumé.

Finally out of boredom and curiosity, Resumé waited until the boy was not inviting him, then he got up and walked over to sniff the moving, silent, small mouth. He tried to get his nose inside where the full secret was.

Little Franklin picked up on it immediately. "Gum" he said and took the well used ball of Zookers Bubblegum out of his cheek. Resumé sniffed at it and before he knew what was coming, five year old Franklin pushed the ball into Resumé's mouth.

The dog made a face and let the gum drop from his mouth.

Franklin picked up the dirty ball of gum and wiped it off on his coat. Then he put the gritty mass back into his own mouth. Resume's head went sideways into canine quizzical. Franklin chewed. Resumé sniffed. Out came the gum and the ritual repeated itself. After three rotations Franklin made a big awkward swing with his arm and threw the gum away. Resumé jerked as he watched. While Franklin was busy getting out a fresh chunk of Zookers, the old dog jumped out of the truck and fetched gum number one.

When Resumé returned Franklin's eyes were shut and he was grinning about the new sugar juices squirting from gum number two. Soon both dog and boy were chewing gum.

The two resident Redbone hounds looked on in disbelief.

As backdrop to this little obicular odyssey, adults were scurrying and gathering arms and supplies, organizing a search party for Helga's shooter. Everyone, that is, except for Titus. He had left on an errand.

"She came through the operation quite well. Every indication is that she will survive. We need to keep our fingers crossed that there will be no paralysis. She's still under anesthesia. You're welcome to go in and see her but she won't know you're there. It'll be this evening or tomorrow morning before she'll be alert." The doctor left Enno and Sloop and Titus.

Odd, the deliberate intensity, the military mood that Enno felt. Titus took Sloop's hands into his own. Enno couldn't see the slip of paper pass between them.

"Will you go back to Jefferson's and let everybody know?" Asked an exhausted but steady Sloop, "and take Enno with you."

"Carl's downstairs. He brought Marvin in. Just a shoulder flesh wound. He'll go with us. Here's the keys to his pickup. Oh, and the police were there. Pretended to take interest. Figured it to be a hunting accident. Will be here any minute. And when the sheriff's deputy heard your name he remarked that somebody had been in his office asking about you earlier."

Sloop was thinking. "I won't be going back to my farm tonight. Enno, can you see to the chores?"

"Where can I get a hold of you, if I need to?" Asked Duden.

"Titus knows," he turned and addressed Titus, "the station, my friend."

Titus Ibid nodded and they left.

Shirley drove slowly up and down each Mascara street. She was looking hard for the sedan. For this reason she didn't notice the black Lincoln tailing her. And she wasn't going to find the sedan because it was carefully tailing that same Lincoln. Her Papa would've gotten a chuckle from the image. He would have reminded her of the time the Polar bear her uncle tracked followed the curious Caribou which actually followed the drunken, weed-caped Aachuck. The three made one big circle in the falling snow. Over and over again.

Sig, meanwhile, was reading his just-received wireless fax while carefully tailing the Lincoln. It read, "Big Bad Fish. Call on secured line ASAP. Do not intercept. Do not interfere with. Important we talk."

Shirley pulled off at the small corner market for supplies. The lot was full so she had to park around behind, near the Porta-potties. As she walked into the market, Brice's Lincoln drove back behind and parked next to her pickup. He got out and stood behind the portable toilet. She wouldn't see him. And she had to pass here.

Sig saw it all. Later he'd explain to *them* that the fax came after the incident. Right now he knew he had to 'interfere.' Parking on the main drag he trotted around behind the gift shops and quietly pulled himself up and over the fence. Crouched, he snuck alongside the Lincoln. A chop of the hand to the back of the neck, Brice never felt it coming. Sig slid out the wallet from the prone Armani coat and went quickly back to his sedan.

When Shirley came back to her pickup with the orange juice and toothpaste she saw the suited man laying by the outhouse. Looking closer she recognized the brute from the Deli. Looking around she made a mental note of the black Lincoln. She then drove to the Sheriff's office and reported a passed-out drunken tourist, behind the market.

Sig dropped the wallet in his lap and whistled. He knew what this stuff meant. Big Bad Fish indeed! He was glad he had not been seen.

Resumé was sitting on the porch of the Fork home. Next to him sat little Franklin. He had his arm around the dog and both of them were chewing gum. Only Franklin blew gum. And each time they popped Resumé would almost choke on his own gum. He wheezed with a stock dog's difficult laughter. The Redbone hounds stood off a little watching and wondering.

Brenda Fork was coated and sitting on the porch rocker reading to bundled Mahalia and Jackson. She was worried to genuine sickness about her friend Helga.

Up the drive came Titus' rig, a delivery van. Today it had no sign on the side. Hidden in the back of the van was a big thin flat box containing a dozen pairs of different magnetic signs. Titus could be a baker, plumber or polka band as it suited him or his assignment.

The kids, Resumé and Brenda ran out to meet them and get the news. When she heard Helga was alive Brenda sat down and cried.

Just then through a cloud of cold dust, charged the dapple grey stallion Glass. He ran right up to them snorting and blowing.

"Jackson, fetch me a big halter, quick!" ordered Titus. He turned to speak to Enno,

"I'll pen him up here. You best get over to Sloop's and check on stuff. Since they've got no phone there I'll be expecting to see you in no less than two hours. Otherwise I'm coming to check on you. And, Enno, no monkey business, no hero stuff. Just take care of chores. Okay?"

Duden and Resumé loaded in the old five window Chevie pickup and headed out, with resignation, to be useful, to be nothing more than a farmer and his dog.

Sloop was perhaps driving Carl's Ford pickup too fast. The bullet shattered passenger window let go of little shards at each bump. He had memorized the address. Outskirts of Redmond. His derringer was in the ankle holster. The gravity knife was in the sleeve slit at his armpit. He was trying hard to remember where he had recently run across that old homestead. The one with the deep, wide, hand-dug well.

The copter ride to the hospital had put him back in 'Nam. And this truck ride was keeping him there.

The hunter's truck had been registered to a Charles Hopkins. If he was the one Enno had grabbed by the ears... Mr. Hopkins would never be seen again.

Chapter Ten

Siletz

"Fellows, try to understand that your model is not your final aim,
but the means of giving form and strength
to your thought and inspiration."
- Charles Dickens

Brenda and Titus watched Enno drive off with his gum-chewing dog. Under her coat "Yummy" wore a quilted apron. She pulled up the corner and wiped tears from sepia-toned cheeks. Helga would make it. She willed it.

"Will he be okay, you think?" Slipping her arm into Ibid's and watching the boy drive off.

He looked at Enno's dust, thinking.

"Life surprises us. How we react to those surprises, that's what makes our story. His ... yes, his is a quiet story, but an important story. Yes, he'll be okay."

Enno needed the company. So Resumé rode up front with him. The dog noticed something was bothering his friend. Right now, gum chewing was uppermost in his canine brain but the sadness in his young man's eyes invited Resumé to be cautious. He turned a plan into a rhythm. He watched with earnest concern, mouth still, until Duden looked away. Then he chewed furiously, quitting instantly when Enno looked his way.

Enno wasn't really looking at anything. He was lost in thought. That picture of Helga crumbling to the ground. It was as if he had watched her die. He shook his head hard to rid himself of the picture. That bullet had been meant for him. Waves of nausea pulled at him. Forced himself to think of other things. Flipped through his mental rolodex, looking for just the right counter-pull. It was difficult this time, his gut wanted to stay with the horror but his brain said find another place. He found it. The memory of his time driving Sloop's team of horses on the manure spreader. The animal power. Power. Something primal. Connected. Pulsing. Power. He could feel it even now, right into his blood and up into his skull, up between the brain and inside cranial bone where the juices measure heart odors and retain memories of awakenings.

The unlikely grace of that system. The basket-like harness of leather straps ornamented with peanut-shaped brass spots green and tarnished except where a movement played at rubbing and polishing. The jingling sounds layered between the sound of breath and the pungent almost burning horse sweat smell. He loved that smell. It oozed down deep inside of him and reminded of nameless times before and ahead.

The tightening of the system, of the harness, of the muscles, of the attention. The tightening resulted in movement. Resulting in a job possible. Resulting in a following machine's response. Resulting in a piece of a plan. Resulting in a pace which matched his heart beat. A system understood as appropriate. Thrilling.

Like buckets of laugh drippings. Thrilling. Like the touch of an attracted beauty. Thrilling. Like that song which creates a floating space. Thrilling.

And unknowable. The ever present threat of that power going completely out of control. The skin-held assurance that his time at this job was stolen. Stolen because he had not the skill to control, truly control, the horses - the system. Without Sloop's presence he did not feel he could handle the horses, work the spreader. He was stealing a ride on the thing. And it was thrilling. Even now, driving his truck, he could remember the feel of the lines in his hands and arms and neck. The exhilaration. The absolute exhilaration. Softly, carefully, so as not to disturb the loveliness of his remembering he asked himself, 'what was it?'.

Some day he wanted to be just as good, just as casual, just as certain, just as connected as Sloop was with his horses. His mentor had a calculated determined calm. Enno thought he wanted that for himself. At least he wanted to be able to call it up when needed.

Sloop. Sloop. Back, slam, to the horror and the guilt and the questions. Enno thought about the conversation at the hospital. It bothered him inside and out. He found himself wondering what Ogdensburg meant. What was it he was planning on doing? Pictures came to him, pictures of vengeance, pictures of terrible things. Enno shook his head. "NO!" He heard himself shout. And he stopped his truck and stepped out of the cab. He thought about what to do and realized he didn't know where to go if he could do anything. He felt helpless. He wanted to reach his friend and stop him before anyone else was hurt. Before Sloop got himself into trouble. He leaned on the hood of the truck, hands carrying his weight, head bent. A prayer stance.

The late winter afternoon chill was mixing now with layers of an intruding warm breeze. Then an announcing whoosh noise. Suddenly wind blew. Blew progressively harder. It altered Enno slightly. He recalled he had chores to do, animals that needed tending. He jumped into the truck and proceeded to Sloop and

Helga's farm. For some people responsibility is relief. Enno is that way.

John B. "Sloop" Ogdensburg was driving Carl's yellow pickup. He was driving it hard. He had something to do, right away.

The pickup felt the wind. Hard, pushy, warm Chinook wind. Two miles ahead an irrigation wheel line was feeling that same wind. Broken free of a single restraining wire. Rolling, heading to intersect at a 45 degree angle with a 3 strand barb wire fence which separated it from Highway 97. The same highway Sloop was racing on.

Jimmy Three Trees was back in his cardboard house in the woods. He was crying. It was the sloppy disjointed pathetic crying of those self-inflicted with homelessness and social disorientation. It must be differentiated from the quiet containered sadness of the terribly unlucky.

In the corner under a pile of rags he found a rough metal container, looking like a galvanized tin suitcase. It was padlocked shut. He pulled the grimy string from out of his shirt and put the little key in the lock. Slowly he opened the case, careful to keep his eyes shut. Sitting back he slowly opened his teared eyes and feasted, agonizing feast, on the view of the inside of the box lid. Taped there were the remains of tattered photos. Several of a handsome young couple obviously very much in love. And dead center were recent pictures of Victoria Wood and Enno Albert Duden.

As he pulled into Sloop's place it felt different. He noticed for the first time the frailty of the place. The power of the beauty and magic emanating from this farm ... still there. But now he saw it for the first time as a fragile power. It depended on an overlay of regular touches, regular chores, regular adjustments, regular monitoring, regular realignment, regular appreciation, regular strokes, regular wonder. The power of this place slipped perceptively with the uncertain absence of Helga. It was as if something was falling.

Enno leaned forward and instinctively looked through the windshield and up. He readied himself to catch a falling piece of magic. He winced in confusion as he thought, not of Helga, but of Sloop and his vulnerability.

Resumé watched him and clicked his gum. There was a world of difference between this young man and his former human, Riven. Both were sensitive to a fault. Sam's fault was to use his sensitivity as a weapon. Enno used his like a glove.

Duden parked his truck. He pulled a notepad from the glove box. He would walk the farmstead just checking things out. Perhaps he'd make a note or two as reminders. Once he'd seen everything then he'd make sure all the necessary chores were done. Plenty of daylight. He couldn't forget to check out the workhorses in the barn pasture, Sloop's prize heifers and the cow herd.

Resumé jumped out of the truck cab and leaped up into the back of the pickup. There, he knew, was a large plastic bag wrapping some of Enno's extra blankets. Into a loose corner of that plastic bag he deposited his severely chewed wad of gum. Careful to fold the plastic over it for protection. He had a big challenge ahead of him. How was he, a dog, going to come up with a regular supply of this wonderful bubblegum stuff?

Enno first checked the house. Inside. All okay. Then he walked all around the outside. He didn't think about why, his insides told him this place was at risk. He would have done turns if he knew that he was being watched from a quarter mile away. Bo Coin was on a ridge with binoculars. Brice had told him what to watch for and note.

Resumé's nose was in the air. He caught wiffs of deodorant

soap, cinnamon musk aftershave and hair spray. The dog's upper lip curled. He nudged Enno's loose hand and only received an absent minded head pat. So he decided to follow his nose and check out the offense on his own. Off he went at a lope.

Enno moved from the house yard to the kitchen garden and green house. He made a note to build a little fire in the greenhouse stove that evening. The ventilating windows were fine till later.

Adjacent to the garden Helga had a poultry compound which housed her ornamental birds, Ring-Necked Pheasant pairs, Speckled Hamburg trios, and four Royal Palm Turkeys. All looked okay so he went on to the large layer house.

Charley was scared. He was scared bad. He would never forget the sight of that woman being hit by his bullet. He wasn't remorseful. Didn't have that in him. But he was darn sure scared. He hurried to finish his packing. He was going back to Minot, North Dakota and his Uncle's welding supply store just as fast as he could get out of town.

In spite of the Chinook wind Bo Coin was cold. This spy stuff. He wasn't cut out for it. He was a businessman, a successful one, important in the town. How on earth had he let himself be pulled in to this nonsense? He knew how. He was scared. Scared and fascinated. He'd never actually met anyone like Brice Liner. Oh, he'd seen the movies and read some of the cheap fiction but in the flesh these guys were different. They were, or at least Brice was, really threatening. Bo had a clear sense that Liner was someone who was capable of repeated, casual violence. So Coin was doing surveillance because he was scared and because, like a stupid hormonally-challenged teenager, he wanted to feel like he was part of what ever intrigue was going to happen. Just so long as no hard work or pain was involved.

On a rocky ridge overlooking some quirky little farm, he stood with binoculars waiting for some farm couple to return. He was told to watch and see what buildings the man goes in to. Write it all down, Brice had said. But Bo was surprised because instead of the couple he was supposed to be watching, the kid shows up. The same one his wife claims rescued her on the mountain. There was indeed something fishy here. Now he was really curious. And a dog, what's this? The dog is coming up the rise towards him. He fumbles in the pockets of his Eddie Badger coat thinking he might find something to use against the dog. The only thing there is is a box of breath deodorizing gum. Here comes that dog straight as an arrow. If he didn't know better he'd say that dog could see him. As the dog gets closer there is something reassuring about the scene. Bo smiles. This dog is no threat. He's some old cowdog, half feeble. He goes back to watching Duden. 'Where'd he go?' He sweeps the farmstead anxious about having lost sight of the kid. With his eyes glued to the binoculars he doesn't see that Resumé is within twenty feet and has slowed to that crouching, herd dog, slow stalk. Bo drops the binoculars for a minute and sees that he's being "eyed." Resumé is attempting to 'hold' Coin absolutely still by staring at him with an inherited, hypnotic visage.

"Get out of here!" Bo offers halfheartedly. Resumé keeps coming each step taking a full second. Never taking his eye off the chubby, Realtor eye sockets.

"Go on, beat it!" Bo stoops to pick up a rock to throw and Resumé knows it's his opening, his only chance. He leaps at Coin. The Realtor falls backwards and crab crawls struggling to get out of the dog's reach. Resumé sinks his teeth into the first thing he can. Bo scrambles up to run off and Resumé ends up with a coat pocket in his mouth.

The dog thinks. 'Man, now that was fun!' As Coin runs off Resumé shakes the coat fabric as if to say "I am truly mean!" Something falls to the ground. A little box of gum. Resumé sniffs, chews the box open and goes nuts over his score.

The Mascara chamber of commerce always struggled with slow season concerns. Tourism for this tourist town ratcheted up in May and held its own through September. Sometimes, weather permitting, they would enjoy some good income from Thanksgiving through Christmas but only if adequate snow brought in the skiers. The slowest time, usually without fail, was from mid-February through mid-March.

Luther Yankone, and his conniving wife Reba, had come to town in a flurry of press releases raining down on Mascara's slow January. They were wealthy developers of a very specialized sort. They built and franchised up-scale church resorts combining a faux rusticism with high stakes bingo and a pyramid sales approach to profitable political activism. One of their more dramatically successful adjuncts had been the idea of a gated community of time-share, condominium garage units for monster mobile homes. People could drive their fifty footers right into a glassed-in super garage and atrium with all hookups including cable television and coin-op Canadian pharmaceuticals. Each one included a luxurious large basement apartment. And these units were all connected by a private tunnel system set up to be traversed by fancy golf carts. Each unit typically sold for half a million direct or much more when a time share composite was structured. Six could be located on one acre.

The Yankone's had purchased an option on several thousand acres of prime forest land just outside of Mascara and proceeded by reverse publicity to let the public know of their plans. Small town investigative reporters, with the intelligence of parking attendants, had been leaked stories about a massive new development. They rushed to interview Luther and Reba who were both very pleasant and condescending and quick to say that the reports were premature, or ridiculous, or imaginative, or wildly speculative. The reporters followed up with interviews of county and state officials who were forced to say 'no comment'. Further inquiries into the dealings and doings of the Yankones unearthed 11 successful 'creative' developments in several countries. Newspapers accounts appeared all over the state of Oregon. Within four weeks of their arrival everyone was convinced that the Yankone's proposed "Wild Rose Land and Cattle Company" was a smoke screen for a development that would surpass even the Vice President's "Big America" above-ground casino and membership retirement community outside of Jackson Hole, Wyoming.

So when corporate types, accountants, architects, landscape designers, subterranean engineers, bankers, hair-stylists, cabinet ministers and international contractors all suddenly filled every available motel room, bed and breakfast unit and trailer space in Mascara in late February, the Chamber of Commerce made adjustments in its projections declaring a "new" season and reason for tourism. They identified their challenge; how do we repeat this business level every February? Meanwhile the Mascara City Council had emergency meetings to figure out how to alter the long range urban plan to allow for the trebling of the city limits to incorporate the Yankone optioned property.

Peggy Youngquist, a single thirty year old mother of one two-year old son, drove her battered 1967 Ford Torino wagon through the Mascara industrial park on that chilly Saturday afternoon. It was her one day off from working two different waitress jobs and she most always spent it going through the dumpsters and throwaway corners of the businesses. Here she found some light duty wooden pallets which she busted apart and stomped on to break into small pieces for her wood heater. Her son, Tyrone, was buckled in the car seat in the back of the wagon, humming to himself and kicking the driver's seat ahead of him. Christmas had not been fun this year. Her mother in Cincinnati had passed away and there was no money for her to get back there. It was no longer about her or her mother. It was all about her son.

Affluent housewives, many of them artistic and with lots of time and not much happening. That's what tweaked Linda Glimpse to consider a combination art center and gallery for Mascara. It had been moderately successful, financially speaking, over its first two years. If enthusiasm from its participants had been any measure, it was a smash. Eighty five women and three men were eager regulars of the Glimpse Art Center and Gallery doings. For the first week in March Linda had come up with a way to hurry spring up. It would be risky but she was sure she could make it work. Her members would each bring a pot-luck item and their acrylic paints. Plus a white T shirt in their own size. After supper they would, all of them, paint a design on their shirts answering the question "Why I love Mascara?" Later they would auction off the shirts and donate all the proceeds to the Glimpse Gallery's Homeless Artist Fund. To anyone's knowledge there were no homeless artists in Mascara at this time. Jimmy Three Trees was the only homeless person and he was certainly no artist. But this didn't stop Linda. She was convinced that this Fund would bring in homeless artists that they could then help.

Sloop was driving too fast. He didn't see it. How could he. A twenty foot length of four inch aluminum pipe sticking out across his highway lane at a height of 3 to 4 feet. It was the end of that runaway irrigation wheel line held up in the air by the last wheel and the fence it had crossed. It was a windy, dusty, late winter, Central Oregon afternoon and the aluminum color blended with the highway colors. He hit that pipe doing 75 miles an hour. It smashed the windshield into his face and spun the pickup more times than any evidence would indicate. The cab door opened and John Ogdensburg was thrown into a stack of hay bales. But he didn't know that. The steering wheel had temporarily slammed his lights out.

Chapter Eleven

John Day

"One would have faith that the unjustest thing
Had geometric grace past what one sees."
- Richard Wilbur

Barren. Sterile. Infertile. When the culture becomes barren it suspends, it never comes to ripening. There is a last swirl in a cup, a life cup. The swirl slows, stops, becomes gone. And the fluid which remains stagnates and feeds on itself, eating first its memories, later its hopes. Death never comes, only further stagnation and evaporation. Death never comes because nothing follows to lament, promise or curse. Death is the province of the remainders not of the passing, just as law is designed to protect property and property owners, so corporate ethic has been designed to escape death. Barren, sterile, corporate ethic throwing off the bonds of possessive passion, the nested comforts, the family familiarities, the shirted friendships, the luxurious unaffordable generosities, off the poignant memories, off the small personal successes.

The *Unison Society of Talking Colors*. Next time around we do it different. No cyber space, no download, no upload, no naive feeding of the tools of the control monster. Even so we will remain culpable.

Titus quotes Camus: We are all murderers. And adds: Some of us are musicians as well. Those who are not, those with lightless eyes and hollow hearts, they get left behind forever.

"Alright gentlemen. Now we shift gears. What we call 'those eco-terrorists' may not have succeeded yet at affecting public opinion, and that is good news, but they're definitely starting to affect the guts of our operations."

Winston Brogue hoped none of the board members noticed his shaking hands. He opened the file folder and began to pass around the copies. His future, his bonus, the revision of his stock option package all depended on his appearing to be completely in control.

This Chicago room took up the entire upper floor of the skyscraper only allowing space for the reception/restroom/elevator area. Paneled to window height in a rare Indonesian wood, and windowed all around, the room was flooded with an other-worldly rose/ amber/ blue light created by the gossamer thin flat refractory yet transparent silk shades. Through them Adi Zarabresi could see the tankers' trail on the dead, grey surface of Lake Superior.

Adi was a junior vice president of the Gee Whiz Corporation. (He hated that name. He would change it.) His purview was public relation, image, all the details of image. That included anticipating negative publicity and then turning it to favor. He was exceptional at his job. He loved the abstract concepts and the little details. For example, this was the only board room table on the continent with three hand blown glass bowls filled with organic California pomegranates, organic Muscat table grapes from a corporate property in Lebanon, and a sprinkling of organically grown edible Nasturtium blossoms from France. The fruit and blossoms all had exquisite flavor. Adi knew, he had sampled. But no one at this meeting would dare to touch, let alone eat, any part of the display. The etiquette in this space, at this time, was guided by an expectation for rigid formality. Nothing casual would be permitted. As for the "organic" distinction it had nothing to do with ecological concern, or health consciousness. This distinction was sought solely because it was a distinction. The best people paid good money for "organic." So Adi wanted "organic." And he didn't care if any of the other board members even knew. Depth, that was the secret of his success. depth, details with depth. He knew that he'd never allow any of his own company's genetically altered farm products to ever grace his tables. That would be tacky, bizarre, no depth.

Wilson Brogue cleared his throat. "You hold a copy of a letter sent to our attorneys. It is, as you see, again signed *The Glass Pirate*. We haven't yet figured out the significance of that choice of names. I'm going to ask Mr. Zarabresi to read this missive out loud."

Adi started to stand and then decided otherwise. He paused for effect then began in a perfect middle-eastern radio voice.

> "*Gee Whiz Big shots,*
>   *Oxidation. That's our goal. Through exposure to the light of day and by untraceable internal means, we're working to oxidize your corporate image. Dry you up. Bleach you. Shrivel you. Drain off excess fluid...*"

Adi's reading eyes had moved slightly ahead of his recitation. At this point he stopped and looked up at Winston, worried.

"Go ahead," the CEO ordered.

Continuing,

> "*... Mr. Zarabresi should appreciate how we choose to*

close you down. And close you down we will. But not
before we destroy the net worth of each and every board
member starting with the avaricious and incompetent Mr.
Brogue. Kiss it all goodbye. Signed the Glass Pirate."

Winston jumped in, "That's it for today, gentlemen. Be here tomorrow morning for a legal review as we set a course of offense. Yes I said offense. Adi, I want to see you in my office."

Sloop's unconscious body had no ID papers on him when the paramedic checked so he took down all the information off the pickup's registration. Later at the hospital the check-in nurse saw the truck owner Carl Seesaw's name in the ambulance notation box. She remembered they had a Marvin Seesaw with a bullet wound.

It was Marvin who identified Sloop. It was Marvin who called Carl and Titus. It was Marvin who told the hospital that they also had John Ogdensburg's wife.

When Helga came to, she saw an unknown and unknowable person in the bed next to her, unconscious and with his or her face covered in bandages.

Winston was angry and worried. Adi was neither, maybe a little excited by the letter's reference but certainly not angry or worried.

"You will be in on this with me. Read this summary report. Its from our man, Liner. When you're done there's someone I want you to meet. Oh, and I intend to know where they're getting information on us."

No one had told Helga her husband was hurt and in the bed next to her. With her hopefully temporary paralysis, head injury and trauma it was felt that she should wait a short time for the news.

She awoke on her side looking at the bandaged person in the bed next to hers. She couldn't roll over to see Brenda Fork sitting with a book. Brenda noticed the slight movement of Helga's head and moved around to see her friend.

"Hey, honey!" She took Helga's motionless hand. "You're gonna be okay. Just fine."

. "What happened, Brenda?"

"You were shot honey. Accident we figure. Luckily it was a .22 caliber. Passed through the corner of your upper neck."

"I can't move Brenda!"

"I know babe. You've got some paralysis but the doctor's say you've got an excellent chance to return to 100%."

"And John? Where's John?"

Brenda struggled to hold an impassive face.

Helga blurted, "Oh, Brenda, I knew this would come. You know I never wanted to have anything to do with John's crazy schemes. There's a great deal I don't know. But I always knew it would someday bring violence - right into our world."

Under the facial bandages John was alert and heard every word.

Adi liked this. This was good. Depth. It had depth. Standing before them was a little, scrawny, long-necked man somewhere between fifty and sixty years of age. He wore a snap-buttoned khaki shirt ironed to a starch finish. Around his neck he wore a chain with a coach's whistle. His khaki ball cap had ear flaps turned up. His grey, curly hair was mid-length and covered his collar. He had bug eyes and a pursed mouth chewing boiled peanuts which he pulled, one at a time, from his little bag.

Lint Fumes didn't seem to care. Two suited corporate execs were analyzing him as if he were an animal in a zoo cage. When

Lint spoke his voiced cracked, crawling up and crashing down in pitch.

"Goober? They're good. Ooee! Don't know how you boys survive up in the frozen north without the better foods of life. Had to smuggle these on the plane."

Lint Fumes enjoyed his boiled peanuts like a three year old enjoys its favorite food.

"Mr. Fumes, you've read the report?"

"Yep."

"You understand that it is imperative we learn the identity of all the key players of this 'Glass Pirate' business?"

"Yep," another peanut went in. "You know these are even better when they're hot, real hot."

"I'm sure they are," answered an impatient and condescending Brogue.

Adi saw it. Plain as day. Lint Fumes' face went slack and the eyes bugged more. The look gave Brogue a small window of opportunity: 'Apologize in some way or we are done.' There was something else there too. It was a deathly look. Brogue did not pick up on it, not at all. He started to continue with directives but was interrupted by Zarabresi.

"May I try one, sir?" The perfect question and the 'sir' were both directed to Lint Fumes who wiggled and fussed to gladly get one for Adi. In that moment his similarity to TV's Deputy Fyfe was amazing. Adi tasted the goober as if he were savoring an expensive hors d'oeuvre. Lint leaned forward, eyebrows up, small mouth poised to smile. All a question.

"Oh yes, this is good!" As Adi said this, he swung an elbow away from his body and in the direction of Winston Brogue. To Lint and Adi it was a clear signal that Winston would never appreciate these finer things.

"Can you spare one more?"

Lint was beaming.

"Can we continue?" Broke in Winston, "After you have

identified all of them, you will dispose of them. You are not to take Brice Liner into your confidence on this last point. Work with and around him to discover these people but don't let him know the intended conclusion. Depending on how this business proceeds we may have you take out Mr. Liner as well."

Fumes was chewing, smiling and wiggling his eyebrows in Adi's direction.

"Did you hear me little man?" The spitting words barely passed through Wilson's lips when, in an imperceptible flash Lint had produced an open knife. Slashed it across Brogue's upper belly cutting his expensive coat, tie and shirt and barely scratching the skin. Just enough to produce a thin trickle of blood.

Brogue fell backwards on his desk, stuttering in fear and confusion.

"Yep, I heard you, big man. And when your job is done we'll talk more." Turning to go he winked at Adi and offered one more peanut. The two men smiled and nodded to one another. Adi was breathless. Brogue in a wave of fear, anger and indignation wondered who he could get to 'do' Fumes? Obviously there was only one man, Liner.

———————————————————

Enno had completed his review of Sloop and Helga's farmstead and now headed for the big layer house. It was Helga's project. Sloop had helped to design it. The building was about a hundred feet long divided into three sections. In the middle there was a tall tower section which served as a bulk feed hopper. All in wood, the bottom of the eight foot square tower funneled down to a point where bags or buckets were filled. This middle section, with the hopper dead center, was also home to hand tools, a refrigerator, a washing counter, a veterinarian supply chest, a hose spool and faucetry for the automatic waterers. As Enno stepped inside, the ammonia from the sawdust, mixed with manure, reached up inside his nostrils.

Standing in the center section there were two doors on opposite sides of Duden. Through the left door was a large well-ordered layer house with roosts and nest boxes and five hundred contented brown hens. Enno took down the two wire baskets and walked slowly and quietly in amongst the hens. He collected brown eggs from the nest boxes. When a basket was full he went back into the center of the building and placed the eggs into large flat cardboard trays, all but the dirtiest ones which went on to the washing counter. The full trays were set into the old refrigerator, one on top of another. After he was done he counted the trays he had filled, multiplied it out, and noted with the day's date 271 eggs. That number was added to Helga's morning note of 111. He wondered if he'd be making the egg deliveries in the morning. Pencil still in hand he calculated it out. Surprising. Helga's little egg operation grossed $50 a day every day. That came to $18,250 a year.

All five hundred of these hens were young layers. In the other half of the building, Helga had 550 young pullets which would start laying in a month. At that time, they'd be moved to the layer half after the current layers were sold. In this way she always had 500 hens laying strong and several batches a year of young laying hens to sell.

The birds had all been fed and watered that morning so Duden just checked to make sure everything was okay. Resumé, his dog, sat outside the chicken house chewing his new gum.

Adi Zarabresi is talking on a private line. One he knows is not being bugged. (At least not by him.)

"Can't say too much now but Winston's in over his head. Glass Pirate again. He's got the two hired guns going after each other." Laughs.

"Yes."

"Yes."

"Oh, and I saw the report from Liner. Milk Man's resurfaced. Thought you needed to know. Yeah, just remember me at merger time."

Sig's in his hotel room. He's sent off a fax demanding to know who Liner's working for. Doesn't like his suspicions. As he carefully, meticulously puts on his fake beard he thinks about taking time off.

Nettie Coin had dropped off Sam Riven in town. He was going to try to find Enno. She was going to tell her estranged husband that she would be transferring title of the snake flats acreage to one Enno Duden. And for good measure she planned to throw in a demand for a divorce.

When she went into Coin Bros. Realty no one was sitting at the reception desk. She went upstairs and when she heard voices from her husband's office she sat down in the chair just outside the door. She could not help but hear.

"I don't know who the broad is but I will find out!" It was Brice's voice. "I can't believe I was rolled in this yuppie tourist trap! I'll need your phone for at least a half hour."

Nettie didn't recognize the voice but the man sounded mean.

"Well, it's a cinch you aren't gonna get Mr. Realtor Man here to go back out to your suspect's farm." The voice belonged to Billie Blue Chevie but Nettie couldn't quite place it. "The dog sounds like the one Duden got from a man called Sam Riven."

Now Nettie was leaning and listening with every pore.

"This is what you're going to do. Chevie you tail Duden. And you, Coin, you stick with Ogdensburg," said Brice.

"Well I don't know where he is," whimpered Bo.

"I don't care!" shouted Brice, "find him! And while we're at it, what do either of you know about this kid?"

Billie shook his head noncommittally.

Bo mumbled "He's nothing. A drifter. Has some nutty idea that he's gonna have a farm of his own. My silly wife seems to think he saved her. I don't think he has anything to do with your stuff."

"Coin, you're an idiot. The boy is at the center of all of this. We tail him and he'll tell us things. The more the boy knows the more likely he'll have to disappear later."

Billie thought hard. He wouldn't deliver Enno. But now it was plain. He had to find out who this goon was working for. Was he for real? Disappear? What did that mean exactly? They'd pay big money for this Armanhope. Billie'd find him and deliver him direct for the money and to set Enno free.

It was the effect of Sam on her. Before she might have stormed in demanding an explanation. But Sam's shared intrigues had already begun to corrode her useless naivete. Nettie got up and walked as quickly and softly as she could. If she couldn't find Sam she was heading for the sheriff or perhaps Duden's friends.

Shirley Intoit could not find her stalker. She decided to try later, after her meeting with Vicky. There was a bar behind the Fur River Restaurant where they were to meet. It was one of two places in Mascara where local, small town businessmen went to avoid facing worries on the job and at home. When the two women entered there were only four customers present, two men trying to best one another with a woman and, in the back corner of that bar, Sig Maltesta, in bearded disguise, nursing a glass of wine and a plate of mediocre fried oysters.

"So tell me about this Helga woman," asked an anxious Shirley as they sat down.

"She's a strange, quiet woman, strong. Works real hard.

Married to a funny old farmer. They do things sorta old fashioned. You know with work horses and stuff. I've heard some people say he doesn't know any better. But he seems far too crafty."

"Do you know if she ever lived in the Bay area?"

"Can't say, don't know much about her."

"And I take it you're sweet on this guy Duden?"

"It shows, huh? Yeah, I can't quite figure it out. I get goose bumps when I'm around him. It's like I've known him all my life. And he acts so strange around me. Interested, and then not." Vicky was looking down and playing with the beer nuts.

Shirley was watching Vicky.

So was Sig. Forty year old Sig Maltesta who had known women from Bogota to Calcutta and who had cultivated long boughts of celibacy as an aid in his mercenary work. Sig Maltesta whose success was built on being half chameleon and half tactical surgeon. Whose success had been built on his being completely in control of himself. Intellectual, art collector, marksman, demolitions expert, surveillance professional, Tango instructor, physchological warrior, highest paid mercenary in history, tactical wizard, chess champion, and degree carrying theologian, Sig was looking at Vicky in a way that he'd never felt himself look at anyone or thing before.

Sig was looking from across the room. His usually taut mouth hung loose and open. His eyes hurt as he reached with them to see more of this spectacular woman. Every nuance, every little move, every shadow, every curve, every hair of this woman transfixed the mercenary monk. He was instantly a mess, instantly a prisoner. So much so that he failed to see Brice's unmistakable bulk enter the bar.

He heard Shirley's scream of pain. Then regaining focus he realized Liner had both women by the back of the neck and was squeezing hard.

Sig went wide and cautious as if he were a frightened customer looking for a way out. Grabbing a bar stool he came at

Brice from behind and swung hard into the backs of his knees. Before Brice toppled over Sig had a small round table upside down and slammed its flat surface into the prone man's face.

He then took both women by the arms and hurried them outside. To both he said,

"You better get out of here."

Leaning towards Vicky he whispered,

"I'm falling in love with you."

And then he left at a trot swinging around behind the building.

Shirley tried to remember the voice. Vicky felt a pain in her neck and confusion.

Part Two

Wet

Chapter Twelve

Snake

Can a conscious man, Dostoevsky asks, respect himself at all?

The high desert is home to sand dust.

The absence of regular moisture has laid bare the soil particles without the glue of rot. Water and air are regular companions to decay. Water absent - the high desert is sand dust. It knows how to behave when it's dry. It lays there. It knows what to do when the wind blows. It does not know how to behave when it's wet, always wet.

It's late winter, early spring. The dry soils, only teased by the gradual melt-off of light snows, are loose from frost heave.

And it begins to rain.

Steady.

Constant.

With no let up. In this open dry country the rain draws a curtain and makes every passage slow for the toll.

The colors change. They get heavy. Countless layers of transparent colors mixing and refracting light. The iridescence of 'too late'. Dark. Wet. The dusty reds of the pines hurry to burnt umbers, yo the nutty blacks. The brittle dusty greys and silver greys swell, darken, sog and murmur.

When the high desert is dry and the sun shining, winter or summer, the human posture naturally tips back to allow the skin under eyebrows to dry and warm.

When steady rains come to the piñon and sage the stance curls forward and eyebrows become awnings perhaps to protect viewpoints but certainly to curl hairs back into the skin.

When the rains come to the dusty rim rocks, store-bought priests and thickening housewives are angered by the momentary pressure of poetic flirtation. Accepting 'never agains' often sets the resigned to ducking hope.

And the endless parade of droplets pushes those previous into rivulets. The landscape seems to undulate with the pushed rivulets as though massaged. And the creeks and rivers gasp and roar.

People in the rain are the same only different, wetter, slower and yet prone to dodge and run, run heavy with high splashing unforgiven steps.

The rains began as Enno Duden finished Sloop and Helga's farm chores. He was heading back, with his dog Resumé, to the Fork Holding to talk with Titus. He thought of farms and farming. It comforted him. Resumé thought of coat pockets and chuckled.

The rains began with downcast Jimmy Three Trees huddled under his pile of rags inside his house in the woods. The one made of refrigerator boxes. He thought, in cold wet fits, of both of them.

The rains began as Shirley Intoit and Vicky Wood drank tea in Shirley's Airstream. They laughed a lot. But their individual breathlessness came from the recent and continuing chase. They, separately and to differing degrees, tried not to cry from fear. They thought of him and him. And he was the same *him*.

Sig lay propped on one elbow on his motel bed. Curtain pulled open with one finger so he could watch the rain. He thought of her. His insulation, his restraint, his courage, had been stripped away.

Titus stood in the open barn doorway puffing a pipeful of Old Chippewa Kinnikinick and watching the rain fall. He thought of her.

Jefferson and Yummy Fork lay on their big bed with Franklin, Mahalia and Jackson reading books and listening to the rain on the roof. Each thought of another.

Helga lay sleeping in her hospital bed. The medicine sleep which cheated her of the fullness of her dreams. It rained outside.

As the rain began John B. "Sloop" Ogdensburg stared at the hospital ceiling and remembered how jail time worked. And he remembered the human reasons he had to do his "work." And he hungered for the 'disguise time' of farming. He worried about Helga and his horses and his cattle. And he thought hard about his choice of Enno as successor. He had forgotten Hopkins, for now.

The rains began with Nancy Simmons thinking she was getting tired of waiting for her life to begin.

The wipers on Nettie's car were going high speed as she drove around anxious to find Sam.

The rain on the metal roof of Lloyd Shoulder's ranch sculpture studio made a loud racket which matched the crackling rhythm of his arc welder.

The rain seemed to calm Sloop's Percheron stallion "Glass" as he stood in a stall at the Fork Holding.

The rain worked itself around Sam's coat collar and down his back as he walked fast and bent. In search of Enno. From the market towards the restaurant. The rain put him back to a familiar anger. One which had been too long a constant. In a flash he understood that a woman had changed him. He thought, with alarm and surprise, of a life with Nettie.

The vacuum wipers on Enno's old '52 Chevie pickup pushed

hard and slow on the upstroke. When they reached the top there was a wheezing release and a fast slapping return to begin the slow climb once again.

Enno Duden had just moved from Oregon's wet west side, over the Cascade mountains, into the Ponderosa Pine framed edge of the great basin, into the climate of the arid high desert. His move was only a day old but the sense of escape from mold, mildew, rust and drip had been almost complete. For Enno, fresh from the permanent grey wet gloom of the rainy Willamette Valley, the socked-in quality of this local weather change was sad. Not of the same magnitude. But it was another small sadness to add to the horrible shooting of Helga and the incident with the hunters. He felt himself sliding into a depression, That depression. The one which had visited him often as a teenager and with such crippling effect.

He remembered the hospital and how he had come to meet the French monk. It brought an involuntary smile. Every time he thought of Sig he could feel the puppet strings. He could feel his movements gently lifted.

Back then. He had been a finished fifteen year old. Had run away from the foster home three times. Finally successful. Painfully hungry by the third day. Cold, unable to think of anything to do. Depressed to immobility. At least until that night when he heard her scream. He followed that scream until he found, behind the big alley dumpster, the two guys forcing themselves on the girl. Enno lost it. The blood in his head made him a rhino-like automaton. He said "no, no" and plowed in, pulling at the men. Pushing them. Though the girl was able to escape, Enno lost the fight.

Hurt bad. The next thing he knew he was in a county hospital bed with a broken arm and a concussion. In the bed next to him was a tall, thin, fit man in a dark beard and big eyebrows. A man who seemed to wear silence. A man who appeared to be waiting patiently but who gave the clear impression of pending explosion. A man who wore contradiction. Perhaps a comedian/

gardener/butcher.

His second night in that room Enno was brought awake by the gentle shoulder motion.

The man's name was Sigismondo Maltesta. Hard to forget a name like that. Also hard to remember. An odd and very old name. The man had been unable to sleep because of Enno's whimpering dreams. So he woke him and asked an insincere if necessary "what's the problem?"

Enno looked back from a peculiar hollowness mixed with hunger.

They talked. They talked all night.

'A kid' Sig thought, open blank book, a dry well. Sig wondered if seeding the well might magically create substance. So he shared pieces, shards, of stories. Windows into a life beyond anything Enno could imagine. Speeds and patterns and births of philosophies with absolutely no parallel in the youngster's experience. Instead of being fascinated by the particulars, Enno was mesmerized by the man himself. A man who began his early adulthood as a Catholic monk only to be emotionally destroyed by the repeated forced witness of hideous atrocities in Central America. Then to be recruited as a spy. Learning, in disgust, from new peers of the business opportunities and profits stemming from those same atrocities.

Sig Maltesta left the cloth and his vows and struggled, within espionage, to make a difference. He figured that if he couldn't be the man holding the scale he could be the balance beam. Change things from the inside, that was his thought.

He became a master of martial arts, disguise and transparency. Oddly, at this time he discovered an insatiable hunger for the fine arts. Disillusionment with 'the company' shoved Sig in the direction of Zen Buddhism. For the second time in his life he dedicated himself to the pursuit of a specific grace.

It was fine arts and his hungry study of the visual chicanery of the painters Matisse, Bonnard, Rauschenberg and Hockney which brought him, in a classic moment of disconnect and Zen nothingness, to realize he should sell himself into service as an independent mercenary. This gave mercury to the idea of *balance beam*. Be handsomely paid with the bonus of opportunities to have a positive secretive 'gumming' effect. Ironies of ironies upon ironies within ironies.

So Maltesta came quickly to be paid to work for the 'big and official companies' as spy, as ringer, as saboteur, as assassin. He was sent, like an explosive spear, into the middle of feeble anarchies, into the bowels of rebellion, into the stomach of unrest, into the innocence of non-violent protest. It was his job to report what he found, to unravel any stability he discovered, to destroy leadership. He was paid to go into the middle.

Once early on he was able to convince three nuns to disappear rather than be assassinated. Bloody habits, he made sure, were found. Another time he convinced an enigmatic rebel leader that to fake his own death would gain him time to regroup. In both cases he received undue credit for successful acts of cruel, social surgery. It appeared he had heartlessly murdered for hire and then vanished. The truth was that Sig had never killed whether for hire or self-defense. He was, though, quick and clever in the ways of accepting credit for cruelty. He had always artfully positioned himself to casually 'deny' completion and thereby attract credit. In small wars, terrorism and espionage circles "The Monk" was a poison cloud. If he belonged to you, you were the winner. If the other side employed 'the monk' you knew it was time to negotiate.

So here, in this hospital room, is 'the monk,' a human cataclysm sitting with a teenager devoid of all but nonspecific longing and holding a hair trigger in the presence of cruelty. In his six-way hospital bed, head and arm bandaged, sat an empty cup of a human. Enno reminded Sig of porcelain. A porcelain cup which Maltesta filled with snatches of stories.

At one point, well into talking to himself, Sig said,

"I have this old philosopher/historian/polemicist friend who says we're all restless and with no clear idea where this culture should go. I enjoy disagreeing with him and am reminded of that whenever I cross paths with an innocent such as yourself. Our culture should be going after injustice. But it doesn't. Our culture thrives on injustice, it fuels the economy and it peoples our myths." He paused and a sad thought temporarily changed the color of his face.

"What's a polemicist?" asked Enno.

"That's someone who studies the relationships of apology and propaganda to formal argument."

"Huh?"

"Doesn't matter. Or when it does come to matter to you, you'll find a way to understand. What should matter to you is that other thing I was talking about - that stuff about injustice. The point I was trying to make is that most everybody, your young friends included, don't seem the least bit upset about injustice and they should be. You on the other hand seem to have this inbred inclination to right wrongs. The only way to get our culture to go after injustice is reach young, naive, natural, good samaritan souls (such as yours) before 'they' do." (With the word *they* he threw a hitchhiker's thumb over his shoulder.)

Duden was drunk with tired, with thinking, with a tidal wave of unfamiliar images, with a cautious reach for unearned, unwarranted friendship otherwise he never would have taken the chance to comment.

"I'm confused. I thought you were claiming to be some sort of mercenary soldier, international bad guy..." He got slower and let his sentence run to *'oh-what-have-I-done'* drips.

"You should talk, kid. You know what you did in that alley? Those guys, if they wanted to, could file charges against you for assault - doesn't matter that they beat you up. You started it. The girl's gone and I guarantee she'll never come to your defense. If they pressed charges you'd be in jail, sure thing. So, what you did, in this society, is not considered an act of bravery or rescue - it's considered a stupid act of aggression."

"I had to..."

"I know. The only difference between us is that if those two were still alive after 'our' meeting they'd wake up each night in a cold sweat with the face of fear etched in their brains.'

"Then you'd be an outlaw too..."

"Yes, I **am** an outlaw. It means working outside of the law. It doesn't necessarily mean working on the outside of decency or morality. You must realize that LAW is no guarantee of anything, it is nothing but a rule structure. Never forget that people in power make laws, not the little guys. And the law really protects only one thing, itself. Law protects law. Some say that's a wonderful truth because they believe it means the law is impartial. In some cases that may be true. But impartiality doesn't stop bullets, it just pretends to catalog where and why they were shot and dole out punishment and property settlement."

They went on this way until, tired to the next level, Sig began to slip into reminiscence.

It was when he fell into longing for the Nicaraguan farm which served as one of his personal safe houses that Enno's eyes opened a little wider and lips quivered slightly. Sig had learned how to concentrate on the tiniest facial changes to gauge his adversary. He noticed the subtle change in the boy and fed it with questions and suggestions.

It was during this hospital stay that Sig helped Enno identify and embrace a passion for farming. This post-modern Jesse James with appendicitis became Enno Duden's signpost. A foundation was laid below the young man, inserted like an inflatable sheet of paper. The ideas of crusading against injustice - of new definitions of *outlaw* - and the notion that the robes of justice often conceal complicity with the accountants for evil.

Enno thought of all this as he drove slowly through the rain to the Fork Holding. And he wondered if he'd ever run into Sig Maltesta again. He hoped so. He smiled thinking about how Sig would get along with his new cast of friends and acquaintances. With Sloop, with Sam, with Titus. He knew one thing. Sig would like Resumé. And Sig was someone who could help Enno 'deal' with Helga's being shot and all that unfortunate business with the hunters.

His mental wanderings had found him a small piece of comfort. Enno patted his dog's head. For a split second he thought he saw a little bubble poking out between Resumé's lips. But, naw, it was probably just the tip of this tongue.

"Oh, no!" Said Vicky changing the subject. "I completely forgot about Jimmy. It's been raining hard and he lives in a cardboard box." She reached for her coat.

"I'll go with you," offered Shirley. "Where will you take him?"

"I don't know. Last year he didn't show up until mid-spring, came here from a shelter house in Redmond. This year the tail end of winter's been mild and he's been around for a couple of weeks. But all he's got is a box in the woods."

"Does he belong to anyone?" The question sounded strange to Shirley even before she asked it.

Vicky wondered why the innocent question bothered her.

Sig couldn't handle it. He had to see that woman again. He left his motel room and pulled his coat collar up against the insult of the rain.

Titus saw the lights of Enno's pickup as they made silver knives of the rainfall. He was glad to see him coming. It meant Titus could stay in his barn apartment tonight. But he wasn't looking forward to telling the boy about Sloop's accident.

Sloop didn't care. Sleep was not an option. He didn't care.

About the pain, that is. He hurt all over. A pain which might have distracted someone else. In his case the pain served to sharpen his long range focus. And dull the immediate. He thought about this work.

He had never been interested in the mythic outlines of folk creatures like Robin Hood or Zorro. They belonged to children. Yet he could not deny the similarities.

'By day a quirky quixotic subsistence farmer--by night the mysterious Glass Pirate striking terror, confusion and profit-loss into the bloodless hearts of corporate boardrooms. The Glass Pirate - diverting ill-gotten gains via a sophisticated maze of computer transactions and bank transfers until they safely and securely and secretly benefitted little people, primarily seedless, toolless farmers.'

In a world and time of nihilism and spiritual vacuum, Sloop's history flirted with comic book proportions. Before him, before the Glass Pirate, there had been his mentor, his predecessor - *Victor* aka *the Milk Man* aka *Titus Ibid.*

Though simplicity had always been the valued operative, they together had watched their operations expand dangerously into a complex web. Now Titus was in semi-retirement, enjoying being a farmhand and musical backup to both Jefferson and Sloop.

It was soon to be Sloop's turn to fade back. That's why so much rested with Duden. Sloop had been certain the young man was the candidate for training. It would take a half dozen years to bring Enno up to the necessary speed. Was he right? They could not afford to waste the time on someone incapable of understanding all the complexities and illusiveness required.

Sloop was worried. It has taken years but the Milk Man and the Glass Pirate had succeeded in quietly bringing down four huge corporations and funneling hundreds of millions of derailed and embezzled dollars to small farmers in Bolivia, Ethiopia, Cuba, Chile, North Dakota, Afghanistan, South

Africa, Columbia, Uruguay, Guatemala, New Mexico, India and Mississippi.

Their work helped many people. Just as their work destroyed some stock portfolios.

At the restaurant a line of wet tourists waited for seating. Sam Riven shook his collar and hat and entered looking for any familiar face. None he wanted were there. He proceeded to the restaurant lounge. Standing to gaze around he overheard a conversation from a booth. They were talking about a shooting. A farmer's wife had been shot, maybe an accident. She was in hospital. Sam recognized the names. It was Duden's friends. That 'Sloop' guy. Before he had a chance to digest the information, a nervous man whispered in his ear.

"In the john. We have to talk."

It was one of his 'brokers.' A man from out of town who brought to Sam 'Ids' to construct. Sam didn't like this but the urgency had suction. He followed and he learned. The man had many moles, many ears, many noses. He'd come to Mascara with a packet of easy work for Riven. And he had quickly learned that the small town was crawling with dynamite.

"Listen! You have to get out of here now!" He was puffing hard.

"Calm down, breathe, talk slow. Details, I need details."

"AFT agents, Treasury agents. On their way here. There's a mob hit man already in town and another on the way. The second one, Fumes, is by far the more dangerous."

"What's the mob want in this toy farm?" asked a frowning Riven.

"Words out. Your burg' is home to a crazy eco-terrorist organization. Some big corporations are in bed with the mob on this one. Turned the creeps loose. They got orders to make minestrone out of any old hippies they find."

Sam instantly thought of his friend Titus.

"But that's not the worst of it!" This man was obviously scared to the point of staining himself. "*The Monk* is on his way - if he ain't here already. *The Monk*! I'm telling you Riven, get out while you can. There's going to be a massacre.

(Sig Maltesta *a.k.a. The Monk,* sitting at the bar, noticed the two men leave the restroom.)

Outside the restaurant Sam flagged Nettie's slow inquiring car.

"Baby, we got to talk. It's time to get those tickets for Central America. We'll leave in a week. Meanwhile there's gonna be a mess of excitement and some nastiness. And you and I, love, are going to have some fun directing traffic. Oh, and I think I know where we can find your boy. We'll take care of that business I promise. First let's find a place warm and dry where we can talk. I need to make some plans and get some messages out."

Nettie was curious. She'd forgotten about her urgency to tell Sam of the conspirators. But it seemed obvious he already knew. He knew so much. Nettie was glowing. Nettie felt gymnastic and in love, but confused and worried. This was such a different world for her. In a matter of days she had gone from sedate to seditious, from lonely to deep in romance, from middle-aged to well-prepared. But everything she had come to accept as proper and normal was sliding away like an avalanche. All these in-trigues... Was the world always like this and she'd been asleep? Where was order, where were the authorities, wasn't anyone in charge? None of her casual lady friends back in Eugene would believe this, any part of it. She hoped that underneath it all Sam wasn't some militia kook. Well, really, for today and tonight, she didn't care, it was all too exciting, too much fun. She'd sort it out later.

Chapter Thirteen

Coos

"A celebrity is someone who is well known for being well known."
- Daniel Boorstin

What makes the change, the shift? Do we go safely mad? Or
is it a gathering of tossled through which, by gathering, collects
us to a marketable sanity? Crest, is it ridden or do we kid ourselves? When we pretend, is it thievery? When we lay claim to
circumstance outside of our influence, do we deflate? What law
of physics would have like energies work over time, distance and
pattern to converge in temporary explosive clusters?

Upon arrival at the Redmond airport Lint Fumes got the
names and addresses of a local used car dealership and the
funkiest motel in Mascara. He called the motel. Reserved a room
for a week. Then he took a taxicab to *"darned used cars"* where in
the rain he paid cash for a dark green, beatup 1980 Ford four
wheel drive pickup. Not too much different from what he drove

when he was back home in Mycanopy, Florida. He asked the attendant which were the classical and jazz radio stations. He was disappointed when the attendant didn't have a clue what he was talking about.

On to the floor of the pickup he threw his duffel bag. Then very carefully he set his aluminum hard shell case on the passenger side of the seat. He took out a handkercheif and smiled bittersweet as he wiped rain drops from the case.

His plan was simple. Even before checking into his room he would proceed to the two busiest gas stations in Mascara and apply for work. Two non-competing eight hour shifts as pump jockey. His research had discovered that Oregon was one of the only places left where attendants had to pump the gas. It was Lint's plan to plant himself where people and information would come to him.

Jefferson and Brenda Fork had decided together. Sloop and Helga needed to be in their own home. That would be the best place to convalesce. Titus would do the 'pickups' and the 'meetings' reporting back to Sloop when he was well enough to help with planning. The young man, Duden, could certainly be able to handle the farm chores. But Helga would need professional physical therapy. And Sloop, for the short haul, would need nursing care. So Brenda left word with the hospital nursing station that the Ogdensburgs would be looking to hire a live-in nurse. In this way word got to Nancy Simmons. At first blush her hesitation was a slam. She shook that off and decided to go to the hospital and get particulars.

Enno took the news of Sloop's wreck poorly. He turned around several times, like a dog might. He put his hands in his pockets several times. He didn't know how exactly but he was certain he had to have caused this latest accident. Titus watched him and found himself frowning. They needed to see more

strength in this young man if he was to inherit the mantel. Enno
needed to show a strong bottom side to his emotions. For his
own sake as much as for Enno's, Titus tried to engage him, draw
him out.

"Hey, you are taking this much too personal. Sloop's going
to be okay, it was a fluke, a bizarre accident. The wind kicked a
runaway irrigation wheeline out into the highway and the setting
sun made it impossible to see. Sloop's going to be fine. It'll take a
while for him to heal up. Luckily he got thrown into a hay stack
otherwise he might have more broken bones. The windshield
filleted some of his facial skin but it should heal fine."

"And Helga?" Enno's voice broke as he asked.

"That's equally a miracle. She's lucky to be alive. At first
there was concern she'd be paralyzed for the rest of her life. But
the doctor's now say that its definitely a temporary condition."

"So she's conscious and everything."

"Conscious yes. Groggy from drugs. And immobile. She can
talk and move her head slightly. Brenda went to see her today.

Enno felt welcome waves of relief.

"So, does Helga know about Sloop?"

"No son, doctor's figured they'd wait til tomorrow. He's in
the bed next to her. But she doesn't know it yet. His face is all
bandaged." Pause. "Least ways they don't want her to know just
yet about his accident." He looked at Enno sideways.

"You okay to camp at Sloop's tonight? The chores go okay?
Any problems?"

"Uh, no, no problems. Everything seemed fine. Yeah, the
dog and I will go back." Enno still seemed dazed.

Titus made up an invitation, "I was hoping you'd stay a
while and have a bowl of stew with me? Some of Yummy's"

Enno looked puzzled. "Yummy's?"

"Oh", smiled Titus, "that's our nickname for Brenda."

Enno smiled. 'It fit.' He thought, 'yes, that giant Jamaican
woman - a beauty.'

"I guess I am hungry but I should find something for the
dog."

Titus said he had stuff. They went in to the barn apartment.

Large rocks interrupted the rain-darkened pine trunks as they speared the forest floor. And an odd lace curtain fog wove at certain height altering the knife edges of the falling rain. This honest, indifferent forest. Nearby the arrogant concerned town.

Most communities of modern men and women are steaming incubators for mob cruelty. Not Mascara. The trinketization of idleness and the glamour of casual elite snobbery had dulled those classic mid-ranges of vengeful envy common to most small towns. That stalwart if bestial quality of latent mob madness had been replaced by the true lower depths of lazy acquisitive stupor. Lots of wealthy early retirees. As long as these mail-order-worshippers have espresso drinks and cable television, the streets are moderately safe for an occasional high definition person or incipient uprising.

Vicky directed Shirley on how to drive to the little spot in the woods near town where Jimmy Three Trees camped. The rain was slowing. Everything shown with the new wet.

The dogs barked once. They heard Jimmy's grunt just before they caught sight, in the flashlight beam, of the cardboard hovel. Vicky gave a soft holler.

"Jimmy, its me Vicky. I brought the nice lady. We're going to take you someplace dry for the night. Okay?"

His head came out slow, reptilian, blinking. Then retreated.

"I guess I'll see if I can get him out," said Vicky as she went to her knees and crawled in the dripping prone pile of refrigerator boxes.

Shirley waited just outside, looking around, still nervous about being followed and about the big, dumb, angry jerk. She could hear them mumbling inside. Then a haunting, instant, absolute silence. Vicky came out quick. Ashen faced.

"What's wrong?"

Vicky couldn't speak.

"What's wrong Vicky?" asked Shirley now with a hand on her shoulder.

"I don't believe it." She was looking at the ground.

Shirley dropped to her knees and looked in to Jimmy's cardboard tunnel. There he sat, on a pile of rags, dog to one side. And on the other side, lid open, was his little metal suitcase, photo shrine. She could clearly see the pictures of Vicky on one side and the young man, Enno Duden, on the other. With the old picture of a couple in the middle. ...Photos of Vicky and Enno?

Jimmy struggled with a smile, pointed and said one word, "brother."

Sig played with his wine glass. The busy restaurant lounge was an interesting and idiotic place for attempts at meditation. He had done his sleuth work and found no clues as to 'her' identity. Behind dark glasses, a false beard and cupped hands he did an old tried and true visualization 'ponder', holding on to the image of a wet white rose. At another level he 'felt' his insides match the imagined soft flutter of wet laundry hung in a breeze. And with his ear he further imagined the tonal ironies of Satie piano music. In these ways he had been able to set the image of the woman back, just far enough to regain some control.

He opened his eyes and did a 'business' assessment. He *had* been sent on a 'business' matter. The 'company' *had* assigned him to the D.B. Cooper matter and the path *had* led to a drunken, hyprochrondriachal Alaskan native named Ahchuck Intoit. *That* had sent him to find the niece, Shirley Intoit, which brought him to this prim little tourist town in the not-so-wilds of Central Oregon. Here the piece of a day told him he had stumbled on to something much bigger than the antique Cooper caper. If Cooper was still alive he would wait. If not....

Organized crime's number two ugly man of the month was

here, Brice Liner. Why? The 'big boys' were ordering him, Sig, to stand clear. Why? Wrong thing to do. It was time to play his brand of chess. He would return to the motel room for a computer check and a tool kit (especially the sealing wax).

Brice Liner was a simple man and not unlike a junk yard dog. When a junk yard dog is tormented, his rage swells beyond proportion. First it had been that smart-mouthed Indian girl. Then somebody had blindsided him twice. But who? Who was tailing him? Attack dog that he was it didn't matter much who, he needed to hurt someone, anyone and now.

He was in this mood when Bo Coin reported that he'd found John Ogdensburg. The man had been in a car wreck and at that very moment was in the Bend hospital. Bo was lucky to have this news to report otherwise Brice would have been happy to practise on the pudgy realtor. A wave of an idea diverted the bad guy: he'd go to the hospital and snuff out this old farmer. If the *glass pirate/milk man* business slacked or quit he'd know he had his man. If not, so what, he'd just keep looking.

Over a couple of bowls of exotic stew, laced with tamarind-flavored peppers, Enno and Titus visited. It was no particular surprise that Titus should reveal himself to Enno as a complex man. They talked about Sloop and Helga, Titus careful not to say too much. They talked about farming. Enno melted into the discussion with genuine anticipation and enthusiasm for the *how-to* portions. Titus was eager to talk about any and all aspects of farming but seemed to direct the conversation towards big farms *versus* small farms - diversity *versus* homogenization and specialization - industrial process *versus* craft - corporate ethics *versus* accountability - farm fertility *versus* sterility - patenting of life forms *versus* natural harmonies. Enno was fascinated, confused, exhausted. He just wanted to farm. But he heard a whisper coming up from inside him and surprised himself when he asked, "Is this all about, like, injustice or something, more than about farming?"

Titus picked his teeth, looked sideways at Enno, and answered, "Yes, I guess you could say that. What brought that to mind?"

"Oh, on the way here I was remembering a friend, or at least I call him a friend, I doubt he remembers me. We were in a hospital together once. He was a monk." Enno stopped himself recalling his promise not to divulge secrets of Sig's story.

Titus felt his ears stiffen and rotate along with the toothpick. He eyes were sharp lasers pushing all but clarity out of the way. "A monk?"

Enno looked at Titus much too long. A look that broadcast the question, *is this someone I can trust*? That's all Titus needed, he had his answer.

"But, its really about farming more than any question of justice." Titus offered. He was a master at the game of the fake. "What do you think you might want to raise when you get your own place?"

Enno felt an easy smile come. Titus had worked the switchyard with brilliance.

"Oh, I get a little confused when I think about that. I know what I want, It's not that. It's just that there's so many things. And I feel my plans shifting around. I know I want to work the land, I want to plow and plant and grow crops. And livestock, yeah, I want livestock..."

"Any particular ones attract you?"

"Draft horses, definitely. Cattle probably. I never thought about water buffalo til I saw them here. Why do you folks raise them?"

"Cheese, milk, meat. They are different in unique ways. Low cholesterol meat, all mozzarella string cheese comes only from the milk of water buffalo. And they do better with marginal feeds like our dryland brush pastures."

At this level of talk Enno became fully engaged. Titus took note and tried to calm his own need to contact some important people immediately.

Back at the motel Sig tapped in to some special connections via his lap top computer. While the requests were being sent he went through his tool kit. He removed a small waterproof pouch and unzipped it to check the contents. He had two sticks of red sealing wax each of which had wicks running through them. He reached into his pocket and pulled out a handmade French pocket knife. He picked pieces of dried sealing wax from its carved head. Sig used the knife head like a signature ring to mark hot sealing wax. The design it left might be mistaken for an upside-down trident or fork. But it is actually meant to portray an arrow pointing down to a lower case m. A photo of that symbol, as it appeared pressed into red wax, was doubtless resting in dozens of file folders frequently handled by dozens of professionals paid to identify, trap and/or destroy *the Monk*.

The lap top beeped and Sig learned that very large bounties were out on a list of possible residents of Mascara and the surrounding country. He might have recognized more of the names if his vision hadn't narrowed around the name of *Enno Duden*. It had been a few years but the paternal instinct remained. Why on earth would the boy's name be on *this* list, he thought. He scanned down quickly and discovered that his own employers, the big boys, were offering amnesty to any professional bad guy who could deliver the goods. It was a race between a huge corporation and the big boys neither of which knew they had the same objective and the same hit man working to destroy everybody and everything associated with something called the "Glass Pirate."

And the company was anxious to talk with him. Seems they had a highly sensitive assignment in Mexico. To him it felt as though he was being pulled off the scene.

He always figured that when the moment came he'd be overwhelmed. This, instead, was just a casual passing acknowledgment. After this one operation (this one he'd do for himself and the boy) his career would be over.

Especially since he alone knew everything about the big boys, those nameless intelligence directors for the Worldbank and the World Trade Organization, the secret police for the new world order. They used to be a manageable joke. Not any more.

And especially now that he knew his heart was no longer his own to direct. He felt an innocent smile and a pleasant adrenaline rush. They were new to him. So too, was his subsequent anxiety about seeing her again.

Sloop lay in the hospital bed bandaged and trussed in casts, immobile. There were only three movements he could feel; his eyes, his thoughts - and her tears. He felt them each as movement. Helga cried silently now Brenda was gone. For Brenda, Helga had whimpered and sighed to give her clear evidence, to share clear evidence, of her misery. Now she was alone, except for the motionless shape in the bed next to hers. She had no idea that person was her broken husband, the man she cursed with her tears.

Sloop knew she was crying. Forced to deal with her silence for so many years he came to feel its subtle movements. To distinguish between sadness, tragedy, anger, terror, confusion and stubbornness. All emotions which shut Helga down to a silent shell.

In this broken confined state, Sloop tried to keep his eyes open. Whenever they shut he felt his thoughts rush as though wind through a freshly opened window. A wrapping, cloying, wind turning the hot sweat of his anxieties to a cold, sticky nervousness. At those times his thoughts circled around sources, stories, beginnings. He remembered so vividly the discovery from Charmaine of the key to Helga. It had taken years to understand its full meaning.

It was on that trip to Berkeley with Titus many years ago that he first met Helga. Helga of the full-body smile. Helga of the loud infectious laugh. Helga of the flirting eyes. She was living with a family and in nearly constant company with a strange young woman named Charmaine.

Charmaine Lebow, natural if unwilling mother of Shirley Intoit, might have had one true love in her life if she had let Titus in. But she was broken, emotionally incomplete, incapable of sharing any part of her soul because her soul was not hers to share. Perhaps that was why she felt such an instant and complete kinship with the new emigré Helga. Here was a young woman who for different reasons and in different ways was also intensely incomplete and working with every ounce of her fiber to make of herself a joyful simple normalcy. Helga of the full body smile was a fraud.

Sloop forced his eyes open. Wondered if his beautiful heifers were okay. Today was the day he was to move them to the upper crested wheat pasture... His eyes sagged shut.

On that first trip, bright shining John Ogdensburg had failed to attract Helga. In the months which followed, months of training and travel with Titus, John (Sloop) had been frequently sidetracked by hungry thoughts of the exotic beauty and her smile. Too late he would learn how that fragile smile's intensity came from desperate disguise rather than joy or understanding. Too late because he found, early on, that he didn't want to live without the smile. Titus had tried to warn him. Titus knew. He knew because in this regard Charmaine and Helga were true sisters

Once Titus had remarked, "when you take an ordinary, average person and burn her through extreme cruelty and horrible circumstance, you get an extraordinary baked shell around an empty soul. It is our curse, our weakness, perhaps our death, that we are attracted to these gorgeous zombies."

It took Sloop a long time to absorb and understand his friend's observation.

Charmaine was angry when she said to him, "She's only going with you because she blames herself for his death, that crazy boy who killed himself over her. She doesn't love you - she can't. Don't you understand? She spent several lifetimes with a sad, withdrawn mother and a needy, drunk father who was always pushing her away violently and pulling her back in inappropriate ways. She was broken and she fixed herself. Now she's beautiful, now she belongs to herself. She cannot, she will not, ever belong to anyone else. Leave her alone. Leave her with me, she's mine!"

All that stuff from the past excused and explained but it never satisfied. In spite of it all Sloop held her and cared for her and deep inside longed for that full-body smile that so completely consumed his youth. She was, after all else, his cripple, his wife, even if she would never be his lover.

As Sig left the motel in search of Brice, he spotted an all too familiar little face in a green pickup. Last time he saw Fumes was in Tunisia. He immediately turned and went back to his room careful not to be seen. When he opened the laptop lid there was a message waiting. CIA, FBI, AFT were all descending on Mascara as well as the right wing militia group - Bald Mother America or BMA. (They made it their job to know where feds were going and to show up and be felt - a new and dangerously effective intimidation tactic.)

Sig wheezed, "Oh, Buddha. This is getting crazy."

He typed in a search code, gleaned a numerical access number, decoded that and placed a land-line phone call.

"Luigi? Sig here. How's my girl Estell?"

"Holy cow! Sig? She still has stinky gas from your last visit and those moldy tamales you fed her. Holy trash burners, you still alive? Where are you?"

"No time to chit chat. I need you to go *code translucent*. Remember Tel Aviv in January? Got another story for you. May not be the biggest but it darn sure looks like the most dangerous.

Don't let anybody know it's you. Are you listening? Good. I need you here within twelve hours. Six faces. Three identities. Go to the usual place. You'll find the story posted. You'll need the reverse mirror. How's your delectus? I need you to see that LA, NY and London all coincide. And the faucet should have appropriate damage. Oh, and this time buddy, you can have all the action you can handle. Time's up."

He rang off and went to the laptop where he commenced to typing in Latin. Luigi Longstroke was a free-lance journalist and dog trainer who, on occasion, worked as the Monk's double. They were perfect physical twins. Luigi would be translating this message which read in part;

"From reliable sources we learn that all major federal law enforcement agencies, several guerilla operatives, terrorists, and corporate police are converging today on a quiet, small, mountain town in central Oregon in what appears to be a covert military operation involving organized crime figures. Anyone anticipating traveling to the area should check first with authorities."

Sig added more details and made up some. Luigi would see that the information made it, nom-de-plume, to the major newspapers and news services. It was Sig's goal to have Mascara's population treble with an influx of news media and just as fast as possible.

Enno and Resumé, back at Sloop's farm, sat in the travel trailer, bunk house and stared at one another. Resumé's bones ached, he knew something big was going to happen. Enno shook the confusing cobwebs out of his head. All that talk, whooee, it was just too much. He'd like to have more time with Titus and keep the conversation to farming.

All Enno wanted was to farm.

Chapter Fourteen

Siltcoos River

"Most things that are done good in this world are done accidently."
- Lord Dilling

As Titus Ibid drove to town to check the computers, he
thought hard and instinctively kept any evidence of the thinking
process down inside. He was a picture of tortured, accepted
nothing. He drove like a tired husband after a wife's demanded
late-night, solitary, grocery item. He drove as a sleep walker. He
drove like a postal employee to a performance review. Deep
inside was a hidden infestation of thought. A tumult inside.
Outside, calm, artificial resignation. Poker face. It was one of his
secrets of success. He could not be read from the outside. Not
yet, anyway.

One more time. He would have to work the smokers and
the calibrations one more time. The entire organization might be
at risk. No evidence, just a small pile of "coincidences" suggesting convergence. He had a strong instinctual sensitivity to the
subtlest readings of convergence. His work invited danger and

Titus was alive this day because he trusted instincts. Sometimes the messages came from real signals, real evidence. Other times odd convergence pushed him in unlikely directions where he would discover evidence. He didn't worry any more whether the "impulses" were solidly based. He trusted them regardless. Maybe *The Monk* was no where around. Maybe the boy didn't know the same monk. It didn't matter.

Titus knew *The Monk* only by reputation. Whether that reputation was fact or fiction it demanded careful attention. *The Monk* was for hire to the highest bidder and his brand, that burnt trident shaped M, was said to guarantee certain terrible outcome. *The Monk* appeared to align himself, by virtue of the identity of his paymaster, only with greed and power. Titus had to admit a certain intrigued admiration for the style and skill of his competitor. It was Ibid's conviction that consistent style, increasing flourish, an apparent devotion to a controlled projected identity, were the hallmarks most frequently of a principled intensity which bordered on insanity. A powerful realm of spiritual balance which he, Titus Ibid, courted cautiously with shame and relish. Shame and relish carefully pocketed out of view, never to interfere with the needs of a given moment.

This moment had needs. Titus was on a wave of impulse and had to ride it out. The impulse said "check your flanks now!" That's where he was going, to check his and everyone else's flanks.

Titus felt a new vulnerability seep, rust and rot in to the old familiar chainmail of his protective shell. For most of his adult life Titus had been able to send his concerns into an instant nose-dive to the very bottom of "so what" - to the core of "it doesn't matter" - to the naked end or beginning. It stripped him of the dangerous need to protect and hold. Once he had given up any hope of a life and love with Charmaine Lebow, those many years ago, he had carefully avoided property, affection, ties. He *had* been able to do what he did because he had nothing to lose. And because the excitement and the accomplishment of the "work" had filled him just enough. But, just like with certain foods, he had to "eat" more often, "work" more often, to avoid the hungers.

Now things had changed. Now "so what" was an emotion denied to him.

On the outskirts of Mascara, the toy town, Titus saw them and their car. Long before they saw him he saw them. So out of place. This pretend town, even on a slow, late winter/early spring rainy, dirty snow, evening, was a sharp contrasting backdrop for these men. They could have been a pair of Jr. Amway salesmen or twin motivational speakers heading for a Holiday Inn clambake but then their odd talents would have been wasted, their talents for cold detached, premature justice or prejudice under the veil of information gathering. These were agents of the Federal Bureau of Investigation. A suggestion that the inherent beauty and nobility of the human spirit is often susceptible to the deflating, demeaning, influence of mindless militaristic obedience.

Titus saw these two and felt a cautious sympathy for them. Then he saw the others. Not more than one town block behind, as an obvious tail, here came three young, bald mercenaries staring intently ahead over a pickup hood, plexiglass bug-guard with the reverse inscription "America for Americans." Combative naivete. Young fascists. Members of *Bald Mother America*.

Something was definitely up. Titus had to be careful. More careful than in the past. He now had things he didn't want to lose; his music, the mules, the Fork family, his farming. His new ideas, his new still-formative ideas. Thoughts about farming.

Fred English was listening to the public radio broadcast. The scientist was saying,

> "We've messed with the genes of the fruit fly and of
> mice and doubled their life-span. If we can map the genes
> of humans I believe it is conceivable that, in the future,
> people will live much longer. Many of the principles which

160 Lynn Miller

*have improved agricultural productivity; things such as
hybridization, gene splicing, programmable chemical
tolerance--could all be applied to the human species..."*

Fred picked at the thread of breakfast pork chops stuck
between his teeth. He wasn't sure he wanted to live to a hundred
and forty. He was certain he didn't want to share a pork chop
dinner at Brenda's Cafe with any mutated or cloned individual.
Nope. Keep it simple. That was Fred's motto. That's why he was
pleased as punch to retire from the Oregon State Police and take
his present job as Oregon State Livestock Patrolman, "Cow Cop"
suited him fine. He could be just as diligent and inquisitive as he
wished - be "detecting" - without all the risk and tragedy.

Fred English's mother looked like Fred MacMurray the
actor. His father looked like Bob Hoskins the actor. Fred did not
look like an actor. Fred looked like both of them combined with
that acquired *feel* of a tired cop. He was maybe short, maybe tall,
maybe thick, maybe thin. A personality like caramel chews,
definitely sweet and sticky. Not much schooling. Lots of voca-
tional stuff. His education was his own. Whether it was a clue on
a case or a thread of a disconnected idea Fred would follow it to
beyond its clear evidence. He pursued, studied, everything on
the subject. Then, he acquired, by consummate unrelenting
curiosity, the habit of backing up along his own trail of inquiry
until he found that last little piece of the string he had followed.
He would pick up his idea, or suspicion, or clue and give it a
gentle tug watching, as though looking down a string or tangle
of water hose, to see where that tug influenced the jumble. In his
mind he saw it like a hose, tangled and laying mostly out of sight
in tall grass. Finding the two suspected ends and gently tugging
usually gave him that first little excitement of discovery. That
lovely "Aha!" that he could not get enough of. In another's hands
that buried, half-hidden hose might be rudely yanked out of its
hiding place. Not so with Fred English. He worked, no played,
gently at the disentanglement. He was very much like a master
catch and release fly fisherman, playing, no working, as slow

and gentle as possible with the completion. Ah, yes, Fred English loved detecting.

Lloyd Jerald Shoulders was an electric, aesthetic force in New York City and London. His sculptures and drawings made the gums of art critics bleed. The urban hunger for his oeuvre, his inexcusable, unexplainable, inexhaustible work, was further influenced by the fact that no one in the art world, except his dealer, had been able to discover just who this man was and where he lived and worked. He'd arrive twice a year in Manhattan smelling of manure and welding rod, looking like Steve McQueen's uncle, like Sean Connery's drinking chum, like a kidnapped Argentine statesman, like Paul McCartney's painting instructor, like a logger, like a preacher/farmer, like a rancher/sculptor. He'd arrive just ahead of his truckload of recent sculptures as though by embarrassing coincidence.

Back home on his ranch some distance outside of Mascara, Oregon, L. J. Shoulders was a curious hermit rancher hardly worth mention. The residents had no way to deal with this satellite individual seeming so aloof, so untouchable, so unknowable, so 'superior', so insulated, so harmless, so disconnected, so silly. Occasionally the local curious, when overcome by their own lazy emptiness, would harbor snippets of cheap vengeful vindictiveness coloring the ammo of gossip and prefaced with slamming rhetorical "who does he think he is?!" snarls. To this Lloyd reacted as though he were immune. The deflection worked and the jackals turned their taunts to other prey. Prey that would squirm, scream, cry and run. Suitable prey for small mobs of small frightened jackals. Prey that oiled the intestinal workings of a modern tribal society with corporate license and no vitality, no fertility, and borrowed creativity. Later, when the mob was large enough and brave enough and drunk enough they would return for the weird old hermit. They'd return and straighten him out. Yes they would.

Many years ago young Shoulders, the once reluctant modern messiah, had gone to the desert for forty days, deep in to the desert, the allegorical desert, the proverbial desert. Way back until he found a door at the back end and passed through to a living heaven of his own design. He never returned from or through that desert. How he came to become the Donatello of modern sculpture is another story.

This evening he sat in his low ranch house surrounded by modern art works and cowboy memorabilia. Not to mention his own works, he sat amidst the sculptures of Brancusi, Giacometti, David Smith, and a trio of Brigitte Pelen masks. There were paintings, prints, drawings and posters of the works of Georgio Morandi, Jules Bissier, Arshile Gorky, David Parks and Don Weygandt. Amidst the cowboy artifacts were McChesney, Buermann, and Garcia bits and spurs. One glass top table protected seven blacksmith-forged Spanish Ring bits. Between the art works hung chaps, chinks, woolies, braided reins, and Deer Lodge Prison horsehair braidings. Bare spots on the walls were written on in pencil and ink with the borrowed words of T. S. Elliot, Dylan Thomas, Italo Calvino, Henry Miller, Lawrence Durrell, St. Augustine, Shakespeare, Bob Dylan, Machiavelli, David Hockney, Desmond Tutu, James Baldwin and Steve Martin. There was a freshness to the clutter, as though everything had been carefully placed over the preceding week. It felt like an aesthetic pack rat's prayer chapel and storage unit.

Lloyd sat in this space with an old book of Caribbean sketches by the artist Jules Pascin, his own notebook and a glass of *Argueso Pedro Ximenez* Cream Sherry. Outside, along the edges of his benchland pastures, coyotes yipped like distraught shopping women warning errant offspring. Outside the rain wet things. Outside, it was dark and cold and formidable to most people, a protective 'empty' which wrapped Shoulders in isolation. His well-ordered and bohemian cowboy isolation. Shoulders swelled, shoulders up - eyes closed, in silent prayerful gratitude for his aloneness.

Nurse Nancy Simmons was a thoroughly modern woman, self possessed yet insecure. Bright without the unnecessary baggage of intellect. Sweet yet incapable of unselfish sympathy. Attractive enough to conceal her pettiness. Aggressive unless met by force. Submissive in a lazy self-serving manner. This was a woman who concealed her feelings. A woman who apologized to no one, ever. A woman of manageable ambitions. A plaid sensibility admired by other women, sometimes desired by men if only briefly. Frequently invited along on dreams but always too late for the boat. Vacuously convincing herself they hadn't been dreams she was interested in. They weren't boats she wanted to be on. They were not up to her measure. She didn't even bother to wave the boats good-bye.

There were isolated moments when alone, in the bathroom, she leaned over the toilet, wept and vomited. She'd deny it. She conveniently didn't remember these moments, they were quickly wiped clean from her selective memory by the damp cloth of "no."

———————————————————————

Enno couldn't sleep. He got out his large utility sketchbook. The one with farmstead drawings. The one Resumé hadn't seen yet. Enno sat next to Resumé on the foam pad, trailer bench seat with the little collapsible formica table. The rain was loud and comforting on the trailer's metal skin.

The book laid open on the table. Enno thumbed through the last several sketches as if reading notes. He opened a fresh spread and began to draw. Using a matchbox as a template he outlined a rectangle with three sides, moving the box he made the shape into an "L" and wrote "house." To the dog he said

"I'm thinking maybe I'll make the house be like a corner of the compound."

Resumé did not respond.

Enno drew another outlined rectangle and wrote the words "woodshed/rakeshed." It was a short distance from one side of the house outline. Next he drew a larger rectangle freehand and

labelled it "garage/shop." He kept doing this until he had
smokehouse, forgeshop, chicken house, root cellar, barn, wagon
shed, pighouse, and others all forming a square compound with
a large garden in the center. Then loosely he drew in shapes to
represent trees, bushes, hedges, fences, roadways, and even an
aerial outline of a team of horses plowing.

He looked down and saw that the dog had fallen asleep. He
sketched in an orchard and pond and felt his eyes get heavy. He
wondered about Sam, Sloop, Helga, and the others. Just before
lowering his head to his waiting folded arms he felt that unreasonable hungry attraction for Billie's half-sister Nancy.

Bo Coin was angry with himself for being frightened. He
was a successful realtor, an important man in town. Billie and the
old hippy farmer were nothing to him. Why should he worry
what Brice might do. Unless he, Bo, was to be next.

Once again Sig leaves his motel room. He has to find Liner.
Town this small maybe just cruising around he'll come across the
conspicuous black Lincoln. It would stand out in a village of
SUVs and pickup trucks.

Mascara's a small particleboard false-front, quasi-western
tourist town of expensive yet cheap specialty shops, high suction
real estate offices, and eight espresso outlets. There are no true
ethnic restaurants, no laundromats, no mass transit, no garment
district, no wharf, no courthouse, no projects, no slums, no
financial district. In other words no place where well dressed
thugs might hang out to pick at each other's noses...

There it was! Parked in front of Coin Bros. Realty. Piece of
luck. Sig backed into an alley parking spot behind a neighboring
title company and waited.

He took out his small sketch pad and tried to draw what he
remembered "she" looked like. Didn't work. What he remembered was a palpable sense of heat and fruit juice and clean.

How could he draw such things?

After years of celibacy - actual, qualified and metaphorical - how could he think of such things? Feel such things? Not that it went against a code, it went against his personality. How could he? As a mercenary of peculiar motives and methods, he had experienced similar questions, similar doubts, and he recalled his Buddhist teachings and his Catholicism. This moment the words and poem of the activist Jesuit priest, Daniel Berrigan, hummed in his lower throat.

"Thus the victim becomes a witness to (among other, more sublime truths) the failure of the destroyer to destroy. The dead man walks abroad."

A Penitent Speaks
You come toward me
prestigious in your wounds
those frail and speechless bones.
Your credentials -
dying somberly for others.
What a burden, gratitude, fake and true vows,
crucifixes
grislier than the event -
and then the glory gap -
larger than life
begetting less than life,
pieties that strike healthy eyes
blind:
Believe! Believe! Christians
tapping down a street
in harness to their seeing-eye god.
Only in solitude
a passing tic of insight
gone as soon as granted
-I see You come toward me free,
free at last.

Can one befriend his God?
The question is inadmissible, I know.
Nonetheless a fiery recognition
lights us;
broken by life,
making our comeback.

With the remembrance, Sig Maltesta felt his breath stutter on the intake. His helpless human self... He was that close to his own weakness, his own truth, his own *new*.

He was exhausted with himself when he saw it. There came *thug* Liner strutting to his car and unbuttoning the suit jacket. From 150 feet Sig could see the pistol holstered on Brice's left side. Liner pulled out in his 'Chicago' car and Sig followed in his budget rental

---

After Jimmy Three Trees surprised them with the revelation (if that was what it was), Shirley and Vicky went their separate ways. Vicky's confusion needed solitude. Shirley went to her trailer excited and apprehensive to have learned the whereabouts of her mother's old school chum, Helga. Tomorrow she'd head to the hospital where Helga Ogdensburg was. Tomorrow, maybe she'd finally learn something of the mother she's never known. She was frightened and surprised. Surprised to feel a hesitation. Maybe she didn't want to know what she was about to learn. What an exhausting day it had been. She stroked the glass horse on the window sill and asked him for answers.

Seems Victoria Wood was learning what she didn't want to know. Could the boy she was so interested in actually be her brother? She had to know, whatever the outcome, Vicky had to know.

Same thing with Shirley, wherever it took her she had to learn about her mother, Charmaine Lebow, or exhaust herself trying. Exhaust herself. She was hungry and tired and remembered the corner market with the Chinese takeout sign that proudly said *no MSG used*. She put on her coat and hat.

Jimmy Three Trees tried, on foot, to follow the half-breed girl. He needed to know where she lived. He needed to thank her for the raincoat and sleeping bag she gave him. He needed to tell her a secret. She, he knew, would understand.

Sig was thankful for the rain. The shots of bright, from headlights, bounced and flashed across wet surfaces helping to conceal his car as he followed Brice Liner.

Heading east out of town, Brice Liner didn't see the cow ambling the highway shoulder ahead him. Didn't see or didn't care. He was accustomed to everything moving out of his way or he plowed through it. Just as he had done earlier with that "Billie" idiot. The high water in the road slowed him as it splashed over the windshield and drug at the wheels. The cow moved towards the road center to avoid the spray. The collision of the Lincoln and the cow, even at reduced speed, caused the big man from Chicago to crease his forehead at the steering wheel. It also bent the front corner of the vehicle in to rub on the tire. Caved in the nose and hood. The cow was barely alive, legs jerking.

An oncoming car pulled to the opposite shoulder just as Liner stumbled out, cursing and waving a pistol which glistened in the reflective light of the rain. The car pulled away slow, then fast.

Sig stopped well back from the accident and watched what followed through his binoculars. The rainy night forms made what followed look like a modern dance caricature. Over it all was ugliness and death.

Brice jumped around. The distance and the rain absorbed all sounds. The big man kicked at the mud, the shining wet air, the car and then the cow. When the cow moved he shot it. Brice shot it over and over again. Seeing this, Sig leaned across the driver's seat of his rented car to get to his own pistol. This move saved him. At that very second, Brice Liner, noticing the headlights of the parked car a hundred feet back, took aim and fired two rounds into the windshield where a driver should have been. He then kicked the dead cow again, shot it again, and got back in the crumpled Lincoln. The tire rubbed and squealed against the bent metal and broken plastic as Liner pulled out on the highway. He lowered the passenger window and took one last shot at the cow.

Sig's windshield was a disaster from the bullets. He had crawled out the passenger door and moved, through the rain, in a crouched position towards the accident. Before he got close enough to do anything, he watched and heard as Brice pulled away in his limping squealing Lincoln.

Titus stopped at the corner market and went to the bulletin board. He found a note stuck up with a thumbtack. It read, "Reward for return of my tongueless cat. Don't wait too long." And it was dated but had no address or phone number. Outside at the payphone he dialed the number he had memorized a couple of years past.

As Shirley Intoit walked past him and into the market, Titus caught a glimpse of her face. He had to grab the edge of the phone box. Wave after wave of loss, sadness, fear and surprise rushed through his old taut frame. He was leaning to look in the glass market door while the phone rang...

Sam Riven jumped when he heard the phone ring. He had cleared an area of his large worktable and was organizing colored scraps with notes to explain things, as he saw them, to worried and curious Nettie Coin. More importantly, the scraps helped him to "see" what was coming and what he could affect. This process had him nerved up. The phone's ring had cut through several of Sam's nerve bands. He jumped.

"Yeah! Geez that was fast. Put up that stupid note less'n half hour ago. We've got to talk right away! But must be extra,

extra careful. Everybody's following everybody, I think."

Yes, that's true, thought Titus. "Where do you suggest we meet?" Sam did not know about Sloop's hideout and Titus knew he must keep it that way.

"There's that chain-up area west of town 3 miles. I'll be with a woman in a caramel-colored Olds. We'll talk there. Half an hour okay?" asked Sam.

Titus was still looking in the market. "I might be a couple of minutes late, but I'll be there. Don't approach me until or unless you see me standing by my cycle like something's wrong with it. Otherwise go on and we'll connect again later by phone. Right?"

Lint Fumes had finished a slow cruise around the little town. He kind of liked it, reminded him of home. He was amused to be able to pick out all the obvious visiting "professionals." They were watching each other watch each other while looking for "the prize."

Tomorrow he'd start his two new jobs. In the morning it was at *Carl's Gas and Cigs*. Mid afternoon, across town, it was at *Lupe's Chevron*.

Right now he was looking for some good takeout food and time alone in his motel room with the contents of his aluminum case. He saw the Chinese takeout sign on the market gable and pulled in. When he reached the door, a man who looked like a grey-haired version of Abe Lincoln was hanging up the phone and turning towards the door. Lint thrived on first impressions and this man he liked the look of. "Allow me?" he said in a slow southern drawl as he held the door open for Titus Ibid. Titus smiled and nodded, distracted, as he craned his neck to see the girl again.

Back in the corner of the small market, an inset deli featured a small visible kitchen and steamtable with trays of Chinese food. Shirley was paying for her Hunan chicken, mushrooms and rice when two separate men approached her from behind. She turned and noticed Lint Fumes, a little bone-thin man in pressed Khakis and a jerking smile. A pleasant exaggerated little man, comic, reminded her of some old TV character. Wally Cox maybe? No, no, it was that other guy, that deputy character. Her casual thoughts were pushed aside, her spirit was being yanked on, being threatened. She felt watched. All her muscles tightened. Was that ape back? Was she trapped? She'd let her guard down about the other guy, the monk character. Was it him? 'Don't turn around,' she told herself. Fidgeting with her canvas bag for the spray mace, she glanced up to the nearby polished stainless back wall of the kitchen and caught the reflection of the tall, sad, grey-haired man standing behind her. He was so intent. Her sense of threat passed and was replaced by an odd sadness. Then the screaming started.

"Must! Must! Must!" hollered the ghastly, dripping, coughing apparition that was Jimmy Three Trees. The thick-set young man who had been at the register vaulted over the counter and grabbed the vagrant.

"No, no, not in here. You have to leave."

"No, must must see her!" screamed the old vagrant.

"Sorry Bub, but out you go." The cashier was dragging the flailing man to the door and suddenly Jimmy went limp and slumped to the floor unconscious.

"Thelma, call 911!" he hollered.

Shirley, Titus and Lint all walked towards the door. When she saw who it was she said, "here, pleas,." and handed her parcels to the startled Titus, rushing then to Jimmy's form to cradle his head in her lap.

There it was. Titus had heard it. The sweet and sour lilt of Charmaine's voice came from this young woman's lips. The tears started to pour out of him. He was out of control. Lint stood near by soaking in the drama. 'This is good,' he thought, 'I like this.' In genuine sympathy and because he wanted to connect to the mysterious depths and sincerity of the odd moment, he set his hand on Titus' shoulder.

The touch was all it took. Titus came as though awake. He looked from Lint to the wall clock and reconnected.

"Have you a piece of paper?" He asked the surprised Fumes.

Lint nodded and took out his little flip pad with the short stub of a pencil.

"Please write this down for me and give it to her." He nodded in Shirley's direction. "I must leave right away. Give it to her after I leave, please? Write; *Charmaine Lebow? 504-4732*".

Titus handed Shirley's canvas purse and Chinese food to Lint with a genuine smile of gratitude and loss and walked around and out of the market.

Titus had to prepare something before his meeting with Sam Riven. And he definitely had to prepare himself. Part of him was floating, part of him was an aching death.

Lint watched the man go. Oh, yes, he liked this man. Life was so short and jumbled up. Why couldn't he have friends like this man. Why'd the world have to be peopled and run by garbage like Brogue and Liner? Why were they the ones to pay the bills and decide who lived or who died? He needed time with his music, with his case.

Jimmy was coming out of his faint but completely incoherent and more disoriented than usual. Shirley stroked his forehead and heard the siren and then saw the emergency lights flicking around the rainy shimmering cold outside. Reminded her of what sunlight did to her glass horse. She looked up and didn't see the man she'd given her stuff to but quickly noticed Lint with it. He approached. "The gentleman gave me this for you." He handed her the note. The note he'd already copied. She read it and her wide-eyed head flew round, right and left.

"He's gone," Lint said.

Sig looked down at the poor dead cow, riddled with bullet holes. His prayer was silent and weightless. He took his sharp, French pocket knife out and set to work. He removed the ears, half of the tail, and the square foot patch of fatty hip hide which contained the brand. These he took back to the damaged rental car.

It was almost impossible to see, but he drove. Head in and out of his window. Hurrying to catch up with the Lincoln.

Brice's head was full of blood fever. Anger had taken him over. His damaged car wouldn't go over thirty. The rain sizzled on the rumpled hood, hot from all the broken functions. He aimed himself at his purpose, unwilling to think or see anything else. He was heading to the hospital to finish off Ogdensburg.

Fred English sat in his single-wide mobile home cleaning his sawed-off shotgun and watching a video-taped episode of the Waltons. By his side was a hot spiced rum and his much loved science terminology dictionary. He was researching *anemometry*, the Beaufort scale and wind measurements for a cattle rustling case. The phone rang, it was the County Sheriff chuckling. Fred looked out into the rain as he listened to an account of a possible alien abduction and mutilation of a cow on the highway not far from his place. Sheriff figured it could wait til morning. Fred knew otherwise. Fresh clues. Fresher the better. He would go out right away.

Duden was dreaming. Walking along a roadside barbwire fence with Resumé running ahead. When the dog turned, Enno saw he had a big wire stretcher in his mouth and under his paw was a pair of wire pliers. Instantly an apple tree appeared, loaded with ripe fruit and shading a tall ladder. Enno climbed the ladder and as he reached for any apple that portion of the tree would change to bare branches.

Chapter Fifteen

Tillamook

" We have found the truth and the truth makes no sense."
- Chesterton

The secret of the universe is the ruling question of exception. The exceptional owes its existence to exception which governs form through anarchy. And exception makes of the exceptional an apology for predictability which we know as mutation. Exception is known as mystery. And governing anarchy is the flux of the weld.

Enno came awake in a sweat, gasping for air. He pushed at a suffocating wrap of confusion and restraint, only there in his dream. He flung his right arm in a sweeping arc struggling to protect himself. There was nothing but that darkest black of night's final hour. His arm went limp to the side of the bed and came to rest on Resumé-the-dog's, head.

"Are you watching me? Have you been watching me, boy?

Good dog."

"Good Dog" seemed inappropriate, inadequate.

He rolled over to try to go back to sleep. Not the same sleep please. A better one this time. The one he had come from was worrisome, tiring. He demanded a restful sleep.

It wasn't to work out that way. Flat on this back, eyes wide open, he tried to get a clear fix on what was bothering him. Sloop's accident? Helga's trouble? The run in with the hunters? They were enough but it was something else. Nameless. Ahead of him, not behind. An apprehension for what was coming. What was it? What was happening? These new people, the Fork family and Titus, they treated him with familiarity that was both troubling and comforting. What was it they saw in him? What was expected of him? He didn't want anything expected of him. With Sam Riven, the testiness, the taunting all seemed to fit the New Zealander's angry personality. But even there, Duden felt he was being watched, measured and clung to. Why? Enno Duden - orphaned carpenter's helper and future farmer, nobody important, what could these people want from him? See in him? With Sloop and Helga it was different, it was what orphan Enno wanted to believe were family sensibilities, friendship in some simple form, shared values. Sloop and Enno always spoke, commonly and economically about the life of farming. Their kind of farming.

Watching Enno through the wrinkled tops of his eyes, Resumé plopped to a prone position beside the bed. He crossed his front legs to form a cradle for his chin and, with rear legs akimbo almost limp with relaxation, he let loose with a deep sigh.

Enno heard this and looked down. The second their eyes met Resumé was on his feet and pushing his nose into the young man's arm.

"And then there's you, dog. What am I to make of you? Want to be my partner? Huh, fella?" He stroked Resumé's blissful agreeing head.

It was more than how these new people saw him, treated him, listened and watched him. There was a thick, dark feeling like that felt before a battle or as a child's first bedtime concern for closets and the undersides of beds. It was that apprehensive prelude to giving a nightmare a shape and a voice. Something was coming. And for Enno this meant change which threatened his plan, his dream, his one purpose, a farm of his own. He couldn't let it take hold.

Running right along side of this apprehension, the young man felt a contradictory or complimentary samaritan-like surge. Sloop and Helga needed him, now. Though he had no doubt the angry vengeful bullet had been meant for him he, none the less, felt Helga needed protection from what was yet to come. And Sloop needed both a helping hand and someone to protect him from himself. Neither of those feelings came from a place of experience or strong logical thought on Enno's part. They both came from that same spot that sent him to help anyone or thing, helpless or threatened, even at his own risk.

Being able to select protective duty over anxiety gave relief. If he was busy taking care of business, it was difficult to dwell on the dark unknown.

Shirley always rose early. Sometimes four thirty, sometimes five thirty, never later. Her daily rhythms were punctuated by a comfortable anxiety. She was anxious for each day to begin. Her father said it was her southerly genes. He said she must be like the trout he had heard of who exploded into excited activity at the first suggestion of morning light. Shirley had no animals to care for, no farm chores, no fishing trip planned, no job to go to. She could have stayed in her comfortable travel trailer and slept until the swing shift hit the espresso shacks but she wouldn't. That was too much like being sick. Too much like waiting to die. Whether she knew it or felt it, her anxiety was a constant, vigilant preparation for a life she was speeding towards.

This morning, however, had two new twangs. Helga

Ogdensburg and the old man from the market. The note had her
mother's name and a phone number. Shirley had tried, from the
phone booth, several times after the ambulance had picked up
Jimmy. But there was never any answer. She would try again this
morning before going to the hospital. She'd also call Vicky to see
if she knew about Jimmy's stroke. In a town as small as Mascara
maybe this old guy knew Helga and Charley both.

Her morning toilet ministrations were a model of stylish
efficiency. She sloshed cold water from the greystone enameled
basin onto her drum-tight face. With a handmade whalebone and
caribou hair toothbrush, she used an exotic sweet powder to
clean her teeth. This morning she was definitely going to shower.

Her thoughts flung themselves on all the stuff of yesterday.
Her new friend Vicky, and the episode with Jimmy Three Trees in
the woods, plus his terrible trouble at the market. Shirley Intoit's
gaze fell to the Glass Horse in its rubber seat on her window sill.
Her hand followed her gaze and she stroked the form.

This morning she could actually be talking to one of her
mother's old friends, Helga. Odd, she didn't know this woman,
Helga Ogdensburg, but the difficulties of her search for the
mother who had abandoned her worried Shirley. For unex-
plained reasons she felt that everyone and anyone who could talk
with her about Charmaine Lebow were poised to disappear at the
mention of her name,...

She went into the tiny trailer shower stall still thinking.

...the story this time was that this Helga woman was confined to a hospital bed. Shirley felt she didn't have to run up and
grab the sleeve of a fleeing person and plead. This time was
different.

So much to think about this morning, she'd almost forgot
about the thug and the monk. She dried herself from the shower,
put on an old oversized sweatshirt of her uncle's as a robe and
pulled her luxuriant black hair back with two large tortoise shell
combs. She thought about her promise to the Payout shaman to
contact this Victor character. Later, that could wait.

The Bialetti pot on her gas stove burbled to say her espresso was ready. She poured her strong coffee and spread a thick layer of English marmalade on a slab of whole wheat bread.

She dropped the bread startled by a knock on her trailer door. Stupidly preoccupied, she unlocked the door at the same time as she pulled the little curtain aside to see who it was. He pushed his way in and closed and locked the door behind him. Sig held a single bloody finger to his lips requesting silence as he went from window to window looking outside for something.

There is something about the color and attitude of Sage that suggest berries. Those soft pungent bluish-grey knarled irregular shrubs ought to have berries. Blue berries, edible little blue berries with those exploding crowns and that unexpectedly sugary-safe taste. He loved the look, smell and feel of Sagebrush and wanted them to have berries, thick hanging-down-low berries. He imagined bears laying down on their backs and scooting backwards, mouths open, shoving their heads in under the Sagebrush until the fruit tickled their noses.

He loved the high desert. Many obvious hack-kneed reasons; the colors, the space, the surprises. But most of all he loved how this landscape drew the insignificance out of him, like the way oil works its way out of a Chicana's hair. Here he could be the dope he wanted to be without any fear of contradiction. Here he could flirt with consequence fully appreciating the fact that his future was stuck in the night deposit drawer.

He saw himself as a writer, worked at it, tried to behave as one, invested entirely too much in a spendable writer's tomorrow. His day job was a necessary mistake. His wife saw him as delusional but otherwise acceptable. She knew first hand that a good man was hard to get and harder to keep since the passage of the sanctity of marriage amendment to the constitution. Besides, little Toopack, their son, needed to at least have the appearance of an accessible father, otherwise it would be Shelly's price to pay with all the other moms. The price she had to pay to keep her family resembling convention was a daily non-committal nod towards Roger's early morning pencil-pushing. She had to make sure he didn't go off half-cocked with some weird idea that he had a manuscript which might be published, might pay real money, might allow him to quit his day job. She could see him mumbling to himself 'so why not go ahead and quit today'. No, no, no, no, no, no, no. Play at it, okay, but she would make sure he was always around with a regular paycheck and a lawn mower. That was in her version of the contract.

Earlier that night: Fred English believed that science was a tableau of rationales. Smart people deciding that there had to be an explanation for everything, a rationale, worked in their heads to devise principles by which phenomena came to be. Then all the envious competing "scientists" set about to disprove or discredit that new law or rule. But someone forgot to tell mother nature, or so Fred felt, because time after time he witnessed how the obvious wasn't, how the actual rationales of the natural world would align in curious ways which seemed to encourage patterns of synchronicity which, some times, altered natural law itself. Little men rushed to convenient deductive fear pockets, such as *alien intervention,* while big men simply removed the exceptions from their line of sight believing that in so doing, by assignation to suspense accounts, they had cleared the work area and allowed the world to continue well explained. For Fred English, Cow Cop and arbitrary deductician, the little men were to be preferred. You could talk to them and along with the fantasies they retained relevant information rather than pretending it wasn't there.

He saw the flashing patrol car lights first. Closer in he saw the officer, flashlight in hand, appearing to argue with a short man. Then he noticed, before he reached the scene, the glitter of windshield glass some distance away from the patrol car. He drove up to the pile and looked down then proceeded to the flashing lights. He parked and stepped out of his state issue pickup. The directed force of the trooper's flashlight hit him in the face.

"Hey, Bub there's nothing for you here. Move on." The officer was angry. The little man drew him back around with his insistent squeal, "I'm telling you I saw it all. That cow dropped from the sky with a man on his back flashing a bloody knife!"

"And I'm telling you you're nuts! I've been patient with you. Now this is how it's going to play out. You are going to get back in your car and drive away from here or I'm going to handcuff you and you'll spend the night in jail. Got that?"

"I'm a doctor, you can't talk to me that way!" came the shout.

"Excuse me, officer?" The rapidly approaching Fred English was holding his open wallet up with its glistening badge. The angry trooper's eyes slowly altered to confusion as the Cow Cop whispered introductions and jurisdictional observations in his ear.

Turning now with a genuine grin Fred asked, "What's your name sir?"

"Sam Fistula, Dr. Sam Fistula. I have a practise in Mascara."

It took great control for English not to laugh about the name. "Do you mind my asking what sort of doctor you are sir?"

"Chiropractor. I specialize in small animals and people."

(Not horses? Fred wondered.) He was looking down at the head-light illuminated mutilated body of the cow as he listened.

"So, are you going to need me any further?", interrupted the officer.

"Yes, yes, hang on for a little bit please."

"And, Doctor, I am very keen to hear your observations. Can you wait just a few minutes by your car. I need to examine the sight?"

Fistula hurumphed past the trooper.

Fred used his own flashlight to canvas the perimeter and the carcass, careful not to step on the wet ground which was punctuated with footprints.

Fred started to speak in that voice some men use to talk into a voice recorder.

"Two men, multiple shots fired, surgical precision where the parts and hide were removed. Evidence that the bovine was probably involved in a collision with a vehicle. See the glass and this headlight ring? But the best news is that we have a fresh crime scene. Note the blood. And lookee here, skids marks, hmm hmm? But, they're leaving the scene? Officer, I need you to fence a wide perimeter with incident tape and alert Redmond and the state police to be on the lookout for a late model luxury sedan with a broken windshield, plus right fender and hood damage, traveling slow as it drags a tire. Also, advise extreme caution. Suspect alcohol or irrational behavior, firearms. And watch for a second vehicle with a broken windshield in pursuit of the first. I want to protect this sight in case this warrants casts of those prints."

"Yes sir." The trooper was pumped up, he knew now he was working alongside the legendary English.

"Dr. Fistula, your observations will be extremely important to resolving this incident. I am inclined to suspect that your conclusions of bizarre foul play may be accurate. But right now I need to follow a very hot lead. May I visit you later to get your testimony?"

"Yes, yes. I'm going to a string quartet performance at the high school and should be back at my home," he handed him a business card, "some time after 9:30 this evening. Please phone before you stop by."

"Thank you, Doctor." English smiled internally noting there was no way he would call ahead first.

After exchanging radio information, Fred drove off towards Redmond, stopping every two hundred feet to examine the pavement.

Sig had succeeded in following Brice Liner to the Hospital and watched as he canvassed the parking lot looking for something. Brice came to a car, nodded to himself, opened the door and took out a set a keys that the owner had left in the ignition. Then he looked around before he went in the emergency entrance.

Sig waited a few minutes.

Lint went into the small town liquor store. He was in need of a bottle of Dubonnet. This store had a front lobby with comfortable chairs divided from the store shelves by a counter. The building had been a doctor's office in a former life and the liquor store owner found the waiting room too much of a community feature to remove it. Two men were seated in the lobby talking with some animation.

"Turn it around. Do the means ever justify the end? For example, you work at gathering data about raptors. You love your work and you're a purist. You're always saying how it's your chosen work to collect the data with no thought as to its eventual use. You don't want to be influenced, you don't want to skew the numbers to make any point or assist any possible outcome. You call it science." He wore a perma-press sky-blue shirt with silver vertical pin-striping, rough cotton draw-string pants, Italian loafers and no socks. His ankles were artificially tan. As he spoke he waved his cell phone around as if he were spraying for bugs. Their wives were shopping for liquors, gossiping and frequently laughing at their husband's conversational antics.

"What's your point?" This second half of the conversation wore a down vest over a hooded sweatshirt, hood down. His blue jeans had a bronze-plated name tag which read *Edizione Antonio Beechy*. He wore his cell phone in a velcro-assisted holster at his belt. On his feet were striped socks and Birkenstock sandals.

"Just this, your data may very well lift protective restriction, endangered species ... you know what I mean ... all that crap, and you will have effectively destroyed the species you love."

With a roar of laughter "What a load of feces!"

"Ben, I'm serious!"

" I don't doubt it, Parker. Listen if we labor over all the possible effects of everything we do, we'll do nothing."

"Now, you're going too far."

"Oh, yeah, well take your work for example. You have to go through your day shielding yourself from what might happen or it would kill you. You can't convince me that practising law doesn't have myriad hidden and unwished for consequences. You are always focused on the end..."

Lint inserts himself at this point.

"Gentlemen, forgive my intrusion. Could you direct me to a music store and some place that sells rifle shells?" Smooth, deep southern drawl with high pitched squeaks.

"The hardware store on Hyde street's the only place for ammo," offered the attorney.

"Yes, and there is no place outside of Bend for a reasonable selection of tapes and CDs. You don't sound like you're from around here," asked the college professor.

"Chicago, just blew in. May I ask you gentlemen a question?" Lint's eyes squinted down around twinkles. "If principled man were to end up dead because of those principles would the abstract notion of morality have been well served?"

The attorney chuckled, "Where did that come from?"

"You sir. I overheard parts of your discussion about means and ends and it reminded me of Camus and his notion that ..."

"You don't sound like you're from Chicago..." interrupted the professor.

"Speech impediment. When I was younger I kept interrupting my teacher. He used pliers to pull my tongue out and hold it while he whacked it with a ballpeen hammer."

"Jeez! What did you do?"

"I shot him. Dull, I know. I've never forgotten that he showed far more style and demonstrated greater effectiveness with his measure." Lint held on for a while and then burst into a soft subdued laugh.

The other two laughed nervously at first, anxious to acknowledge the strangers perverse joke.

"Well, now I've lost my place which probably does higher honor to Camus. May I suggest gentlemen that argument is ill-served by heat. It is always an indication of wasted energy and selfishness. Law and science afterall are both complex sets of apologies for acts of wasted energy and selfishness. With that I thank you and bid you good day."

Lint Fumes, contract-killer and bon vivant, pointed at each man, flicked his thumb as if firing a pistol, and walked out of the Liquor store's waiting room with his Dubonnet.

Helga looked on horrified as a big man in a dirty blue suit pushed a pillow down over the face of the bandaged person in the bed next to her. She screamed a broken piece of a weak scream when a second man entered soundlessly and hit the pillow assailant hard at the back of the neck. Helga passed out in a dead faint. Brice crumpled to the floor.

Sig worked fast, first checking to see if the bandaged Sloop was conscious. He was, just barely. (He had visited three rooms down the hall before coming here, careful to press the nurse call buttons at each of them. This would keep them busy for a few minutes.) Then he struggled to lift the limp form of Brice Liner on to the gurney which was against the wall of Helga's hospital room. He strapped him down, ripped his shirt open and lit a square red candle, aiming hot wax on to the man's chest hairs. When he had a significant pile of hot wax he pressed the carved end of his knife handle down hard, making a clear impression of a trident shaped M.

Still moving fast and purposeful, he removed from his backpack the cow's ears, tail, and hide patch. Brice started to move and Sig hit him hard on the head with the table lamp. Liner went limp. Taking a needle and thread from a small tin, he took two stitches through Brice's ear lobes and through each cow ear pulling tight and tying firm. Liner looked like some Picasso-

esque cariacature of Grecian dispute with two bloody animal ears
hanging from each side of his face. Next he opened the man's
pants and lit the red candle again this time dripping hot melting
wax on to the hairs well below the belly button. Into this he
pressed the branded cow's hide patch tugging to see that it was
firmly stuck. Next he took heavy string and stitched the cow's tail
around Brice's neck like a necklace. Next, as an afterthought, he
took his razor-sharp French pocketknife and scratched a message
on Brice's belly.

*"There is no justice, there are only limits, you have exceeded yours.
Monk"*

With one last tug at the gurney restraints, he went to check
the two patients. First to the woman. Her pulse was good, she
was fine. Next he went to the person with the bandaged head.
Sloop had been conscious for a few minutes and had silently
watched Sig's ministrations with Brice. Two eyes looked out
through the wrappings without divulging a clue as to identity.
Maltesta looked into the eyes and suppressed a shiver as he
thought he recognized himself. It was a different game now. He
patted Sloop's shoulder and left the room with all of his tools
and the set of keys he had taken from Brice's pocket.

Fred English sat in his pickup truck in the Hospital parking
lot looking at the battered Lincoln. He saw the man with the
back-pack leave through the emergency door and walk to a small
sedan, get in and back out. It was Sig. He slowed and took one
last look at his rental car with the bullet-smashed windshield.
Then turning his head right he saw English looking at him. He
drove off calmly.

English ran for the hospital entrance and followed the
muddy footprints to the room where Brice Liner mumbled into
consciousness and cowography. English was in clue heaven.

Little and large overlapping eccentric circles of the power-politics of style, pure poison.

Where does original thought begin? In the belly? Outside, down the road somewhere? As waste product of the push of life? Or in chorus as contrived, improvised, counterpoint and harmony?

Anecdotal evidence is to science as creativity is to intelligence. The perpetually rewritten novel with tangental variants published. The novel as textural pictograph. The narrative a tide-like flood wrapping around islands of thought, nuggets, revelations, quotations and diagrams plus images.

And then we step backwards to the ordinary, to be fed the tiniest slivers of possibility because in the beginning we are human and in the end we are unknowable.

"Never fight evil as if it were something that aroze totally outside of yourself."

- William Sloan Coffin

Chapter Sixteen

Jordan River

Sig said to Shirley in a whisper, "Cat and mouse is over, we need each other. I perhaps more than you. A surprise to both of us. You came here to launder your Cooper money, I came here tailing you. People paid me to get to the Cooper thing. And as you already know, there are people here who want to hurt you. I don't think there's a connection, but there might be."

He reached for the roll of paper towels on the counter and began to wipe the dried blood from his hands. He noticed what had escaped her this morning, a plastic ketchup bottle lay nestled on the counter top in a bed of scattered raisin bran, maple syrup and broken glass.

"You're a messy one," he observed.

"Who are you? Really, I mean who are you?" she insisted.

He ran some water on the paper and continued working the dried cow blood off. He stared at her a little too long. "You don't want to know. And I can't afford for you to know." Long pause.

"I think we may be able to help one another. And beginning some time yesterday, I quit one set of my former employers and began working for myself."

She, by all rights should have been scared out of her wits by him but she wasn't. Instead she looked around the trailer and noticed that several things were scattered as if she'd been driving hard down a rough road. Curious was the expression on her face. "Well go ahead and talk, I'm going to finish getting dressed."

After leaving the corner market, dizzy with remembrance and confusion, Titus had moved to the industrial park and eventually into Sloop's hidden computer office. It was a long and convoluted process. First, even dazed, he had managed to complete the ritual of the wounded Killdeer, drawing the invisible predator away from the nest. Rather than pretending to have a broken wing and squealing in a false fear, he went from casual walk to a nervous hopping limp, ducking in and out of shadows, to the loose post of the slatted tow service chain-link yard fence. Somewhat certain that he was not being followed, he lifted the fence flap and ducked inside, navigating the maze of crumpled vehicles until he reached the decrepit forgotten 49 Diamond Reo Log truck. Inside the cab, the rusted spring-loaded shard of a seat, released by button to hinge upwards, worked as a trap door revealing a shielded portion of the ground beneath which was covered by two tack-welded sheets of old galvanized siding. Under the siding, which swiveled sideways on a hinge pin driven into the earth, was a diagonal shaft dropping down in the ground and against which lay a wooden ladder-stair. Titus, small flashlight in mouth, lowered himself down the hole, carefully lowering first the seat then the roofing sheets. Once down, he marvelled as he always did at the curious inverted shape of this lava tube cave. Thousands of years before, hot lava from a volcanic eruption had burnt its way through the ground and cooled creating this stone-lined, three headed snake of a cave. They, Sloop and Titus, had always been careful not to leave any evidence of their coming and going. This was an access route they used only when absolutely necessary, only when they suspected they were being watched. Following his memory and the tiny battery light's plume, Titus Ibid took the rapidly narrowing left passage until, on hands and knees, he passed through a tight crack and climbed up to the sliding board roof of the shaft which allowed him access to an outer chamber of the abandoned gas station shop. Once up there, he would gather some information from Sloop's computers, two important tools, and leave by the regular side entrance which came out between the two anchored, locked, dumpsters. Opening the special front door of the one fake garbage dumpster, he would remove the 1968 Berlinetti touring bike and head out the back gravel forest service road, to meet Sam Riven. He would have to be doubly watchful for patches of snow and ice.

Bundled up in the sheep's wool lined coat, riding on the bike, he remembered that one time in California many years ago when Charmaine had squealed with delight, arms wrapped around his middle, hair flapping and slapping in the wind. They were racing to Tiburon. He had been blissfully happy with promise. That sensation, sensation as a raw emotional memory, had never completely left him.

Vicky woke up with an odd taste in her mouth. Something like rotted herring mixed with burnt coffee and detergent. Up until this morning she had always enjoyed the waking flavors. Hers were usually strawberry jam and pasta salad with vinagrette dressing and clorets. But this morning she had a mean headache, meaner breath, and a swelling anger. She had to find Duden. He must have known all along, the butthead! Now she understood why he had always deflected her advances with such blushing embarrassment. "Gawd, I can't believe it!" she said as

she slammed the bathroom door. She thought the slamming had
caused the upheaval she found. There were medicines and
toiletries strewn over the sink and floor.

Nettie sat behind the wheel in her car waiting for Sam. He
had warned her to keep a lookout for anyone who was watching
and not to stare at Sam and his contact. They would, he said,
wander off in the darkness to talk. She wasn't to get squirrely and
slip up on the vigilance, everything was going to be okay. Still,
she couldn't help but wonder what she was letting herself in for.
Above and beyond the adventure, there was a sense of over-
grown boys playing at dangerous even stupid games. Sam hadn't
given any specifics but she got a general sense that a couple of
men were directing some kind of global economic piracy against
large corporations and government agencies. Sam was providing
false IDs and various "patents" of history like college degrees,
marriages licenses, credit histories, etc. Sam seemed to believe
that it was all serious enough business that people were in line to
get hurt, especially now that "professionals" had been spotted in
town.

"Whether or not the Monk is actually in town, I do agree
that things are getting thick. Too thick. Maybe, just maybe, this
will work to our advantage. Imagine for a second that perhaps
other things are happening coincidentally in this town and
region, separate from our organization, and that the other things
are drawing folks in. I saw boys from B.M.A. tailing what must
have been feds. Any militia stuff going on that you know of?"
Titus seemed preoccupied as he spoke.

"I think so. Herman Sholtz's boys have been trying to get me
to do some papers. I've been avoiding them. They've moved their
camp to somewhere in the Steens. They'd be funny if they weren't
so deadly. Talk is they are trying to team up with B.M.A. on some
constitutional tax strikes." Sam was a different Sam. He spoke
one half-beat ahead of an anxious calm.

"Can you shut your place down completely, make it look like you've left town? Any place you can hide for a week or two?" Titus asked nodding towards the waiting car.

"I take it you want me gone but nearby?"

"That's right."

"Yeah, I have an idea I might be able to do that. But Buddy I think I'm fixing to leave for good, some time soon. Got a whisper of a handle on a new life. I'd like to try it out," said Sam.

"As a favor to me, hang on for a little bit, okay? I want to see what shakes out while we run deep and silent for a spell."

"Not so smart, you riding that cycle this time of year."

"Dumb makes a good disguise."

At the hospital room of Jimmy Three Trees:

"When *Zapata* met *Golda My Ear* he was wearing crossed ammo belts over a button-down oxford shirt, pale blue, which matched the color of his socks in his sandals. The blue socks were hidden by the long leather chaps and bit straps. He wasn't interested in her or her politics and she wanted to be able to tell everyone in a future life that they had met. Chocolate cake is good, better with cold milk, but good just the same, especially with frosting flavored by vodka. The challenge is to leave the first person out of serious talk. But what is a first person but someone who comes before a second or third person. And isn't that arbitrary? More so than even television. There is no rhyme or reason for the late night news being broadcast so early un-less..." Jimmy droned on underneath their own soft overlaid conversation.

"He just sat bolt upright, staring off into the distance, and started to talk like this. He's been at it now for nearly 20 minutes. Doesn't seem to hear us or acknowledge anyone in the room with him. His voice is different, clear and sweet. Notice how dilated his eyes are, Doctor?"

He ripped off an instruction slip from a pad. "I want you to give him this, should knock him out so he can rest."

Jimmy was still talking and the gruesome subject stopped the Doctor and nurse for a moment.

"...done it. So the muscle man hit him again with the tire iron, over and over again and the Billy boy just flopped around on the ground limp like all the strings were broke. Then the muscle man picked him up and threw him in the market garbage bin and laughed. One foot sticking out still. If Winston Churchill had been left alone we'd know him better today as a poor painter rather than a parliamentarian or queen-pecked ruffian..."

The nurse administered the injection.

Earlier that evening and in the same hospital there had been quite a lot of commotion. Nobody on the staff could remember anything so bizarre in the history of the hospital. It seems that a large man was discovered only partially dressed in torn clothing, tied down to a gurney. There was no record of him having been checked in as a patient. Conjecture was that emergency admissions must have been asleep or absent without leave when someone brought the unfortunate man in. The local radio news had reported that this man had appeared at the local hospital with cow parts stitched or welded to his person. Along with that there was some sort of demonic symbol branded to his chest. He was delusional and dangerous, so it had been decided to sedate him heavily. Police had cordoned off a set of rooms and were waiting for the opportunity to question the man.

The Chiropractor, Dr. Fistula, still miffed that the detective had never shown up for the promised interview, caught enough of the radio broadcast to know that he belonged at the hospital to identify the alien.

The doctors, on police instruction, had told Helga that the bandaged man in the bed next to her was her husband. After an emotional silence and hiccuping with short breathes, she in return had identified the man with the cow ears as having attempted, during the night, to suffocate her husband with a pillow. She tried to describe the second man who had hit the assailant but it was difficult as she had fainted at that moment.

Sloop pretended to be unable to hear or to respond.

In an office building in Los Angeles.

"I don't have much time. This sounds too far fetched," came the authoritarian voice.

"We've triple-checked. Our sources are all direct-connect."

"Okay, give me the two dollar version." He sounded insistent, impatient.

"Mike Merced is a successful wealthy 40 year old California contractor married to the daughter of a well placed Mexican family. She has four children from a previous marriage. She divorced her first husband. That's the only reason her old-world family would go along with her second marriage to Merced. They live in California and Mexico, two estates. He is fluent in a clumsy militaristic Spanish. She is ambitious, well educated - speaks four languages including Chinese - and married him for his money. He's head over heels in love with her and her children."

"Too much detail," he interrupted. So the informant sped up his delivery.

"Merced has political ambitions and a criminal record. He also has loose marbles and a loose tongue. He's decided to make a long distance run at the Presidency of Mexico. Filed to have his name officially changed to Miguel Merced. He has people who've drafted a complex plan to deal with *issues*. The plan has caught the attention of the U.S. administration. They have taken dangerous steps to assist Merced. They have also attempted to put a lid on any further public discussion of his "plan."

"Briefly, the plan, tell me about it?"

"He says 'war on drugs' is backwards. Plan calls for U.S. to leave dealers alone and instead arrest ALL drug users and put them in agricultural work camps. Make THEM do the work the Mexican migrants have been doing. Frees up a couple of million prison beds and provides indentured labor to the large farmers while removing a huge chunk of the incentive for Mexicans to sneak across the border. Central to this part of his plan is a positive working relationship with the current U.S. administration, one which he secretly sees as, in his words, 'tight-assed, short-sighted, bible-thumping, and Mommy-driven'. He views, in the near future, the U.S. as being perhaps the only significant country, besides Mexico, outlawing all hallucinatory drugs. Feels it works into his short term goals. He calls for the legalization and registration of soil-based drug production in Mexico. Production not use. Wants to have stiff criminal penalties against any Mexican users and the death penalty for meth production and chemical exotics. His people say that Mexico could provide 85% of the organic drug needs of the world within three years. He plans to go after venture capital for field and factory and believes he can create a couple of million new Mexican jobs within 18 months. Says this will knock out the drug lords and put a big crimp on activities in Columbia, Northern California and Afganistan. Feels that this action alone will destroy 65% of the international funding for terrorist activities. In the future, he sees Mexico as the next super power."

"Geez!"

"The White House got wind of the plan. Invited the Merceds to visit. The Merceds politely declined. So reps were sent to them. Our President wants Merced to succeed, at least in part. Offered to assist with political planning and funding if Merced would quit talking about his 'plan'. All but assured them they could win, and sooner rather than later. Of course all the usual *white house deniability* is built in."

"Did they agree?"

"In a way sir. Conzuela appears to be the brains and she's taken serious steps to insulate their plan from too much Washington influence. What we know, and Washington does not know, is that Aqualita, the first lady's maid, is Conzuela Merced's illegitimate half sister. Aqualita and the president are VERY close, sir."

"Oh, brother! .... You mentioned dangerous steps?"

"They don't know everything, but they have identified Conzuela as something to control, so the White House (Rover to be precise) made a call to the *pultenado* team in Mexico City contracting them to kidnap 6 year old Mary Jimenez Merced. They were told to pull no punches and make it real and expensive. Little Mary is Mike and Conzuela's daughter."

"Oh, Gawd!"

"Rover's plan is that the kidnapping will draw favorable sympathetic attention to the Merceds. Give Mike a platform for running and scare the conniving out of the woman."

"Wait a minute, that suggests she will know who's behind it and he won't?"

"Precisely, sir. Plus, we believe we are the only ones who know that Conzuela, Senora Merced, is actively working on a political alliance with the Chinese, something to do with franchising third world governments and dividing east and west territories."

"Okay, before I go, this is what I want. What are our chances of being able to get the girl first?"

"Fifty fifty with the right operative. May I anticipate you? We haven't been able to locate the Monk."

"Two options: either Monk or some other operative snatches little Mary right now! Or we find some way to convince Conzuela who took her daughter."

"On the latter, we have two pluses: first we have an audio of Rover's call to *pultenado* and second Aqualita wants out of the relationship with the President."

The geologists admit that for that 160 acres of forest ground to swell and rise at the rate of six inches per month is both significant and insignificant. The Volcanologists are saying nothing, partly because they are too excited to make coherent assessments, and partly because the harried minutiae of attaching and adjusting many high tech stethoscopes to appropriate fissures, caverns, snake holes and root systems have them mentally scattered. At the end of a new gravel road, a locked gate and chain link fence prevent the unauthorized from getting far enough into the cordoned area to see the space-age quadrant of mobile laboratories within which tractor-fed graph paper inches through rollers and past dancing needles. Two science-types work at complex computer stations running scads of variables. The whole interior of the facility has the antiseptic death-watch aspect of an infectious disease control center.

Early on a decision was made not to needlessly worry the public. It was agreed that press professionals would be only releasing confirmation of any geological activity that the public might already have heard about or actually felt. Explanations without depth would perhaps be given. In four short years a low area on the east side of the Mascara peak known as Lumpy Lash had risen a total of twenty feet. Barely perceptible to the naked eye. On the southeast side of this rise the ground temperature had risen to 55 degrees at a depth of 6 feet. Mother earth had a serious pimple rising.

What escaped the notice of everyone was a slightly more distant anomaly. Eighteen miles north and west of the swelling/warming ground 'activity', not more than eight hundred feet from the house, and well within the deeded acres of the Fork Holding, hot water was struggling to find its way to the surface. There was terrific upwards force causing the erosion of loose materials between the deep layered rock strata. Had the volcanologists been monitoring this site, their enthusiasms would have repeatedly represented missed dinners at home.

As Titus rode his classic motorcycle carefully down the long, bare, paved, night-dark road, as detectives did their detecting in the hospital, as Shirley dreamt, as Enno sketched farm plans, as Sam and Nettie lay side by side in bed discussing postponements and intrigue, as Luigi and Estelle sped down the highway in the rented minivan, as Sig conferred with his controller about the need to snatch a little girl in Mexico, as Lint Fumes listened to Coleman Hawkins and read in his motel room, as Marvin Seesaw dreamt of a sweat lodge built of the scalps of bureaucrats, as Nancy Simmons got up to get a glass of warm milk and purge herself of the crippling sentiment that had disturbed her sleep, as all these things and more were happening, the bulge beside Lumpy Lash shook a nervous shudder and for a hundred miles in any direction, the earth adjusted itself without concern for human comfort or retirement planning.

In the morning the volcanologists would tremble with excitement and work feverishly on the wording of a statement to explain the earthquake and necessary precautions the public should take. They suspected that this was just the beginning of a series of ever more serious quakes. They were more concerned that their instruments were detecting that the activity below the surface was shifting laterally to directly below the Lumpy Lash peak. An eruption at the bulge would have been a manageable curiosity, an eruption high up on Lumpy Lash could destroy property for miles, taking out the town of Mascara. They were excited and frightened. Consideration was given to contacting the Secretary of the Interior and thereby the White House. But this whole business was more important than that. This was urgent and potentially devastating. The executives at the White House had shown zero capability with disaster preparedness. They believed it was high time *'we privatize the emergency alert system.'* They knew who they needed to notify everyone, the voice of authority, the best publicist on the planet, someone who could deliver a list of precautions and be heard, the one calming and steadying influence in white America's media landscape, Oprah Winfrey.

Lint Fumes was an expensive private investigator and hired assassin. His perfect disguise was the simple fact that he did not look nor act the part, not on casual view. Lint was a man of precise passions, calibrated rationales and self-control. Within his polished aluminum case Lint carried not a disassembled firearm but the most magnificent custom-built Bang and Olafsen portable sound system imaginable. That and hand-tooled copper cases holding an array of classical jazz recordings. Late this evening Lint sat propped up in the motel room bed listening to Coleman Hawkins on the saxophone and reading from a new book which interested him. The book was "Looking for Spinosa: Joy, Sorrow and the Feeling Brain" by Antonio Damasio. He found a passage he marked in brackets. It read;

> "Imagine, for example, meeting someone who, as a result of damage to a certain location of his brain, became unable to feel compassion or embarrassment - when compassion or embarrassment were due - yet could feel happy, or sad, or fearful just as normally as before brain disease set in. Would that not give you pause? Or picture a person who, as a result of damage located elsewhere in the brain, became unable to experience fear when fear was the appropriate reaction to the situation and yet still could feel compassion. The cruelty of neurological disease may be a bottomless pit for its victims - the patients and those of us who are called to watch. But the scalpel of disease also is responsible for a single redeeming feature: By teasing apart the normal operations of the human brain, often with uncanny precision, neurological disease provides a unique entry into the fortified citadel of the human brain and mind."

Lint chuckled as he marked the passage.

Enno had been awakened by his dog Resumé, who had been frightened by the earthquake. The dog had been sleeping lightly, troubled by dreams of a great canine beauty taunting him with her sideways glances. Enno had been dreaming also, but it was a solid, comforting dream of walking behind a big team of draft horses as they plowed a fine clean furrow. The dream had been awash in the scent of new spring earth and horse sweat. Enno felt each step of his booted feet fit perfectly into the newly drawn trench. He felt his life project forward in time, borrowing from his anxious past the energy of want to be supplanted now by the energy of appreciation.

Chapter Seventeen

Chetco

*"I have often tried in my work to show the mercy of God.
You cannot show it by portraying only virtuous people:
what good is mercy to the virtuous? It is in the drunken
priests that you can see mercy working. And I call that
optimism."*
                                          - Graham Greene

"Hulloooo, hulloo, hulloo, hulloo! Paper or plastic?" She was
wildly enthusiastic, shaking her cashier's apron to the disco
music piping out from the back corner of the market, across the
aging lettuce, oranges and onions, as if it could retard the mold.

"Wood," he answered.

"Excuse me?"

"I would prefer a wooden box, if you're asking."

"Oh, I get it, you're being funny. Good one," she rolled her
eyes, punctuating her sarcasm, and shook open a paper bag as
she swiped bar codes across the register reader. "Are we going on
a picnic or something? Kind'a kaaaa-old for this stuff, ain't it?"

"My boy and I are going sledding this morning, way up on the
mountain. So, what's wrong with what I've got here?" answered
and asked Roger the writer.

"Nothing, not a thing. Just making conversation. This time of
morning we don't get many people in here. You from around

here? Local?"

"Yeah." He was looking for his son who was still getting some items from down an aisle.

"Not meeee." she sang. "I drive all the way from the other side of Bend, every blessed morning. Don't you feel sorry for me?"

Roger looked at the red-headed cashier. He thought, 'She was a brunette two days ago, wasn't she? If I were to write about her, nobody would believe the description. No that wasn't it. It was that nobody would care.'

"Are you going up by the bulge?"

"The what?" He asked.

"The bulge, you know, that little volcano thing they keep talking about on the news."

The night before, Fred English went straight home and turned on his three computers. He lived in a new 'craftsman-style', double-wide, mobile home, only one hundred feet back of Highway 20. In between towns, out just a bit from 'congestions'. You couldn't see his place from the road. It was hidden by a carefully cultivated hedge of evergreens and a wall of hand-stacked lava rock. What you could see, if you were looking, is a small grey satellite dish just above the junipers.

When bachelor Fred had moved into these new digs, it took him only a minute to decide that the big living room would become his office and 'staging area'. He would use the little den for his limited TV viewing and light reading. In his big room he had custom-built, at drafting table height, a corner workstation which encased three separate but interconnected computing stations with large flat screens (these could, when desired, be linked in one continuous wide image), two scanners, a large format ink-jet printer, and assorted external drives and electronic goodies. His chair adjusted both ways: up high then down, and back and forth. Nothing too special about that. What was unique was the spring agitator he had rigged from off a discarded washing machine. When he was mentally blocked, or tight-necked, or drowsy at the inappropriate or bothersome moment, he pressed the lever on the side and the chair whipped right and left, shaking him violently. He had to be careful not to do this when the chair was set up high as it would throw him off.

When seated at his corner station, Fred could turn around and glide his chair a few feet to a large table on wheels. It was four feet wide by ten feet long and featured flat document drawers under each end. The top of the table was piano-hinged length-wise and could be jacked up to a 45 or 90 degree angle when he needed a "clues" wall. Tonight the table was flat and empty except for a copy of a state directive on *Mad Cow Disease*.

While the computers were booting up, Fred tilted his "clues" wall up and affixed a large, thin, synthetic chalk board to the screw clips on the top edge of the table-turned-wall. When he heard the appropriate beeps, he signed on to the internet to check his emails while reaching for a box of round-headed colored pins and a regional map.

He had figured out this much; the big man with the cow ears and the brand on his belly had been driving the Lincoln - had killed the cow - and had probably shot out the other man's windshield. Motive unknown. Suspect some sort of mental imbalance, maybe. Just yet, he could not fit in the story line why this man had apparently gone from scene A to scene B where he attempted to kill the hospital patient. He knew that the silent guy in facial bandages could be a big piece of the puzzle. The second man, the follower, had carried himself artificially, with a pretend gait, as if he were a circus performer leaving the tent or an actor back stage or someone accustomed to disguise and in between characters. The second man had probably cut up the dead cow and most definitely did the perverse things with the cow parts. But Fred suspected this was not a perverse man. Dangerous but not perverse. First questioning thought; innocent bystander driven by stray gunshot through the windshield to creative act of vengeance? No, English didn't accept that. There was something more here. A lot more.

It was clear that this was not a classic case for a "Cow Cop." He was probably, theoretically, out of his jurisdiction. Technically, he was supposed to track down cattle rustlers, and nothing more. But Fred English knew that if he didn't follow the clue trail nobody else would. So this would be his baby and he was energized.

The things that caught him up were those marks on the man's belly. The curious trident shape melted into the red wax. And the words scratched, no, more like they were cut into the big man's belly. The only part he could clearly make out was the word "justice" and then, further on down the line of blood, the words "you have exceeded yours. Monk." He typed in the word "Monk" into the Interpol criminal data file he had accessed off the internet. One of the several pictures that popped up was not of the big man. It was of the other guy. As Fred read the accompanying text he felt himself begin to twitch and quiver.

He typed in what information he had on John Ogdensburg, the silent patient. Uh oh. Now he knew he had something. Here was a man with no history, none. A blank slate. Time to tally up.

He wrote on the blackboard, not what he knew but what he suspected. Later he would cross out what he suspected, check facts and look for patterns. He wrote inside a drawn circle; "Large Armenian-type, city boy, football player, mean, expensive clothes, hit man?" In the next circle he wrote; "Medium, athletic, Hispanic-type, cosmopolitan, actor, known 'mercenary', suspected cannibal, on every most-wanted list on the planet, yet protected by U. S. federal government." In the third circle he wrote; "Invisible man." In the fourth circle he wrote; "dead cow." Outside of the circles he wrote, "Something very bad has come to town." He smiled only briefly, remembering Dr. Fistula's notion that the man and the cow fell out of the sky. Maybe the crazy chiropractor wasn't too far from the truth.

Then he wrote "Doesn't compute" and added "YET."

When Sam Fistula got to the hospital he followed a newly arrived police officer. On the third floor a man in a suit and two uniformed sheriff's deputies were standing by a room talking low. The policeman Fistula had followed was apparently relief for one of the others. As they spoke to one another Sam made an attempt to pass them and enter the room.

"Hey, you can't go in there!" insisted the suit.

"You have the cow killer in there?" asked Fistula, smaller than usual and nervously fingering a rubber-band.

"Yeah, so?" offered the young uniform.

"I'm a doctor. Talk to officer English. He knows I'm the one who can identify this man."

"I don't care if you're Mother Teresa, you ain't going in there! Got that! If you want to go wake up Fred English and bring him here, that's your stuff. Now beat it!" Spit out one of the deputies.

"Wait a minute Jim," interrupted the tired and efficient suit. "Sir, would you come with me a minute. I'd like to ask you a few routine questions."

Luigi was young enough that driving all night was an acceptable physical inconvenience and challenge. And when Sig called, everything else came second. It wasn't just the money, which was fantastic. It was the intrigue of occasionally playing a punk-rock Robin to Sig's French-existentialist Batman. Luigi was in love with Sig but certainly no more than Estelle. He realized that she would gladly die for him.

Maltesta had said "six faces, three identities." Longstroke had added to the count. In the back of the minivan, all ninety pounds of Estelle's tawny muscular frame lay limp and slumbering. Luigi had brought twice the usual poundage of her cosmetics. He had chuckled for an hour when he realized the two of them would be descending on Mascara, he *the* consummate amateur makeup artist would be stage center in Mascara!. And she! My gawd, they had no idea. Before he had left he made sure that his physical appearance would discretely match Maltesta's. It was important

to look like *the Monk* thinly veiled. He even practised walking
like a testosterone-overloaded heterosexual male. He pictured
himself as half Frank Sinatra, half Lance Armstrong. It made him
giggle.

He was a gentleman of the old school. Slow moving, silver-
haired, big-tipping, smiling Piero Gambizzi had his reasons.
Commerce was at the top of the list. And the single most profitable commerce remains insurance. Frighten people enough and
they'll pay any price for insurance. Terrorism insurance, he loved
it. The idea that he might move quickly to destroy attorney
general Larry Berry and the Justice department while giving
credit to "enemies of the homeland" struck him as beautiful. The
idea that such a move would eventually bring him great riches
seemed appropriate.

It had been easy for his operatives to find the three whacked-
out Yemenie political science majors and convince them they had
been chosen from above for a mission to purify Persia and re-
store control of the Caspian Sea to bearded males. They were
each given an easily traceable cell phone which had been stolen
from legitimate Arab charities. They were also given tickets to a
Celine Dion concert, cases of hard lemonade, and bags of dried
apricots. All they had to do was drive camouflaged trucks loaded
with explosives to somewhere near the Jackson Hole Holiday Inn
during the Justice Department's awards ceremony. The trucks
would not be hassled because they were also delivering liquor
and dancing girls to the doings; liquor which would have to be
sampled by the security guards. And it really didn't matter if
they were sloppy and short of target on delivery because regardless of where they were, Gambizzi's men would be detonating the
trucks by remote control at exactly the moment that the several
hand-held rocket launchers would lob thirty or forty rounds into
the motel conference center.

The planning had been immaculate right down to making sure
no Italian-Americans were working in hotel management or

service at the complex that night. Piero knew that such measures would be looked upon favorably by a just catholic God. Never forget your own, that was his credo.

Piero was occasionally successful, enough so as to guarantee his life-style and reputation. As he wished, and as he willed, people were generally afraid of him. Truth be known, however, Piero relied regularly on fortunate and unfortunate idiots.

As the plan played itself out, the Yemenies drove the trucks in the opposite direction to a motel on the outskirts of town to drink the alcohol and "talk" to the dancing girls one last time before going to meet their heaven. And the Jersey bad boys who had never been in the Wyoming woods after dark and never handled rocket launchers, "accidently" blew up the private vacant compound of a supreme court justice. When the trucks exploded, the only living thing injured was a marauding black bear looking through garbage cans. Not far away, the vice president of the United States was hiding, with a supreme court justice and four stenographers, in a luxuriously appointed bunker beneath his Big America Casino and Resort. Within thirteen minutes his official security detail, special forces four hundred strong, had arrested and brutalized all parties responsible, especially the dancing girls. The Yemenies were promised leniency if they agreed to say that their facial injuries were the result of a traffic accident. Also they were required to act as informants, translators and test dummies for the defense department's new politically correct interrogation techniques. And last, they had to change their college majors to art history.

Luigi had done his job of peppering the news media with bits and pieces of political and criminal intrigue centered in and around Mascara, Oregon. When it became apparent to media conglomerates that the White House was trying to slow down the release of that information, independent investigative journalists smelled stink under the drying paint. Travel plans were arranged. But it seemed that media would have to bring their own motorhomes or stay 20 miles away. Mascara had become a very busy burg.

Almost every single accommodation in Mascara had been filled with or reserved for the organizers, manipulators, Realtors, developers, architects, designers, bankers and speculators linked with or fastened to Luther Yankone's proposed mega housing development. What few available rooms there were in town had been scooped up by Liner, Fumes and Maltesta who had arrived just ahead of the FBI, the CIA, Bald Mother America, and a Quilters Reunion. Bend and Redmond were enjoying a "shoulder" season lodging boom. This influx had not escaped Reba Yankone. She successfully argued for a 25% increase in the scale of their proposed development and a waiver of the city's developmental charges.

As for the descending media; the fact that Mascara, in winter a normally sleepy tourist town, was full of people just seemed to prove something big was about to happen. From the standpoint of attention magnetics, it didn't hurt any that a minor earthquake was reported in the Mascara mountains causing some alarm for volcanologists monitoring a suspicious growing bulge in the ground. (No one yet knew that attempts were being made to contact the Oprah Winfrey Show.)

Then, to put whipped cream on the day, news squeaked of a terrorist bombing in Jackson Hole, Wyoming, somehow involving the casino-owning illusive U.S. vice president. It was going to be a good several days for the internet, radio, print and television.

They had talked for some time. Shirley was suspiciously attracted to the narrative. Sig had asked her to get Vicky Wood and go with her to find a man named Enno Duden. The two women were to convince Duden that his life and their lives were in danger. Shirley was to tell Duden that Maltesta needed his help but first he, Duden, needed to stay well, stay hidden, and protect Shirley and Vicky until Sig returned in two days.

"We don't need protecting, at least I don't. Where are you going?" demanded Shirley.

"Mexico. And when I return I hope to have a six year old girl with me."

"What? This gets stranger by the minute. I don't need any of this. Look, I've got one little connection to make in this town and then I'm out of here. Nobody's after me but you. And if I can believe you now, you're on to something else. So why should I listen to any more of this?" Shirley shook her head.

"The man who has tried on more than one occasion to hurt you is a professional contract killer."

"How do I know you aren't one also?" Shirley asked half joking.

Sig looked at her for a long moment without saying anything.

"Oh geez. You leave my trailer right now, right now!" She felt silly hearing her weightless words.

He kept staring at her. And she slowly began to understand that complicity is multidimensional.

"I'm not going to hurt you and if you do as I say there is a good chance nothing bad will come of this. I know you are bright enough to see that ... eventually. Know this, Brice Liner, that's the big guy from the restaurant lounge - the one you found unconscious in the market parking lot, he is incapacitated for the time being. But there is a second man of the same profession in this town." He pulled a computer photo of Lint Fumes from his pocket. "You see this man?"

Shirley caught her breath going in and then going out. It was the little man from the market, the one who had handed her the note with the reference to her mother and the phone number. She told Sig. And Sig told her a very great deal. She came to believe the urgency and the danger.

"But why do you have to go to Mexico right now, and why the little girl," she asked calmly.

"It's totally unrelated, or at least I want to believe it is. It's my job, it's what I do. If I don't nab little Mary within 12 hours and bring her here to hide with us, our government has arranged to

have her kidnapped and killed. Certain people need to believe
that the girl is dead. And I need to convince the mother that she
must keep that terrible secret.

"It's circular. I build circular rooms around the ones who think
they are players. So long as they all believe we have hidden what
they want in the corner of the room, they'll keep running around
until they finally see it is a circular room. We buy time and
disorient them. And they get meaner by the minute, meaner and
myopic. Oh, I almost forgot. For the next two days while I'm
gone, you might think you see me, but it won't be me. Trust me
on this. Don't talk with *me* until I talk with you. Now go quickly
and get Vicky and find Duden!"

"Oh my god! OH, MY GOD! You know, it's like, you know, like
I really care or something." She was bony thin, blonde, and
pretty in a lifeless sort of way. So was the girl she was talking to.

"I know, I know, I know... Like, what does he want from you?"
As she said this, a tinny version of *Piano Man* sounded, alerting
her of an incoming cell phone call. She pulled out the little flip
phone, looked at the caller ID display, opened her eyes wide as
hubcaps and blurted "OH MY GOD! IT'S HIM!" then, looking at
the device she pressed a button, held it up and said in a deadpan,
don't-care voice. "Yeah? Oh. Hi. Yeah. No. Yeah. No. I don't
know. Okay." And she hung up.

"What did he say? Oh my god! Tell me what he said, tell me,
tell me! OH MY GOD! I can't believe it! He called you, like, he
really called you!" The words shot out in squeals and shrieks.

Nettie and Sam stood waiting behind these two at the market
checkout. Nettie watched them amused. And Sam watched
Nettie. A few days ago this little intrusive, teenaged display of
moronic hormonal imbalance would have set him off like a rat
terrier with a cornered squirrel. Not now. Time had slipped
sideways and Nettie's delight was all that mattered to him. He
leaned forward and in an inviting whisper said,

"We need to get going. How far didja' say your cabin was out of town?"

"It's up by Amethyst Lake, you know, that private lake where the church camp is." She smiled at him over her shoulder as she leaned back against his frame. "You don't seem too worried any more."

"Should be. It's serious stuff. But..." Leaning forward and placing his craggy head on her shoulder he gently bit her ear lobe.

Chapter Eighteen

Millicoma

Expectation is the curse and the blessing. Words picture for us.
Pictures float us. A list of films would include, "The Widow of
Saint Pierre," "Girl on the Bridge,", all the films of Jacques Tati.
Remembering Michael Caine's superb performance in the film
rendition of Greene's "The Quiet American."

It is in the amazing horizontal connections that we find the
vertical as wide, the frivolous as significant, and the apology as
breath.

Young man dreaming of a farm, the very boyishness of it is
exclusive. It is, after all, an unacceptable picture for a time of
decodified impulse, perforated instant gratification, industrial
imperative, and the forced transitory hieroglyphics of a wash and
wear angst. He was not of his generation, he was of the lost
dreams of previous generations. And perhaps, as such, poised to
give us a glimpse of the best opportunities of a past's future.

Enno Duden woke early to a late-winter crystalline fog
undecided in its temperature offerings. It could melt later into

the low forties, or it could sharpen and harden in the low thirties. He had chores to do and a specific urgency. He wanted to get to the hospital and check in on his friends. Enno was prone to single-mindedness. Sloop saw it as a strength. Riven taunted him about it, saying he'd never see the forest for the trees unless he widened his view to take in more of life's periphery. Though the sentiments registered, neither specific observation touched him. He wished he knew what Sloop saw in him and he wished Riven would go away and leave him alone. But he didn't think about it too much. Wasn't time. He spent his waking, and many of his sleeping hours, dreaming of his farm to be.

This morning, he had a glass of juice and a piece of buttered toast before heading out to the farm shop. The dog Resumé bounced on spring-loaded toes and kept right at his heels. The shop building was an early tin structure over which Sloop had layered a board and batten skin of rough-cut Pine. The young man went through the little door and unlatched the big sliding one. Inside, the old galvanized sheeting was visible over the reinforced I-beam frame-work. The structure was forty by eighty feet with a high ceiling. And every square inch of its interior perimeter held tools, chains, ropes, cables, materials and storage. In one of the four, loosely-defined bays sat an old International horsedrawn manure spreader, half disassembled.

One corner of the shop had a separate, stand-alone, six by ten foot, double-walled room where John B. kept his veterinarian supplies and feeds. Just outside the feed room door, a bicycle-tired garden cart sat parked with a stack of black rubber buckets. Duden filled one bucket with a rolled corn- oats -barley mix grain ration. The second bucket got cracked corn to the halfway mark. The largest bucket he filled with Alfalfa pellets. All at the ready, Enno pulled the cart out of the farm shop and headed for the guinea fowl pen. He stopped, turned and looked at the dog, Resumé. Should he tie him up? Warn him not to chase the livestock? Resumé, as if to indicate that he understood the young man's concern and was deeply hurt by the inference, sighed deeply, smirked, and dropped to his belly so that he could chew on his own butt. Enno got the message.

The guinea palace was a wonder. To Helga's imagined design, Sloop had built an eight foot by sixteen foot sled frame. Crossways, from 4 x 12 runner to 4 x 12 runner, he had built a five foot by eight foot structure appearing tall and skinny with a steep shake-roofed peak. It had an Alpine or Czech feel of dis-proportionate comic balance. From the corners of this structure stretched a chicken-wire fenced enclosure which matched the foot print of the sled runners. It was like a netted, runnered cube with a pretty and precarious little wooden tower house in which, at night, guinea fowl roosted safely. Enno had watched Sloop once when he had hooked his team of Percherons on to the front and had drug the entire structure an eighth of a mile to the corner of a nearby field. To start the load, Sloop had pried up each runner and jammed a ten foot long two inch pipe in crossways. As the sled moved ahead it rolled on the pipe until passing over it completely. By that time, enough forward inertia was in play to allow the horses to finish the difficult draft.

Back to the task at hand; first, as instructed, he opened the pen gate to let the twenty-seven guineas out for the day. They cackled their odd half squawk/half burble and filed out for the morning bug hunt. Then he went around beside and into the tall house filling the feed trough with the cracked corn and checking the watering cans. Next he stuffed a handful of clean straw in the bottom of the feed bucket and set to gathering the guinea eggs. There were only twelve.

In the next, more typical shed and pen he found the three ewes with their lambs, all of them separated from the ram. Two of the new babies were sitting atop their mother with little legs buried in her heavy winter wool coat. He divided the Alfalfa pellets between the sheep and filled their water troughs and hay feeders. The ewes bleated and the lambs cavorted.

The speckled, vulture-headed, pea-brained guinea fowl hadn't much interested Resumé, but the sheep, now that was a different matter. The old dog felt himself jerk and stare and stifle a whim-per. This was too much. He knew what he needed. He nudged

Duden's leg by way of excusing himself and ran off towards the old blue pickup where he had stashed his chewing gum. Enno continued with the chores.

Anything he could do to get away from that house. Roger hated it. And why did he call it a house. It wasn't. The sign out front said Cottonwood Condominiums. They weren't even that. They were six pair of duplexes. All brand new, all crammed together in a line, with tight little assigned parking places and the circumference cordoned-off by a three rail, white plastic fence. Plastic. Everything was plastic. The garage door was shiny, dusty-pink colored plastic, the front steps were textured slip-proof plastic, the front door was a shiny, washable white plastic with a plastic door knob and plastic knocker. Once inside you were walking on a plastic floor stenciled to resemble new oak. And the stucco-like walls were actually covered in a washable, plastic wallpaper. The kitchen and bathroom counters, sinks and cupboards were all shiny washable plastic. His wife loved it, so easily cleaned, no waxing, always shiny. Ironically, contrary to its puerile appearance, it was a perfect environment for killer pathogens because humans always provide beautiful, hovering crumbs for a germ's perfect satellite-like habitat. And because in that microscopic world of occasional nasty bugs, this all plastic world offered no biodiversity, no natural predators, no molecular meanies, no atomic acids, no subatomic monsters, no crud-eating mites or mold. In fact, the all plastic environment made life catatonic for even spiders, webs stuck no where. Not to mention silver fish, the ugly little northern cousin of the cockroach. The shiny plastic surface provides a constant mirror image for the downward looking creepies, and they simply cannot stand looking at themselves for very long. So the only thing which survives is the occasional insular bacteria, happy to grow in such a protected environment with large warm blood and tissue rich mammals floating about begging to play host. Maybe that's why he had writer's block. The papers kept sliding off his plastic desk in his plastic den and onto the plastic floor. And the hidden pathogens, the thirsty bacteria, the microscopic copy editors, leeched the imaginings from his brain.

Adi Zarabrezi of the *Gee Whiz Corp* had contracted a team of software wizard's to check into whether or not his company computers had been infiltrated. It was the only way he could figure that this *Milk Man* character had been able to garner inside dope on the firm.

"Yeah, you've been had. Not only have they got in and taken data, memos and emails but, are you ready for this?..." The man who spoke had flaming red hair and food particles at the left corner of his mouth.

Zarabrezi felt a cold chill. Maybe it had been a mistake to hire these guys. No. No. There was no way they'd be able to determine that **he** had skimmed funds to an offshore account. No way.

"Yeah, I'm ready, let me have it," he said, regretting his choice of words.

"They, who ever they are, are robbing you blind. So far to the tune of 120 million plus."

"What?" Zarabrezi rubbed his temples and muttered, "That's not possible!" He had only taken one and a half million. They were wrong. They had to be. "You're wrong, you have to be!" he insisted.

"Sorry, but we're definitely right. Well, there is good news. We stopped them. Or, to put it more accurately they stopped themselves, right when we were getting close enough to capture some source data. Here's the story.

"There is no defense against this hack attack because it is impossible to fully analyze the scripts. The math is set to some rolling set of matching numbers and combinations and lasts only for a split second. When the numbers match, kinda of like a slot machine, access to the designated target is instantaneous. And it lasts for a second or less. Then the rolling numbers start up again with a whole new random pattern. Plus, something is written in to self-activate a protection. When the numbers feel any probe or questions being asked they revert to multiplying by zero and the whole program spins off into a black hole of cyber infinity. This invasive software disassembles encrypted, electronic, wire transfer routing codes, changes assignations in a pulse always reverting back, in random sequence, to beginning form. Every third dollar is skimmed electronically and routed to a different legitimate account where it is instantly routed to a third revolving account.

"As the skimming occurs no accounting is affected so that your records show all the money made it there or back again, whichever was the directed case. However the bank balances don't jive and there is no traceable connection back to indicate where the discrepancies occurred.

"I think we may have discovered here, with your problem, just what happened in Texas a couple of years back. In that case their own people were hustling to skim their own ill-gotten gains into juggled off-shore accounts and suspecting their cohorts were doing it as well. There was a kind of silent complicity to cover up the whole problem. And, perhaps most important, there was no suspicion that there might be an outside raider. In that case implosion occurred, files were destroyed and no one will ever know where all the money went. That's what happened with that energy trading corporation down in Texas."

"Are you saying that there may have been a third player, an outsider, someone who skipped out with a pile?" Adi asked feeling a little pressure release but a new queasiness.

"I'm not saying maybe, I'm saying most definitely. And it's a whole lot more than a pile, I'd say a mountain of cash. See these numbers in these coded equations and how they scatter at this point? We saw the same pattern at that other firm. Only back then we just figured it was a coincidental consequence of all those execs tweaking the bank computers. This is something big, huge possibly. I suspect that the only people who might be able to pull something like this off would be a very big IT corp working on, or building and selling, operating system platforms. That way they would have immediate residency on the computers. This is no little operator, this is complex and involves some sort of cyber syndication."

Adi thought about this briefly and discounted it. His information had come from some solid detective work following a single piece of credit card information. And it had all led to a small Central Oregon town and a cluster of old hippy-types. It would appear that some highly creative left-wingers had figured out how to make an altruistic organized crime pay and pay well. Adi Zarabrezi asked himself how he might switch sides. He belonged with the winners, no matter what. He placed a phone call that would seal his fate and tip the *Milk Man* that someone was close to knowing too much.

Lint had purchased a bumper sticker for his rented pickup truck. It said *"Re-elect the Bozos, They Didn't Mean to Steal From Us."* And he purchased an oversized hooded sweatshirt which featured, front and back, the words *Robin Hood Was Right!* Throw in his Grateful Dead tin lunch box and his personae was complete. Lint didn't believe in disguise, he believed in fly attractant.

Sloop had time on his hands, or in his brain. He couldn't move much and was anxiously waiting for the doctors to remove his facial bandage. His thoughts went forward and backwards like the needle on a seismic graph machine. He tried to settle his thinking and position his priorities. Titus would have everything under control. Certainly he would have already set *PIN FLIP* in motion. Threatened? He couldn't believe it possible but they had to protect *Pascal's Revolver,* that's what they called the software programs they used to divert funds from large corporations. And *Pin Flip* was the self destruct and scatter safeware they had devised to use only if and when they were about to be discovered. They would always be able to reinstate *Pascal's Revolver* later but only if the entire operation escaped scrutiny.

He quickly took a mental panoramic of the complex system
he and Titus had set up and maintained. They were always on
the lookout for any corporation which demonstrated rapid
growth and unreasonably high fluctuations in profitability and
loss. Once they found a candidate corporation they reviewed the
product and customer base of the company. If there was no
indication of a concern for social justice, and/or environmental
stewardship they unleashed their invasive software *Pascal's
Revolver*, named after *Pascal's Triangle* - an inward looking
mathematical triangulation. If the corporation was involved in
the rapid electronic transfer of funds, back and forth, the *Milk
Man* program diverted every third dollar through different
legitimate and illegitimate accounts until it finally came to rest
momentarily in an electronic bank of their own design. This
bank, *NexDoor Financial*, provided a specialized, profitable service for ventures which had large amounts of untraceable and
traceable cash filtering in. *Nexdoor Financial* 'purchased' cash
from sixteen traveling carnivals, the Republican National Committee, the Democratic National Committee, the Consortium of
TV Evangelists, four pari-mutuel horse and dog tracks, and
twenty-three Indian casinos. Besides the 10% premium paid, the
sellers had the added advantage of no taxable trail, so long as
they themselves did not report it. The cash funds were picked up
by teams of *Milk Man* operatives and divided three ways to *Glass
Pirate* accounts for distribution to principals working with
Cuban farmers, Ruwandan farmers, Tibetan monks & farmers,
Vietnamese farmers, Central American aid organizations, U.S.
political prisoners, Chiapas revolutionaries, U. S. farm aid,
among many others. And no field operative knew anything
beyond his or her contact. The agencies, organizations and
individuals all thought they had their own quirky but appreciated anonymous benefactor.

Reviewing all this in his hospital-fog brain, Sloop still
couldn't figure out how their operations in Mascara had been
found out. Maybe it hadn't. Maybe something else was going on.
It was important to hunker down and trust their tight organiza-

tion to conceal them. Still, why had that obvious professional tried to kill him with the pillow? And, the man who saved him? Who was that, doubtless someone he needed to know.

"Mr. Ogdensburg. Good morning. It's time we took those bandages off and had a look," offered the hospital team.

"I am attracted to appreciation. I love to see the happy smile of children when their lives are going well. People in love, for me that's all about appreciation. I am especially drawn to the third party glow, that's when it's obvious that the appreciation has no direct investment. I'm not talking about gratitude, appreciation, the way I'm thinking of it, is different. You know, like watching a woman smile as she in turn watches a couple kissing." Shirley was speaking in a distracted tone to Vicky. Then her voice became directed. "And this mysterious man, this Monk character, he's funny... In a dangerous sort of way... He conceals, or uses, his emotions well except when it comes to you. He's got the bug bad."

"This is all so weird. I don't know this man at all. And I really don't care if he is attracted to me or not. What I care about is Enno. If he is my brother, and I'm not convinced of that yet, I want to know. And if he's in trouble and somebody is trying to hurt him, I definitely want to help. Hey, did you find out anything about Jimmy?" Vicky looked distracted, disheveled, and no less lovely.

"No, everything's been happening so fast," Shirley said.

"And did you feel that earthquake last night?"

"So, that's what it was."

In the middle of the night, before the earthquake came, the Percheron stallion, Glass, had felt an infinitesimally fine humming vibration enter his body at his hooves, up the navicular tendons and quickly through to his heart. It was the same sensation which had caused him to escape his own stable at Sloop's earlier. The horse began to pace nervously around the Jackson box stall in which he had been confined. He nudged the gate repeatedly. When the earthquake finally hit he was wound tight with anxiety and jumped sideways enough to throw himself to the straw-bedded floor. When he jumped up he began kicking wildly at the stall walls. Every instinct in his body said 'let's get out of here!'

Brice Liner was strapped to a hospital gurney, which was parked next to a bed, in what appeared to be a private room. He had the presence of mind, when he came to, to keep quiet and take a measure of all that surrounded him. The straps crossed his arms and chest at the upper torso and again at the hips. He tried and found he could move his legs laterally. He saw in the mirror across the room that the gurney straps passed into and through a round ratchet-tightener, anchored on the side of the rolling bed. There was a lever rod extending out at a 45 degree angle from each of the mechanisms. He listened and heard voices just outside the room door. Cops. Door was probably locked. Using his feet, he tried to move the gurney. He was in luck, the idiots had not locked the wheels. He inched and fudged and wangled until he got the gurney lined up with a side-bar anchor of the regular hospital bed. He then pushed up against the lever rod of the ratchet. Nothing. But he could feel a springing. He kept trying until he finally released the upper torso strap. Arms free he released himself entirely and stood up. The sheet fell away and he saw his torso in the mirror. He read Monk's inscription in reverse and noted the trident brand. His determination and hatred took a firm wrap-around hold of his anger. Examination had shown that his ear lobes were torn and that other parts were sore as well. He was on the third floor with no easy exit out the window. He had no clothing available. He would have to use the element of surprise. He lay back down on the gurney and covered himself with the sheet. He could wait as long as it took.

Fred English had asked the doctors to advise him of when Ogdensburg's bandages would be removed. When the doctor entered the room to do the job, English had followed quietly and sat in a corner out of view of the two patients.

"It's bad but not as bad as I thought it would be, bad enough though. Hard telling what it will look like when the healing's complete." The doctor was holding a hand mirror up for Sloop to see his glass-shredded face. John B. 'Sloop' Ogdensburg took the mirror in his own hand and caught a glimpse of a suited round-faced man sitting in the opposite corner. The man was looking out the window and didn't notice he was seen.

"John. John. I want to see. Show me, John." It was Helga's voice from the next bed over, choking on emotion.

Sloop looked at the doctor with a questioning gaze.

"Yes, I think we can roll you over. If you wish. But Mrs. Ogdensburg I need to warn you..." John interrupted the doctor,

"Please ask the stranger to leave."

"Of course, I had no idea. Excuse me please. I'll come back later." English offered, off guard because he was slightly embarrassed by the privacy of the moment.

When her husband rolled over, Helga was surprised to feel overwhelmed with gratitude. He was there, he was alive. He had gone through this for her. Brenda had explained how after the shooting John had raced off to find the shooter only to have a freak auto accident. How their being in the same room at the hospital had been another unexplainable coincidence. Her next emotion was sympathy. His face was crisscrossed with dark blood-scabbed lines and a raw patch seemed to suggest he had lost a portion of his left jaw line. Both eyebrows and his nose were swollen. His eyes however were more him than usual, more intense, moist. And his eyes were talking, in soft tones, of his own gratitude and concern.

He knew he had almost lost her. He needed to tell her she could not go, could not leave him, not in any way, not now. He needed to tell her something he had never felt before, never communicated before. It couldn't wait any longer. He had to tell her.

"Doctor, may we be alone?"

When the doctor left, John said to Helga, his wife,

"I need you."

Fred English had gone from Sloop and Helga's room to the third floor to talk to Brice Liner's guards. He ran into the tired suit.

"Fred, we've got a Dr. Fistula in the waiting room. Been here most of the night. Says you'll okay his visiting the half man/half cow character. Let me tell you, he is a nut case! You hear his theory about extraterrestrial intervention? What a waste of time. Anyway I'm going home. It's all yours buddy. Oh, by the way, expect local TV and newspaper reporters here in half an hour. Sorry, it came from above. I told them there was nothing to tell."

"You might be wrong. Maybe Fistula has something to entertain them with," offered English.

"Nah, you wouldn't do that, not to our sainted local press, would you?"

"Might be fun. Let's find out. Is Liner still restrained?"

"Yep, tied to the gurney."

"Okay, tell Fistula he can 'identify' the alien. I'm going to interview the assailed. Ask Fistula to come talk to me after he's done."

"Okay Fred, it's your pension."

Marvin Seesaw, Payoute chief, stopped in, early that morning, to visit the mini strip mall construction site outside of Mascara. His son Carl worked there. It seemed odd to him that the big dumpster lid was propped open by the handle of what appeared to be a vacuum cleaner. He was close enough so he peaked inside and on second glance noticed what looked like a human hand down below the sheet rock scraps. It was soon after that the police confirmed that Marvin had found the body of Billie Blue Chevie. He was obviously beaten to death. Two rounds of questioning had turned up only one curiosity that might have relevance. The local vagrant, Jimmy, had been seen filling the dumpster with odd loose ends of sheet rock from around the site. And no one seemed to know where Jimmy had gone to.

Dr. Fistula, Chiropractor, was very glad and more than a little proud to finally get clearance to identify the suspect. Fistula arrived at the hospital room door. One of the two guards announced he was going to the cafeteria. The remaining guard informed Fistula that he had just five minutes and asked if he wanted company.

"No, I'm a doctor and I prefer to do this alone." He entered the door after it was unlocked. Inside he saw the form on the gurney and approached. The man had straps across his body and lay sleeping or unconscious. Fistula hesitated to come close as if this was a corpse he found repulsive. Then he noticed the bloody torn ear lobe and moved closer to inspect. In less than a quarter of a second Liner had his hands closed around the little doctor's throat preventing any sound, or air, from escaping.

When the little man slumped to the floor, Liner got up and went behind the door, tapping lightly to get the attention of the guard.

A slight wiff of warmish, deep-earth, odor drew the two Redbone hounds to a spot not eight hundred feet from the Jackson farmstead. As they approached, they felt the planet hum under foot. It was an inviting sensation, just a little ticklish. When they were certain they had found the spot of ground from which odor and vibration emanated, each hound took its turn to urinate in a circle as if to say *'all other mammals stay clear of our spot'*. Then they set to the canine motions of trying to understand this attraction.

"Franklin!" Hollered Jackson 'Papa' Fork, "where are the hounds, son?"

Little, black, five year old Franklin Fork was supposed to keep a watch on the old Redbone hounds. Nine times out of ten, if he really kept an eye on them, they went nowhere. (The notable exception being whenever Papa left the house with a rifle.) So, Franklin pretended to be watching them, that way they'd more likely wander off and he'd get the adventure of pretending to find 'em. It was his favorite thing. Almost equal to chewing gum. Of course when they just wandered off, old and curious, it was nothing like when Papa took them hunting. Hunting they would bay and howl and yap and yip as they ran. Franklin didn't get to go on the real hunts, he was too young and his legs too short to keep up. But he loved to hear them sing out and sorely wished he could run after them. When they wandered off to sniff a new cow plop, or a windfall fruit, no one got excited, except Franklin. Every opportunity he got, he'd try to egg on the hounds. At the most inopportune times he'd yell out "Get 'em boys, go get 'em, sic 'em, go on get 'em!" Usually banging a stick against the noisiest thing he could find. Franklin was sure that if the dogs would start to bay and run, something, surely something, would flush out for them to chase. But the old dogs had long ago differentiated between young 'uns and the men with rifles. And when the kids would egg on the dogs, especially little Franklin, the old hounds would take it as a cue to walk slowly and quietly back to the underside of the front porch.

This time, as Franklin hollered (his Papa smiling to himself from a short distance away) "Get 'em boys, go get 'em, sic 'em, go on get 'em!" The dogs ignored him entirely. Franklin actually had to look for the dogs. Lucky for him, he could see their long-eared solid red ochre bodies some distance away.

"Papa, the dogs is longer away then you said I could go," offered Franklin.

"Where they at?" Jackson asked.

"Over by the far edge of the orchard."

"Okay son, good work, let's you and me go get them together. Wait just a minute." He knew that if the dogs were solidly held by some attraction, chances were that a varmit was involved, so he got his rifle and loaded it. Franklin saw this and was jumping for joy. He was going hunting with Papa, wow!

Big Jackson Fork walked in long sure strides, the rifle laid across his shoulder, just like little Peter from Peter and the wolf. Franklin skipped by his side, looking ahead and then looking up. There was a distinct rhythm to the procession. It made smiling Jackson, the jazz pianist/farmer, wonder after the inherent rhythmic design of most things human. Then he thought of his friend Sloop, a man completely devoid of rhythm, at least in any obvious musical sense. He certainly had a rhythm of sorts to his hidden work.

Then his face stiffened. He had somehow gone back in time, before the accident, before the shooting. He felt odd as if his deference and concern had slipped away to expose his own selfishness.

When they got close Jackson called out, "Woody, Louis, come. Come. Come, heel."

The dogs hesitated only momentarily and finally gave way to the command.

Looking around the spot, Fork saw nothing much unusual. Bunch grass, wolfy and dry, partially concealing a minor, low, outcropping of lava rock. Not enough cover for a large or medium sized animal. Too cold for sage rats or snakes. Probably a small rabbit. Then he caught a scent. Like a mild earthy tea, warm smelling. Then he saw the slightest wisp of steam escape the rock pile.

Chapter Nineteen

Clackamas

"There they go. Them speckled-belly geese. Why would anyone shoot at them? Might be good eatin'. But so? Can't they just wait for the windfalls, you know, the old ones that fall out of the sky from a heart attack or stroke? Eat them. Don't be shooting the young ones. Dudn't make no sense. I had a goose dinner once, before I knew what those lovely birds had to go through just to live. You know, they fly thousands of miles to have babies? How 'bout that?"

Jimmy Three Trees was standing in his hospital gown looking out the window. A flock of geese were going by. The nurse went over to see what he was looking at.

"We're sure glad you're feeling better. So, you're some kind of environmentalist are you?"

"No, I don't know what a *runmentalist* is. No, I'm an old wino, or I was one. Now I'm just waiting for a train, or a bus or a horse to get me away from here."

"Hospitals can be unpleasant but you need to stay until we

can stabilize your condition." Offered the nurse.

"I don't mind the hospital none, its Mascara I gotta' to leave, leave right away. Before they kill me too."

Out in the hall, two doctors were conferring.

"He has no next of kin, his liver won't last long, and he has a list of wasting afflictions that would kill a horse," said the young, angry doctor.

"Yes, but I still don't like it. We don't know what this *Ciarebral* will do," said the older, cautious, transparent doctor.

"That's right. That's why it's experimental. And that's why they are going to pay us, indirectly, to administer it and chart the reactions," replied the smug little doctor who looked, with pursed lips and head tosses, like he thought he should have been an actor instead.

"Who exactly are **they**?" With emphasis on the 'they.' Asked the doctor who looked like a man dressed like a woman pretending to be a man.

"We aren't supposed to know. But it's a big family-and-chemical products firm, you know, they make like soap, rat poison, house paint, agent orange, potato chips and recyclable clothing. You know, the *Gee Whiz Corp.*"

As they approached Sloop's farm or ranch, ('What's the difference anyway?' thought Vicky) the two young women had vastly different thoughts, feelings, anticipations. Just before getting a look at the farmstead, Shirley was regretting not reaching the old man on the phone, the one who had left his number at the market. She feared that if the ball were dropped now, and she missed a step in her pursuit of information about her mother, she might quit the search altogether. What? Quit when she was so close? She had to keep after it, she had to. Then she saw the first tantalizing little declarative snatch of tree line and roof top. She went directly to wonder. Her musical brain switched momentarily to tones rather than words, to tonal patterns rather than pictures.

From the slight rise, she saw the silvery tops of rows of wintering Poplar trees, humped at each crown, marching in triple rows, single file in a man-made pattern set more to play than purpose. It reminded her of that Alaskan boy she knew, the one who couldn't go to school because he was highly susceptible to any germ or bacteria. She had been paid once to keep him company and it had been a difficult process requiring her to shower twice, put on a disinfected gown, wear cotton gloves, and then a face mask to prevent her breath from contaminating him. She enjoyed his company, though it was all very sad. The reason these rows of tree tops had reminded her of him was because of the dominos. He spent days lining up dominos, just 1/2" apart and standing on end in long spiraling and squared off rows, going up ramps and down, going through cardboard tunnels and creating a vast maze-like pattern. Once he was done he'd photograph it from every angle. Then he would have her over and he'd push over one domino at the end of his pattern whilst she pushed another over at the beginning. Those two dominos would each fall into the neighboring ones and those in turn into the next ones and so on, in a cascading running rhythm of collapse. She knew it wasn't so, but it seemed like the dominos actually picked up speed as they fell. Racing, as it were, to meet in the middle in a final gasp. It was always an anticlimax. And when the domino suicide march was over, he always cried and laughed and asked her to leave.

The tops of the Poplars protecting the Ogdensburg farmstead reminded her of him and the marching geometry of his dominos. Going down that slight grade, as the road curved, she also saw the reflections of metal rooftops with curious shadows. Later she would see close-up that each roof had at least one clay-pot chimney-top in lanternesque design. And that there were also several rooftop birdhouses, custom cupolas with glass-balled lightning rods, and weather vanes perched above homemade wind-measuring rotating cups. Except for the pictured memory of the domino boy, all these things registered in her brain as tones in an opening orchestral strain she'd never heard nor imagined before. Her driving slowed to a crawl as she hunkered forward over the steering wheel. It was as if she thought she might see (or hear) more.

Then they came to the rock-framed gateway and the sign, "Please Go Away, This Miracle is Fragile." As she turned to offer confirmation to Vicky, Shirley discovered that her own mouth was open. Vicky was white and staring blankly ahead.

"You okay?" asked Shirley.

"No, I'm not. I'm scared half out of my wits. I don't know what I'm going to say to him."

"Who?"

"Him," Vicky said, nodding her head forward as a pointer.

Shirley turned and saw a boy and a stock dog walking towards the front gate and her pickup.

Luigi and Estelle arrived in Mascara late morning. They had stopped at a cafe in Bend for breakfast and preparations before the last half hour's drive. Breakfast for him had been granulated Lecithin, whole wheat bread, and soy milk. For her; two pork chops, hashbrown potatoes, a three-egg ham and cheese omelet, biscuits and gravy, plus water.

As for costume preparations: it had been decided that Estelle would make her first sashay into Mascara nude and without a hint of cosmetics. Luigi on the other hand affixed a Sig-like beard to his lower face along with thickening his eyebrows. He changed to a dark muslin shirt with an Italian leather vest, done-up with expanding pockets and quick snap flaps. It was as if he were packing compasses, notebooks, dusting brushes, magnifying glasses, signalling devices, and an Egyptian phrase book. Instead he was packing small smoke charges, a retractable piano wire, a .22 caliber Derringer, a global positioning device electronically connected to an internet organization which kept track of valuable canines, and a chewing tobacco can full of longish carpet tacs.

Enjoying a post-prandial dip after her satisfying breakfast, Estelle was taking advantage of the last little minutes of languor, spread out across the back seat of the minivan like the shameless egomaniacal starlet she was. Luigi slowed as he entered Mascara. This was great fun. The uncertain certainty. The high drama of another Monk caper. He swore he could hear strains of *the Pines of Rome* in his head. This media manicurist and cosmetician felt sad for the bulk of humanity because they so quickly discarded romance and drama from their meager lives. Not he, he would hug every drop of sweet juice from its goat-livered shroud. These shudders he felt had to be controlled, they would trip up his disguise. He had to remind himself to walk from the shoulders with legs spread apart, not his natural way which was to walk from the hips with legs close together and knees rotating around one another.

For him, the traces of snow and ice, in shaded and protected spots, gave a *harlequin-like* random-pattern note to the landscape. A tunnel of tall second-growth pines formed an entry of sorts to the busy little tourist town. On the right a funky RV park, on the left commercial construction. Then a small expanse of forest pieces before the full blown nastiness of a dirty convenience market and gas station, *Carls Cigs & Gas*. Luigi pulled in, not for gas but for a little test flight. He pulled up to the market and went around to open the back door for Estelle. People were coming in and out of the market, and driving to and from the pumps. Everything stopped and everyone looked when she stuck a tentative leg out of the door and then poured herself out as if she were a cougar descending rocks. Except for a braided horse-hair collar she was completely naked. Her creamy tan coloring was a perfect match for her aloof disdain. Estelle, largest most magnificent Great Dane anyone in this two bit town was ever likely to see, sported shellaced toenails done up with the slight-est tint of lavender coloring (Luigi's masterful touch). Her small eyes were circled by a soft black coloring akin to mascara but very much her own. Her small velvety pointed ears lopped over at the tip ends to form a crown of sorts for her magnetic eyes and unusually large mussel and lips.

A slight, nervous little man in a khaki uniform-shirt with a name tag which read *Carl* approached the dog with a smile of appreciation. He seemed totally unafraid of the Great Dane. Unusual for anyone new to Estelle. She usually worried folks.

"Magnificent animal," offered Lint Fumes, newest employee of *Carl's Cigs and Gas*. Then he looked up to acknowledge Luigi. Lint's eyes narrowed for the slightest fraction of a second. Luigi, on the other hand did a superb job of concealing his recognition of recognition. He made a mental note of the fact that an employee of the gas station *made him*, here was a definite 'player'. Without breaking his fluidity and nonchalance, Luigi took a full measure of Lint, 'Great disguise,' he thought. 'This man could be a tropical fish salesman or mechanic in some backwater, deep-south garage'.

"Thanks, could you tell me where the Mascara Motor Lodge is?"

Estelle always had difficulty with people assigning her as the property of Luigi. They were partners. In fact, if it weren't for her, he'd escape notice by all but male interior decorators. Estelle was looking around for someone. She understood the rituals and her partner's nature, they were going to meet with Sig and she was excited.

Chapter Twenty

Sixes

"It works this way: two tones at high volume produce a third tone which is ultra sonic. So you have the distraction you need and, within it or from it, you have the communication you require." The technician was explaining, over the phone, a new hyper-sonic sound emitter to Titus who in turn was imagining how the concept might be used in other ways. They needed to be ready with a distraction. That was more important than the communication question. They could setup two big events which would demand a lot of public attention and, when examined by the media, would appear to have a relationship which would be even more worrisome than either stand-alone event, or the two combined. Then he saw, on the third computer screen the scrolling news bulletins, and the impossible synchronicity of it all hit him. He was being offered a buffet of possibilities.

The news reports said that in or near a small town in Central Oregon, his town, there were concerned reports of seismic activity - with volcanos and earthquakes named in the same breath, and there was news of an unsuccessful raid on the white supremacist church camp of Bald Mother America by the FBI with a possible hostage situation, and there was the scatter-brained story of a UFO depositing a half man/half cow on the state highway, there was a hunting accident involving a seriously wounded woman (that would be Helga), a freak traffic accident involving a high speed collision with an errant irrigation wheel line (that would be Sloop) plus an unidentified male body was found - suspected to have been murdered in a terrorist plot gone awry. (Who could that be? not Enno, he knew where Enno was.)

All this today, here? And then there were those who seemed to be on his, Titus', trail. It began with the email he received a couple days back identifying one Brice Liner as a corporate mercenary, a muscle man, hooking up with the local Realtor to dig into rumors of an underground, anti-corporate, leftist organization somewhere in the vicinity of Mascara. Liner seemed to know, by name anyway, just who he was looking for.

Coincidence? Or not? Regardless, maybe there were a couple of big events here that could be combined to "produce a third tone." The last thing he should do is go to the hospital to speak with Ogdensburg. If someone, or some corporation, had members of his organization under surveillance it would be critical that he and John keep clear of each other. If the tables were turned, if Titus were in Sloop's shoes, he knew what he would want. He would want John to proceed as though he, Titus, were dead. So for Titus, Sloop no longer existed. Titus was on his own at the controls. Titus had to return to habit and keep everything tight against his chest.

Chest. He felt a pang remembering the girl at the market and how she looked so much like Charmaine. The phone number he had left behind was for the land-line into the barn apartment at the Fork Holding. Titus felt some small relief. He knew he needed to return to the Jacksons and play out a normalcy routine. It helped knowing that he might be there when she called. He didn't for a second think that she had any connection to this other convergence. Or that the hand off of that phone number might cause him risk.

Feelings are not to be excused. Neither are they to be blindly obeyed. Feelings are, on occasions, to be survived, on others, to be embraced, and still others, to be mortar for the subtotals of a life.

The sculptor/rancher, Lloyd Gerald Shoulders, was a creature of filigreed habit. Unless there was some sort of emergency, special circumstance or distraction, he wrote, and drew and meditated for two hours each morning. This morning the sketches were for a sculptural, or wall-relief, idea he had visualized; a fluttering, louvered, wall piece. Only the illusion of flutter. And the whole thing was subverted as a violated background for a puncturing, jabbing, line of steel which took the form of a fight with entanglement, a fight with the apologetic dimunization of a whispering background. The idea was exciting, it stepped away from his usual geometric, anthropomorphic, figurizations or his bisected totems. This idea was tableau, it was scenic, it was allegorical, it told a story, it allowed a glimpse of a private struggle, it offered no quarter to thinking voyeurs, it would pat the backs of the casual observer, it would push children off the cliff of boredom. It was Duchamp, Giacometti, Calder and Martha Stewart all locked in ideological embrace.

He took his Moleskine notebook and made notations with his Monte Blanc fountain pen;

> "Harmonic Challenge... Stand Clear...the garbage cans are overflowing. Shorn Anguish. The mysteries of nature point always toward interconnection, complexity, depth, intelligence, genetic memory, necessity, beauty, perfect design, humor. Temporary answers. The artist swings out on the end of a transparent string, sometimes in a flowing arc, sometimes bouncing hard against the excrement of his own vanity."

He put down the notebook and spread out the drawings on the

floor ahead of his rocking chair. The morning light came in the lower studio windows at right angles raining illumination on the sheets of drawn paper. He drank in deep breaths and let his eyes follow his floating brain back inside and out of focus. He floated there nearly in sleep state until his eyes came to rest and into external clarity. They took in the pair of spurs hanging by their leather straps on the back of the chair across from him. Each of the two snowflake-shaped rowels were graced by little hanging jinglebobs. He reached over his shoulder for the Bailey hat. It was time to strap those spurs on, saddle up Juniper, the snake bitch, and go check on the cattle.

"Look it, look it, look it..." As he pointed, Little Franklin Fork was giggling so hard he was choking. Woody the Redbone hound was sitting down hard on his butt, rear legs splayed out sideways, and front legs a reachin' and a pullin' as he drug himself around the front piece of dirt parking area with his eyes shut tight and his nose pointing at a bird dog's angle.

Brenda offered, "His hind end is itching and he's trying to scratch it, honey. That's what they do when they get wormy. Their butts itch. It's time for some tobacco." She kept tobacco leaves in a greasy lard tin in the cellar. Fed them occasionally to the dogs to kill internal parasites.

"Hey, baby, you goin' in to the hospital today?" asked Jackson, "I'm wondering' if maybe we ought to stay clear of the folks for a while?"

"I was gonna go. You afraid things are connectin' up, honey?" asked his wife, Brenda "Yummy" Fork.

"Yeah, I want to talk to Titus first. And, that steam heat comin' from the ground out there. It ain't right. Too much's happen'n too fast. Today I say we keep the children home from school, okay. I want us all close together."

"Whaddaya feel baby, tell me?"

"I feel a storm, a different sort of storm. I noticed that Sloop's stallion is all sweaty this morning, been kickin at the stall all night. And buffalo cows are snorty and confused. It's gotten warm and it's gonna get warmer yet, you notice that flock of Robins? Thousands. It's still winter and I found slugs on the bottom side of the dog's dishes. Add to all that what's happened to Helgie and Sloop and this business that's got Titus nervous and I say something's coming."

"Are you going in? No? Then get out of the way!" The shrill, demanding, middle-aged, thin, muscle-lumpy, humor-less woman in the form-fitting, winter jogging suit had her sunglasses perched up in her hair, which had been gathered, top-middle, through an elastic band and out in a fountainesque vertically-challenged ponytail. Her winter skin was the radioactive, unnatural, crispy red that is the result of an electronic tanning-bed nightmare. On her vest was a button which read *My President Rocks My World!* Her key ring had a big florescent ID flap which read *Wolves R Beautiful*. Out on the post office curb her parked BMW SUV sported *Deschutes Land Trust* and *Weight Watchers Rule* bumper stickers. She had the demeanor of someone who had just come from a firing range ticked off after having missed every paper target while the giggling fat lady next to her had landed every one of her shots in the circle. In spite of the tanning accident, she was beautiful in a regrettable way, regrettable because her personality was pure poison. Beauty in a woman is only serviceable if it is approachable, and this woman would continue to frighten most humans and needy animals away. Hers was an unserviceable beauty.

Her indignant insistence was leveled at Nettie who was talking to Brad from the Realty office. They were standing near the front of the post office. There was room to pass. Sam Riven caught the *tanning accident's* words as he was coming out the Post Office door with a handful of mail. His hackles came up.

"Ooooooh, what have we here? Let me guess; your diet pills are fighting with your metabolism because your sweat can't find a way out of your broiled lizard skin and that has your brain reminding you that bitch rhymes with witch for a reason." Sam delivered the words in a rapid-fire, mocking tone while leveling a blistering gaze on the woman.

She backed up quickly, opened her mouth to say something, shut it, opened it again and said, "What did you say?" in a loud accusatory tone.

Sam put his arm around Nettie, tipped his hat and smiled, "I said, have a wonderful day." They walked off.

Nettie's shoulders were shaking slightly as she did a nickering, silent laugh. She pinched Sam's middle.

"I shouldn't encourage you," she offered.

"Ah, but you should my dear because in this plasticene world the only thing with half a chance at removing the capitalist caste system is the relentless abrasion of sarcastic humors. Who was that you were talking to, not the aging Barbie doll, the guy?"

"He works at the office, Bo's real estate office. I had heard from the other kids that Enno Duden had met with him about land. I asked him if Bo had a hand in refusing to show him the acreage at Snake Flats. And he said something very interesting, something you might want to know. Seems a big, polished, suited man, who looks like a cross between a football player and a banker, has come to town and met privately with Bo on several occasions."

"Hmmm, was there more?"

"Yes..." she hesitated.

"Come on baby, you have to tell me."

"Yeah, but promise me you won't jump to any dangerous conclusions? OK? There was a third person at those meetings, a young man who I met and who I think is a friend of Enno Duden's, someone named Billie."

Sam marvelled at this woman. The wider she opened her eyes the more she saw and, in turn, the more she trusted her own basic goodness.

He didn't recognize the pickup truck at the front gate and

figured it was just someone lost and needing directions. Then Enno saw that Vicky was a passenger and that the driver was a dark haired girl. He walked towards them with mild, guarded curiosity. Resumé stopped and pointed his nose upwards sniffing in all directions.

Sig was in a motel room in El Paso with his sophisticated laptop computer and high tech gizmo array. He had spent twenty minutes before the mirror applying a complex disguise to his face to match the photo on the false ID. Now he was checking, by hyper-relay, messages which had been left at fourteen different email addresses spread across the planet. The hyper-relay caused an encoded message to arrive at one station as undecipherable but to be instantly forwarded in full code to a random selection of three of the other stations. Two of his stations had detonated when hackers attempted to access their memories. He had programmed each of his satellite computers to send back instantaneous messages reading *'dinner party'* the very second they exploded. He had been careful that the detonations be enough to destroy the hardware and perhaps disfigure the intruder but cause no serious collateral damage. On his twelve remaining stations he saw a pattern that confirmed his dread of the last several days. Ever since the US administration had declared war on all forms of terrorism, and ever since the legislative branch had succeeded blaming the terrible security errors of the last ten years on failed intelligence infrastructure, 'intelligence' agencies and organizations had been hardening their perimeters and preparing to defend their respective turfs.

Sig knew that when it proved helpful the FBI, the CIA, and even the Defense Department called upon the Dons of the Mafia for special operative assistance. It was they who, at great profit, had expedited the flow of narcotics to and from Central America, South America, Asia, and Afganistan from the sixties through to the present. Sig, through his own various assignments, had long ago learned that with amazing continuity and through various political ideologies and party affiliations the White House had consistently orchestrated the use of death, drugs and derision in its efforts to 'shape' the world. The Coast Guard, the Secret Service, the Border Patrol, the Customs Service, the Immigration and Naturalization Service, and the Federal Emergency Management Agency had frequently been unwitting accomplices in White House orchestrated acts of covert & overt terrorism. He also knew that in all instances, except perhaps the failed Bay of Pigs Invasion, federal executive stupidity and short-sightedness had reigned supreme. Case in point was the formation, to save political face, of the Department of Heartland Safety which was a confusing mishmash of phony oversight which only succeeded in providing cover for the increasing turf wars between agencies. He also knew through his employment arrangements that the World Bank, Britain, Israel, China, Russia, pharmaceutical companies, Chemical companies, and a consortium of producers of television reality shows, each had their own deadly and effective intelligence organizations all infiltrated by various double and triple agents. What he didn't know until this morning is that the U. S. Department of Agriculture had formed its own extended surveillance organization utilizing Alcohol, Tobacco and Firearms operatives as trainers and that the Supreme Court and Department of Education were putting out feelers about independent intelligence operatives they might pull in. The web was growing quickly.

Gweneth Heartstone, on the surface a highly effective, bureaucratic, administrative secretary, had been a skilled operative of the CIA. Her day job had recently been to work as a secretary to the head of the U.S. Defense Department. In this capacity she had been able to send regular reports back to the CIA about the specific ways that Defense was usurping the *company's* turf. When she had been found out, she had been *offered* an opportunity to be an undercover operative for the Pentagon in a new third location. She had been found dead at her new job, just after she had been able to fire off an undetected message to her old friend, and the only person she thought might be completely outside of the web, *the Monk*. The message read;

> *"The meaning of meaning is lost, the dogs are eating*
> *one another, utility is lost, you were right - the priests are*
> *cowards and opportunists. The meek will have to wait*
> *another millennium. This cloud will be around for a very*
> *long time."*

A saddened Sig Maltesta understood. Each and every agency had declared, by way of self preservation, cold war on the other agencies. Pre-emptive strike had become the operative stance. The CIA would stop at nothing to harm and/or discredit the Defense Department. The FBI sought to bring down both the CIA and the USDA not to mention Piero Gambizzi. The Israeli secret service was out to prevent the Department of Education from creating any intelligence capacity. The Pharmaceutical companies had targeted China and Russia while drawing a clear bead on the USDA and FBI. And the World Bank operatives had targeted the White House and renegade megalomaniacal chief of staff Charles Rover. The first order of business would be to root out the double agents. Gweneth had been part of that first wave. Sig had picked the right time to become a free agent. He would have only a few weeks to use his connections before the cloud covered everything. A terrible, cleansing, cancerous anarchy may be on the way.

Back to the task at hand. He had to nab little Mary and get back to Mascara as quickly as possible.

Before these two men had entered the service, one had been a new car salesman and the other had been studying for his doctorate in agricultural economics. They both now featured buzzcuts, squared unnatural shoulders, squinty sunglasses, ear pieces, calluses on the edges of their hands, patent-leather wingtips, Hoover-blue suits, shoulder holsters well-filled, company credit cards with no limit, and tiny microphones affixed to the back

side of cuff links. They drove a blue-black Chevrolet Caprice
with federal issue license plates, mat-black wheelcovers, bullet-
proof glass, heated cup-holders, and an electrically operated
divider screen which scrolled up from the inside top of the front
bench seat. The two men rode in the car, sitting bolt upright and
looking all the world like two crash test dummies. All this consti-
tuted the *company's* guidelines for undercover. These two men
believed they were incognito, that they blended in.

As these two operatives pulled in to Carl's Gas and Cigs in
Mascara, a ten-year-old, tomato-soup red Ford pickup with a six
inch lift-kit and over-sized tires pulled in behind them. The truck
featured a plastic bug screen attached to the front lip of the
engine hood. The screen had words on it. They read, *Bald Mother
America*. Sitting in the pickup were three young men, all weight
lifters, all shaved bald, all wearing tee shirts, big hoop earrings,
tatoos, squinty-eyed sunglasses with a rakish tilt, and a fast food
version of a neo-Nazi attitude. They also thought they were well
disguised, that they blended in. Truth be known, all five of these
goons were peas in a pod, from their circumcisions back, they
were all brain-dead.

The two operatives in the Caprice looked in their rear view
mirror and chuckled menacingly.

The three 'boys' in the muscle truck looked forward, at the
clowns in the Chevie, and chuckled menacingly.

From his chair in front of the station's market, Lint Fumes
picked his teeth and watched the scene with a cherubic calm.

"I know this rancher, see? Coulda' got himself in a lot of
trouble. Guess, come to think of it he did get himself in a lot of
trouble. It was a couple of years back. I was helping him with a
drive. We had to move 125 feeders 'bout three miles to permit
ground. He was horseback, I was driving the truck. We were
moving slow, down the forest service road that crossed his
ground. Feeders had been on irrigated ground. Nice set of 700 lb.
reds and blacks 'cepting for the guacamole patches oozing down

their rumps and hind legs. Happens that way; summer, irrigated ground and such.

"Then comes this car, real fast, around the corner and hits the brakes when she sees the cattle. There's fence on either side of the road, and a wide old shoulder, but still with this many cattle, quite a few are gonna walk right down the middle of that gravel road. She leans on the horn as if that would have everybody say 'scuse me, here, you want to come by'? Dumb broad. Mean too. She kept leaning on that horn. She looked like an intelligent, well turned out, middle aged lady. As if that tells you anything, huh? Jeez, she was stupid, and mean, did I say she was mean?"

"Yeah, you said mean." Roger was glancing at the newspaper while he listened to the stranger sitting next to him at the restaurant counter.

The old cowhand could tell that this guy was only humoring him, pretending to listen. He smiled knowing that what he had to tell next would get and hold the man's attention.

"She was on that back road driving a little Japanese car, not cut out for the washboard gravel. Had her window down and sat there leaning on that horn. The cattle started up again and moved forward a little edgy, crowding her car on both sides. Joe, he just stiffened in the saddle and kept his pace. Then it happened, she started screaming obscenities. 'You f-ing idiots, who the f-ing hell do you think you are? This is a public road, you have no right to have these animals blocking traffic! Get them out of my way NOW, do you hear me you stupid f-ing pig farmer!'

"She was on a roll, I was back a piece, driving drag with the pickup and I could hear her bettern' I wanted to. Heard Joe too. He put his hand to his hat and said 'Mam.' Kind of like hello or something and then said 'Don't get out much in the country, do we Mam?'

Boy'd that jerk her chain! She yelled something I didn't understand at Joe, and made like she was gonna get out of her car only the door swatted a steer and it let loose with a guacamole gusher right on her door and into her lap!"

"Guacamole?" asked Roger, now interested.

"Cow shit man, poop, manure."

"She finally got out the car and I guess seeing Joe try to hold in a smile must of pushed her over the edge."

"Sounds like she was over the edge even before she got to you guys," offered Roger fingering his last piece of toast..

"Yeah? Well wait til you hear what happens next. She's screaming at Joe to get off his f-ing horse. Now, Joe is a strong man in his prime, known to clear out a tavern or two when he gets riled. No, I know what your thinking but your wrong. Joe's different. Almost like he's spiritual or something. To him a man's pride's a holy thing. And pride challenged? Why, to him that's what decides a day's work."

Roger's hooked. He can see a dozen ways he'd write the scene...

"Joe turns his horse to face her. She's not more than five two and doesn't appreciate looking up at a man on a horse. She looks around, still yelling and muttering obscenities, and walks over to pick up a rock or something. What she finds is a long dry juniper limb with lots of sharp twigs all over it."

Now Benji is hooked on his own story telling. He twists his torso on the bar stool and slaps his open hand with the back of the other hand.

"She turns like she's gonna attack him with that stick, so he says 'easy now Lady, this is getting out of hand' and swings his leg out to get off the horse. Right then, when he's a little off balance she swings that eight foot branch and hits him and the horse. The horse bucks, Joe falls off to the ground backward and gets up slow to inspect his arm, shirt torn and blood trickling down. 'God you people make me sick' she screams almost cackling, 'You think you own the gawd damned earth, you make me f-ing sick. You've got no right. You're gonna pay to clean this car and my clothes and then I'm going to see that your sorry ass gets arrested, you f-ing ass...' Right then's when he did it for the first time, he slapped her and pretty hard too. She made like she was gonna hit him back but he caught her wrist and slapped again, twice, fast and loud. Should'a seen his face, it was cold, not

angry, just sort of matter of fact. Real scary, much more so then
that crazy mean woman.

"Her face was swelling up quick from the anger and the slaps
he was giving her. She broke loose of him and started to make
jerky, sobbing sounds like she was having trouble breathing or
something while she got back in her car. Joe had turned to fetch
his horse. Me? At that point I was enjoying all this. But it turned
ugly real quick.

"She had found a pistol somewhere in her car and was
screaming at him all over again and struggling to get back out of
her car. Maybe it was 'cuz she had both hands on the gun butt,
whatever the reason she lost her balance and fell forward out of
the car and fired a shot. One chance in a million, like that. The
shot hit Joe square in his upper left leg and he went down. But
not for long." Benji stopped, took a shot of his coffee, and
seemed to lose himself in the memory of that storied moment.

"That can't be the end of the story," complained Roger.

"No, I learned that a story like this, well it just dudn't want to
end. Know what I mean? No, it was far from the end. The woman
seemed stunned by the shooting. Limping, Joe walked up to her
and yanked the pistol out of her hand. Then he emptied it by
shooting out her windshield."

"You boys want refills?" asked the tired waitress. They both
put their hands flat over the tops of their coffee cups and shook
their heads no.

"What happened next?"

"Joe calmly hands the lady back her pistol. She's shaking and
cussing but her words don't come out right, it's like she's talking
a foreign language or something. Joe says, 'shut up' quiet like
and she just gets louder, dumber and meaner. So he grabs her
hair with his left hand and with his right he swipes a handful of
the cow shit off the car door panel and mushes it right into her
face! She throws the pistol at him but misses by a mile. Now she's
screaming and stomping around, looking for some kind of
weapon. I've gotten out of my pickup, don't know why, but I did.
And Joe, he walks over to her, she's got her back to him, and he

takes her by the shoulder, wheels her around and slugs her in the face, hard, like it was a man or a horse. She slumps to the ground unconscious. He turns to me and asks for a couple of piggin' strings from the truck. So we tie her hands and legs and dump her back in her car just as she's coming 'round. Jeez what a sight that was; car's windshield shot out and a fancy lady in hiking clothes, all tied up and knees high, face covered with fertilizer. And her all quiet as a mouse and eyes wide open and scared.

"He puts a tourniquet on his leg and insists on finishing moving the steers. When I get up where there's a phone signal Joe has me call the police. I ask him what I'm supposed to tell them. He says 'tell 'em the truth'.

Benji looks down at his breakfast tab. Roger sees him do it. "So is that the end of the story? What happened to the both of them?"

"You a gambling man? I'll make you a little wager. If the end of the story comes as a surprise you pay my tab, deal?"

Roger is chuckling, "Deal."

Benji stands up. "They got married."

"What!?"

"She wouldn't press charges, he wouldn't either. She visited him at the hospital when he had the bullet removed. She took him home. And she's never left his side since. Quietest, sweetest little wife a man could ask for. But the darndest thing is, they hardly ever speak. Been working for them for four years now and can't say as I've heard them exchange more than a half dozen words with each other. Smile alot, but no words." Benji looks down at the breakfast tab.

Roger laughs out loud and says "You win. A good one, yeah, should of seen it coming. Classic, almost Grecian. Best entertainment I've had in some time." And he picks up Benji's tab.

"Our thoughts and our art reach so feebly toward the texture of our passion."   - *Jim Harrison*

Vicky stepped from the pickup truck with a jerky deliberation that announced her anger and discomfort. Shirley slid out hesitant. Enno looked at Vicky with empty eyes. When he turned his view towards Shirley he filled instantly with unexplainable inappropriate anger and confusion. Resumé went to Shirley's side and sniffed her finger tips. For the young half-breed woman the moment was a mysterious carving of purest jade.

Chapter Twenty-one

Clatskanie

What Gustaf Sobin calls "the realm of the eventual"

"Not everything that can be counted counts."
Albert Einstein

Shirley's sensors flitted from reading the dog's silly vibrations to digesting her rapid runaway drinking-in of the young
man's just standing there, and then she went back to the dog
presence. Weather can tone a moment, rain dampens, sun bright-
ens, etc. Other more powerful forces, forces which come of recall
and rejoining and a pressurizing emotional dovetailing, forces of
exploding susceptibility, can tone a moment. Shirley will never
be able to recall the weather of that particular moment. It could
have been night, or storm central, or a hot summer day, none of it
would have reached her. Everything was black except for blinding light around Enno, a light which made his features hard to
bring into focus. She stood both rigid and limp, like the prover-

bial deer in the headlights. It could not have been the look of him because she couldn't see him. It could not have been the sound of him because everything was silent, and he said nothing. It might have been something emanating from the dog, a hypnotic sub-liminal hum with picture transfers. What she saw, besides the haloed back-lit young man, were a series of flipping picture stories as if a slide show was running in her brain. And the stories seemed to yell relevance though none of it made any sense to her. The story pictures included an image of a man falling from Hoover Dam, a woman sleeping on a prone horse, a judge in a courtroom presiding over a room full of hovering great blue herons, a long narrow bed of flowers slung on a piece of canvas being carried by dozens of children, three cats walking abreast on a small treadmill powering an old-fashioned ice cream maker, and a Polar bear walking around with a small black boy in purple striped pants riding on his back.

Shirley never felt Vicky catch her by the shoulders. It was as if the black-haired half-breed girl fainted. But her eyes were wide open and she seemed to be awake and somewhat alert. She never went completely limp, more like her body went into a floating, double-jointed fluidity. She was cognizant, but to an-other dimension. Vicky seemed to have difficulty holding her up.

"Enno, don't just stand there! Help me!"

Duden obeyed with a dumb blush, cradling Shirley's back in his arms and scooping her up. She was hot to his touch and featherlight. He stared down at her face and form. He was com-pletely without expression, red on pink but expressionless.

"Let's take her to the house," offered Vicky, feeling an odd tinge of sad jealousy.

The chopped, lowered, louvered, candy-apple red late model Toyota Celica featured custom chrome wheels which spun in directions opposite of the car's trajectory. Music, so loud it screamed back at itself, shot out of the open windows and into the mountain town's morning.

You couldn't make them out by listening to the music, all the electronica screeched and thumped over the screaming singers, but if you read the liner notes to the latest hit by 'Lovely Planet and the Shrinks', *"punk divorce environmentalists,"* you saw these words;

> *The planetary weave has announced,*
> *God's moved on to suspender another world.*
> *The muddy stains went everywhen til there was no overthere.*
> *The front geese pulled up in flight, butts plugged by followers.*
> *The attorneys could no longer bend at the knees.*
> *Cue met Cue, segway bam into segway, flitten and bitten.*
> *Gardener gone, mold and fungus ate the remaining children.*

If you were musically inclined and cared to dissect the melody, this rock mayhem could be traced directly back to the melody in Stephen Foster's "I Dream of Jeannie." The basic thesis of the songwriting and recording effort seemed to make a bold claim that if Kafka were alive and living today in Gary, Indiana, he would be into garage rock and skateboarding. Poetry belongs in the gutter, meaning works only if it is hidden 'neath layers of cloak. As the lead singer and song writer Jethro Widgit was fond of saying, *"relevance, it's all about relevance, otherwise what does anything mean, man? Don't give me no hip hop less'n' it's deep e'nuff, know what I mean?"*

For the crater-faced sixteen year old Toyota driver, the music meant nothing, it was just fly paper. He wanted to be one of the boy flies attracting reee-spect and girl flies, so he used sonic flypaper. And even in sleepy Mascara it frequently worked. But his dream was to move himself, his sound system and his Toyota to LA. Then he'd be in a heavy flies zone. But for now he'd just cruise the Mascara gut looking for love. Right now necessity ruled. He pulled into Lupe's Gas Station. Stereo blaring, his arm out his window, between two fingers he held up a twenty dollar bill while staring deadpan straight ahead. He could feel the attendant approach and then disappear. He looked around the left side of his car and missed the entry of Lint Fumes into the passenger side of his vehicle.

"What are you...?" These were all the words he got out. Lint had jammed his sharp elbow deep into the youngster's stomach. With his right hand he slammed the car stereo with a ball peen hammer until the 'music' stopped. Then smiling he reached over and took the twenty dollar bill saying, "Tweny dollars regular?" as he exited the car.

When the boy caught his breath he started yelling obscenities and pushed to open his car door. Lint slammed the door back at him and leaning through the open window explained, "I could be forgiven for smashing your sound system. Or you could be found shot to death, face down at the local dump. You do have a choice. Can I get that windshield for you?" Always grinning, never once did Lint look the part.

Sig and little Mary made an uneventful crossing through Lyndon's Lizard, the CIA operated tunnel under the U.S. Mexico border at El Paso. His eye and finger prints were still current on the door-lock optic scanners. It had been surprisingly simple to convince Mary to sit in the large zipped up duffle bag with the base rollers. (This way the video cameras in the tunnel would not immediately discern two people.) Sig had charmed her and told her it was all part of the game. Conzuela, Mary's mother, had told Mary that the nice man would take her on a fun trip and that she would be joining them soon.

Now they were sitting in a private chartered plane, heading first to Oklahoma City and a repair hangar where a large-scale shell game would have them appear to transfer and leave by one of three planes exiting the hangar. When in actuality they would be leaving by snack truck and transferring to a tinted-window chauffeured Mercedes sedan for the ride to Fresno, California.

That's where Sig had told Conzuela Merced he would be

taking her daughter for safekeeping. He had agreed that they would make the last leg of the trip in one of her cars. And he had listened, without comment, when she had threatened him should anything happen to Mary. She, the mother, had been a tough customer, but there could be no doubt how she would react later when her own agents would detail just who the Monk was. She would come completely apart.

It had worked well. His plan to kidnap Mary, and then communicate to Conzuela, began with a silent switch in the private school yard. He hired a young girl, same size, shape and general appearance as Mary. Dressed her in the same school uniform and had her join the children when he enticed Mary away. Not until recess was over did the teacher panic and notify Conzuela's secretary. Then, child in tow, he, Sig, managed to hide in the mother's office and wait until all her aids and secretaries had been dispatched to find Mary. He had locked three doors and was reaching for the fourth before the distraught, crying Senora Merced had even realized he was there in the room with her. His coaching of Mary had been perfect. She stood, quiet as a church mouse, out of sight in the coat closet. He locked the last door just as she pulled the 357 Magnum from the desk drawer.

"I have your daughter," he said.

"You are a dead man," she said.

He stood calm, focused and silent. He would wait. Then he saw what he was waiting for. Her shoulders began to shake, then the two hands which held the revolver pulsed violently.

"Damn it! Where is she!" she roared. Then she caught herself with one hand on the desk edge and whimpered the same words again.

"She's here with you and she's fine." He stepped forward casually while calling out, "Mary, honey, you can come out now."

When the closet door opened to reveal a smiling girl, he completed his path and gently removed the pistol from a compliant Conzuela's hand.

He gave her the evidence and told his story of being hired

by the White House to kidnap her daughter and worse. He apologized for doing it this way, but he felt certain that it was the only way to convince her of the danger.

"If I can snatch your daughter so easily, in broad daylight, imagine what they might do - especially if her care is of no consequence?"

"Who are you?"

"I cannot tell you that," he answered. "What I can tell you is that you need to send your daughter with me. Allow me to take her away and hide her. Then you must pretend that she has actually been kidnapped and is in great danger of being harmed. I'll tell you who to contact. With them, you will pretend that you are willing to do whatever they say. They must think that everything is going according to their plan or there will be worse consequences and immediately."

"Mary, querida, go and see Paco. I want to talk with this man for a minute."

Child gone, she turned to Sig with tight angry eyes and looked at her pistol by his side, "Why the hell would I agree to send my daughter with you?"

"First of all, it is because I am the only one who can keep her safe right now. I am the first one they sent. Others are already here, prepared to take over if I should fail. For them, failure is not an option. In their minds, if I should fail and you should find out that they mean to do this thing, they will have lost the advantage of surprise and any chance of holding you in check. You see, they are attracted to you, not your husband. And they fear you and your influence. They are too stupid to understand courtship. They understand coercive power. And that makes them dangerous in the short run."

He slowly raised his hand and offered her back her pistol. She took it.

Looking down at the gun she asked, "Why would you do this thing?"

"For money and position. I don't like working for idiots."

"Are you asking to work for me? You frighten my daughter and me and expect I should hire you?"

"Ask her yourself, your daughter was never frightened. As for a job, I don't need work." He smiled a dry cold *don't-ask* smile, "But if I am to take risks in hiding and protecting your daughter, I expect to be compensated handsomely. If later you should have additional need for my services, I work on a pre-approved project basis."

"You said money and position. What did you mean exactly?"

"You are already a powerful woman. And you already are in need of the best of people. If you should find that you need me, I will have my favored 'position'."

"You know in a different situation I might find you amusing, but this has gone long and far enough. So that we understand one another..." now she was pointing the pistol at his face, "I will offer the courtesy of telling you that your body will be delivered to those who hired you with a note explaining that I am not such a coward as to hire others to do my dirty work."

"You do me a great disservice Senora, thinking I had not planned for just such an eventuality. You, obviously, will never understand me but I see right through you. I will make you my offer one last time. Please allow me to protect your precious daughter."

"My daughter is right now here, safe in our home, protected by my staff and our security. What happened today was a fluke. It won't happen again, I will see to that. I don't need you..."

Right at that moment, behind Conzuela, a small frightened man burst into the room stuttering. She wheeled around to face him while keeping the gun pointing in Sig's general direction. "Dios Mio, Senora, little Mary has disappeared. We cannot find her anywhere." Conzuela turned to face Sig only to find that he too had disappeared.

Chapter Twenty two

Mollala

Coincidence is God's way of staying anonymous.

The ugly headed insecurities feed on the insecurities of others growing in satisfied alarm and emotional dysentery. Vulnerability is both the corrector and the bait. Understanding is haunt. Sigismundo Maltesta understood this.

Conzuela Merced, immediately after the second disappearance of her daughter, found the phone number on the scrap of paper with the initials SM and the words "if she is still alive, only I can protect her." She dialed the number and got no answer. Slumped in her chair, she wondered if he had taken her again or if, as he had warned, the second wave had taken her. She avoided thinking of her daughter's condition. The second call had reached him. "Rather dramatic. You win. Bring her back and we'll talk," she had said.

"Your daughter is safe and hiding in the kitchen pantry. It is a game I rehearsed with her. A game that I thought might be necessary to make a point. Obviously, I misjudged you. Not your capacity for administering cold-blooded death, but your capacity for intuitive reason and your maternal instincts." She hung up on him and raced to the kitchen and her daughter.

A large, suited man entered the kitchen. "Senora, I thought you should know. We feel certain there are two cars with two people in each which seem to have the estate under surveillance."

She called *him* back. "We must talk. I have need of your services. I want to discuss my daughter's safety."

"Hang up and do not discuss any of this further over your phone, it is tapped," Sig said.

She trembled as she held her daughter. She was confused about this man. She was determined to get even with the U.S. government.

Enno Duden carries with him, at all times, a latent impulse towards corrective violence held in near absolute reserve by a personalized, purified law of corrective ambition, of correct goal. This law becomes the filter for every invasive assault, every strange impulse, every unexpected desire. He is a mystery to himself. And never more so than when he found a strange new woman in his arms, there from a faint-like stupor.

For Enno there is always the risk that he has found a place in longing that he will not easily be rid of. Wishing and projecting so hard, so intently, for a farm of his own creates an ephemeral world of 'possibility'. He has grown comfortable within his own single-mindedness. Whenever he feels threatened or challenged he goes back to that wished-for vision of the farm. If he should ever find a farm of his own, whose is to say whether or not that will give him the ardor to replace the 'daydream' as his source of strength. As with the man who consciously or unconsciously backs out of consummate romance in an effort to rediscover the poignancy of longing, there has always been that risk that Enno will wish a certain failure for himself, the risk that

Enno is now exactly where he wants to be.

He sets Shirley down in one of the many rocking chairs on Helga's front porch. When he looks up, he notices that Vicky has fixed a stern eye on him. He assigns her look to the difficulty that her female friend is having and to that general dismay all women seem to have for men in awkward social settings.

"Who is she?" asked Enno.

"Hello to you too," spits back Vicky.

"Mind telling me what's going on here?"

"Her name is Shirley and I just met her the other day. She and I are here for several reasons. Number one: Who is *the Monk*? He wants us to tell you to lay low because someone is snooping around looking to hurt you. Number two: how long have you known that we are brother and sister? And number three; What is going on around here?" Vicky red face suggested either anger or tears or both.

"You are Sig's sister!" asked a startled Enno.

It was too early to check into the Motel so Luigi and Estelle cruised up and down the small town's streets, checking out the area. This big town journalist couldn't remember the last time he saw so many up-scale SUVs; BMWs, Porsches, Mercedes, Lexus, Hummers and Cadillacs to name but a few. And every single one of them with a driver and no passengers. Must be because it's a school day he thought, and Moms are out doing shopping chores. The four dark blue Ford and Chevrolet sedans transporting teams of either proselytizing evangelists or FBI agents (or some combination thereof) struck him as a bit too obvious. He figured it would be like some of those remote Northern California towns and had expected to see lots of cowboy, farmer and logger pickups. But, except for a Bald Mother America Ford, there weren't many of them. There were dozens of newish, contractor pickups zipping from the lumber yard to the dozens of construction sites scattered all over the town. Even he could see that this community would triple in size within the year.

Where she sat, upright, in the front passenger seat, Estelle-the-Great-Dane had to lower her head to see out the window. That posture suggested an attentiveness but her eyes were bored. Bored that is until she saw the little city park and whimpered in a lacy, dusty baritone voice reminiscent of Lauren Bacall.

The sun was shining and it was thirty-five crisp clean degrees Fahrenheit. A temperature and weather condition that the truly local, actually somewhat indigenous folks loved most about the high desert's collision with the Cascade mountains. Peggy Youngquist sat, wrapped in a second-hand sheepskin coat, on the park bench, watching her little Tyrone scamper over the plastic park-model gymnastic furnishings. In forty-five minutes she would be dropping him off at a friend's house for baby-sitting while she worked the mid-day waitress shift at the Fur River Cafe. She was so tired that, though she loved watching her son play like this, she couldn't bring herself to smile.

Luigi saw them and then the park sign which said dogs must be on leash. He parked and went around to Estelle's door. He clipped a short leather leash to her elegant spiked and rhine-stoned collar. "You know the routine," he said while placing the end of the leash inside her mouth. Estell lowered herself grace-fully from the minivan seat and proceeded to "lead herself" into the park. She trotted to a cluster of trees which begged pre-violation sniffing. Tyrone stopped in his tracks and stared at the biggest dog he had ever seen in his very young life.

"Good morning," offered Luigi as he sat on the other end of the bench opposite Peggy.

She pulled her head down deeper into her lined collar, rotated her eyes his way momentarily, and nodded in acknowl-edgment.

"Mommy, mommy, doggie, doggie!" hollered the boy as her raced to her knees.

"That's a beautiful dog, Great Dane?" asked Peggy.

Worked again. Luigi never ceased to marvel at how

Estelle, as subject or verb, could immediately pop open otherwise nonexistent communication channels.

"Thank you, yes, but don't let her hear you say that. She sees herself as above all that."

From a pleasant and casual conversation Luigi learned a bunch of stuff about this little town's interior map; stuff like where to eat and where not to eat, when things shut down, to watch out for the soccer moms in big SUVs who drove erratically, that there was some kind of big developer's convention in town, that creepy white supremacists were showing up, that he really should take the drive up the Cascade Lakes Highway to see the mountains up close, and that the Thai restaurant had a local Jazz ensemble play on Monday nights, and that she worked there those nights.

Peggy found *Lou*, as he had introduced himself, to be exotic and funny and comforting. Lou found Peggy to be lovely, tragic and wasted. Tyrone fell completely in love with Estell who could care less about the ear tugging rug rat. They agreed with smiles to meet back at the park same time next morning.

Before they had arrived in Fresno, Little Mary and Sig had given the limo driver the slip and boarded an Amtrac for Oregon. It was while riding the train that Sig took the time to read the papers his research had unearthed. Too many coincidences. So, as is his habit, he had followed an obscure one. How did the Cooper girl fit into the Duden mess with these heavy hitters? This girl, Shirley Intoit, was looking for information about her mother, Charmaine Lebow. The last thread she had was something about the Berkeley campus decades ago. A search of the University records had accidently turned up an illegal, secretive, political action group the mother had been linked with. Something called *Aisle of Dogs*. The only thing he could find was a list of suspected members and a fragment of a manifesto that had been painted on a coffee shop bathroom wall and signed *Giggleswick*. It read:

*a structural theory for the construct of corrosive guerilla
action.
draw a diagram of a root system, look at the tip end of tap
root or first action.
build a fictional set of indicators - suggestion - several
disparate germinations.
use those illusions to suggest greater efforts.
liken to two men pretending to be an army.*

The membership list included what appeared to be nick-
names. He saw Charmaine Lebow with the nickname *'Canary'*
and next on the list he saw Titus Ibid with the nickname
'Giggleswick'. A search of *Giggleswick* turned up a small town in
England. A quick search of several sets of Central Oregon records
turned up a passing reference to a Jazz Bassist performing at a
Thai restaurant in Mascara, his name was Titus Ibid. Bingo.
Through this crack he was sure it would all become clear.

Mary was napping. He had to remember to send the con-
firming emails through the circuit to Senora Merced. She needed
to know Mary was fine.

Meanwhile back in Mexico, Conzuela Merced struggled to
hold her composure. It would be easy to play the part of the
distraught mother of a kidnapped child because right now she
really didn't know what was true. When the Washington operative called her, she let loose with a torrent of invective that would
have neutered an alligator.

Just as Sig had expected, Enno clammed up and gave next to
no information to Vicky and Shirley. He stood against the porch
rail. Vicky leaned against a chair back. Shirley sat in a chair. And
Resumé sat bolt upright next to Enno's right leg. The dog's head
moved back and forth to register words and emotions.

Shirley was feeling better, only a slight weakness remained

of her 'experience'. She was keenly interested in the dog and its connection with the boy/man.

They had reached a difficult understanding or non-understanding regarding the question of whether or not Enno and Vicky were siblings. Enno had forcefully said he knew nothing of the matter. Yes, he knew Jimmy and liked him but put no stock in the suitcase revelation. He became quite nervous when he heard that Jimmy had passed out and been taken to the hospital.

"You know, and another thing, she," Vicky was pointing at Shirley, "actually understands him?"

"I want to see him; he can't be in a hospital. It can't work that way for Jimmy." insisted Enno.

Part Three

Dust

Chapter Twenty-three

Deschutes

*"Every shred and ounce of nature equals mortality.
We must not stand up to this but absorb it." - Jim Harrison*

The advance team from the television show were being 'guided' through the technical and geological jargon jungle as it regarded the little volcano and the earthquakes of Mascara.

"So, are the earthquakes and this volcanic activity related or not?" she asked.

"We believe they are related. But you have to understand that this might be purely a bizarre coincidence. Nothing here is making any sense, although much of it does seem to be following a series of recognizable patterns," answered the young scientist.

"That's a mish mash of contradictions..." she replied.

"I know how it must sound, but please bear with me for a moment. We have what is technically termed as the beginnings of a *shield volcano*. These are formed along the rift valleys and ocean ridges of constructive plate margins or areas where plates are moving apart. They are also formed over hot spots. We believe this to be a hot spot. At some point we expect magma to break-through the surface out here and flow slowly but freely for some distance. As it cools, it will form a low broad volcano. With this kind of volcano we don't see violent eruptions, as in the case of Mt. Saint Helens. Instead we see a kind of oozing flow of magma."

"So you're saying this thing isn't going to blow up in some dramatic fashion?" She was apparently disappointed.

"Correct. At least that's what we think today. Look," he said. "There's a bunch of other stuff happening here and we are still measuring and extrapolating data."

With refreshed excitement she asks,

"Are people at risk, here? What about the town of Mascara? If this thing turns out to be more violent than you 'want' it to be, how much advance notice will people have?"

"Allow me to show you something?" He went to an erasable white plastic display board and drew a diagram beginning on the left with a pronounced mountain or volcano shape meant to represent the Cascade Mountains, then moving gradually to a foothill plateau where he drew a very wide and slight hump to represent the shield volcano site. Next, the ground line continued gradually down to the level of the town, and beyond to the next lower level. Under this ground line he drew several wavy, nearly parallel lines.

"We are experimenting with something different. Trying to get a read on what's happening below the surface. We are taking readings with a gravimeter. It's a device that geologists use to measure the force of gravity at a particular location. These readings can tell us about igneous intrusions," (he drew an upward blip in one of the parallel lines) "and salt domes. These structures are felt to affect just how plates interact underground. We need to understand why some of the activity suggests plates moving against each other and other phenomena suggest that the same plates are pulling apart."

"Is that just your scientific curiosity at work, or is there something here that really worries you guys?" another reporter asked.

"Well, we're really worried about a lot of things here," answered the boy clinician, immediately regretting his blurt. "Erase that, please. What I mean to say is that we're being asked to monitor the volcanic activity and explain the seismic variables and relationships. But, in this local case the ground is doing things quite different from what we usually see and seemingly in curious concert with contradictory phenomenae."

The television people were all chewing the ends of their pens trying to figure out whether there was a story here or just another case of jacketed scientific hysteria. I mean, let's get real, who cares if, one mile down, the seismic plates are having a moment of harmless dyspepsia?

The young academic was obviously upset by the turn in this presentation. He was loosing them. This, he had known, could be a big opportunity for his career. Media exposure to fan the latent charisma of his brilliant young mind.

"We have *'abiotic activity'* here which just might have, I said *just might have*, dramatic telling effect to the landscape for hundreds of years. The scientific community has long held that most significant geological changes occur gradually, over a very long time. The situation we have here could alter the landscape and watershed almost overnight.

"You see this layer here?" he pointed to between two of the wavy parallel lines on the erasable board drawing. "Imagine this to be a pervious (water containing) rock (aquifer), like a sponge blanket under the surface beginning here up on the mountain side and running downhill. Below, and above this, we have impervious rock layers we call an aquiludes. There is hydrostatic pressure at these lower levels. If you puncture the top layer of aquilude, water will come up to the surface in artesian fashion. The landscape and climate of this region are affected by this subterranean reality. If it should change dramatically, domestic and agricultural wells could all dry up. And just such a scenario could be caused by what's happening with the shifting plates. That's one concern.

"Our core samples have brought up Cinnabar or Mercuric sulfide mineral, HgS. This stuff is the only commercially useful ore of mercury. We usually find it deposited in veins and impregnations near recent volcanic rocks and hot springs. It's the hot springs we're interested in. The Cinnabar is telling us that our aquifer is being affected by great temperature, not surprisingly, near the shield volcano. But we're finding this to be also true 20 miles distant and that's not good. We could be having volcanic and seismic activity running along some distance of a fault line."

"Hey, I thought the plan was to have California fall off into the Pacific? Are you telling us that western Oregon, from the east side of the Cascades west, is getting ready to sluff off?" laughter in his voice.

The television science reporter meant it as a joke. The young scientist didn't know how to respond to such a ridiculous observation. He was trying to keep himself on track with his presentation. So he did not respond.

"Honey, did you hear the man's question?" the woman asked nervously.

"Yes." was all he said.

At the back of the entourage a young hot shot muttered 'oh geez' and slipped out to make a cell phone call to the editor of the Chronicle in San Francisco.

"May I continue?"

"Wait a minute. Why won't you answer this man's question?"

"I guess I thought he was just being ridiculous. Did you really mean for me to answer? Because the answer is obviously no, the western third of Oregon is not going to 'fall off' into the sea. What may happen could be far more exciting than that." Again he regretted his blurt. "I mean to say from a scientific perspective."

"Please, do tell Doc," came the reporter's jab.

Sighing with realization that the moment was completely lost, the suddenly less ambitious young man said, "Destructive margins or convergent margins in plate tectonics refers to activity always seen under the oceans, never below the continental crust. At least not until now." He just wanted to get through. The heck with trying to bring it down to their level. "We've got the asthenosphere and the lithosphere or oceanic plate. Volcanic activity or the buildup of magma can cause a set of circumstances or conditions with friction and increased pressure forcing the lithosphere to dive beneath the asthenosphere and melt. Normally the subduction zone required for this phenomenon only occurs on the ocean floor. However, we appear to be having this happen here, under the aquifer. We are measuring both reverse and normal faults. That's never occurred before in the same zone."

"Okay Doc, cut to the chase. Are we to expect a big earthquake soon? And second, will there be any kind of volcanic eruption soon?"

"You just don't get it, do you!?" He was rasing his voice. "Everything is out of whack! We don't know what is going to happen!"

"Okay, calm down. Give us the worst case scenario. Talk about people, cities, fires, that sort of stuff."

"Several quakes, 7 point on the Richter scale, massive damage within 150 miles of epicenter, may or may not happen. Concurrent with earthquakes we could see magma flow breaking out in many spots. Perhaps most dramatic we could see startling changes in the landscape, almost overnight. Lakes could dry up and new ones form and large areas collapse or break open. There is every reason to suspect we may have a bunch of new hot springs with geyser activity a'la Yellowstone. And if the conflicting fault activity aggravates, we'll have pronounced new canyons and perhaps even rivers."

Every journalist mouth in the room hung open for a long second and finally succumbed to the impulse to chew at nonexistent gum.

Fred English found the dead, partially clothed police guard in the hospital room. Dr. Fistula was there also, unconscious but still alive. The second guard was down in the cafeteria and came up at a run when he received the radio call. The area was secured and a Doctor was brought in to treat Fistula. State and local police were notified. English went into a wide, low, intense posture scouring with his eyes for any clues before he took off for the parking lot. He found two ambulance drivers angry about their missing rig. Fred called in an all points on the ambulance.

Ten minutes before, Brice Liner had dressed in the guard's clothes and walked out the front door of the hospital. He saw the ambulance idling by the emergency door with flashing lights. No one was in the unit. He got in flipped off the flashers and drove out of the parking lot and towards the Redmond airport. From experience he knew this to be the best place to hijack a good car.

At the departures curb, three cars sat with their engines idling; a Dodge pickup, a Ford Explorer, and a Lexus sedan with its trunk lid open. The Ford and Dodge owners were both at the airport front door helping people with luggage. The Lexus driver, a software thief from Tacoma, sat behind the wheel playing with his Blackberry and ticked off that he had to wait for *her* to come back for the second suit case. Liner pulled in behind him, flicked the ambulance flashers back on, got out and walked to the Lexus. He slammed the black luxury car's trunk lid shut, the insulting sound of which brought the driver out in a heat. Brice hit him sideways at the neck with a slicing chop from his flattened hand. He got in the Lexus and drove off as he dialed the mounted cell phone for Piero Gambizzi.

"What do we do?" asked a somewhat less agitated Vicky Wood.

Shirley's wary eyes were glued on Enno.

Duden was surprised at the clarity and complexity of his thinking. He instantly thought about that patch of pants fabric Resumé had brought him.

"They know we're here. We can't stay here. Or at least you ladies can't," he said.

"Well, its for damn sure you aren't staying here by yourself!" Vicky surprised herself with her angry possessive tone. Lots remained unresolved for her.

"Chores are done here. Let's head back to town,' Enno said.

"Hide in plain sight," said Shirley.

"Who said anything about hiding?" Enno felt the invasive energy coming up from inside.

Resumé gently bit Enno's loose hanging hand, licked it and ran to jump in the back of the five window.

"No buddy, I think we'll leave old blue here and go with the ladies. Might work as a decoy. Okay?" he directed the question towards Shirley who shrugged her shoulders. This man she definitely didn't like. He was like some shallow, southern, farmboy dope without the accent and swamp smell. The whole damn thing she didn't like, too much hyper-drama, too much butter-wrapped romance.

"I need to talk with Sloop and Helga," Enno said out loud but meant for himself.

"What did you say?!" snapped Shirley who right in that instant reminded Enno of a Greek exchange student he had briefly known. She too leaped directly to demanding anger and without obvious cause.

"I need to get to the hospital, I've got friends there." ('Sloop might know something. Least he'll want to know what's happening.' he thought.)

"And what was that other name? Did you say Helga?"

"Yes. Why?" In that moment Enno looked to Shirley like a cross between a dewy early morning cabbage and a sack of potatoes. Ugly and dumb. He had those pursed, sour cough-drop lips and dull, waiting eyes.

"Who is Helga to you?" she demanded.

"My friend. I live here with her and Sloop. This is their place."

Again, Shirley felt herself swoon.

Gambizzi had goons in Jackson Hole. The ones who had botched the terrorist thing. He dispatched them immediately to assist Liner in Mascara. It wouldn't take them long to drive there.

Liner was a double agent, while on *Gee Whiz Corp's* payroll he had been working to gather information for his other second boss, Gambizzi. Liner's first loyalties would also go to the toughest. Gambizzi was making a move soon to gain control of *Gee Whiz*. Piero told his people that it was time for a talk with Charlie Rover. "*The Monk*, huh?" he asked himself. "We'll see about that."

"While you're at it, get Zarabrezi on the line." he punched.

Luigi had taken care of costumes and makeup. He now looked like Sig trying to look like someone else. As for tawny Estelle, she had allowed him to painstakingly paint her up to look like a deepest, darkest, brindle with beautiful, fading, zebra-like parallel stripe marks all applied by eyeliner pencil. It was time to test the costumes. Together they would go downtown for a little stroll.

Nettie's fingertips traced back and forth along Sam's bare arm as he went from distracted float to focused thought. She wondered at her transformation. So fast, so effortless. And contrary to the external evidence, so self-possessed. Sam stiffened and said,

"I've got it. I know what we need to do." He kissed her quick and reached for the folder.

On November 24, 1971, the night before Thanksgiving,
with the swagger of someone who had just made the deal of his
life, a man somewhere between 30 and 45, wearing dark glasses
and a business suit boarded a Northwest Orient Boeing 727 at the
Portland International Airport in Oregon. The ticket he purchased was in the name of Dan Cooper. It was a law enforcement
officer's mistake, in a later press conference, that hung the handle
of D.B. Cooper on him. In real life his name was Charleton Ibid,
brother to Boston Ibid, father to Titus. He was an amateur pilot,
an insurance salesman, and an avid parachutist. He was suffering
from terminal lung cancer. And he loved his brother and young
nephew, two down and out acrobats for a small travelling circus
camped that fall in a small town on the Iowa banks of the Mississippi.

In the plane, Charleton took seat 18F, ordered a bourbon
and water and, just before takeoff, handed a folded note to the
flight attendant, Flo Schaffner. Flo was attractive and accustomed
to mash notes, she stuck it in her teeth and later in her pocket.
After take off she read these words, "Miss, I've got a bomb, come
sit next to me - you're being hijacked."

Chapter Twenty-four

Umpqua

"I have been robbed. There are no hundreds here."
Cyrano de Berjerac

The Sicilians produce a variety of grape called the Pantelleria muscat which is renowned for its sweetness. There is a dish called 'Sarde a Beccafico' or 'Sardines Stuffed with Raisins and Pine Nuts'. The Panatelleria muscat makes a raisin most deserving of this dish. Start with 2 pounds of fresh sardines, one half cup of the right raisins, one half cup of pine nuts, 3 tablespoons of fine dry bread crumbs, two chopped garlic cloves, freshly ground pepper, two tablespoons extra virgin olive oil, one cup plain flour and oil for frying. Clean and bone the fish, removing the heads and tails, then wash and dry. Soak the raisins in a cup of lukewarm water until soft, then drain and pat dry. Mix the ingredients and then stuff the fish with the mix, reclose them and coat thoroughly with flour. Pour oil into a skillet to a depth of 1 inch and heat. Fry the sardines for 5 minutes or until nicely browned on both sides.

Drain fish on paper and sprinkle with salt. Arrange and serve.

Joanna Mendelsohn Thurber of Perhapshire, Vermont, had written a book entitled *Love Recipes*. It was in hardcover and not doing as well as the publisher had expected. Joanna had agreed to do a book tour. The tour had started ambitiously, with chain store appearances in some major cities; Boise, Salt Lake City, Tulsa, and Bakersfield. Attendance was embarrassing, so the itinerary shifted to independents in upscale western towns; Sun Valley, Aspen, LaPine, and now Mascara. She knew what the problem was. It was the damn editor at Burlinghouse. It started with Joanna's title. What was wrong with *"Eating Apricots in a Hair Coat"*? Then the cover design morphing from the picture of the gloves and the theater tickets into the one of the twenty-something ditsy blonde with the Italianesque ape squeezing her shoulders from behind.

She sipped her gin and tonic and felt her stomach tie up in knots. She had written a first rate novel. She had changed her name to give it a lasting resonance. (Peggy Schwartz, her real name, didn't cut it.) She had left her husband in preparation for a life of anticipated satisfaction. She had fired her agent, believing that the coming success would warrant a climb to top notch representation. She had the Sophia skin treatment and the liposuction and the velcro undergarment thing. All these corrections and additions had made it easier, even necessary to accept the publisher's changes. Now she remembered that cruelest of moments when Dabney had done his rundown on acceptable endings.

"A. Realistic. B. Fanciful. C. Romantic. D. Some combination of the above. Those are your acceptable choices my dear," he had said. Then he narrowed it even further and said, "We want your readers giddy with the ending. That's the only way they'll come back for another round. The part about the dog dying, we have to cut that out all together. And where you have the mother stepping aside for the sake of her son's happiness, I think that doesn't work because we love to hate her and we need to see her taking a big chunk of the prize and choking on it. Fade her destruction to the background and bring up Alonzo (don't you just love that name, it's far better than David, don't you think?) reaching for Greta. I'm telling you, I see film all over this one, film and more film. We've come up with a real winner here my dear. Just hold on. It will be the ride of a lifetime."

And now she was in the Fur River Cafe Lounge ingesting alcoholic nerve to face the six or so people who were likely to show up at the bookstore for her signing. Looking deep into the glass she didn't see Bo Coin until he had already slid in beside her in the booth.

"Hey. Where have I been all your life?" It was rude and stupid. So was he. She smiled a dull smile and questioned him as polite prelude to a "get lost bub." They talked and she was surprised to find she needed to. She saw he was clean, middle class, white, and somewhat harmless. Class considered, he was definitely a small step down but she had his attention. So she unloaded. Bo listened, and listened, and uncharacteristically for him, said little or nothing. Time past in a flutter.

Looking at her watch, she wrapped up her long personal history and said, "So in one hour I go over there and face 'my public'. It's so embarrassing," without thinking, she put her hand over his and felt heat. "My book is good Bo, its really quite good, it deserves better than this."

He recognized an opportunity but was overwhelmed by an odd, unearned sense of kinship.

"Oh, no, you don't have to do that."

"Yeah, I know I don't, but I'm gonna. Right now I've got to run set some things up. Hey, I have a hunch this is gonna be your big night. Leave room for drinks with me later this evening, okay?" And he left.

As Sloop and Helga, in their hospital room, absorbed and fluffed their rediscovered, lesser selves

- as humming and strumming Fred English headed towards Mascara for clues

- as Enno, Resumé, Shirley and Vicky awkwardly headed together into Mascara to gas up

- as Mascara-bound Sig sent a cryptic email to Conzuela assuring her of Mary's safety

- as Sam and Nettie ran off incendiary handbills at Sam's print-making studio

- as Peggy picked at thoughts of Luigi

- as Titus went through the steps, at the 'station', to see to it, maybe one last time, that sub-commandant Marcos received a cautionary note along with the 3 tons of rice, the dozen crates of penicillin, the blankets and the bank draft for three million dollars, all for Chiapas farmers

- as Jimmy Three Trees slipped into a talking panic, worrying about the whereabouts and condition of his dogs

- as Nancy Simmons worried about Billie's whereabouts while reading the Vogue article on Sting's preference in women

- as Lint Fumes listened, while dispensing gas, to Roger the writer's description of this town as all snobs and no class

- as Bo Coin intruded on Linda Glimpse's mid-week art club meeting of 23 women and 2 men to offer to purchase all of their *'art's where it's at'* T shirts if they would attend a book signing in 45 minutes at the town bookstore

- as two FBI agents watched from a distance while two CIA operatives planted a listening device on the Bald Mother America restaurant-parked pickup truck while Revenue agents interrogated two soused journalists in town for the earthquakes and brindle painted Estell lifted a leg on a motionless, street corner anchored, drug enforcement agent painted up convincingly to look like a cigar store Indian standing as still as a marble statue

- as Harry *the Tooth* Langostino and his two frustrated kick boxer friends raced west from Jackson Hole in their Plymouth Navigator

- as Adi Zarabrezi struggled to make contact with *the Milk Man*

- as Reba Yankone adjusted the many various gold bracelets on her jewlery commode

- as all these things and more were happening, the bulge beside Lumpy Lash rippled with another nervous shudder and pressurized subterranean hot water sought release through any fissures it could find.

Brice went into the shopping center parking lot and abandoned the Lexus, walking across the highway to the motel office to demand a replacement key. Once in his room, he called an unlisted number and demanded a black, bullet-proof Mercedes sedan be delivered right away, this he did while selecting a pastel dress shirt to go with his standby Armani suit. There were several more things he would need. He went to the mirror to see what could be done with the holes in his ears.

Piero Gambizzi, cloth napkin tucked into his collar front, drank his brother's estate bottled Chianti and ate his *Sarde a Beccafico* very slowly, savoring the chewy sweet fruit centers of the salty fish. He was on the phone with the White House. He was listening attentively. It was his turn when he decided it was his turn.

"This is what I have to say, it's a mistake. Going into Mexico is a mistake. If they don't trust us, we cannot trust them. It is a bad thing. Bad for business. I say pull out Charlie, now." Pause. "Then you are on your own. If it comes to this, we will protect family and territory. Please understand this Charlie, you and your boss are not family. Say hello to your mother for me. Oh, and Charlie, get a wife. It doesn't look good."

Bo thought hard about how to get more people to the bookstore on short notice. He had an idea. He would call his office receptionist and setup an emergency sales meeting at the bookstore. He'd tell them there was a new high stakes opportunity for the firm with this Yankone real estate development. They'd go for that one. He could wing it later, after they heard Joanna's presentation. Anyway they'd thank him when they saw and heard her. She was fabulous.

Adi had worked hard on the computer and came up with eleven major corporations with serious profit/loss accounting issues; off shore accounts, CEOs and CFOs thought to be draining funds, major money laundering shenanigans. Eleven of them. Four sets of top execs facing federal indictments. Wholesale confusion as to who stole what. Could *the Milk Man* have had a hand in all of those? If so this econo-terrorist group could be sitting on hundreds of millions, even billions, he had to get inside. He belonged inside. They would need him. No matter how hard he worked at it, thought about it, it was clear, he had to go to this little western town himself. He had to learn what was happening and meet *the Milk Man*. Compared to all this, Gambizzi's offer of high position and rewards with the *Gee Whiz Corp* didn't quite measure up. Adi wanted depth. The only way to compete with the rapid economic developments in China and the European Union was to be on the ground floor with siphon action, just like the sort that these hacker-desperadoes seemed to be pulling off domestically, same thing only on a larger scale. Zarabrezi saw it, felt it, he could help them pull it off. Mascara and *the Milk Man* felt deep, his deep. He had to go. He had to do the brain work on his own. But he would need an assistant for the physical stuff. He instantly thought of the little man with the boiled peanuts and smiled.

Little Mary was sound asleep, head in his lap. The train rippled along its xylophonic and percussive path as Sig stroked her head and thought about how things were turning out. Frequently he had told himself he would never be able to leave the game. He was so far into it, no one would let him. The energy which protected him was the energy of being known and feared as the ceaseless hunter, as the merciless stalker. Once he stopped and became the hunted, his fortunes and his reputation would wither. But if his love of art had taught him anything, it was that all things could be seen anew, be rediscovered ad infinitum, be cleaned and resuited, be given new background music and a bracing sarcastic air, be allowed to feather into a background for other endeavors, become a question rather than an answer. After all *the Monk* was the *piece de resistance*. Just as in the time of the Medici, as in the glow of Botticelli's gaze, just as with the original Sigismundo Maltesta, whosoever hired *the Monk* won the battle, oft times avoiding same, oft times by decorative default.

It wasn't that he was tired of the work. He actually still thrilled at inserting himself in complex ways. Inserting himself right into the midst of the awful manipulations and connivings of the powerful, correcting the balance and allowing people to suspect him as the culprit, the assassin, the thief, the cannibal, the agency of fear. Just as with this Mary caper. It had worked well. No, he wasn't tired of the work. He wanted an expanding and contracting change, he could feel the desire for a fulfillment in more storied ways, and more domestic fashion. It was confusing to think about and yet just as certain as his feeling, his longing.

He conjured an intoxicating image of Vicky and felt a protective pang towards the young man, Enno. The boy was like an organic memory stick for him. Though it was a while back and needed updating, he had never in his long active life ever shared so much personal information with one individual. It wasn't that Duden could get him in trouble, He wasn't worried about that. It was that Enno felt like his own personal computer file backup. It was as if Duden was Sig's personal hideakey. Should things get out of hand, the boy would.... the boy would.... the boy would what?

He was accustomed to dealing with espionage, wars, civil unrest, burglaries, kidnappings, feigned assassinations, street fights, and the intrigue as chess match with three opponents (he being one), but this mess in Mascara had a complicated, haphazard flavor to it which threatened to go towards genuine anarchy. He smiled realizing he had contributed in no small measure. By now Luigi's chumming of the media and internet would doubtless, even at this moment, have scores of press snoops racing to the no longer sleepy tourist town. And Brice Liner? He hoped the police had him in custody. He remembered the funny, frumpy man in the hospital parking lot. He immediately recognized him as detective, as cop. This man's posture, even as evening silhouette, reeked of comic persistence. If Liner was not under arrest, this detective would surely have him in his sights.

Then there was *Giggleswick* and the *Aisle of Dogs*. Titus Ibid. He trusted his instincts and this man was most certainly at the core. It all might be a confusing mess but there was no mistaking the presence of more than one architect of intrigue. He began to think that this situation might be a convergence of several elements some as yet unsuspected. Sig had some serious digging to do just as soon as he got back. He stroked Mary's napping head. Hopefully he could count on the half-breed girl and Vicky to watch Mary while he worked. He would have liked to helped them with this small but important chore.

Conzuela had deciphered Sig's message. It only helped a little. She was frightened and angered that he had given her operatives the slip. She understood his point, that no one, not even her, could know where he and Mary were. If they did, then others would follow the trail and it would become impossible to hide and protect. He had said he would keep in touch, and so long as she did not know where to look she should consider Mary safe.

She had followed his instructions and made the stoic, if angry, call to the White House number. Just as he had said, the secretary for Mr. Rover had insisted that she must be terribly confused. No one at the White House would ever be connected with the abduction of her daughter.

But Conzuela Merced was far from satisfied. She called for a meeting with two distant cousins who worked as accountants for Mexican Drug Kingpins. She had use of *El Perro Feo*, the secret enforcement arm of the drug cartel.

The State police had agreed with English and moved the Ogdensburgs to another suite of rooms on the fifth floor of the hospital. In the front room of that suite three plain clothes detectives setup strategy for the return of Liner. Meanwhile, Dr. Sam Fistula wobbled out of the hospital to his Honda Accord, more convinced than ever that great, extraterrestrial evil was descending on them all.

Charleton Ibid, a.k.a. Dan Cooper, a.k.a. D. B. Cooper, relayed dozens of messages to the cockpit of the 727 that November day of 1971. He demanded $200,000 in used $20 bills and four parachutes. He showed the stewardesses his black brief case, which contained a couple of red cylinders, wires and a battery. He said this was his bomb. The plane stopped at Seattle/Tacoma Airport in Washington where the passengers and flight crew were allowed to de-plane but not before Charleton offered a $200 tip to the helpful stewardess. She declined. But she did do him one last favor and explained how to lower the rear stairs of the tail of the 727, the only jetliner equipped with that feature. Before she left, she pulled the curtain shut between first class and coach. When the plane took off, he informed the pilot he wanted to fly to Mexico, landing gear and flaps down, at an altitude of 10,000 feet. Pilot said that would be difficult. They made plans together to stop in Reno for refueling and took off.

Chapter Twenty five

Coquille

"The speeds are human." - Paul Newman

Titus drove back home to the Fork Holding. His tall mind buzzed within a four dimensional maze of preparations and analysis. Early on, in the first trenches of his warfare with corporations, he had learned that his most dangerous adversary would always be himself. Visualization was his conceptual tool, the one to help him stay attentive. He trained himself, even when potentially lost in reverie or abstract thought, to precede, attend, and follow every physical action, no matter how small, with visual snapshots of where he was, what he had just done, what he had thought about doing, what was missing from his view, what he must do when he returned. He visualized himself before, during and after every moment. When things had gone wrong, it was most likely because he had let his attentiveness slide. As a curious and important paradox, he had learned over time that these manic exercises served to actually calm him; they worked to separate his consciousness into three levels or layers. There was this hyper-attentive aspect sandwiched betwixt an upper level of tortoise-like, low-voltage calm and the lower level of intellectual and poetic administration. He would never fully leave any one dimension of his engaged, cognitive, reflective self. The closest he had come to a deadening or separation had been his short, intense ober-season with Charmaine Lebow. And not because in her he had found a parallel intellect or a kindred soul. Instead he was attracted and consumed by her because she was the exact and exacting opposite of him. Literally smart without being intelligent, manipulative while compliant but without a hint of premeditation, unaware of her surroundings, incapable of reflection, devoid of charity, a dull, uninteresting mystery to herself. Titus had fallen in love with someone who, in her being, explained him to himself. Titus had fallen in love with someone who would never be able to love him back. Titus had fallen in love with the intoxicating, indefinable hollow of a promising emptiness.

As a young man at Berkeley, his mathematical brilliance had astounded everyone. He was able to see, in his head, several complicated, interlocking sheets of equations and how they might, in wild and exotic ways, tangentally affect each other. He juggled the math, changing the toss, changing the rhythm, grabbing two thoughts in one hand and tossing them before his internal sight while three pulsing, light-engorged, numerical labyrinths whizzed in close proximity, applying and then peeling light from the oncoming equations. In the fraction of a fraction he could see paradoxical opportunities for the numbers and patterns to impregnate and alter each other. While in these moments of exalted mental discovery and contrivance he was energized and fully inflated. When pressed to follow simple *'a'* to *'b'* progression he deflated and lost energy. He was unable to maintain any sustained interest in the linear. As a young man his enemies had been boredom and a self-defeating, blind samaratinism. Back then when his mind was fully engaged, he was on the front edge of euphoria, an emotional ride which became a controllable, dialable narcotic.

Back in the beginning, when he had first chosen to taunt, corrode, siphon from and destabilize corporations, no warrior or technician or diplomat was ever sent out from board rooms to challenge him. It was shamefully easy to infiltrate and extricate. And, as computers and software and the internet grew more invitingly complex and automatic, the mechanical elements of his work became a walk in the park. Where the danger and hazards, where the challenges and fireplay came into the room, that was all later with his taunts, warnings, assignations, acrobatics, all that signature stuff that, for him, became so critical to the psychological warfare aspect. It wasn't enough, not hardly enough, to filter out the funds. THEY had to know it was being done, and by something shadowy and ubiquitous. And they had to know that these reappropriated funds were going to refill the reservoirs of essential humanity that these very same corporations had drained. They had to be fearful and know that an unknowable energy would adjust for their excesses.

All these thoughts drummed through his head as Titus made the drive back to Preacher's Hollow and the Fork Holding. He took the usual precautions and added a few new ones, certain that with all the different surveillance players at hand someone would be trying to follow him. But no one tried.

Before dropping down the last bit of grade, he stopped and walked to an overlook with his binoculars. From here he might be able to see if anyone was on the ring or rimrock watching Jeff's farm. He was once again reminded of how curiously attractive the geographic setting was. It was his home, he loved it. From above it looked like a gentle crater with one side flattened. And in the center of the crater a low wide hill upon which sat most of the Fork buildings nestled in what is for the high desert an oasis of luxuriant trees, cottonwoods, willows, poplars, pines, junipers and more. The hardwood trees at this time of the year are silvery soft green with only the hint of the coming spring. The dark green pines and junipers glistened with the trace remains, peaking out from under boughs, of the slow thawing, past-freezing, rain. The low swale which surrounded the center hill rise, looked much like a question mark in the earth, starting at its highest end in a spot which held the farm spring. Here native bunch grass came green first. Had there been surface water it would have followed the wide curve of the swale and into the straight leg before leaving the crater at the open wall.

Looking through the binoculars, Titus saw no signs of anyone around the upper ring of the hollow. He was reminded again of the strategic nature of this geography. He noted, as he had in the past, how easy it would be to wreck havoc on any unwanted intruders from spots along the rimrock ravine. But it would have to be people familiar with the area, some of the rock was unstable and would come down mighty easy. Moving his gaze down he was surprised to see steam rising from a spot above and near the spring. Maybe Jefferson had done some burning of debris. He'd have to check it out.

When Titus finally pulled in to the farmstead, Jefferson met him.

"I don't see the boy's pickup. Has he been back from Sloop's yet today?"

"We haven't seen or heard from him. Had some tremors last night, thought maybe he had unexpected problems up there. Did they feel the earthquake in town?"

"Heard about it. Worried about the boy. Hope he didn't get it in his head to go to the hospital. All sorts of things are happening, too many snoops and hardheads in town. Everything okay here?" Titus remembered the steam and looked off in that direction noticing the redbone hounds circling and sniffing. "From above I thought I saw steam or smoke from up by the spring."

"We've got a spot of warm water seeping out up there. Very strange. What do you think about me and the boys going over to Sloop's to check on Duden? Can you hang out here til we get back? Brenda's inside cooking, she'd love to get an update from you."

"Yes, good idea. You go ahead. But, Jeff, be very careful. Scope out the place before you plunge in. People are paying too much attention to Sloop. Or maybe they're watching the boy.

Anyway, be very careful."

Titus went into the barn and across the floor to the door of his barn apartment. Just outside on the wall hung a phone which rang as he entered. Across from the ringing phone, Glass, Sloop's Percheron stallion, looked over the stall door. Normally self-possessed, the stallion looked to Ibid to be in a state of controlled panic.

Shirley guided her pickup truck to the gas pump in town. A funny little man with deep folds in his facial muscles smiled and asked her in a squeaky southern drawl if he could help.

She smiled back, not recognizing him, and said, "Fill it with regular please."

Lint looked into the cab of the truck and saw two other people. In the middle sat a creature who looked like a cross between Helen of Troy and a female pugilist. Her poise was disarming. She looked straight ahead. On the far side sat a young man, arms crossed, staring straight ahead and suggesting by his look that he was lost in thought. Lint smiled again thinking he was witnessing the quiet stage of a lover's spat. Watching people was one of his great pleasures. He overheard the driver ask the blonde, "What do you want to do? Go with us to the hospital or stay here?" Lint slowed the gasoline release, he had a fresh suspicion that there was important information available in this truck, and he wanted to catch it. It was then that he found Resumé's inquiring eyes watching him. The old stock dog threw off the contract killer for just a second.

"I'm going with you. You'll need me to keep the two of you apart. What is it with you, you don't even know each other and you're shooting arrows back and forth." She looked from one to the other. Enno fidgeted and felt the surprise of his sideways pocketknife biting into his thigh. He opened the door and stepped out to retrieve the knife out of his jean's pocket. Vicky had to smile, less than an hour ago she was worried that Shirley and Enno had some sort of animal attraction for each other. Then she frowned, remembering the business with Jimmy and the startling possibility that she and Enno were siblings. While this was going through Vicky's head, Shirley's mouth dropped open as if to say 'what is he doing, leaving? The dumb ass coward. He's such a creep, what does Vicky see in him. And there is no family resemblance between the two of them. All of this is greasy, a pile, a mess of nonsense.' Her disgust projected out from her face.

"Shirley, look at you! What is going on?"

"I don't know. Let's just say I trust my instincts and there's a big stink here."

Enno ignored them both and dug for his knife. Right at that moment Nettie's Oldsmobile pulled up along side. Enno felt sandwiched between two bits of demanding ugliness. Then Sam Riven popped his head up from the passenger side.

"Kid, we've been looking all over for you. Hop in we need to talk."

Without answering Sam, Enno got back in Shirley's pickup and closed the door. Ignoring Sam and Nettie, Shirley was paying Lint for the gas and Lint was paying real close attention to everything. At the opposite pump a van pulled up and at the back window Resumé caught sight of a vision of loveliness. A brindle Great Dane female with Julia Robert's lips, Audrey Hepburn's neck and the eyes of Johnny Mathis. He felt himself yelp even before the sound came out. Luigi stepped out of the van to stretch. He was wearing his Monk-in-disguise disguise. He only stopped for information and to test his get-up, remembering the sparks in Lint's eyes the last time around. Estelle let him know that she wanted out, so he opened the rear door. When she languidly poured herself from the vehicle, Resumé's eyes glazed. He had never seen anything so lovely. His remotest previous live's memories, all the way back to Cleopatra's twin Salukis, could not measure up to this moment.

So there they stood, side by side, a man with an uncanny likeness to Sig madeup to look like he was trying to disguise that likeness and a magnificent, over-large, fawn Great Dane female pencilled by eyeliner to look like a brindle. Lint looked at them and did a soft double take. Shirley looked at them and remembered Sig's warning, "you may see someone who looks like me but it won't be me." Vicky looked at Luigi amused. Enno looked at Sig's double and almost said something but stopped himself when Luigi returned his gaze without so much as a hint of recognition. Resumé's tongue loosely slapped his front knees and he worked at trying to regain his composure. Happy to be distracted from Enno's afront, Nettie looked at the Great Dane and thought 'how lovely'. And Sam screwed his eyes up knowing there was something wrong here. He said, "Honey, drive on, right now, drive on." The Oldsmobile drove off. Luigi spoke,

"Hey, could you tell me where I could buy a big set of nail clippers in this town? My dog is in desperate need of a pedicure."

"Two blocks west, you'll find a pharmacy on the left," answered Lint.

Hearing Luigi's voice, Shirley, Vicky and Enno felt released from their different anxieties. This was definitely not Sig's voice. Then Resumé saw it. She, that tawny beauty, looked at him. Right at him.

"Amy, let's go." As part of her many disguises Luigi also changed the Great Dane's name from Estelle to Amy. She turned her head slowly and looked at him with the complete disdain of a conceited female, then she walked slowly over to Shirley's pickup truck box. First she sniffed the tire, then the side of the truck and finally raised her high head only slightly to come within inches of a trembling Resumé. The old dog, who had earlier been secretly chewing gum, gulped and swallowed the wad. 'My Gawd but she was beautiful,' he thought. Estell (Amy) raised her fulsome upper lip and hissed a teeth-bared growl at him which would have destroyed most unprepared mammals. But Resumé mistook it for a smile and grinned back, slipping off the wheel-well perch onto his chin. The spill, slamming his chin against the truck sidewall, nearly caused him to bite off his own tongue. Estelle turned, unimpressed, and slowly got back in the van.

While this high drama unfolded, Lint watched the Oldsmobile leave and made a mental note of the license plate. He had taken in all of Sam's actions and knew something was thickening. He also had figured out, quickly, that the man with the dog was a fool, possibly by accident in the middle of a deadly game. Shirley he recognized from the Chinese Food Deli. Lint Fumes knew that Sam, Enno and the old stock dog were the ones he needed to pay close attention to.

Shirley, while going through her wallet to pay for the gas, had come across the slip of paper with Titus' phone number and stiffened as she remembered where she had seen the little gas station attendant before. She should have heeded Sig's warning about Fumes, but she didn't want to wait any longer to follow the lead on her mother, so she pulled her truck up to the little station market and got out to use the pay phone.

Luigi and Estelle drove off. Enno was so wrapped up in his own discomfort that he didn't notice Resumé jumping out to follow the van. On the second ring a man answered Shirley's call.

"Are you the man from the market, the one who left me a note?"

"Yes," answered Titus.

"How is it that you know Charmaine Lebow?"

"You, you, you are her daughter." Titus marvelled at how nervous his normally calm voice felt.

"Who are you? Is she there with you now? Do you know where she is?" Shirley felt herself anger.

"You are, of course, the purest biological essence of your mother with none of her personality." He dared to think with excitement that hers might be something of his personality, he wished it were so. "Your mother would never have thought to help that poor man in the market."

Shirley, for the third time in one day felt her knees buckle.

Enno saw her start to drop and watched as she grabbed the phone to hold herself up. He leapt from the truck and raced to her side in the phone booth, gently encircling her waist to hold her up. She had a hand to her mouth, and the other holding the phone body. Her eyes were wide. The receiver dangled on the end of the cord. Enno could hear over the handset a voice asking "Hello?" Over and over again. He took the receiver and spoke into it. "She slipped, I think she's okay."

"Enno, Enno? Is that you?" asked a perplexed Titus phone voice.

"Yes..." Before Duden could finish Shirley snatched the receiver. "Give me that phone!"

"Mister, I don't know who you are or what is going on here. Answer this, do you know a woman named Helga Ogdensburg?"

"Yes."

"Do you know where she is right now?"

"I can't tell you."

"You don't have to. I know where she is and I'm going there right now." She slammed the phone on the receiver and started to push herself free of Enno's hold. Then she stopped and saw him for the first time. The smiles came simultaneously. One to the other and back again. No words. Just smiles. Slowly releasing her, Enno spoke first.

"I know that man, he's okay. He's Helga's friend."

Vicky looked on, from the truck, with renewed sadness.

Brenda noticed the unusual cast to Titus' face as he entered the house.

"Honey you look like you just saw a ghost."

"I heard one, Brenda, I heard one."

Back to November 1971 and the plane being hijacked. Forty minutes after takeoff from Sea Tac the stair signal light in the cockpit flashed on. When the jet landed in Reno, the stairs were down and two of the parachutes, the money, and Cooper were missing. Newspaper reports say that "Cooper dove into a freezing rainstorm at 10,000 feet, wearing only a business suit and loafers. The temperature was 7 below zero, not counting a wind chill factor estimated at minus 70 because of the plane's speed of 220 mph." Truth was that the airlines hid the real facts not wanting a rash of Cooper-like attempts if the public found out that he had actually been remarkably well prepared, with suitable gear and supplies and parachuted successfully minutes after takeoff. Suffering from a broken leg, he had commandeered a car and drove as far south as the Columbia River before falling ill to a fever. It was in a fever that he had hidden his stash, after scattering handfuls of bills around to convince people he might have died in the leap, and stuffing some in his clothes. A difficult three weeks of hiding, running and healing found him in Alaska. From there he sent money to his Brother, Boston Ibid, specifying it was to provide a college education for young Titus.

He survived his cancer for several years until, dying, he passed on the whereabouts of his 'buried treasure' to Ahchuck Intoit.

Chapter Twenty six

Grand Ronde

weaponsalve:
a salve which was supposed to cure the wound being
applied to the weapon that made it. (Johnson) The direction
"Bind the wound and grease the nail," is still common
when a wound has been given with a rusty nail. Sir
Kenelm Digy says the salve is sympathetic, and quotes
several instances to prove that "as the sword is treated, the
wound inflicted by it feels. Thus if the instrument is kept
wet, the wound will feel cool, if held to the fire, it will feel
hot." (Brewer)

"Stranded at the edge of the world, I don't know where to go."
Van Morrison

Those things in nature which, above all odds, break the
genetic mandate, buck the behavioral laws, go against the social
codebook, whether it be a woodpecker drilling and enjoying
watermelon, or a house cat riding dog-like in the back of a ranch
pickup truck, or a mean-spirited dyslexic simpleton elected

supreme democratic leader in a time of great crisis, or the healthy tree growing in an unaccommodating climate, or the person flying in the face of all convention to test basic inherent survival instincts in pursuit of a small crusty bit of spirituality, these things are all molecules in the ruling, blanket, mosaic law of the exceptional.

Brice Liner had received a phone call from the motel office informing him that his car had been delivered. It was fortunate that the delivery person did not hand off the keys in person. Liner was in no mental state to accept the temporary use of the little lavender Dodge Neon as the *firm* worked to locate the required black Mercedes. 'Harry the Tooth' Langostino called from his cell phone to say that he was just past Juntura. His Plymouth Navigator was cruising at 125 miles an hour. Liner told him to go straight to the hospital. Check on the Ogdensburg man. If he attempted to checkout, nab him and wait there. Brice was heading right away for Sloop's homestead. He would finish business there and head for the hospital.

Bo Coin had succeeded in rounding up three and a half dozen people to attend Joanna Mendlesohn Thurber's book signing. Good crowd for a cold, early-spring, week-night, small town, bookstore event. At one level he was excited because he felt certain this would make a favorable impression on 'the broad.' But then there was this new dimension. He actually felt like he was also making a positive contribution to the arts, to culture, to the future of good writing. It was a new sensation for him. And he liked it. He felt his shoulders square up and his eyes moisten just a little bit. He was too close to the arrangement to see that this foolishness, and his part in it, felt all the world like a week-old Twinkie laying on a plate adjacent to a pool of ketchup, with a shiny pile of farm-raised Trout eggs masking as Russian Caviar. And, if he did see it, all would escape notice. Such is the cultural and ethical insulation of *Fortress America.*

When Jefferson had arrived at Sloop's farm with his sons, it was quiet. He saw Enno's pickup but couldn't find the boy. The tracks at the front gate had indicated that something had happened there. Chores seemed to have been completed. Then he saw from three quarter of a mile away, the haze of light dust. A vehicle was approaching. Instinctively he backed his pickup into the equipment shed and turned to his little boys.

"Men, serious time. You are going to stay in the cab of this here truck, NO MATTER WHAT HAPPENS! Do that, until I come after you. Do you understand?" pause, "I don't hear you."

"Yes Daddy," they both said, "But where are you going?" asked Franklin.

"I don't know yet, I won't be far. Stay put! This is very important! You understand? Stay put, no matter what!" Jefferson had a foreboding and wished he had left the little men home.

Brice Liner was big and the Dodge Neon was a little car. He wore a sharkskin Armani suit with pastel blue silk shirt open at the throat and Luchesse loafers made of the belly hide of Grecian goats, chewed for a fortnight by retired Lebanese housewives, all of this beautifully augmented by gold chains and bracelet against the Caribbean skin tones interrupted only slightly by the pinkish earlobe tears. Liner looked all the world like a GQ vision of a bodyguard gone solo. The picture was tortured by the reality of the lavender- colored, tuna-can car.

Jeff watched, unseen, as the car drove deliberately, stupidly, up to the house and Liner stormed out pistol in hand. Kicking pots and chairs out of the way, he tried the door and when he found it locked, he shot it open. Jefferson turned to look at his pickup. The boys were peaking over the edge of the window. He motioned with a flat hand for them to get down, as he bent low and rushed towards the house. With the advantage of knowing the floor plan of the house and the lay of the yard, he was able to sneak up on the entry way with stones in hand, backing flat against the wall to wait for Liner to exit. He hurled one stone expertly and broke the car's windshield. Cursing and banging, the angry intruder came rushing out of the house.

Liner was a big man. Jefferson Fork was a man mountain. The minute Brice stepped out the door, Fork wrapped his two octave hand around the gun toting wrist. With the other massive, muscled piano-player's hand, he plucked the revolver free like it was a piece of lettuce. Liner flung round and knocked the pistol loose. It dropped into the liquid-rich compost bucket Helga kept on the porch. Liner hit Jefferson twice with deadly assurance. Any lesser man would have fallen, or at least stumbled, from the blows. The big black man swayed only slightly, as if he were a three hundred pound punching bag. Checking his swing Jefferson hit Brice Liner hard in the face causing him to fall backwards off the porch towards a rick of stacked firewood. Liner stumbled grabbing a chopping block. He found the double-bited axe and pulled it free. Facing Jefferson Fork he blurted,

"You are one dead bastard."

As the two little boys watched from the pickup cab, their daddy walked right into the swing of the axe.

Fred English, cow cop, with leads from the always competing county sheriff and state police (they wouldn't normally share information, one agency to the next, but somehow felt that the cow cop was neutral in the turf wars) had found the Lexus in the supermarket parking lot. It was instinct that drove him to cross the highway and inquire at the motel desk. There he learned of the lavender Neon delivery and the exodus of Liner. While in the motel office, thinking of calling for back-up, he looked outside and noticed a van-driving man in a goatee leaving the lot with a Great Dane riding shotgun. It was the same guy he had seen crossing the night-time parking lot of the hospital, it was *the Monk*. Purely on prioritizing instinct, English left on the run to follow the van. He didn't notice an exhausted old stock dog panting by the hedge row.

Resumé, the love-struck stock dog, had followed the van to
the motel only to be slighted again by Estelle, the nonchalant
canine temptress. Now he was more convinced than ever that she
was just playing hard to get. He would have to persist, but first a
little rest.

At the motel, Luigi had retrieved, from his satellite-rigged
laptop, an encrypted message from Sig. The message had read:

*"Orlando vacations as low as $59 with bonus coupons and an
opportunity to win a new KIA sedan with a full tank of gas. Your
relatives know about this offer so act now, before they beat you to the
deal!"*

Translated the message read;

*"Arrive Mascara tomorrow with small package. Require temp safe
house. Watch for El Perro Feo."*

Luigi was gone in search of Peggy Youngquist, the lady at
the park. She might be the one to provide the safehouse for the
little girl.

Tools were important to him. He saw them as extensions,
not only of his effectiveness but also of his personality. So Sloop
kept his axes razor sharp.

Brice had swung the axe hard, with a two fisted, two armed
force. Jefferson had stepped inside the swing, wrapping his big
hands all the way around Liner's throat. The axe had come loose
from the grip and continued its' path folding around Forks'
shoulder, free of Liner's hands, and cutting deep into Jefferson's
lower back at the waist, before falling to the ground.

Liner struggled to get free of Jefferson's hold, yanking at the
wrists and kicking at his groin. Jefferson looked down at him

cold, released one of his hands from the throat and took hold of the hit man's belt. He picked him up, by throat and belt, and slammed him into the side of the Neon without releasing his hold. He slammed him twice again until the body went limp. Dropping him across the hood of the car, he noticed the blood, his own blood. He closed his eyes and bent his head up as if praying. When he opened his eyes, looking sideways, he saw the terrified faces of his two little boys still sitting in the pickup truck. Pressing his hand hard against his bleeding side, he went to them. They were sobbing and shaking and confused in their relieved pride. He let them out of the truck and held them close. Franklin had a new swollen appreciation for his giant pop.

"Hey, little men, you did good! I'm so proud of you. Now I need you to help Daddy. No more crying now, that's right, we've got work to do. Franklin, you go into the shop there and find me some rope. Jackson, I need you to sit right here and protect this truck little man? Good boy."

In the house, Jeff had found a bed sheet and tore it lengthwise to make a tight tourniquet-belt around his middle hopefully to slow the bleeding. The wound had first gone cold and now was feeling hot. He fetched the axe and set it in the bucket of cold water. Immediately his side felt cool. (*Weaponsalve*, something Yummy had taught him. He used to tease her about it being just so much voodoo. Time had taught him, however, to never make light of her 'other worldly' knowledge.)

He deposited Liner folded up, in the Neon, but not before tying his feet and legs and retrieving the pistol from the compost bucket. He was so anxious to get the boys out of there that he didn't think to remove the keys from the lavender car.

It had been a national embarrassment. The reports were that the new post-modern white supremacist organization, Bald Mother America, at their press conference had announced total agreement with President Walter. The sound bite had read;

"Fully 99% of the time we find terrorists being non-whites out to kill and discredit whites. We agree with the President when he said recently, 'There's no time like the right timing for making us safe from those who would hurt us.'"

Assistants to aids at the White House had urged that the president distance himself from BMA. The response had been to promote the offending assistants to jobs at the EPA and issue an official statement.

"This president remains true to loyalty and his belief structure and refuses to regret that some would misinterpret him."

They, the White House, also urged that the national press release the full context of the president's original statement arguing that this alone would clear the air. The press released the full statement. I read,

"I was elected by the people to be forthwith and I am. There's no time like the right timing for making us safe from those who would hurt us when we aren't looking and want a free ride doing it."

The unusually spun-air of politics went all fuzzy.

In Jackson Hole, Wyoming, in a secure bunker apartment below his casino, the Vice President, Myron Cooleritch, reread the president's statement and turned to his lap-dancing stenographer, "The man is an idiot. We wanted ineffective and we got egomania without a shred of intelligence. We can send him on vacation and keep him out of cabinet meetings and incident briefings but we can't seem to keep him away from the press. What's he got coming up?"

His stenographer adjusted her bra strap and checked her notes, "Camp David. He makes an appearance at the middle east energy talks."

"Did you send off my directives to Rover?"

"Yes sir."

"Send another. I want them to rig Walter with that micro-phone we used during the debates. Feed him his words, damn it. Don't let him adlib again."

"Sir, Rover is asking what to tell the press. They want to know why you aren't at the energy talks?"

"Same response. National security dictates that both the VP and Prez not be in attendance at the same public event. Now, come here. Where were we?"

"Who will be at the meeting with the president?" asked Conzuela Merced.

"Besides the CEOs of three major oil companies, representa-tives of Egypt, Syria, Libya, Yemen, Israel, the Palestinians, and the governor of Texas," answered the suited man.

She turned to the two who looked like golf pros. "Call the White House contact and advise that no one messes in the affairs of Mexico or my family. Remind them that 20% of their resident population is Hispanic and loyal to Mexico. Tell them details of their act of terrorism will be released to the Associated Press, Reuters and Spanish speaking media immediately. Advise that we are not to be held responsible for the impassioned actions of our people. Once you are sure that the message has been received and we have corroboration that the president is at Camp David, send in the team. I want the president, unharmed, and in our custody as soon as possible."

"Senora, kidnapping the president of the United States will be seen as an act of war."

She looked at her aid with cold intent, refusing to say a word.

The maid entered the room. "Senora, your husband wishes to speak with you."

"Not now Rita."

By the time Jefferson Fork made it back to his place he was

feeling dizzy. He knew it was from loss of blood. Brenda met the truck and waded through a flurry of excited little boy blurts to lay her hands on her husband. Jefferson smiled then looked down to his side, directing her gaze. She saw the blood, pulled the tourniquet sheet back and quickly, quietly, inspected the wound. Helping him, she made it to the house, understanding that the boys must be part of the reason that Jeff wasn't telling her anything.

"Titus?" he asked.

"He got a call, honey. Gathered up a bunch of gear and left. Said something about the hospital. Said he found Duden and that you were not to follow." She gently wiped his sweaty brow with the flat of her hand. Inside the house she laid him on the big leather sofa and ran to the back porch. There, in the broom closet, she swept her hand around in corners, sweeping up a wad of spider webs. Back in the house, with her free hand she wet a wash cloth. Then she wiped the wound gently, watching as her husband seemed to be slipping off to sleep. Next she expertly applied the spider web globs to wherever fresh blood appeared. The bleeding, miraculously, came to a halt.

"Daddy gunno be okay?" asked a sobbing Franklin.

"Yes, sweetie. He gonna be fine. You boys done good. Now, you stay here and watch him while I go make a call."

Liner was dizzy. He hurt all over. And the ropes were tied so expertly that he couldn't get them undone. But out of purest rage he managed to sit upright and start the little car. The windshield was shattered, he pushed a hole in the sticky fragmented glass which he could see through. With ankles and wrists together in pairs, he somehow managed to drive off the farm. At the motel he'd be able to get in touch with Langostino. This was far from over and he intended to even the score many times.

The assault on Camp David came at dinner time. The Mexican operatives, eleven of them, had been surprised to find very little security in place, no electronics, two suited G men, no marines. What they had worried would be an impossible task turned, in the beginning, to their favor. It was as if no one placed much importance on protecting the president. What did surprise them was the strength of the individual bodyguards assigned to each of the visiting dignitaries, including the kick-boxing blond female who stood between them, the Texas governor, and the president. A fire fight ensued, while the Mexicans took out various middle Easterners, the Texas governor managed to place a cell call to the marines. Within minutes the president was kidnapped along with the remaining survivors of the middle-east energy conflab. The marines mobilized quickly and cordoned off Camp David. A standoff was stood. The White House was informed, which in turn informed the vice president, all without so much as a peep to the press. News had got out, however, through private cell phone SOSs to middle eastern governments.

The vice president double-checked the information. His understanding was that Mexico had telecommunicated some veiled threat and within minutes Spanish speaking goons, probably drug mobsters, had stormed Camp David, killed the Jewish diplomat, the Palestinian minister of truth, the Libyan oil minister, and the Texas governor plus a mess of body guards. Kidnapped but alive was the blond, female, kick-boxing bodyguard of the Texas governor plus President Walter, and a handful of middle eastern dignitaries.

Myron, the vice president, was livid. It was time to act, turn the whole mess to advantage. The first thing he did was to place a contract on the head of white house *chief of trouble*, Charles Rover. He wanted him dead, immediately. Second, he ordered, via emergency hookup, special ops to coordinate the retreat of the marine guard with strategic bombing of Camp David. He never liked the place anyway, and this put the President, as martyr, to his highest and best use. As he next considered how to release this information to the press his answer came by diplomatic intrusion. The French president, Charles Perrier, was on the phone. It seemed that the Syrians and the Yemenese had contacted their European trading partners to report that their leaders and diplomats were being held hostage at Camp David. The French president was calling to warn the U.S. that Europe would not look lightly upon any harm to its allies.

Gawd, how Myron hated the meddling, superior French! That was it. There was the answer. He ordered 'special ops" to bomb Camp David and then he called in his stenographer.

"Honey, this is for official release to the press, all the usual channels:

At 6 PM EST, the U.S. suffered a terrorist attack, orchestrated by the government of France, obliterating Camp David and resulting in the loss, amongst others, of President Larry Walter..."

"Oh my Gawd!" Blurted the stenographer!

"Steady girl ...

'Presidential heir apparent Myron Cooleritch, at 9 PM EST, declared war on the renegade nation of France. Cooleritch stated, "No godless nation of snail-eating, fashion designers will deter us, Victory will be ours!"

Do you think that part about 'snail-eaters' was a bit strong? No, leave it in, send it that way."

On the train near Klamath Falls, Sig got word through agency channels of the siege at Camp David. (The bombing hadn't occurred yet.) He instantly thought of Conzuela Merced but ruled it out. She certainly wouldn't be that stupid. He was busy teaching little Mary how to play a card game called Fish. She was cleaning his clock and giggling all the while. Soon she would nap and he would send a cautionary note to Mexico, then check with Luigi.

Enno sat at the window with his arm behind Vicky, along the back of the seat. Shirley drove. He was tilted slightly with part of his back against the door. He felt caramelized. Never had he ever felt himself smile so hard. Oh, maybe, perhaps maybe driving Sloop's horses. But in that instance, he had the urgency of the dynamic at hand to keep him in check, to hold him together. The way she had returned his smile, it was mirror-like. He wanted to talk to Shirley, look at her, ask her questions. He didn't feel anything else in his space, except for middle-sitting Vicky as a physical obstruction. He had forgotten about the dog and he had forgotten why he was going to the hospital.

Vicky sat bolt upright, eyes welling with tears, wishing she could be anywhere else. Shirley leaned into the steering wheel, her smile more hum than muscle. She forced herself to talk.

"These people we're going to see? Why are they in the hospital?"

It was a gentle slap to his silly state of mind. He came partially awake and recounted a brief outline of events. Vicky remembered things.

"Don't forget that Jimmy is in that hospital as well." She felt a warmth towards the little alcoholic which left her in a wheeze when she recalled the tin suitcase altar in the cardboard shack. She dropped her head to her hands. Enno thought, selfishly and for a half a second, about touching Shirley's shoulder with his finger tips, but didn't.

Shirley leaned forward and laid her hand on Vicky's knee. "You okay?"

Vicky, to deflect the moment, reached forward and turned on the radio.

They all stiffened as they heard the report of the body found brutally murdered and stuffed in a garbage dumpster. The report said that federal officials were treating it as terrorist related. The name of the individual was given as William Blue Chevie.

"Terrorist related? Wasn't he a friend of yours?" asked Vicky.

Shirley was wishing Sig was back as she wiped the flat of her hands back and forth across the old steering wheel.

Early in the nineteenth century, Adolf Sax invented an instrument which threatened to replace many old standby horns. By 1850 instrument manufacturers coagulated together in a nervous cabal which hired a hit man to attempt Adolf's assassination. Meanwhile, religious leaders made a case against the Saxophone, claiming it to be an instrument of the devil.

Chapter Twenty seven

McKenzie

"The most exciting phrase to hear in science, the one that heralds new discoveries, is not "Eureka!" (I've found it!) but "that's funny..."   - Isaac Asimov

"Whenever you come into a person's life come in instantaneously and when you must go - go even more quickly." - Lord Dilling

Music would wrap us in the cloth of longing, the cloth of possibilities, the shirt of better times. Paintings can permeate the loose fit masonry of our sensibilities and stop us short of waste. We need superb paintings and magnificent music because the written word so seldom finishes the job.

At the editorial offices of the flamboyant, national network, television news organization, CEO Simpson Burdoch, was holding court.

"So let's see the short list."

- *Fast breaking story about a possible terrorist attack on Camp David.*
- *Seven civil wars in Africa with misery compounded by Aids epidemic and starvation.*
- *U.N. report links pharmaceutical multinational with mercenary contractor in Africa.*
- *Volcano in Oregon.*
- *Terrorist bombing in Jackson Hole, Wyoming.*
- *Gulf war going bad.*
- *High stakes kidnapping in Mexico.*
- *Earthquakes in Oregon.*
- *Corporate finance scandals.*
- *Senate to consider tax cut and pay raise.*
- *Presidential commission recommends consolidation of Education Department with Agriculture, Environmental Protection and Commerce. To be called Domestic Department.*
- *Conservative talk show host fails drug test for fourth time.*

"Lead with Volcano, don't touch the cabinet stuff or the corporate finance stuff. Send people to Camp David, Oregon, Wyoming, and Mexico," said Simpson Burdoch.

"Where are we going to get the reporters? We're over extended. There are only so many people in the journalist pool," someone said.

"Pull them out of Africa. No one cares."

It would be an hour later that the first missiles hit Camp David and Ripley's Advertising department would go into hyperdrive with new prime time rates. Within two days, in Houston, Los Angeles, Miami and Fresno, Hispanics were demonstrating against the 'kidnappers' at the White House.

Marvin's bullet wound allowed him to be excused from the process so Carl did the mixing. Juniper pollen, legume inoculants with dry Kool-aid powder and fine grains of iron pyrite spooned into envelopes also loaded with rubber-band powered spinners set to whip the stuff out when the flap was opened. These were to be mailed to every Gee Whiz laboratory and headquarters with a warning included. The warning would read:

"If you touched or inhaled any of the contents of this envelope you have minutes to get to a doctor, medicine man or priest. You are not our enemy, your corporation is. Stop with suicide genetics or we return again and again." Signed *Glass Pirate.*

They knew the envelopes would attract suspicion. It didn't matter whether hazmat authorities opened the envelopes or some secretary did. The mix was harmless but the emotional effect was certain.

"Hey, Unc. Did ya ever think about it? We could get in a lot of trouble if we got caught doing this." Carl was unsure about Marvin taking the lead with his plan. He was certain the old Indian would be making the others mad.

"So? Our people get in trouble walking down the street. So what's new?" He was reading to himself a directive he had forged to appear as though it came from the Glass Pirate.

Plan to sabotage genetic engineering: Badger dung mixed with ground Nettles needs to be introduced into laboratories as host for time-release hydrochloric acid. Perhaps introduce into squirt bottles of soap?

Marvin was excited about this extra dimension. Crippling them at the bank was one thing, but he had always argued that the actual evil workings of the corporations needed to be sabotaged. Get them in their laboratories, that's where it had to happen.

Roger the writer needed space. So he went to the counter at the Gun Club Cafe and ordered something to eat. Peggy Youngquist served him. She was midway in her shift. Roger didn't notice Peggy. And Peggy did not notice Roger. To him she was insignificant. To her he was another lout expecting to be waited on.

Roger the writer and his wife had argued. He felt he had something to offer the world and she laughed at him saying he was lazy. He couldn't seem to get through to her that his mind contained great riches. He played with his coffee and imagined how his world would be different once he finished his novel. So many people would want a piece of him that he would have to go into hiding. Even his wife would want a piece of him. A photo of him right at that moment would have captured a shallow, self-absorbed smile.

Luigi parked the van outside of the Cafe and 'asked' Estell to wait inside the vehicle. He poked his head in the door and immediately saw Peggy pouring Roger's coffee.

"Hi. Remember me?" He asked.

Peggy looked up and squinted her eyes.

"In the park, big dog. It's Lou."

"Oh." She covered her mouth and blushed. "I didn't recognize you. You didn't have that beard yesterday."

'Oops. Stupid move,' he thought as his hand went to his chin. He forgot his disguise. "I'll tell you about this later. Right now I have something important to talk to you about. Can you take a break?"

"I like it." She had her slight thin fingers at her chin as if imagining hairs there as well. "Your beard I mean. Ah, no, ahm I can't leave right now, I'm the only one here until, let's see, until Rachel gets here, in about fifteen minutes. Then I could maybe take a couple of minutes." She was beaming, her whole body alive with smiles and blush.

"Good." He smiled broadly, responding to her infectious

pleasure. He planted himself on the stool next to Roger the writer.

Roger saw the whole thing. Some obvious romantic sashay. Rather common. Didn't work. Wouldn't play out in his novel. Too sweet. He wanted to somehow wipe the smile off the little waitress' ordinary face. It was too much, too much sugar, too obvious. As for the man, different story. He couldn't remember the last time he had seen a more attractive man. He found himself hoping they could talk.

Lou kept turning around to look at the van parked outside.

Peggy returned to Luigi's 24 inches of counter space, standing back just out of reach with her head tipped down slightly, the obvious pleasure replaced by a look of discomfort and confusion. "Rachel's come in early. Do you want to talk now?"

"Great. Let's go outside. My van's out there. You can say hello to Estelle and we can sit inside for a minute."

As they walked out the door Roger felt himself pulled, he wanted to say 'Don't go. I don't know your name.' He felt diminished. Craning his neck to watch them as they entered the van, he stuck his finger in his coffee and then licked it off.

In the van, in the space of less than five minutes, Peggy Youngquist's life catapulted in an unexpected direction. Luigi explained that he wanted to hire her to watch after a little Hispanic girl. It might be for a couple of days, it might be for a couple of weeks, or who knows, maybe for more than that.

"I, I, I can't do that. I have to work."

"Honey. It's time you took a break and had a vacation. How long has it been since you haven't had to work? Here's the deal. I'll pay you $1,500 a week to watch little Mary. If it ends up being only two days you keep the $1,500. If it goes to 8 or 9 days you get two weeks worth. That, plus your son will have someone to play with. And I will be in regular touch with you."

"But, what if its longer than that?"

"However long it takes, you get $1,500 a week." He watched her face closely. "I can have the first installment to you in cash today, what do you say?"

"Oh, I don't know." She was confused. First of all, she wanted to do anything it took to keep the new attention and favor of this man. That maddened her because she thought she had come clean, had freed herself of any dependency on men. Secondly, she was confused about the money. She had heard him but she hadn't. Fifteen hundred a month was good but as a temporary thing not good enough to have her maybe lose her job.

"You know Peggy, that's $6,000 a month if it should come to that."

Her mouth fell open. "6,000? ... I'll do it." They talked about particulars and setup a time to meet. Peggy went back in the restaurant with the look of someone who just won the lottery. Roger was jealous. She got her man and obviously something more. It wasn't fair. Why did the prizes always go to the unworthy?

As Luigi and Estelle drove off, Fred English, cow cop, made a couple of notations before he pulled out to follow. The reflection off the Cafe picture window had not allowed him a view of what had happened inside, but he had a clear view of the unknown proposal being made to the lady in the Van. As Fred had watched them, Estelle had watched him.

Crisp, clear, and warming atop the stabilizing cold. It was a beautiful day and the Juniper trees knew their place in this high desert world of separate promise and spacial definition. Early spring rabbits, chipmunks and squirrels positioned themselves on road edge, prepared through prayer to make their daring run just before a motor vehicle would speed by. The pastel colored car that approached careened in drunken fashion. The driver's hands were bound at the wrists, as were his feet at the ankles. He fidgeted trying to work loose the ropes as he drove the car. Every jerk had the car veer one way or the other. The little animals were hard pressed to second guess the trajectory. The game was not as fun, and a whole lot deadlier, than it usually was.

Brice Liner was accustomed to paved city streets and free-ways. Driving this gravel and dirt goat trail, with pot holes and washboards, only served to amplify his anger and frustration. Finally he made it to the pavement, not a squirrel or rabbit squashed, and stepped hard on the accelerator with one of his two bound feet. Within minutes he was at the motel parking lot. Forgetting his physical limitations he attempted to exit the car as he always had, only to trip and fall on the pavement.

The attendant in the motel office watched the large round, eave-mounted, mirror which canvassed the parking lot. He saw the man in the torn suit struggle to get to his feet. Then he hopped, legs tied together, towards the rooms. His hands were tied as well. It was the man the police officer had described. The attendant dialed the number on the card.

When Fred English got the call, he quickly changed course, back to the motel.

The call came through. "You made the worst mistake of your life. Your daughter is dead. There is no place for you and your operatives to hide." Conzuela fainted.

Sam intuitively understood that the mess of opposing players swarming around Mascara gave him a great opportunity to 'redirect' traffic. He didn't know if they were all after the same thing or not but it seemed highly unlikely. All he had to do was influence them, suggest that they keep an eye out for the other guy. He had spent the day gathering information about who was staying where. This little town had a bunch of bed and breakfast setups, most of which did not feature phone messaging. So he stuck with the motels and custom accommodations which did. He discovered that most of the bigger federal agencies, CIA, FBI, AFT, ITC, etc, had their boys camped down the road in Bend at the fancier chain lodgings. Nettie had done a bangup job gathering stuff from there. As for Bald Mother America, that was a little

more difficult as they were staying in private homes in one of the
golf-course-justified gated-communities. For BMA, he resorted to
enveloped messages under the wipers of their two trucks. The
developers, accountants, bankers, landscape architects, and
realtors assigned to the Yankone project were very easy to locate.
As were the media teams, the one for the volcano and the other
sneakier one, which seemed to be digging after some other dirt.
As for the hit men, he was a bit stymied. He knew of *the Monk*,
had even seen him with the dog, but he didn't know who the
others were. And he hadn't been able to discover where they
were staying. It might be time for a little heightened surveillance.

His plan was simplicity wrapped up in a confusing road
map. He would leave messages with each of them, pretending to
be informing on a competitor. He would aim them at each other.
He informed the CIA boys that the FBI had ridiculed them at a
local school presentation to fourth graders. He informed the FBI
that the CIA had been overheard in a bar saying that only 'third
gender activists' were encouraged to become FBI agents. He
intended to inform *the Monk* that there was a contract out on him
by Gambizzi and that two or more operatives were in town to
carry it out. He intended to leak to the Yankone operatives that
the governor was secretly working on building an experimental,
federal, prison hospital for drug offenders with Aids. The prison
would be up against the Yankone development. He left wake up
calls for the architects, landscape designers, developers, and out
of town realtors informing them that their competitors had
wiretapped their accommodations. He had left word with a
talkative coffee-jockey in a popular drive-up Espresso joint that a
federal prosecutor was considering a grand jury inquiry into the
land speculation practises of the Yankone development.

Several of these actions Nettie found offensive but she was
definitely in the game with Sam, she was hooked on the necessary, nasty, intrigue and carried by the screwball, righteous
adrenaline. For example; it was her idea to suggest, via the Bald
Mother America window leaflets, that the visiting lady novelist,
whose book Nettie had read parts of and found to be idiotic filth,

was actually an FBI operative in drag. She/he was to make an appearance at a local book signing where other agents would be in attendance to pick up operating instructions in their campaign to disrupt BMA. After Nettie vocalized the idea, she was instantly ashamed that she enjoyed thinking about it. She told Sam she was just joking but he grabbed up the plan and told her they'd have time on southern beaches to talk about guilt.

Meanwhile Sam was getting a doze of his own kind of worried. He was having a whale of a time with this fine lady. They clicked at all levels and she had growing control over his personality by dint of her own. His worries were basic. Number one, he didn't want her to get hurt and this was serious business. Number two, he was concerned that she was getting hooked on this localized sabotage stuff and he definitely had romantic plans that included her, plans that had them far away south in sunny climes and on sandy beaches. And, after decades of being the smart aleck, the lonely shark, here he was babbling about every little thing, past and present, to this magnificent sponge of a woman, one who took a genuine interest and managed to make him see and feel his past and future, including the parts which needed alteration, as exciting. She had worked her way inside. He had even come to agree with her plan to anonymously give the land at Snake Flats to the boy, Digger Duden. They had already begun to have the papers drawn up, careful to establish the value at only $10,000 so that there would be no gift tax. Ten dollars an acre. Nettie's consolation to Sam's concerns was to draw up a mortgage agreement which had Duden 'volunteering' to pay $500 a year to the orphanage where he grew up. They were just waiting for an opportunity to spring it on him. Sam was close to convincing her that it should be done at arm's length, no face to face discussion - no names, arguing that this way Duden would be less likely to refuse the gift.

Sloop and Helga's hospital room had a TV and a radio. They opted for the radio. Music was playing, an eclectic mix of jazz and blues out of New Orleans featuring a bright, engaging, authoritative man's voice offering intelligent insight and delight between each musical cut.

"That was Antoine "Fats' Domino, New Orleans native son giving us his trademark version of Blueberry Hill. See if you can guess which of the blues royalty sends up this new lyric. Let me give you a hint, her red hair notwithstanding she is one of the gentlest fine ladies of song I've ever had the pleasure to share a Shrimp Po'boy with."

The guitar licks were sweet and sour and driven. The lyrics, carried by her 'I will forgive you but I will never forget you' voice, swashed back and forth, laying out a feather bed for unspoken yearnings:

I'm done being down
I'm done being down
   working with
        my eyes wide open
   done being down
   done being down
working with
  my eyes wide open
      done down
      done down
  eyes wide
  eyes wide
done down
done down
  wide eyes
down done.

Sloop was sitting on Helga's bedside, tapping a light, accompanying beat with his finger tip on her bed sheet. Marvelling at how rapidly she was regaining locomotion, Sloop was nonetheless growing more anxious about what he knew was coming down the pike.

"John?" Helga slowly, weakly set her newly rediscovered hand around his hand. "I want to go home. I want to be in our house and with my birds."

He found himself pleased with her statement, pleased and relieved. " I want that too." He closed his eyes and thought about his heifers and the horses. "If we are to be safe, there are things I must finish. I am concerned about doing that without you, but I can't ask you to be by my side on this." He knew he was prepared to relinquish himself to her, finally. But he also knew he was incapable of dampering those aspects of his physicality which made of him his own best weapon.

"Maybe you can't ask me, but I can tell you, John, that I want to help you with what you have to finish. I don't want you going off alone." She had the strangest passing thought about her safety deposit box and the watch which would require soon, by force of ritual, winding. And as if a breeze passed within her, from one dark corner towards an open door, she felt a clarity of release.

"Do you think you might be strong enough to leave today? I want to go to the station office to set some things in motion."

"Can we stop at the bank also?" she asked squeezing his hand. Her strength came through this look he gave her, the look she had waited for, achingly, for her whole life. A new secret she would treasure and guard closely for she understood that sentiment is a possessing which rots when casually shared.

Do human rights only exist if they are enforceable? Isn't it possible that human rights have a poetic force which is diluted through enforcement? Was it Benjamin Franklin who said people who give up their liberties for security have neither? What is enforcement if not policed security? A love of the law does not create a law of love, it creates a hidey hole for the inherent cowardice of power.

Nancy had identified Bille's battered body at the Bend morgue. After the shock and initial terror, she had quickly slipped into her protective cocoon. She had to. She had long suspected he would get into trouble. He was always taunting people and always looking for the easy score. Strange, she felt none of the customary demand for knowledge and vengeance. She did not want to think that he got what he had coming. She didn't want to think at all. So she went to the upscale restaurant lounge downtown and poured two martinis into her blank face.

What now, she asked herself? Back to work? She sure as hell wasn't going home to her apartment for a good cry. No, she'd go to the hospital and see if anyone had heard of a need for an in-house nurse.

At the hospital she got word that a call had come out for someone to help with a couple who would be discharged soon from the Redmond hospital. She drove there in a daze, thinking of Billie's face and the warmth she had felt, knowing in the limited familial sense that she had belonged to him.

Brenda shook his hand, telling the young doctor good-bye and thank you at the door. Franklin was carried aloft by all aspects of the physician's manner and doings. Maybe he would be a doctor one day? Then he could save his daddy's life too.

Back in the bedroom, Brenda 'Yummy' Fork went directly to big Jeff and kissed him hard on the mouth.

"Careful, woman, I'm a hurt man."

"We gonna get you well real fast cause I got plans to hurt you all over agin."

"What d'jou hear fromTitus?" Jeff smiled at her, though it hurt his back to do it.

"Nuttin'. He gonna take care of hisself. He'd be real angry if you didn't do the same."

Titus sat in Brenda's little car, curbside and across the road from the hospital parking lot. He watched and waited. So much to think about. Soon he would see Charmaine's daughter again. Soon he should see some evidence of who all was tailing Sloop. He had left word for Sam to join him here, they needed to talk. Also, with any luck he and Sloop would get a chance to exchange notes. His most disturbing news had been the bit from Carl. Marvin Seesaw had jumped the bounds. Something very unpleasant would have to be done right away. Chaos was entering their own ranks.

The black Lincoln Navigator, covered in road dust, rolled ominously passed Titus. The character who looked sideways and down at him from the passing death wagon reeked of enforcement gone to seed. It made Titus shudder. What he could not have known was how his own persona affected the road-weary Gambizzi thug. (Harry the Tooth shivered and flashed back to his frightened childhood.) Empty of any applicable reference, the image of Titus had the permeating, ethereal, disquiet of an angel of death. It was moments like these that Titus's essential character and purpose, that of the poet as immortal reluctant executioner, oozed out of his pores.

Chapter Twenty eight

Nehalem

*"The redder's lick - the stroke which one receives
in endeavoring to part combatants."*

Mapmaker's Coffee and Art had a radio which was dialed to
NPR. Luigi sat, sipping his flavored latte and listened simultaneously to the radio and to the conversation at the table behind
him. From the voices came:

"With the one exception being war powers, the U.S. long
ago ceased to be a super power." A man's voice.

"Oh, come on! How can you say that? We aren't hated,

globally, because we are weak..." another man's voice.

"No, we are hated for our arrogance, for our politics, for our alliances, for our tacit approval of horrible dictatorships, and for our culture."

"Whoa, now that's a boatload. So, say you're right, how does that make us less of a superpower?"

Radio in the background:

"Local news update, top story; police have identified the body found in the Mascara dumpster yesterday as 29 year old William Blue Chevie. They are asking that anyone who may have come into contact with the murdered man, over the last few weeks, contact the local police station. The FBI is taking over the investigation under the new terror task force directive. There is no official word on how the authorities link Mr. Chevie to suspected terrorist activity."

That "T" word caught Luigi's attention. He made careful notes about the news story to pass on to Sig. The broadcast continued.

"On the national level, Hand-held rocket launchers were found in Wyoming by investigators working on the attempted bombing of the convention center."

Behind him, the two men were still speaking loudly but Luigi only heard snippets. He kept thinking of Peggy; there was something about her that drew him in.

"Because the European bankers control the money. Look, right now, the U.S. consumes and coerces, that's all! The European banking community controls 70 or 80 percent of all international corporate and governmental borrowing. The U.S. manages to control only a percentage of its own consumer borrowing and even that's eroding." Pause.

"Well, the world still depends on us for product. We are the breadbasket to the world, and look at technology and cars and alternative energy."

"I'm afraid to have to be the one to tell you my friend, but you've been asleep for the last 15 years. We're no longer the bread basket to the world. Our government sold us out on that one, too. Today we import more food than we produce for ourselves. As for technology, we have a handful of overlarge companies struggling to produce high end software, and that's about it. All the rest has moved elsewhere. Cars, and tools, and appliances, and even building materials? Follow the string and you'll find we are no longer producers. We consume."

"Oh, come on, man! You're so full of it. Once again, you're blowing it all out of proportion."

"Exaggerating am I? Get this. In China today, the government and business are working together to build the largest paper manufacturing plant the world has ever known. When it's done, in two years it will be the size of Rhode Island! And the only people over here who will still be making paper will be the crafts people doing it one sheet at a time. Our whole commercial paper industry will disappear within two to three years."

"What about shipping? How will they be able to ship that paper over here what with the gas prices going up so high?"

"I'm guessing they won't. Not the raw paper anyway. My guess is that they are already building printing plants with a goal towards doing all the printing, and then shipping only the finished product over here. Anyway, they have scientists working helter skelter, over there, to develop small portable centrifuges that will produce nuclear-powered motors they can pop right in those big freighters they've got."

"So what does that leave us with?"

"College sports."

On the radio came an emergency bulletin which inserted itself, by dint of the urgency of the tone, as the only sound in the coffee shop.

"This just in: At 6 PM EST, the U.S. suffered a terrorist attack, orchestrated by the government of France, obliterating Camp David and resulting in the loss, amongst others, of President Larry Walter. Presi-

dential heir apparent Myron Cooleritch, at 9 PM EST, declared war on the renegade nation of France. Cooleritch stated, "No godless nation of snail-eating fashion designers will deter us, Victory will be ours!" "

"Oh geez! What's that? War number three or four?" blurted a coffee drinker.

"Now is the time to buy stock in California and Oregon wine companies!" Came the shop owner's announcement to the room.

Luigi thought it time to leave *Mapmaker's Coffee and Art.*

Sig had arrived in Mascara with little Mary. Lou and Estelle had met them unseen by the myriad snoops who were now, thanks to Sam and Nettie, too busy watching each other. Lou drove Sig past Peggy Youngquist's home to show him where the little girl would be cared for. While they drove, more workings of *the small town gone to seed* were observed. Lou explained to Sig about some of his observations, especially the three young people at the gas station and Lint Fumes. Sig informed Lou about Lint. Then Lou hands Sig a note he found under his van wiper blade. Note reads:

"Monk, three professionals race each wishing to be one with glory of stopping you forever. Signed Amy Beech's grand nieces."

"Amy Beech?" asks Lou out loud.

"Amazing composer, long deceased."

"Connections?" asked Lou.

"None." answers Sig, "unless you consider obscure humor a connection.

"What about the professionals?" asked Lou.

"I have identified two in town, but I am certain I am not their target, or at least I wasn't when I left." Sig looks at Lou inquiringly.

"Nope, we didn't change the mix, did we girl?" he asks

Estelle who's busy in the back seat letting Mary scratch her ears. Sig sees this in the mirror.

"Lou, do you think Estelle would agree to move in with Ms. Youngquist to act as a bodyguard for her, her son and Mary? Before Lou could answer Estelle's wet nose brushes Sig's ear and he has his answer.

"Thanks sweetheart, I'll make it up to you." offers Sig. Lou looks out the window smiling and thinking, whenever the three of them are together, he, she and Sig, Lou gets the distinct impression she has far less use for her 'master.'

"I'm leaving now. You know what to do, contact in the usual way, and I suggest you change your digs. And Lou, that does not mean moving in with the woman and girl. I need you circling and watching and not drawing flies. Got that?" and Sig steps out of the van and walks off. To his disappearing form, Luigi says in a squeaking falsetto voice.

"Holy undershirts Monkman! You know we're deep-breathing the stinking trails. As for skirts, a boy has to have something to yearn for if he can't have the man of his dreams."

Titus watches the hospital parking lot from his hidden corner and observes:

1. In the second corner, Liner's operatives hanging out in their black Lincoln Navigator;

2. A dark blue Chevy Caprice with two suited men parked in a far third corner and watching;

3. And what he takes as a local sheriff in a white Ford pickup truck in an opposing corner.

They all appear to be observing one another while pretending not to, like school boys watching the new girl on the swing.

Inside the hospital, Sloop is making preparations for he and Helga to 'checkout' ahead of schedule.

Just then, Nancy Simmons pulls up in her Honda Accord thinking she will talk to administration regarding the couple who will require a live-in nurse.

Inside, Jimmy Three Trees is working to force open the window of the janitor's closet adjacent to his room. He's feeling an urge to find his dogs.

Right behind Nancy's Accord comes Shirley's pickup with Vicky and Enno included. Enno sees Nancy who heads over their way to talk.

While all of this is taking place Adi Zarabrezi steps off a plane at the Redmond airport and secures his rented Porsche Cayenne and a map to Mascara. He places a cell phone call to Gambizzi operatives and learns of the activity at the Redmond Hospital.

Across the Atlantic, the French president, George Perrier, demands a special session of the UN security council to review the US declaration of war against France.

As part of a plan to secure the government, the acting president Myron Cooleritch, has four different video-tapped presentations made, each with a different backdrop, and each assuring the American public that the war effort is going well and that sacrifices will need to be made if freedom is to be protected.

Meanwhile contracts have been taken out on the lives of:
• France's George Perrier,
• Charlie Rover of the White House,
• the lady governor of Louisiana,
• Conzuela and Miguel Merced,
• the Commie president of Venezuela,
• Winston Brogue president of Gee Whiz Corp,
• the meddlesome mother of the VP's stenographer,
• the current editor of the New York Times,
•and Lewis Lapham of Harper's.

Fred English, realizing that Brice was heading for the hospital again, put in a call for back up and to alert the security detail stationed in the clinic parking lot. He took a long slow drive around the hospital block and noticed a man, Lint Fumes, also circling the site, but in the opposite direction. Next, also coming his way, he saw the man in the goatee, different vehicle and without the big dog. This time, something about him looked altered. The current version of *the Monk* oozed a contained menace. Sig noticed Fred noticing him and he smiled, the funny persistent cop was on the job, good, Brice Liner fell into the lineup, following Sig's car, this time he was going to be careful, no barging in. He wanted each and every one of them, whoever they were, dead. He would scope out the place before he made any moves. In the parking lot, Langostino thought he caught sight of Liner driving past, he started up and pulled out slow, to see if he was right. The black Lincoln Navigator slipped in between English and a Ford pickup with a six inch lift-kit and three bald mercenaries seated inside. Just then Fred English, nose on fire with instincts gone nuts, caught himself looking too hard and long at the approaching Brice Liner. As their vehicles passed each other, Liner spit and snarled, sending Fred reeling back to his high school days of 30 years past, when dragging the gut in Eugene, as a hormone-charged teenager, he had the same feeling of surveillance, contest, flex spectacle and pending malice. English pulled his seldom used revolver from the shoulder holster and set it beside him on the seat. Next Liner and Langostino were eyeball to eyeball as their vehicles passed, going in opposite directions. Liner jerked his head towards the hospital. Approaching the hospital vicinity, Sam & Nettie made the turn and were focused on the hospital and parking lot, not the traffic. It was Nettie who noticed that there was an odd rhythmic intensity to the parade of vehicles, moving slow in both directions, with most of the vehicle occupants doing the "if I don't look at him maybe he won't look at me" stiff neck. She saw Enno Duden in the parking lot, standing with three women and talking. Sam quickly realized he was in the midst of the beginning stages of a tail chasing party with toughs playing for keeps. The FBI Caprice pulled out of its parking slot, extra slow, moving curbside where the occupants could get a better look at the participants of the "parade." A man and woman, heavily armed costumed CIA agents, materialized out of nowhere to join the parade procession. Then came a large van truck with a radar dish on the roof and the call letters WETZ TV on the side panels. It too joined the circus after an anonymous tip that federal law enforcement was moving, in force, on the hospital. Then came a rented Porsche Cayenne driven by a VP of *the Gee Whiz Corp*, Adi Zarabrezi. Next came yet another media truck, this one however was an electronic surveillance unit manned by Alcohol, Tobacco and Firearm agency technicians. Titus sat still in the small car and watched as the drama built.

Gambizzi's people had informed Charlie Rover's people at the White House that *the Monk*, suspected of having hijacked the Mexican kidnapping, was holed up in a small Central Oregon town, perhaps with little Mary Merced. Charlie sat in his private office, the one which accessed the oval office through a secret panel door, the one which was sound-proofed and featured myriad de-bugging devices, the one which included a bathroom accessible only by Rover, the one which featured a photo montage of Michael Jackson and Pat Robertson. He placed two calls, one to special ops and another to the CIA. He wanted *the Monk* eliminated immediately. Having completed those calls, he went into his private water closet. He would have had to get down on his knees to find the plastics explosive adhered to the underside of the lip of the toilet. It was set to go off the instant that the toilet was flushed.

Rover's eliminations eliminated him. It would take seven minutes for White House security to finally reach the debris site. The French would be blamed, the Mexicans would be suspected, TV comedians would revisit a thrilling diarrhea of possibilities, and news rooms everywhere would feel further taxed. A terrorist bomb attack in a White House bathroom? A crippling embarrassment of riches. When would they catch up, too many opportunities for punditry lost to the pressures of time. Oh, but for just one slow news day! The only segment of the media seemingly immune to the "this-just-ins" was NPR, not to be bothered as it was deep into its early spring fund raiser.

Back at the Fork Holding, Glass, the Percheron stallion, was jerking back and forth, wide-eyed, in the barn box stall. Hypersensitive to the earth's vibrations, he felt a rolling action underfoot, which gave him the sensation of some unknowable evil coming his way. He wanted to run.

Judy Hamlet was publicity maven for "Alliance for a Better Oregon," a land use planning organization whose membership featured a who's who of liberal professionals. She had tracked down Luther Yankone at a book signing in the Mascara bookstore. He was here because a real estate informat had advised him that there was to be a private meeting to discuss his development project. No way he would allow that to happen without his observation and input. And, equally, there was no way Judy Hamlet was going to release Yankone from his promise to talk about ABOs concerns for his project. So the two of them sat on folding chairs in the back corner of the bookstore while folks filed in.

"Mr. Yankone, as a matter of principle, we must oppose" - pause - "but you know, push come to shove, that we are comfortable, if it is inevitable, that you do have the resources to contribute a thing of beauty to the landscape, unlike so many of these low and middle class rural people who have no sense of proportion and no sense of how they affect the landscape."

"You got that right." He did not look at her.

"Ultimately our fight is not with you."

"Right again. It would be stupid to fight us. Will you excuse me?" And he got up to walk over and talk with Bo Coin who had just entered with a big-haired woman in a silk suit.

Joanna Mendelsohn Thurber slipped her hand inside Bo's elbow and squeezed.

"Honey, what did you do? How on earth did you get all

these people to come out?" Smiling, she looked over the room at 35 people jammed in and talking. Bo's pleasure with himself spilled over to form an oil slick that would surely cause a fall. The look on his face was pornographic.

Lloyd Gerald Shoulders was sitting by the wood heater in his welding studio working in a sketch book when the first shakes hit. Cans on shelves rattled, the power flickered off and on, a tin of welding rod fell off the wall bracket on to the shop bench and flipped open scattering, like pickup sticks, the dusty grey rods that looked just like oversized fourth of July sparklers.

He got up, unsure of himself, his knees buckling, the floor slightly curling, everything in the cluttered artist's sculpture studio unstable and rattling. He found his flashlight and gripped the bench while he watched the hot, single-wall, tin, wood-heater stove pipe sway as if moving to music. Some hundred feet away in the barn, his saddle horse, Juniper, screamed like a mare early in weaning.

Sloop was trying to figure how he and Helga would escape the now encircled hospital when a fury of activity hit the desks at every floor. He overheard part of what the nurses were saying. Every available ambulance was needed to go to Mascara at once. A massive disaster was underway. He didn't have to think about it. Sloop put Helga in a wheelchair and managed to get her to the emergency door where, curbside, an ambulance waited. She safely inside, he took the wheel and flipped on the siren and lights and left the hospital as fast as he could drive. Another ambulance and a rescue truck joined in behind him. Sirens could be heard going off at the nearby fire station. Sloop heard over the ambulance radio that a series of earthquakes were tearing Mascara apart.

Titus had been watching everything and saw Sloop drive out in the ambulance. Starting out slow he pulled away from the curb and headed into another parking lot to turn around. By the time he was back on the road going in the right direction, Sam and Nettie had seen him and were getting in behind. Meanwhile, Shirley had gone into the hospital, found Jimmy Three Trees and agreed to sneak him out and take him home. The hospital was in disaster preparation mode so no one questioned their departure. Outside, one after the watchers noticed each other pulling out and very quickly the highway to Mascara was a multi-vehicle, high speed, caravan chase. Ambulances in front, law enforcement - also with sirens and lights - scattered throughout the procession, media trucks, Sig's rig with a frightened but fascinated Vicky on board. Bald Mother America's muscle truck, FBI Caprice, Lincoln Navigator, Fred English, Lint Fumes and Brice Liner, Shirley Intoit being egged on by Enno and Jimmy. Nancy. A Porcshe Cayenne. Four high school kids in a Honda Civic wanting to get to where the action was. Six state police patrol cars. Two deputy Sheriff pickup trucks, and eleven unsuspecting commuters. Forty one vehicles, containing eighty three people, eighteen of them publicly or privately-hired assassins, four open cans of beer, seventy-one cell phones, eleven bottles of oxygen, two shoulder-mounted rocket launchers, thirty-one revolvers, a crate of hand grenades, twenty-four rifles and shot guns, three video cameras, tear gas, smoke bombs, six lap top computers, a Lhasa Apso, a complete set of Coleman Hawkins music, thirteen global positioning devices (only three of which agreed on an accurate position), and thirty-eight radar detectors.

All of them were racing along, bumper to bumper, at 95 miles per hour down that high desert two lane highway. Racing towards earthquakes, volcanic eruptions, shoot outs, fist fights, handcuffs, stretchers, photo ops, hiding places and love. Sloop was in the lead and Titus was tight up against him. Behind them, at every opportunity, certain vehicles were daring to pass each other. Eleven shots were fired, vehicle to vehicle.

Sloop knew just when he would turn off his flashing lights and siren. Titus was anticipating him. There was a road, just past a gradual turn, where it might be possible for them to veer off and lose the rest of the procession. Sloop was heading either for Fork Holding or his own place. He'd figure that out when he had a chance to stop and talk it over with Titus.

Shirley drove, Enno sat next to her, and next to him sat Jimmy Three Trees, a very different Jimmy Three Trees - yet much the same. The phonetic stutter was gone, replaced by a sort of phraseological stuttering.

In a soft insistent voice Jimmy spoke without a breath.

"The heart association is some kind of official thing which, and you know they aren't dog people, goes into people's bodies and measures their parts, inside parts, I've got parts, I know when I was in that heart hospital that they took my dogs and some of my parts, I need my dogs, the parts they can have cause I don't feel them gone, Thanksgiving is my favorite time because of the turkey grease, it makes my dogs burp from both ends. Do you like music? Dog burps are music, but it wouldn't work if you made them wear pants, it would sound different, there was this time when my Sally was swimming across a creek and started burping from both ends..."

Smiling, Shirley and Enno listened but only a little. The heat their touching bodies created caused for both of them, a deafening internal hum, a blinding light of unimaginable possibilities.

Chapter Twenty nine

Santiam

Into the waters of the jawless fish
eyes humming of prominences
He would dowse the firedamp
marking transform faults
for a map back to the
evening primrose oil
and the income of the Brown Dwarf.

Sitting with kerosene lanterns and propane-generated coffee, Roger the writer, was thinking about the man at the cafe and listening to public radio on his hand-crank. He figured he might get some kind of update on the earthquakes. Mercedes Martiniquais was the guest on the fund-raiser-abbreviated, new age radio show, "Blended Dimensions." She had written for forty years about the need for occasional retributive economic slaughter, yoga, the check book, and the higher laws of siphonage.

The interviewer asked,

"But who then is the enemy?"
"The enemy is not a person or a group of people. The enemy is an aspect, an aspect of humanity which holds that it is essential for every

man to believe in wealth beyond reason as a sacred possibility. Over the ages, this aspect has given license to Kings, given power to despots, permitted the vast vulgarities of cornered wealth even at the expense of tortured hungry masses. From the beginning we could see that a great fortune lent opportunity for great power. Governance required great fortune. And great fortune did not exist except in contrast. To have great fortune it needed to sit hard up against great misfortune or the empowering measurement of contrast did not exist. If each man was well in wealth, and goodness was an issue forced by true social balance, man's lust for power would soon poison the human landscape with a power born of more direct cruelty. We believe that man's competitive drive to have more than his fellow man is true to nature and can best be moderated by the beneficial predatory leach."

Roger changed the radio to KKIT, the country channel and Emmett Buxton who introduced LouAnn Brittany's new single "My Baby's Got the Cutest Butt in Rodeo." He changed again to an AM talk show featuring the insistent nasal tones of Doctor Brockly who was screaming through the airwaves that these alternative medicine types were bilking naive idiots out of their hard earned dollars with all this herbal garbage. The show was interrupted by the Emergency Broadcast System's obnoxious honking squawk and a moronic voice, barely audible, which spoke of a series of earthquakes in Central Oregon and the need to stay indoors, away from glass windows, unless the building was unstable. And required that the listener stay tuned to this channel for further instructions. That announcement was interrupted by another emergency broadcast which warned of volcanic eruptions and molten lava flow in Central Oregon and insisted that people stay indoors unless they needed to move out of the way of lava flow. This announcement was interrupted by another one which warned that all exit routes out of Central Oregon were either clogged with traffic or busted up by earthquakes and advised that people stay put unless they were instructed by authorities to evacuate. Next came another interrupting announcement that the Federal Emergency Catastrophe

Arrangements League, or FECAL, were on their way from Washington DC with agents prepared to process earthquake and volcano disaster insurance claims. Next came a news bulletin advising that all power was out to ten thousand homes in Central Oregon as a result of earthquake damage. Roger thought briefly how fortunate it was that his wife and son were off in Seattle visiting her mom. She might be worried. He'd have to make a point of getting in touch with her. He sipped his coffee, thought of the man at the cafe and listened to yet another news bulletin.

"This just in: All of Washington D.C. has been evacuated following the terrorist bombing in the White House which took the life of presidential aid Charlie Rover. Investigators continue to examine the rubble at Camp David for clues about the suspected French bomb attack which took the life of President Larry Walter. Speculation is flying concerning the whereabouts of Vice President Myron Cooleritch. And Hispanic demonstrations against the White House were growing in Houston, Los Angeles, San Diego, Miami, New York City, and Fresno and have turned violent. Three different federal courthouses were on fire. A special session of the U.S. Congress has been called in Philadelphia with the Republicans accusing the Democrats of aiding the enemy by refusing to vote to expel people of French birth from U.S. The senator from Alaska has called for the immediate construction of a French internment camp on the bombed out former site of Camp David. Red state Senator Buckets had publicly accused blue state Senator Wiggins of cowardice and un-American tactics in the latter's efforts to retract the declaration of war and to negotiate with the Hispanic demonstrators. General Burgoyne "Burg" Hershey, head of the joint chiefs of staff, appointed himself as the acting commander in chief of U.S. forces and as such declared Marshall Law temporarily suspending any constitutional restrictions on search and seizure. He also ordered the return of ten thousand national guard troops from the middle eastern front to move into riot-torn U.S. cities. The French president is accusing the U.S. of an attempt on his life and demanding a UN security council meeting to condemn the American declaration of war against France. Britain, Germany, Belgium, Poland, Sweden, Norway, Finland, Holland,

Monaco, Spain, Italy and Luxemborg have all signed a declaration condemning the actions of the US government and calling for European unity in defending the sovereignty of France. South Africa is calling for a convening of an African Congress to consider ways to defend itself against the renegade actions of the U.S. government. The Hollywood Actor's Guild has issued a declaration calling for a cooling down period, condemning the actions of vice president Myron Cooleritch, and notifying the world that it should not see these events as actions taken by Americans but rather as the mistakes of a reckless few. Now for an update on the earthquake and volcanic eruption out in a remote segment of Ore
-gon..."

Roger had heard enough, he switched to the community college station and cut in on the Gipsy Kings singing "Un Amor." He left it there enjoying the percussive harmonies while his subconscious brain tried to sort between panic and confusion.

Sloop and Titus had succeeded splitting off the racing caravan on to a side road. After a mile, Sloop stopped the ambulance, shut off his engine and lights and waited for confirmation that they were not followed. Titus pulled in around beside the ambulance and shut off his engine and lights. After about five quiet dark minutes, Titus got out of his car and entered the passenger side of the ambulance to embrace his friends and bring them up to date.

"Oh man, a lot going on. Well if that wasn't enough, we've been listening to the ambulance radio," said Sloop "and right now there are a series of earthquakes all around town plus a couple of spots where molten lava seems to be breaking out of the ground, at level sites not on mountain tops. Looks like a major disaster sequence. One of us needs to go to the station and secure the computers, we need a current update and all files moved off site."

"That would be me friend. You and Helga need to go to

Jefferson's place, stay away from your own until some of us who
are fully mobile can help you."

"Titus, be safe."

"Put the ambulance in the barn when you get there, out of
sight."

English decided that this whole thing was getting out of
hand. Here he was driving at 97 mph in his Ford pickup, portable
magnetic roof light flashing, with all hell breaking loose. One
thing he knew, the Brice Liner character just ahead of him was a
killer and had to be stopped. Just then Brice's car pulled out to
pass the Porsche SUV ahead of him, even with oncoming traffic,
English took hold of his revolver and pulled to the right shoulder
speeding up. He couldn't afford to lose Liner. Adi Zarabrezi was
driving the Porsche Cayenne, cursing about the idiot passing
him. Didn't he see he had no where to pull in? Then he noticed it
was Liner. At that very instant, he felt something on his right and
looked to see English's cop pickup keeping up with him on the
rough right shoulder. He was sandwiched in a vulnerable position. Up ahead the oncoming traffic was swerving and leaning
on horns as Liner headed straight for them. Liner was steering
with one hand, pistol in the other. Zarabrezi, fearing a wreck,
stepped on his brakes to slow down permitting Liner to pull in
ahead of him except for the fact that English was beating him to
the position. Liner leveled his pistol to shoot at Fred. Fred hit his
brakes, falling back and causing Adi to react by speeding into the
hole, up alongside Liner, who shot Adi Zarabrezi dead. The
Porsche flew off the road into a old Juniper tree and exploded in
flames. A rescue truck and sheriff's cruiser, part of the crazy
caravan, pulled over instantly to take charge of the wreck. Everyone else flew on by to continue the madness. That included Fred
who was now, once again right on Liner's bumper. Up ahead Sig
was hot on Lint Fume's bumper with Shirley and Enno close
behind. Behind Fred, two cars back came Sam and Nettie. And
right behind them was the FBI followed by Bald Mother America,

the Gambizzi thugs, and everybody else.

Near the entrance to the town of Mascara, two highways converge and traffic is normally slowed to a 10 to 25 mph crawl. Long have the city fathers and mothers haggled over what to do about the state's highway running right smack through the middle of their once tiny, sleepy town. Traffic was a monumental problem. Discussions, official and reckless, bandied about the question of a by-pass, perhaps through the bordering industrial park or maybe a conversion of two parallel streets to one-way arterials. And at the state capital the highway department was already into its own plan, engineering the condemnations of private properties to construct a complete four lane by-pass. City fathers, erroneously believed they had the last say and that no commerce-throttling by-pass would ever be constructed. One high school student had been severely reprimanded in church for painting on the side of the city hall one night *"By-pass, Over-pass or Bump-ass."*

It was at the narrowest point of this traffic funnel, adjacent to the health club and movie theater where the state police had begun constructing a road block because of the earthquake damage just ahead. A two foot wide and four foot deep crack had formed in the pavement, running right down the middle of the combination main street and state highway. As they arranged the road block setup, the officers could see the fast approaching caravan, ambulance, firetruck, and media truck in the lead. The first vehicles peeled off into the health club parking lot when they saw the road block. Others followed.

Luigi Longstroke, minus Estelle, sat parked behind the road block watching for Sig. Right behind him, sitting and panting, was Resumé the old stock dog. He had followed what scent of the female Great Dane still oozed out of the van.

In the parking lot, cars, pickup trucks, vans and motorhomes piled in as various people piled out. It started with shouts and name calling, moved rapidly to fist fights, advanced to clubbings, exploded into gun fire, blew up with two grenades, and ended with a swat team's arrival. Brice had seriously wounded Fred English and then backed into the shadows to watch the traffic pattern of the fights and flights. He caught sight of Shirley and Sig and followed them, careful that they not notice. But he wasn't thinking about anybody behind him. Lint had enjoyed watching how all the differing federal boys, and the militants, and the Gambizzi thugs, and the two Vietnam veterans from the media truck, were all randomly and efficiently dispatching each other. He was looking everywhere for the man we know as Titus. He wasn't there. But Lint Fumes did notice Brice Liner following *the Monk*. That's the trail he knew he needed to stay on.

When the fighting had broken out in the parking lot, Jimmy Three Trees had jumped out of Shirley's truck and run off into the dark. Minutes after that, Sig ran up and grabbed a surprised Enno's shoulder and told him that they had to follow his car right away. It was Shirley who pulled Duden's arm and shoved him into the driver's seat of her truck. "You drive" she said, smiling and beaming with emotion that did not jive with the panic and the riot. She slid in the passenger side and after just a few moments of sitting next to the window she slid deliberately over to the middle of the bench seat as if a third person were entering the truck. "Well? Drive!" she insisted. Neither of them saw Resumé jump into the back of the truck. (Lou knew not to follow Sig, not with all these people in attendance. It was his job to be seen elsewhere and mistaken for *the Monk*. He slowly drove to different viewing spots around the fighting.)

Ahead of Enno and Shirley, Sig drove fast and deliberate, stopping once to see if anyone but Duden was following. Brice had been quick enough to pull over and not be spotted. Lint did likewise. Vicky sat in the bucket seat next to Sig, holding the dash in front of her and chewing her lip while wondering at the pleasurable adrenaline rush. Looking for a quiet part of town to have a discussion, Sig headed out to the industrial park and pulled in by a storage unit, all the while speaking in a soft assuring tone to Vicky, but yet speaking offensively and deliberately.

Once again to avoid being seen, Liner turned into an alley and went around beside a chain link fence next to the tire warehouse. Here he could see them through the fence. Lights off, Lint had followed Liner. The only thing he could see was Liner, but that was, by his way of reckoning, quite enough.

Sig, thinking it was safe, got out of the car and went to speak with Enno at the wheel of Shirley's pickup. Vicky followed him. She saw Shirley sitting right up near Enno and she felt her temperature rise. Instinctively, as if high school had only let out fifteen minutes before, she hooked her own arm into Sig's. He looked at her confused and continued:

"Jeez it's good to see you again kid, and to know that you are safe. You've got yourself in a hell of a mess. We have got a lot to talk about. But first, we need to get these girls to safety. Son, you need to take both of them someplace and return to meet me. We're going to need each other."

Shirley wanted to interrupt Sig with some declaration of self sufficiency, but watching his obvious deference to Enno, and with all the veiled references to shared intrigue, it all made her look even harder at this young man who had sucked her in so deep, so quickly. Her father, Oochuck Intoit, had he been there, would have warned her about the blindness that comes from the well of flash love.

"Here's the address of a trailer house on the other side of town." Sig gave Enno a slip of paper with Peggy Youngquist's location. "Where are you going to take them?"

Dizzy from hearing Sig refer to him innocently as *son*, Enno thought about Sloop's farm and decided against it. Then he naturally thought of the Fork Holding with a vague knowledge that Titus, Jefferson and Sloop were all connected and included him and his in the mix. He mentioned this. And they agreed, Sig convinced that Titus Ibid was the third leg, and for the time being a good leg. Sig went around and helped Vicky into the seat next Shirley. Without hesitation he placed the flats of both of his hands on either side of her surprised face and lowered his own to kiss her. Then he returned to his little rental car, the ground rolling slightly under foot, and drove off. The ground rolled under Vicky as well, but she believed it was caused by her heart's loud beat and her mouth aching for more.

In the distance Liner's view of Sig's group had been distracted when he noticed a tall, thin, grey-haired athletic man duck into a hole in the chain link fence. He had seen that man before. Pay dirt! To hell with the girls and *the Monk*. He'd get them later. *The Milk Man* was his! He trotted over to find the hole in the fence and crawl down the trail which led to the lava tube tunnel under the abandoned Exxon station. Lint, on the other hand, having seen all of this, walked to where he could observe exactly where Liner went. Seeing him disappear into the cab of the old truck, Lint returned to his car and retrieved a flashlight and a light-weight, sharpshooter's collapsible rifle. Then he walked over and retraced Liner's path into the tube.

Once inside the abandoned station's hidden electronics center, Titus checked the backup generator. All was well, the power outages had not disrupted the computers. Quickly, he set in motion a process that instantly backed up all the computers onto three external hard drives. While this occured, and he packaged up the laptop he would need, he read the report. The *Pascal's Revolver* probe had determined that the private military-contract corporation, *Helabernin*, was transferring huge amounts of money back and forth from off shore accounts to administration accounts. The report pegged the company as a candidate for raid. No time for that now, as he felt the metal building twist from subterranean forces, time enough later, he thought. He snatched the three little external hard drives and the lap top and thought about which way to exit. Odd, how it seemed to be getting warm with a sulphur smell? He opted to go out above ground.

If it had not been for the wars in the middle east, the Jackson

Hole explosion, the Camp David attack, the White House bombing, the deaths of President Walter and his aid Rover. the declaration of war against France, the disappearance of Vice President
Myron Cooleritch, the declaration of Marshall law and the
suspension of constitutional rights, the defacto move of the
nation's capital to Philadelphia, the financial collapse of *the Gee
Whiz corporation*, and the 50% off chain-wide sale at Walmart, the
earthquake and volcanic activity in Central Oregon would have
warranted an army of press.

The U.S. Congress took advantage of the moment, and in a
late night session voted itself a raise.

Chapter Thirty

Sandy

distinguishing the duty to explain from the desire to persuade

"Met many a woman I'd rather die for
than die with and that is how it is with country."
-Lord Dilling

"He says I have no choice. That I need to get my things in order because he's coming back to take me with him. Something about a farm in Central America." Enno was driving, next to him sat Shirley and next to her was Vicky. Vicky had just spoken softly to Shirley but Enno heard every word.

"What did you say to him?" asked Shirley.

"What could I say? Nothing. I guess I just looked at him."

Shirley thought for half a second and smiled. Then revealingly she asked "What does he look like?"

Vicky looked at Shirley and broke into a laughing smile.

Shirley blurted a short-breath laugh and nodded.

Enno was slipping back into a familiar, emotional correction. He looked into the mirror and saw Resume looking back at him. It was reassuring. (All the while that the old stock dog had been off in pursuit of his love interest, no one had noticed he was missing, not even the dog himself.)

Enno Albert Duden struggled to revisit his farm dream, he needed to tighten the lid on his emotions. Then he felt the back of Shirley's hand, on the seat, resting against his leg, and he slipped off a notch. What caught his slip was the reasonable wonder. Was this a girl who might share his dream? He shuddered at his deep, unreasonable selfishness. Afterall, that dream of a farm, his dream, had always belonged as a duty well ahead of comfort and pleasure.

With urgency Sig drove back into town, around and through that side of the community where little, old, modest vacation and retirement homes still remained as a reminder of the quiet, mountain-forest village charm that Mascara once owned. He came in by a gravel alley to the back of the new movie house, parked and walked up against the building to spy on the continuing fight in the cojoined parking lots. A crowd of frightened movie patrons, taken out of the darkened theater by a flashlight-wielding usher, huddled near the theater door, watching the fighting in the parking lot. The lot was now lit in strange crossing knives of pulsing light, produced by the headlights and emergency flashers of the ring of vehicles. Sig's eyes were drawn to the three movie posters beside him, barely visible. The theater was showing "The Girl in the Cafe" and "The Girl on the Bridge" and "Breakfast and Tiffany's." He thought of Vicky. He forced his eyes to stiffen and he flexed every transcendental muscle in his psyche aiming himself at his training, his experience, his immortality. He stepped into the group of theater patrons and disappeared as one of them.

Out in the lot he saw a familiar form, seated and slouched with bleeding chest, up against a pine tree trunk. It was the funny, persistent, detective, Fred English, nearly passed out from blood loss. He had taken a high caliber round in the central right shoulder. Quickly canvasing the area, Sig backed out of the theater-goers group and went wide to English, pulling back his blood-soaked coat and tearing at his shirt. English, dazed, came around enough to make out who was helping him. Weak though he was, he still managed a surprised smile.

Luigi, still on the periphery of the fighting, caught sight of Sig bent over English. He also saw the two blue-suited feds move into the parking lot's wild, erratic, light ring. They nodded to one another while looking toward Sig, then split apart, disappearing out of the lights.

"Hang on buddy, you're gonna be fine. We'll get you to some help." Sig was talking to Fred while he stood quickly and turned to see where he might take him. In that instant of movement a bullet narrowly missed his head. He dropped and instinctively covered the prone English.

"FBI. Freeze!" came the shout from one of the blue suits. Two of them, one on either side, thirty feet apart, each pointed revolvers, with double-fisted anxiety, directly at Sig and English, lumped as they were together against the tree. Luigi had seen it all coming and took advantage of the moment to do a low tackling dive against the back side of one of the agents' knees, snapping a federal ankle and dropping the man in a painful sprawl. This caued the fallen agent's firearm to skitter across the pavement towards English and Sig.

The second agent was not so fortunate. Grabbed from behind by two waxed, bald-headed, musclemen in fishnet tank tops, the agent went white. The BMA reps were beaming. "Lookee here, I've got me a girlfriend, Bubba."

Sig muttered "thanks" to Lou and they carefully, quickly, drug English out of the parking lot lights. Sig then ran off to tell two sheriff's deputies, coordinating with the just arrived Swat Team, that two federal agents were being held by militants across the lot. Back with Lou, the two of them loaded English in the van. "Find someone to help him, fast. Eventually I'll be with Estelle."

Lou understood.

English had trouble sitting up in the van's captain's chair. The last thing he asked before passing out was, "There are two of you?"

The only light Liner had, when he slipped down through the hole inside the old truck's cab had come from his small Swiss Army knife's red security light. With a pistol in one hand and the light in the other, he read the walls of the tunnel with his shoulders and worked his way towards the last sounds he heard. Then came sounds behind him and he turned to catch a blade of flashlight. Flattening himself into a crevise in the lava tube's wall, and with his little light off, he waited as the flashlight and Lint Fumes approached him. The flashlight stopped moving and seemed to be pointed right at him. He grinned down deep inside of himself and took aim on where a man would be if he held that light. He fired three deafening, echoing shots. But nothing. Then he made the mistake of shooting out the flashlight.

Up above, after destroying the remaining computers, and exiting the abandoned Exxon Station at the camoflauged dumpster, Titus, a laptop case in hand, heard what he thought were four shots coming from up out of the ground. 'Somebody's in the tube?', he thought. The ground rolled again slightly and he heard squeaks and cracking. Just then Marvin and Carl drove up. Titus had an idea.

"Gigs up. You screwed up with that solo act. Feds are in town. Everything's found out. Don't ever come back here. Cease all activities and scatter. Don't ever let me see your faces again." The two Payoute indians looked at each other swollen with embarrassement and fear, nodded to Titus, and drove off. They decided to go to Tule Lake for a while. They knew an excellent retreat there. They had no idea how lucky they were.

As for Titus, time to go, quickly, back to Forks. He heard two more shots from under the ground, thought for half a second about seeing who was down there and then he noticed Liner's

car. He knew that car from the hospital caravan. Time to go,
NOW.

Underground, from southeast of Mascara running north and
a little west, hot pressurized lava, released by the earthquakes,
flowed through any crack, fissure, old lava tube, or excavation.
As it flowed it caused the surface, in places, to roll. Where the
lava came close to the surface and made contact with old
rosinous Juniper tree roots, flames ignited and in some cases
would shoot up through the hollow tree trunks, flickering out
through woodpecker holes.

In the industrial park, the old subterranean lava tubes gave
easy release to the lava to flow. Lint saw Liner one last time,
when the glow of the approaching lava lent just enough light for
one good clear shot.

Sam and Nettie had avoided the mess at the parking lot.
They drove around the town, where they could drive, and were
horrified by the earthquake's continuing damage. At one point
they came to a caved-in mobile home where a young white
woman, a tough looking young white boy and a little frightened
dark-skinned girl were standing with a huge now solid black
Great Dane. The children were shivering in the cold. Nettie had
Sam stop. She took her coat off and had him give her his.

"Here, let's get you in the car," Nettie offered to Peggy
Youngquist.

Peggy looked around nervous. "I don't know. I think I'm
supposed to wait here. Thank you. I don't know. My God, what is
happening? Ty honey, put the nice woman's coat on. Mary,
sweetie let's get this other coat on you. This is so nice of you,
Mam."

At that exact moment Sig drove up and jumped out of the
little car.

Sam's eyes were big as saucers. *The Monk!*

Peggy looked at Sig, smiled and then realized this wasn't
Lou. She started to cry convulsively. "I don't understand, I don't

understand." Nettie put her arms around the woman and looked scornfully at Sig. Then she looked down at Estelle, the Dane, and pointed at Sig as if to say "sic 'em". Estelle walked over to Maltesta, licked his hand, and sat down. As if by cue, Luigi drove up in the van sans English. When he jumped out, everyone looked from him to Sig and back again. Without saying a word, Sig went to the van and opened the door motioning for Peggy to get in. Nettie moved to stand, protectively, between them. Lou offered,

"Hey, its okay, everything's okay. Peggy honey, let's get you and your family to safety." Desperately needing some semblance of security, Peggy fell into Lou's arms. Little Mary ran to Sig's arms smiling and yabbering in Spanish which he returned as he set her in the van. Tyrone took the Dane's sequined collar as the dog led him up into the waiting vehicle.

Sam went to Nettie and said, "Come on honey, they're getting it figured out."

Sig said to Lou, "Done here, Chiloquin, the usual. Go now."

Lou drove off. Sig stood his ground. Sam took one long last look at him and drove off with Nettie. He seemed to come to some understanding, some appreciation.

"Honey, I think the man was right."

"Which man?"

"*The Monk*, the first one who showed up. The real one. He said 'done here'. That goes for us too, I think we're done here."

"So you understand all of that?"

"I think so. Least ways I'm comfortable with what I think is happening. But this place is a disaster, we need to get out of here right now. Think you're ready to travel?"

She squeezed his arm. "Not yet, we need to find Bo first. Remember, I need to get his signature on those papers we drew up and a few others."

"Where are we going to find him, with this town torn apart and the power out?"

"Let's try the bars, there are only four of them in town, it won't take long."

They found Bo in a candle lit booth at the Gun Club Lounge with a Joanna Mendelsohn Thurber. Nettie thought they are perfect for each other. He was enebriated and enervated and flexed up, so it took only minutes for Nettie to coerce Bo to sign all of the documents. Then Nettie and Sam sealed certain forms in envelopes to be mailed later.

"Central America here we come!" blurted Sam.

"Honey, I haven't had a chance to talk to you about that."

Sam felt his insides cave in. He saw his dream crawling off. Sitting in the Oldsmobile on a cold, black night of flashing lights, smoke, fires, sirens, Nettie kissed Sam's cheek and said,

"Have you ever been to Kauai, to Hanalei? I own a bungalo in the jungle just north of there."

"Sweetie, I happen to know that the jungle just north of Hanalei is a roadless wilderness."

"Yes." She smiled.

"And you're telling me you own a bungalo in that wilderness?"

"Yes. Crummy little bungalo. That's what one of those signatures from Bo was all about." Still smiling.

"Right on the edge, near the roads?"

"Nope."

"Deep?"

"Yes."

"Near a beach?"

"Only separated by a thicket of palms."

"Pretty beach?"

"Magnificent beach."

"How do you get there?"

"Only way in is by boat."

"Boat?"

"Yes." She took his hand. "And I have a motor launch berthed in Hanalei."

"Are you suggesting that..."

"Sam honey, this is how it's going to work. I'm taking you to Hawaii. We are going to live in my bungalo, with a stock of Rum, in the jungle, on a private beach, a long ways from any other spies, spooks, counterfeiters, assassins, wise guys, realtors, or young women. For a period of several months I have every intention of not letting you out of my sight. When we boat into town for supplies, I will be on your arm. There's an art supply store in Hanalei where we can both stock up. Let's say three months, yes, three months, we'll hide out together. If at the end of that time you want to leave, or we want to leave, we can. I know you've always had your sights set on Central America..." Sam interrupted her with his finger on her lips.

Chapter Thirty one

Siuslaw

Writing is all about attendance.

*"A work of art is a corner of the creation
seen through a temperament." - Emile Zola*

The darkness stole from Shirley and Vicky those new views, afforded in daylight, of the entrance to *Fork Holding*. Even so the magic, the purposefulness, the music all flavored the specific, coagulated, atmosphere of the place and its guarded entry. Enno remembered how the meandering drop into the canyon was sheltered by opposing red rimrock punctuated by the scaley, red-plate bark of the Ponderosa pines, and how the fuzzy, silver-gray winter tops of Cottonwoods and Poplars, ribbing as windbreaks the lower orchards, confused the perception of depth. He recalled for some unknown reason how that unusual box canyon seemed to form, with its higher gradual back end, a long question mark with the farmstead cluster as the concluding dot.

In the headlights, they caught sight of an unusual animal.

"What was that?" Shirley asked, reaching across herself with right arm and wrapping her hand gently around part of Enno's upper arm.

He looked down at her hand, unaware that he was smiling and answered, "A Water Buffalo cow and calf. Jefferson and Brenda raise them. Titus lives here too. If he's here, maybe you can find out about your mother."

Their shared driving and talking time had given him a chance to talk hesistantly about that dream of a farm of his own, and in turn Shirley had spoken of her mission to find her mother or at least information about her. She had also encouraged Vicky to speak of the discovery in the woods of Jimmy's shrine and the question about she and Enno's relationship. Duden understood that Jimmy's mind was laterally fluid and he still couldn't put much stock in the idea.

They arrived at the long, low, unusual house and Resumé woke up. He remembered this place fondly. Resting his sore lower chin on the edge of the pickup box, he gazed down at the two incredibly stupid Redbone hounds and was thankful for them. Then the door opened and little Franklin came out on the porch chewing feverishly. The bubblegum man. Resumé was flooded by the comfort of inappropriate yet simple pleasures and carefully lowered his tired body out of the truck.

"Frankie, you come back here!" A big, statuesque black woman came out the front door of the house. "Enno, honey! Am I glad to see you! Jeff's in bed, been hurt bad. Sloop's in with 'im. He's going to be okay but they needs to talk to you right now." She wrapped her arms around Digger Duden and smothered him. " You go in there now. I'll take care of your ladies."

"Shirley, Vicky, this is Brenda," said Enno as he moved into the house.

"*Yummy* is what my man calls me, 'cause I earn it every day, you call me whatever comforts you. Come in ladies come in. Now you," she looked at Shirley, "are you that girl that called Titus a while ago? He said you might be Charmaine's daughter?"

"You know my mother? Is she here?" Shirley squeaked nervously.

"Calm down sweetie. No, I don't know your mama, but I

know my Titus and damned if your Mama isn't that good man's
only love light. And they's someone here who knows your mama
real good."

Shirley went into the low cavernous front room of the Fork
home and was hit by a wonderous kaleidoscope of sights, sounds
and smells. Two small boys came to her side and took her hands
and pulled on them gently.

"She's over here, in our room. Helgie's over here."

Helga laid in the single bed propped up slightly at an odd
angle, still partially paralyzed. She moved her head as if it was a
separate living thing, separate from her still sholders and torso.
Her hands clutched at the coverlet.

"Boys? Leave 'em be. Come back in here. Shirley, not too
long, honey. She's needin' her rest." Brenda turned and saw the
other young lady at the door.

Vicky stood in the entryway, absorbed in the smells, sounds
and look of the Fork Holding house. In a brief period of time her
life, once shaped and guaranteed by her appearance, her animal
intelligence and the maneuvered desires of so many men, now
morphed to a crazy-quilted hunger. She wanted to be a part of a
life of meaning, texture, choice, chosen vulgarities, adrenalin
pudding, and beneficial intrigue. She no longer saw life as
something she might have for herself, but rather felt life as
something to be a part of. And she could see beneath the curtain
corner of her future that there was an infinite array of lives to
choose from, some of them as yet unimagined by anyone.

Jimmy Three Trees had made the limping, swerving run
successfully and was delighted to find his old digs in the forest,
his refrigerator-box house, still intact. He was happy, cleanly,
clearly, happy and that confused him around the edges. His life
for so long had been a series of twitches, stutters, jerks, unknowable half hungers, itches, neck-shortening fears, that this clarity,
internal stillness and freedom were foreign to him. First off, he
went inside and found his old dog whistle and blew it three

times, once for each dog. (Though little Sally was dead, he would always include a blow for her.) That done he sat, crosslegged, in front of the old galvanized tin suitcase and opened the lid reverentially. When he saw the pictures of Vicky and Enno he quietly wept. How much they looked like her! And yet they didn't much look like each other. He saw in the boy's ramrod-straight, wide-shouldered, athletic posture her own tall beautiful figure. And Vicky's face, eyes, hair, and smile were all her mother. The differences could all be explained away by the two different, long gone fathers, but the similarities! Ah, the similarities, they kept alive for Jimmy the sweet grace and beauty of his long dead sister. His life had been and would continue to be haunted by wondering if he couldn't have saved her. He had been too busy when she pleaded with him. Too busy! And since her death, he had been incapable of returning to his lost former life, so poisoned by alcohol and shock and grief that he couldn't do the one thing he felt he still needed to do. He couldn't tell the kids about their mother. Not until now, now maybe he could do that, maybe.

At that very instant the ground shook violently and Jimmy, crawling out fast, narrowly escaped being crushed by a giant Ponderosa Pine, torn free at the roots and crashing down dead center on his cardboard home and suitcase shrine. He rose slowly to his feet and looked in shock at his loss. First he thought it was tears running up his dangling hands, and then, looking down he realized it was his two dogs licking them. He dropped to his knees hugging and kissing the frightened hungry, happy mongrels. Everything was going to be okay now, they were together again, and he would be able to talk with them, answer them, listen to them without the old frustrations. He had so much to tell them, so much to thank them for. They were going to be okay.

Sig received a text message and, while waiting for Enno to join him, booted up his pencil-thin, battery-powered, notebook computer. Taking the usual precautions to circumnavigate cyberspace, he received several news items:

1. Conzuela Merced and two of her bodyguards had been found dead in a limousine in El Paso, Texas. The inside word was that CIA operatives were suspected.

Sig closed his eyes and said a small prayer for Mary.

2. Unbeknowst to the general public, Vice President Cooleritch was in jail, under arrest for ordering the bombing of Camp David which killed the president amongst others, the bombing of the White House washroom which ended the political career and life of Rover, and for the contract killing of Mexican nationals. Seems that a certain executive stenographer had been long in the employ as an undercover operative for special prosecutor Fitzsimmons, who in turn was able to use the Grand Jury to speed a warrant process and keep the information, for the time being, from a much-frazzled general public.

3. General Burgoyne "Burg" Hershey, under his Marshall law edict; had ordered the withdrawal of U.S. troops from middle eastern operations, sent formal apologies to France, after withdrawing the declaration of war against her, established negotiations with U.S. Hispanic community leaders to quell the riots, shortened the terms of Supreme Court Justices retroactively from life to 8 years nonrenewable, while ordering a special constitutional crisis session of the congress to consider a ream of revisions. And to top it off, requested the resignations of each and every cabinet member after he called for a special presidential election. At a press conference, the General was quoted in response to a question, as saying "We ain't got much time to turn this ship around, boys. Work to be done. Let's do it."

4. And for *the Monk's* eyes only: Piero Gambizzi, suspected head of organized crime in North America had managed to corner controlling interest in the now financially embattled, legally embroiled *Gee Whiz Corporation*. He had put out contracts on the lives of Sigismundo Maltesta, a.k.a. *The Monk*, General Burgoyne Hershey, and three individuals in a small Central Oregon town.

Sig sent off a flurry of notes and with the message to Miguel Merced, thought again about little Mary. He arranged to have her

immediately and safely returned to her father, careful to make
sure that there was no way to trace back to Luigi, Peggy, Mascara
or Sig. He had to finish the business here and then move to pinch
off the head of the dragon.

Titus saw the strange pickup at Jeff's and recognized it from
the hospital. He suspected who it was but took precautions none
the less, leaving Brenda's car out away and moving on foot he
circled behind the house. On that trek he noticed a familiar
silouette out near a pile of irrigation pipe, it was Glass the
Percheron Stallion. Must have finally broken free of his stall.
Seemed calm enough, eating early grasses peaking up under a
Juniper. And then there was that smell, sulphur mixed with
kerosene?

The swat team had most of the remaining riot participants
and innocent trapped bystanders, forty or fifty people (counting
town drunks, loggers and bullriders, who had walked over from
darkened bars to join in the brawl) encircled and somewhat
quieted for the state police and sheriff's deputies to herd into
waiting cage trucks. A few of the federal agents deliberately
failed to indentify themselves, hoping to get information as
fellow incarcerit. Harry *the Tooth* Langostino, his two goon partners, a dark-eyed drunk former bullrider, the French foreign
exchange student who had successfully set fire to a Plymouth
Navigator, a short scrapy grandma (who had been seen decking
two CIA operatives and who smacked the sheriff as she climbed
in), and nurse Nancy Simmons were all pushed, despite loud
complaints and protestations, together into the back of a police
van.

As if by stage instructions, a confused Enno stepped out of
Jeff's room with Sloop at exactly the same moment that shell-

shocked Shirley stepped out of the room where she had been visiting with Helga. They had two seconds to look at each other, devoid of any recognition, when Titus came quietly into the room from the service porch. Sloop saw it. Shirley, with different hair color and a slightly wider nose, still looked exactly like her mother Charmaine Lebow. He felt a pigment-loaded, brush of emotion wash over him as he looked at his old friend and mentor, Titus. The smile Sloop saw there he had never seen before on his partner, it was poignancy and frailty and exposure nerved to the normally stoic man's entire body.

Enno sensitive to the moment, and feeling his usual protective, and now possessive self, moved to Shirley's side. Her eyes were filling with tears.

"Enno, would you intoduce me to your friend?" requested Titus. The silence in the room was bright white. Enno looked confused.

"Yeah. Shirley, this is Titus Ibid." Turning to her he aplogized, "I'm sorry I don't know your last name."

Shirley's eyes had widened when she heard Enno speak. "Intoit, my last name is Intoit." She stepped forward with her hand fidgeting in her deep coat pocket, and spoke directly to Titus.

"You knew my mother?"

"Yes."

"Did you love my mother?"

"Yes, I did."

"Why did you let her go?" She shouted now. "Why?" She was crying.

Titus ached with immobility. Sloop stepped forward.

"Young lady, Titus did not let her go. He never had her in the first place. She went off on her own. What become of her was of her own doing. If it had been up to him..."

"John." Titus held up his hand. His face had cleared the cloud. He reached his hand forward, palm up, towards Shirley. She, hesitantly laid hers on his. "Shirley, we have a great deal to talk about. But right now is not the time. There are pressures we must respond to." Without releasing her hand, he turned to Sloop. "John, your stallion is loose out in the back paddock, seems to be okay. Has anyone noticed that smell? Did Jeff speak of it?"

"Yes. He says a new hot spring seems to have materialized, just up a bit behind the house. That'll keep. Did you clean us out?"

"Yes. Barely in time. All is shut down." Titus.

"Enno and Jeff have told me all about what's happened today. Enno, you said something about having to get back to a friend? How important is that?" Sloop asked.

"Sig! I almost forgot. yeah, I need to get back there right now."

"Sig?"

Without thinking, Shirley regretfully offered, "I believe you might know him as *the Monk*."

Titus and John's mouths dropped. Vicky found herself glaring at Shirley.

"Enno? *The Monk*? Do you mean a man named Maltesta?" asked John B. Ogdensburg aka Sloop.

Sloop felt wild, general, conflicting emotions. There was Helga to protect and the entire Fork family. If *the Monk* knew this boy, the boy had led him to them. His first blood-crazed thought was to kill Enno. Titus saw this and moved to John's side whispering in his ear.

For the first time Enno felt Sloop look at him with hatred, with fear, with loathing.

"Mr. Duden, please take the young ladies and leave us. Go to your meeting. I have seen you for the last time." And with that he turned and went into Helga's room. Titus followed but looked over his shoulder smiling and nodding to Enno and Shirley as if to say, 'it'll be okay, go now.'

Chapter Thirty two

Umatilla

"Tilly nope - a small quantity of anything left over."

It is the mean season at the front of the next dark age. We greet it thirty times empty and heedless of the Babylonian confusions. All the same tongue and none. Vast store houses of empirical knowledge and no sensorial advent, no impossibilities, no dark gradutes.

The music of this new old age is often moronic, repetitive, simplistic without cause. There is seldom reach, seldom sweep, seldom chances taken with the artistry, with the craft. Outside of the followers' toothless apology for the rationale of cheap tricks to postulate pretense, we are left with beautyless beauty, colorless color, formless form, soundless sound. There is so much thinner in the paint that pigment has become a nuisance factor. There is so much water in the soup...

The ladders we were climbing are now all laying flat on the ground. And the false acrobats and pretend mountaineers of this new shameless time step between the prone rungs laughing at how easy it has become to move the entire length of the ladder. By removing the ascension and charging rent, they believe they have redefined life to its accurate and most correct aspect of Sisyphisian commercialism.

Life; bloody, greasy, granular, spastic, freezing, gasping, cozy, molten, closeted life - all of it vertically challenging - exists and is punctuated by the evidence of silly, predictable, individualized vignettes which when witnessed always burst with the power to say something startling. Give us this day our daily Fred.

The master technicians, the master craftsmen, the professional artists will never get the "witnessing" right if they insist on looking over their shoulders and in the mirror for reassessment and self-congratulation. It must be painted fast and violently, nailed to a tree before dry, and left to be found, or not.

Witnessing and creation are pure energy, tranformed and gone when touched in any fashion by the social virus known as commercialism.

Enno, Shirley and Vicky returned in Shirley's truck to Mascara. They met Sig at the address he had provided and saw Jimmy and his two dogs scoot off.

Sig noticed the changes in all of them. Shirley's was painful resolution. Enno's was painful confusion. And Vicky's was a virtuosic freedom of connection, she was in her new zone.

"Enno, I may need your help. Are you up to it?"

"Why has it taken me so long to figure out that you are the good guy? Aren't you?" Asked Shirley of the Monk.

Laughing lightly Sig answered "No, actually we, the two of us," and he pointed to Enno, "are the bad guys, the outlaws if you prefer. So, I suspect are Titus Ibid and Enno's other friends Jeff and John. And my dear, you and Enno's sister, yes Vicky it is true, are on the verge of joining us." Sig was looking deep into Vicky's excited, smiling eyes. "And your suspicions are right, it is a helluva ride of horrible consequence and delicious awareness. Right now, I need you two ladies gone. Tell us where you are going and we'll join you soon."

The earth continued to shake and pull apart and the lava continued to seek conclusion. The crack in the ground, down the middle of Mascara, now ten feet deep, was widening in places to full street width. From certain elevations three glowing humps surrounding town, could be seen with fires around their perimeter. Pressure had moved from the early bulge to across town and beyond into the outskirts, heading towards the canyons which were home to Lloyd's, Sloop's and Jeff's ranches.

Sig and Enno drove quickly down every passable street in the town.

"They're here someplace. And we have to find them before they find us or...," he paused looking at Enno, "ours."

"What are we looking for exactly?" Duden asked.

"You'll know."

Then, in a sweep through the industrial park he saw something. A form, it looked human, crawling along a fenceline. It slumped and stopped moving, not as though hiding but as though finished. Sloop and Enno ran to it. They found the charred and maimed body of Lint Fumes, nearly dead. Sig rolled him over and put his coat behind his head.

"Liner's dead." choked Fumes, nodding in recognition of his competitor.

"Sorry, Fumes, if I doubt you, he doesn't seem to die so easily."

"Have to take my word for it," coughing, "he's under us. Feel that heat? I shot him then lava buried him, burnt me, tunnel's sealed off forever." He coughed again. "Hard to ask, but maybe ... take me to my motel room, I'd like to die there listening to Coleman."

Together they carefully took the blackened body of Lint Fumes to his room. Enno followed instructions and setup the Bang and Olafsen system to play Coleman Hawkins while Sig arranged Lint as comfortable as possible in the bed.

"Maltesta, there is a side room, an antechamber in hell for us. I will be waiting there for you, my friend." Turning to Enno he said, "leave him kid or you'll be sharing sweet cocktails with us in Hades."

They had no doubt Lint would be dead soon. Sig stopped at the motel desk and suggested someone check his room in one hour.

They had been sidetracked by roadblocks and emergency vehicles. It took a while for Shirley and Vicky to get to the trailer park, there they found two burning units in one corner and a large Pine crossing several others. Shirley's trailer was still fine, at least to outward appearances. Inside was another story. Stuff was scattered all around as if the trailer had rolled sideways down hill. In the middle of the small floor, mixed in with food and utensils, were pieces of broken crystal.

"Oh no." Shirley went to her knees to gather just the crystal parts. Shirley looked over her shoulder.

"What did it used to be?"

Shirley looked up with a pouting face, "In the very beginning it had been a glass unicorn. I had broken the horn off when I was fifteen. One of my tribal friends had explained that the unicorn was a lame mythological creature that European girls assigned all sort of magic powers to. I had always loved the way light bounced around inside but I didn't want any of my friends to tease me about owning a Unicorn figurine so I snapped the horn off his forehead. For me he has always been my glass horse, nothing more nothing less. He's gone everywhere with me. Well, I guess now he is something far less." She carefully placed the cluster of glass pieces on the little table and set to cleaning up the floor and counter. She stopped, on her knees, and looked up at

Vicky who was seated by the table.

"Will you go with them?" she asked Vicky.

"Them?"

"Yes, Sig and Enno."

"Sig AND Enno? What are you talking about. Enno's not going anywhere. Haven't you figured out yet that he's joined at the hip with that Sloop guy, not with Sig? Enno only cares about farming, work horses, that old dog and..." She was smiling at Shirley who was frowning. "...and maybe you."

"So what was all that threatening talk back there? A lover's spat?"

Just then a rap came on the trailer door, seconds before Sig opened it and poked his head in.

"Might as well come in," answered a surly Shirley Intoit.

"Gosh, did this trailer get rolled?" asked Enno.

"Looks to me like someone came in here and busted everything up looking for something." observed Sig.

"Oh geez!" gasped Shirley who looked under the fridge door. "Thank goodness."

"Cooper's stash?" asked Monk

First she looked cold then she started to laugh. "Caught me, haven't you? Yes Cooper's stash."

"And you're certain its still there?"

"Here's a screwdriver, you take the heater door off and check for yourself." Sig complied. "Let's get something straight here. Are you some sort of policeman or insurance cop? Are you going to be throwing me in jail or fining me? Or what?" Shirley asked.

Sig was smiling, "Let's just see what we have here, shall we?"

"An old metal box with clippings, a letter in a sealed envelope and somewhere's around $125,000 in twenty dollar bills." Offered Shirley.

"You mean to tell me you don't know exactly how much is in here?"

"That's right Mister Smarty Pants. I doubt if you're gonna believe me but I had no intention of keeping that money. I had planned on giving it all away by now," answered Shirley.

"May I?" He asked and went ahead and dumped the contents on the table top. He separated the bills from the clippings and picked out the browned envelope.

"And you haven't opened this?" Sig asked as he read the names on the cover and looked up quick.

"I don't open other people's mail," she sneered, continuing to cleanup the trailer.

"Are you also averse to delivering mail?" he said holding up the enveope which read **Boston and/or Titus Ibid.**   That had her surprised attention.

He ripped open the envelope. "Well, we outlaws have no problems reading fellow outlaw mail."

He read out loud:

To whom it may concern, and any creeps who are poking into what doesn't concern them,

My name is Charleton Ibid, under the psuedonym of Dan Cooper I extorted this money from the Airlines in a hijacking. I'm dead by now, the big C, so give up the search. My brother Boston Ibid, and his son, my nephew Titus Ibid had nothing to do with any of it. They're good people, leave them alone. Hey Bos, if you get to read this note, I just wanted to help out the kid. Don't think too bad of me. Live twice as hard to make up for my short shrift. Charlie

He handed the note to Enno. "You need to give this to Titus." Then he turned to Vicky, "How soon can you be ready to travel?"

She pinched his sleeve edge and said, "Twenty minutes, unless my apartment fell into the crack in the ground or is sitting under a big old tree."

"Hey, wait a minute, not so fast," said Shirley, "What about the money? What about Enno and what about me? There's quite a bit of unfinished business here."

"You're right. From what Enno tells me I need to set some things straight. So here's the deal, you keep the money IF you can convince Enno's friends that I am not a threat. And I'll even give you a leg up. Tell Ibid these words, *Giggleswick and the Asile of Dogs*, it should cap it." Sig.

"*Giggleswick and the Asile of Dogs?* What does that mean?" Shirley asked.

Sig looked extra mean.

"I know, I know, if you tell me, someone will have to kill me to keep me silent. God this is all so ridiculous." Turning to Vicky she asked "Are you going with him?"

"Damn right. Where are we going, by the way?" she asked Sig.

"First to Chicago to fulfill a contract on the life of the head of the Mafia. Then to my farm in Central America."

Chapter Thirty three

Willamette

rainbow: Arch in the sky displaying the colors of the spectrum formed by the refraction and reflection of the Sun's ray's through a rain or mist. Discovered by Theodoric of Freiburg in the 14th century.

"I don't think we should go back to Forks just yet." offered Enno, sitting in the driver's seat of Shirley's pickup. "I need to get back to Sloops' whether he likes it or not and check on the stock. My truck's out there. But it doesn't seem right to expect you to go all that way, this late, and have to come back into town?"

"Thank you, yes, you're right. So, ..." she slid across the bench seat, up against him, and attempted to kiss his mouth, only he ducked and she got him square on the upper right cheek. "Hold still, you!" And she got it right that time. "There, that wasn't so bad, now, was it? Okay, this is how it's going to work. We're going out to Sloops', do the chores and find a place for me to stay the night. Tomorrow we'll deal with the bad stuff. Okay?"

"Nope. Just changed my mind. Doesn't work to put it off. We're going to Forks to have it out with Sloop. That's me having it out with Sloop. You don't need to mess with it. Then we get my dog, Resumé, and the three of us go do Sloop's chores, if its all right with him. Where the three of us spend the night we can all vote on, okay?"

"I like how you think mister farmer-man." And she kissed him again only taking a little longer and getting it pretty doggone soft. Hell, she thought, who needs a puppy. Anyway, this is a whole lot more fun.

Mascara was a disaster. A wretched and complex disaster. Within weeks after the earthquakes and volcanic activity, most realtors moved on to new destination resort towns. Bo Coin, after a brief wild encounter with J.M. Thurber, lost the local lust and pulled up stakes, moving East in search of Johanna's wispy literate trail.

Luther Yankone, (after setting his wife up in an assisted living ranch for the mentally fried - she had lost her marbles when she lost her lavender Poodle 'Precious' - it jumped from her bosom into an opening earth crack), returned to Mascara and purchased every distressed lot he could find. He hired Roger the writer who gave him his signature visionary idea. No money would be spared to widen the 'crack in the ground' which ran up the length of town. He would pave its floor into the new two lane "underpass" through town and design it with every cross street featuring a venetian style bridge with western trimmings. He lobbied unsuccessfully to have the town's name changed from Mascara to *Torn*. But all that was later.

Resumé had been so tired that when Enno left he hadn't even noticed. But after his short power nap, and the vibrations he was feeling in the ground, plus the new stinks he was smelling, he felt apprehensive. Eventually he went looking around the farm-

stead for his partner Enno. At the back door, he found young
Franklin snagging a stick of firewood for the heater while chewing a wad of bubblegum. The dog wagged his tail, and Franklin
looking around for adults, wiggled his finger signifying that old
Resumé was to sneak into the house behind him. Once inside, the
youngster sat the dog down by pushing firmly on his shoulders.
Then, with twinkly-eyed ceremony, he produced a wrapped
chunk of the pink pleasure, the jaw's-joy, the gum! Resumé made
a quick move to snap it up, but forceful, little Franklin stopped
him with a flat hand to the snout. He wagged his finger back and
forth and in a whisper said "Bad Doggie Bad." Then, as a good
little flirt, the boy made the Dog watch him slowly, ever so
slowly, unwrap the chunk of pink sweet rubber delight. He held
it between thumb and finger, enjoying the view of the squirming
dog. Next instant, he heard his mother holler his name and he
jammed the gum hard into the poor dog's mouth. Holding a
finger to his lips, as he ducked past the washing machine and
into the kitchen, he made exaggerated chewing motions with his
mouth. It was as if, by example, he thought he had to reteach the
old dog the new trick.

Checking through the battery units, Sloop and Titus had
gotten favorable indications that things were moving away from
them, or at least for the time being, in their favor. Titus had gone
outside to check on the stock and the new hot spring. His head
was full of thoughts of young Shirley, looking forward to getting
to know her. Somewhat absentmindedly, he first went to the barn
to get a halter and long lead rope for the stallion. If the horse had
wandered far, he would double the rope around to both sides of
the halter, like a riding rein, and ride Glass back. He fetched his
wide, flat brimmed hat, gloves and a coat while listening to the
battery-operated radio. The news bulletin suggested that the
volcanic activity at Mascara was subsiding.

Back in the house: It was Helga who, after hearing the conversation between Titus and Sloop about Enno's alleged transgres-
sions, took her husband's hand and said, "John trust Titus on this
one. I'm asking you not to throw away the love you have for that

boy. We are still healing, you and I, and its not just our bodies which need time." John said nothing in response.

In the next room Yummy was checking in with her wounded, bed-ridden husband. "Honey, I like that girl young Enno picked out for hisself. She's got color down deep inside her and if I know my sauce, and I KNOW my sauce, she's got it baby, know what I mean? She's gonna curl that boy's toes, uh huh, curl his toes."

Titus walked out with flashlight, halter and rope, in search for the grey Stallion. It took a while but he found him nearly a quarter mile off. Glass stood still while Ibid placed the halter around his head and fastened the rope at both ends. Then he whispered to him, blew in his nostrils lightly, rubbed his forehead and led him to a downed tree where he could get on his back. Once mounted, he gained height which gave him an improved vantage point. There was a glow up the canyon. He rode that way to check it out. It wasn't a regular fire, but he didn't have to go far to feel the heat. Glass was getting nervous. What Titus found was a lateral crack in the box canyon wall out from which was oozing an increasingly wide flow of slow moving molten rock, lava. Glass reared when they got too close and it was difficult for Titus to stay on the big horse. Just as they turned to run back, a Juniper tree burst into flames from the heat. Titus could see what was happening, he couldn't understand it but he could see it. The lava was coming down that deep curving canyon heading right for the Fork Holding, all the buildings, the livestock, everything was in its direct path. He rode off a distance, calmed the horse, and turned to try to figure out what was to be done. That was when he remembered the stashes of dynamite hidden in the opposing rim rock walls, there to maybe deter the most unwelcome guests trying to come down the road to do harm. Well, what could be a more unwelcome guest than this lava? He had an idea, which became a plan with a price tag. He turned Glass around and ran him back to the house. It was at this time that Enno and Shirley were driving down that road and saw the lava flow from above. Enno gunned the truck for the last three quarter mile.

Titus and Enno arrived at the house at the same time. Nothing needed to be said between them. He handed the boy the reins of the horse and ran inside. When he came out he took the horse and asked Enno and Shirley to help get the folks ready to leave, now.

Titus next went to the shop, tied the horse and went in to find what he needed. He fetched a 14 foot long section of light weight 1/2 inch PVC pipe, drilled a quick hole in the end and pulled wire through with which he tied on three greasy shop rags. Next he put a mess of matches in his coat pocket and went outside. The canyon was now a wall of fire moving slowly towards them. Even from here, both he and Enno could see the bad news, the road out was impassable, flaming Pines had fallen across it. There was still a chance they could get out, overland, through the canyon floor, but it would be rough. Titus had to give Enno the long pipe while he mounted the stallion. Once up, Enno handed him the long staff with the rag end. Titus pulled his hat down tight, nodded and smiled to Enno and said,

"Take care of that girl for me, I'm sorry I won't have an opportunity to lie to her about her mother." Then he rode off, jerkily at first, as the stallion didn't know what to make of the long pole up and out ahead of him. People started to pile out of the house in preparation to leave. Jeff on crutches, stood beside Helga's wheelchair. Brenda had the children in tow. Sloop came down the stairs with Shirley. They all stood mesmerized by the sight.

In black silouette framed by the firey glow of the approaching yellow orange wall, marched a magnificent Percheron stallion upon whose back rode the long sinewy frame of a hooked-nose, pointy-bearded man in flat brimmed hat with a long, pencil-thin, blunt-nosed lance under his arm. They rode sideways as if folding themselves into the flame. And they disappeared. Within minutes a massive explosion was heard followed by raining rock, and then minutes later a repeat from the other side. Avalanches proceeded, more from one wall than the other, filling the deep canyon throat with rock, up against which flowed rapidly cooling magma. He had done it, he had sealed off the box canyon. From high up on the canyon wall they heard a familiar scream and then saw the stallion lose its footing as it raced down the gravel pitch. He fell and rolled, and got up, shook, stood a minute and then walked down the rest of the way. There was no man with him.

Chapter Thirty Four

Columbia

Epilogue

Inventing by analogy

acuminate = long-tapering at outer end
appressed = lying close and flat against
globose = spherical or nearly so

Save for the imagination of angels,
there are no pockets in a shroud.

The cataclysm at Preacher's hollow continued to produce natural wonders. Perhaps the most brilliant result of which was the formation of a deep, three quarter mile long, crystal clear, curving, narrow lake butting up against a magnificent stone dam sealed by lava rock. They named the body of water Glass Lake.

The next result of note was the pastel-hued basin surrounding the bubbling hot spring out of which spewed a natural geiser with peculiar regularity. A mathematician finally proved that the timing of the geiser seemed to match a patterning akin to the numerology of Pascal's Triangle. They named the spot Ibid's Spring.
When seen from the air, the lake and hot springs formed a perfect question mark with a steaming, spewing point.